Farewell, Aylis

Aylis

A Non-Traditional
Novel in Three Works

Central Asian Literatures in Translation

Series Editor
REBECCA RUTH GOULD (University of Birmingham)

Editorial Board
ERDAĞ GÖKNAR (Duke University)
JEANNE-MARIE JACKSON (Johns Hopkins University)
DONALD RAYFIELD, PROFESSOR EMERITUS
 (Queen Mary University of London)
ROMAN UTKIN (Davidson College)

ACADEMIC
STUDIES
PRESS

Farewell, Aylis

A Non-Traditional Novel in Three Works

AKRAM AYLISLI

Translated by
KATHERINE E. YOUNG

Edited by
REBECCA RUTH GOULD

Boston
2018

Translation of this manuscript was funded by a 2017 Translation Fellowship from the National Endowment for the Arts.

Library of Congress Cataloging-in-Publication Data

Names: Əylisli, Əkrəm, author. | Young, Katherine E. (Poet), translator. | Container of (expression): Əylisli, Əkrəm. Yəmən. English. | Container of (expression): Əylisli, Əkrəm. Daş yuxular. English. | Container of (expression): Əylisli, Əkrəm. Möhtəşəm tıxac. English.

Title: Farewell, Aylis: a non-traditional novel in three works / by Akram Aylisli; translated from the Russian by Katherine E. Young.

Description: Brighton, MA: Academic Studies Press, 2018.

Identifiers: LCCN 2018023271 (print) | LCCN 2018042874 (ebook) | ISBN 9781618117953 (ebook) | ISBN 9781618117946 (hardcover)

Subjects: LCSH: Əylisli, Əkrəm—Translations into English.

Classification: LCC PL314.A46 (ebook) | LCC PL314.A46 A6 2018 (print) | DDC 894/.361—dc23

LC record available at https://lccn.loc.gov/2018023271

Academic Studies Press
28 Montfern Avenue
Brighton, MA 02135, USA
press@academicstudiespress.com
www.academicstudiespress.com

Dedicated to the days and nights of Aylis,
for which my soul bitterly weeps

Table of Contents

Preface

It is a great pleasure to introduce the first volume in Central Asian Literatures in Translation, a publishing initiative that aims to broaden the scope of world literature by introducing new and classic texts from Central Asia and the Caucasus in English translation. Each title in this series redefines what literature can be and mean in a region wherein geopolitics too frequently mutes aesthetics, yet which has inspired an astonishing diversity of cultures, languages, literary traditions, and imperial formations.

We are inaugurating the series with the novellas of Akram Aylisli (b. 1937), a courageous dissident writer who has suffered greatly for his commitment to peace in times of war and to cosmopolitan values amid ethnic strife. The magnificent stories of Aylisli translated here deserve to be placed alongside Soviet classics such as Konstantin Gamsakhurdia's Georgian classic *The Right Hand of the Grand Master* (1939) and Boris Pasternak's better-known *Doctor Zhivago* (1957). This is particularly true of *Stone Dreams* (2011), the publication of which resulted in the author's continuing de facto house arrest, as detailed in Joshua Kucera's foreword. Like these predecessors, the stories Aylisli has to tell are fundamentally concerned with freedom under constraint and the role of the visionary artist in making a better life, and a better society, possible.

As detailed in Andrew Wachtel's afterword written especially for this volume, Aylisli's aesthetic is informed by the Russian literary tradition's commitment to justice under tyrannical regimes and solidarity with the underdog. At the same time, the novellas in this volume open up new frontiers in the literature of the post-Soviet Caucasus, as well as in our understanding of the hybrid Azeri-Russian cultural milieu Aylisli describes. As such, they make a fitting opening to a series that will showcase the achievements of writers whose names are in many cases only dimly known to the English reader, yet whose works expand the possibilities of literature and culture across the former Soviet Union.

Rebecca Ruth Gould
Series Editor, Central Asian Literatures in Translation,
University of Birmingham

Akram Aylisli's Lonely Battle for Reconciliation

On February 10, 2013, a crowd gathered in Azerbaijan to burn books. Book burning may seem like an activity out of another era or a metaphor for past censorship and dictatorship rather than something that really happens today. But a video of the event shows a gathering of a couple dozen people, mostly middle-aged and older, many wearing suits and ties.[1] With little apparent enthusiasm they methodically tear up old hardcovers and throw the pages onto a pile. A balding man in jeans and a leather jacket pours some fuel out of a reused vegetable oil bottle onto the books and then lights it in several places with a cigarette lighter. The crowd watches stoically as the fire rages brightly and eventually dies out, leaving the books in ashes.

The target of this sad episode was Akram Aylisli and his novella *Stone Dreams*, which had just been published in the Russian literary journal *Druzhba narodov* (Friendship of Peoples). The books being burned were mostly old editions of Aylisli's other works—there was no copy of *Stone Dreams* in the pyre because it hadn't even been published in Azerbaijan.

This particular book-burning was in Ganja, Azerbaijan's second largest city, but similar events took place in the capital, Baku, and other cities around Azerbaijan. And the reception of *Stone Dreams* was not limited to book burning. One politician offered a reward of more than $10,000 to anyone who cut off Aylisli's ear and brought it to him; others demanded that he undergo a blood test that would determine if he was truly Azerbaijani. President Ilham Aliev, citing Aylisli's "deliberate distortion of the history of Azerbaijan by his entirely slanderous work," issued a decree formally stripping Aylisli of his title as "People's Writer" and revoking the

---

1 "Azerbaijani Writer's Books Burned over His Controversial Novel," Radio Liberty's website, February 11, 2013. https://www.rferl.org/a/azerbaijani-writer-books-burned-akram-aylisli/24898784.html.

special pension that he had received as a distinguished artist.[2] His works were removed from school curricula and his plays were pulled from theaters.

Aylisli's "crime" was that he wrote about his own country's crimes against Armenians and not the other way around.[3] Over more than a century of bloodletting, there have been plenty of atrocities on both sides. That Aylisli chose to focus on the blood shed by his own people makes him almost unique among Azerbaijanis (and, for that matter, Armenians).

Aylisli had been a leading Azerbaijan literary figure since the 1960s, one who managed the rare feat of enjoying both official and popular support in both the Soviet Union and in independent Azerbaijan. His works were in school curricula, and he served as a member of Azerbaijan's parliament from 2005 until 2010.

Aylisli had previously spoken out against anti-Armenian hatred in Azerbaijan, most notably in a 1989 debate published in *Druzhba narodov*, a time when many more intellectuals on both sides were instead whipping up nationalist hysteria against the other.[4] But *Stone Dreams* went much farther in grappling with the conflict.

The novella alternates between two narratives. The first is the history of Aylis, Aylisli's hometown in Nakhchivan, a landlocked exclave bordering Armenia, Iran, and Turkey. It was here that Armenians were massacred by Ottoman troops, who had invaded to support local Azeris in a fight for control with Armenians over the region, in 1919. The massacre—a relatively little-known episode in the Armenian genocide, in which up to 1.5 million Armenians were killed—wiped out what had been a vibrant Armenian community in Aylis. Its Armenian churches, once

---

2   *Rasporiazhenie Prezidenta Azerbaidzhanskoi Respubliki o lishenii Akrama Ailisli (Akrama Nadzhaf oglu Naibova) personal'noi pensii Prezidenta Azerbaidzhanskoi Respubliki* [Azerbaijani President Ilham Aliev's decree on the cancellation of Akram Aylisli's personal "Presidental Pension"], President Ilham Aliev's official website, February 7, 2013, https://ru.president.az/articles/7230.

3   Some, including Aylisli himself, have suggested that it wasn't actually *Stone Dreams* that got Aylisli in trouble with the authorities, but the next installment in the trilogy, *A Fantastical Traffic Jam*. That novella portrays a dictator who resembles Heydar Aliev, the former president and founding father of modern Azerbaijan; it was published in Baku in a small Russian-language edition in 2011.

4   The debate (or, more precisely, that part of a very long public discussion dedicated to the problems of nationalism) began with a letter by Aylisli and a reply to it by then-editor-in-chief of *Druzhba narodov*, Sergei Baruzdin, both published in the March 1989 issue of the journal. Later this debate continued with a collective letter of the Azerbaijani Writers Union that appeared in the October 1989 issue. Akram Aylisli, "Poka v dome budet sushchestvovat' liubov' . . . : pis'mo S. A. Baruzdinu" [As long as love exists at home . . . : Letter to S. A. Baruzdin], *Druzhba narodov* 3 (1989): 170–171; Sergei Baruzdin, "Emotsii i fakty" [Emotions and facts], ibid.: 171–174; General Committee of the Azerbaijani Writers Union, "V redaktsiiu zhurnala 'Druzhba narodov', glavnomu redaktoru S. A. Baruzdinu" [To the editorial desk of *Druzhba narodov*, Editor-in-Chief S. A. Baruzdin], *Druzhba narodov* 10 (1989): 233–235.

famed around the region, were abandoned, and Armenians' homes were occupied by Azeris, often the ones who had abetted the Turkish slaughter.

The second narrative concerns the pogroms that Azerbaijanis carried out against Armenians in Baku and other cities in Azerbaijan between 1988 and 1990. As the Soviet Union was falling apart, interethnic tensions rose in many peripheral parts of the empire, and some of the worst tension was between Armenians and Azerbaijanis. This tension would eventually lead to a war between the two sides; among the most notorious episodes was a series of organized slaughters of Armenian residents of Azerbaijani cities, most notoriously in Sumgait, carried out by bands of Azerbaijani men. The pogroms themselves killed some unknown dozens and forced virtually all Armenians who had been living in Azerbaijan—including 250,000 in Baku alone—to flee. "If a single candle were lit for every Armenian killed violently, the radiance of those candles would be brighter than the light of the moon," says one of Aylisli's characters in *Stone Dreams*.

To a generous reader of *Stone Dreams*, the dominant impression of Azerbaijan is of the humanity and decency of the main characters of the novel, people who respect their Armenian neighbors and lament the cycle of hatred that has swallowed their country. But many of its readers were not generous. Some in Azerbaijan accused Aylisli of trying to mimic the Turkish novelist Orhan Pamuk, who won the Nobel Prize in Literature and had been the subject of controversy in Turkey because of his frank acknowledgement of the Armenian genocide. A group of prominent academics nominated Aylisli for the Nobel Peace Prize in 2014, crediting him as "the first Turkic author to write a novel about the Armenian genocide" and praising his "amazing courage in the cause of overcoming hostility between the peoples of Azerbaijan and Armenia."[5]

Aylisli anticipated the accusations that were made against him in his text. The wife of Sadai Sadygly, the hero of *Stone Dreams*, asks her husband about his sympathy toward Armenians:

> Yes, I was in Aylis, and I know the Turks dealt brutally and cruelly with innocent people there. But you've also been in those places from which *Armenians* drove out thousands of unfortunate *Azerbaijanis*. Have you thought even once about how it is for those unfortunate people, those Azerbaijanis, homeless now and living without the slightest hope for the future? Do our Azerbaijani instigators, the ones who stirred up this bloody

---

5   The Nobel Peace Prize 2014 nomination, unofficial website of Aylisli, http://akramaylisli. info/english/nomination/.

trouble, really think about them, the Azerbaijanis whom the unfortunate Armenians themselves now curse? I mean both the Karabakh Armenians and the local Baku Armenians who don't care about us because, according to their thinking, we're also Turks? If the Turks slaughtered your people, go ahead, fight it out with them, why are we Azerbaijanis even involved? In what way are those Armenian screamers better than our homegrown ones? Why don't you think about that, my dear?

Elsewhere in the novella another character, seemingly channeling Aylisli, articulates Sadai's attitude on this question: "What today's Armenians are like is beside the point—the point is, what we're like now."

These sorts of sentiments are vanishingly rare today in the Caucasus, where a quarter century of nationalist propaganda by both Armenians and Azerbaijanis has fuelled a deep hatred on both sides. But the history of Armenian and Azeri cohabitation is much longer than their history of enmity. For centuries Armenians and Azeris peacefully intermixed throughout the South Caucasus, the region south of the Caucasus Mountains (which extends along what is today Russia's southern border), northeast of Turkey and northwest of Iran. The Caucasus is one of the most ethnically diverse regions in the world, and Armenians and Azerbaijanis are just two parts of an immensely complex ethnic patchwork. Azeris (who now are divided between the Republic of Azerbaijan, founded in 1918, and the Iranian province of Azerbaijan) are mostly Shiʿa Muslims and speak a Turkic language closely related to modern Turkish. Armenians belong to the Nestorian branch of Orthodox Christianity and speak a language that is its own branch of Indo-European. Despite these basic differences, centuries of shared history under Ottoman, Safavid, Tsarist, and Soviet rule have brought them together. Much Armenian and Azerbaijani traditional music and many of their dances are very similar. Armenian and Azeri literatures are similarly informed by a shared Persianate and subsequently, Soviet ethos. The regular quarrels that the two sides now have over the provenance of their favorite foods—like stuffed grape leaves, thin lavash bread, and meatballs—only serve to demonstrate how similar their cultures are.

The comity that Armenians and Azeris had with one another began to disappear in the late nineteenth and early twentieth centuries as ideas of nationalism—a European import transmitted via Russia and Turkey—took root among the region's intellectuals. As the Russian Empire declined and control from the center weakened, disorder spread across the Caucasus.

The first major clashes between Armenians and Azeris took place in 1905 in Baku and then spread to other parts of the South Caucasus. The fighting began as labor disputes but took on an ethnic cast. The clashes would be reprised in the chaotic years following the 1917 Russian Revolution and collapse of the Russian Empire. This time they were exacerbated by the invasion of the Ottoman armed forces, who sought to take advantage of the chaos in the former Russian Empire and took the side of Azeris against Armenians.

Eventually the Russians—this time reorganized as the Soviet Union—reconquered the Caucasus and managed to tamp down the violence. Under the USSR the South Caucasus was divided up into three Soviet Socialist Republics—Armenia, Azerbaijan, and Georgia. The Soviets were thus forced to decide which land to allocate to Armenia and which to Azerbaijan. The solution was necessarily imperfect, and Soviet Azerbaijan was a particularly curious creation. It included Nakhchivan, an exclave roughly the size of Delaware, separated from the rest of Azerbaijan by a swath of Armenian territory. Another territory that ended up in Azerbaijan was Nagorno-Karabakh, an enclave slightly smaller than Nakhchivan, which due to its Armenian majority population was given a special status (it was an "autonomous oblast" in Soviet terminology). This awkward division appears to have been motivated by a good-faith effort to assign, as best as possible, the region's manifold nationalities into unitary boxes. But both Armenians and Azerbaijanis would later complain, along with many other Soviet peoples who suffered a similar fate, that their forced cartographies were instead deliberate time bombs set by the Soviets to explode in case of the Soviet Union's disintegration.

For most of its existence, the Soviet Union managed to keep a lid on the ethnic tension between Armenians and Azerbaijanis that had plagued the early twentieth century. Baku was one of the most cosmopolitan centers in the entire USSR. The chess grandmaster Garry Kasparov, who grew up in Baku with a Jewish father and Armenian mother, described his nationality as "Bakuvian." Interethnic marriages were common with Georgians as well as Armenians. Baku Armenians commonly spoke Russian as a first language rather than Armenian.

Still, Nakhchivan and Nagorno-Karabakh underwent significant demographic shifts as a result of being assigned to Azerbaijan. In Nakhchivan, the Armenian population—which had been roughly 40 percent before the Soviet takeover—dropped to only 11 percent by 1926 and barely 1 percent by 1979. In Karabakh, the proportion of the Azerbaijani population grew as well, but Armenians still accounted for about three-quarters of the population at the end of the Soviet era.

During the second half of the twentieth century, Armenians' consciousness about the genocide—which had been largely repressed in the decades
immediately following—grew, both in the Armenian diaspora and in Soviet
Armenia. A mass demonstration in Yerevan in 1965 marked the genocide's
fiftieth anniversary. The sense of loss that Armenians had experienced as a
nation grew to encompass other lost lands, including Nagorno-Karabakh.
As nationalist movements blossomed across the Soviet Union in the 1980s,
one of the most powerful was the Karabakh Movement among Armenians,
which sought for Nagorno-Karabakh to be removed from Azerbaijan and
united with Armenia.

This movement snowballed and eventually led to war between Armenia
and Azerbaijan, which ended in a ceasefire in 1994 after an estimated 30,000
were killed. Nagorno-Karabakh and some surrounding territories of Azerbaijan
came under the control of Armenian forces, and the populations on both sides
were ethnically cleansed. The legacy of the war has had a profound impact
on Azerbaijan today. Just as Armenians were forced to flee their homes in
Azerbaijan, over 600,000 Azerbaijanis who had been living in areas now controlled by Armenia also were forced out.[6]

The sense of resentment over the war has been nurtured and manipulated
by the Azerbaijani government, which has developed into one of the most
repressive states on the planet. In the widely respected Polity IV rankings com-
piled by political scientists, only 10 countries in 2017 were more autocratic
than Azerbaijan, which ranked alongside Iran, China, and Cuba.[7]

Hatred of Armenians is virtually state policy in today's Azerbaijan. In prac-
tice, no one with an Armenian name (easy to spot, as they end in -yan or -ian, as
with Alikhanyan, Kocharyan, and Petrosyan in this volume) is allowed into the
country; if they arrive at the airport, even if they are from a country for which
visas to Azerbaijan aren't required, they are turned back. Police have even investi-
gated Azerbaijanis who vote for Armenia in the Eurovision Song Contest.

At the same time, Azerbaijan also has become relatively wealthy, earning
billions from its oil and gas reserves on the Caspian Sea. It has spent heavily
on flamboyant architecture, attempting to turn Baku into a sort of post-Soviet
Dubai, as well as on its military, with which it regularly threatens to take back
Nagorno-Karabakh by force.

---

6 *Azerbaijan Factsheet*, UN Azerbaijan, May 1, 2018, https://unazerbaijan.org/wp-content/
uploads/2018/05/Factsheet_Aze_1-May-2018-v1.pdf.

7 *Polity IV Individual Country Regime Trends, 1946–2013*, website of Center for Systemic
Peace, http://www.systemicpeace.org/polity/polity4x.htm.

In Armenia, meanwhile, victory in Nagorno-Karabakh has turned out to be a Pyrrhic one. Its borders with Azerbaijan and Turkey (a close ally of Azerbaijan) are closed, stifling its economy. The constant military threat from Azerbaijan has forced it into an alliance with Russia, which has a military base in Armenia and gives the country military aid to help make up for Azerbaijan's substantial military spending advantage. (To add to the humiliation, though, Moscow also sells Azerbaijan the large majority of that country's weapons.) As in Azerbaijan, hatred of the other side has only grown since the war.

International mediators (led by the US, Russia, and France) have been trying to hammer out a peace deal to resolve the Nagorno-Karabakh conflict, but diplomatic talks have stalled and become more focused on preventing another war than on a lasting peace. On both sides, rising nationalism has made it virtually impossible for the respective leaders to make the kinds of compromises that would be necessary for a real peace deal.

One of the many low points in this sad history is the story of Ramil Safarov. On the evening of February 18, 2004, Safarov killed Gurgen Margarian with sixteen ax blows to the head while the latter was asleep in his bed. The two men were participating in an English-language training seminar in Budapest organized by NATO. Both were young lieutenants in their respective armed forces: Safarov for Azerbaijan, Margarian for Armenia. During his trial in Hungary, Safarov's lawyers explained that their client had suffered from post-traumatic stress as a result of his family's expulsion from their home during the war between Armenia and Azerbaijan. Safarov's home region of Jabrayil, adjacent to Nagorno-Karabakh, was occupied by Armenian forces and the entire ethnic Azerbaijani population, including Safarov's family, was forced to flee. The Hungarian judge was not moved by that justification and in 2006 gave Safarov a life sentence in prison, with no right to appeal for thirty years.

In 2012, however, shortly after a state visit by Hungarian Prime Minister Viktor Orban to Azerbaijan, Hungary extradited Safarov back to his home country. He was immediately pardoned and set free, promoted to major, and given eight years of back pay and a free apartment. "It is very touching to see this son of the homeland, [who] had been thrown in jail after he defended his country's honor and dignity of the people," said Novruz Mammadov, Aliev's top foreign policy adviser, upon Safarov's release.[8]

---

8 "Agreement during Hungarian Premier's Visit Decisive in Ramil Safarov's Issue," News.az, September 1, 2012, https://news.az/articles/67397/print.

The pardon was widely condemned internationally: the US Department of State and White House, French and Russian foreign ministries, the European Union foreign affairs representative, and United Nations secretary general all issued statements criticizing the move. In Azerbaijan itself, however, critical voices were scarce. And this was what prompted Aylisli to release *Stone Dreams*. "When I saw the crazy reaction and the artificial fueling of hatred between Armenians and Azerbaijanis, which went beyond any borders, I decided to publish my novel," he said in a 2013 interview.[9]

Even after the initial furor over the publication of *Stone Dreams* died down, Aylisli has continued to be the subject of an intimidation campaign; in 2016 he was on his way to a literary conference in Venice when he was stopped at the airport and accused of attacking a border guard. For the most part, though, he has kept a low profile. "Let some in my motherland think I'm not a writer: so be it," he writes in the afterword to this edition. "I don't need honor or glory in a country where they burn books and a killer with an ax is elevated to the rank of hero."

Meanwhile, the tension between the two sides has continued to grow. April 2016 saw the heaviest fighting since the 1994 ceasefire, with over 200 killed. And the inclination to take responsibility for crimes committed by one's own side is vanishing. Azerbaijan's government has begun to embrace a conspiracy theory that the pogroms in Sumgait, Baku, and elsewhere were in fact orchestrated by Armenians as a provocation. Armenians have done something comparable with the most notorious war crime on their side, a massacre of over 400 Azerbaijani civilians in the Nagorno-Karabakh village of Khojaly; Armenian politicians have frequently either denied that the massacre happened or have claimed that Azerbaijanis themselves carried it out.

Aylisli said in interviews after the release of *Stone Dreams* that he hoped Armenian writers would write about the crimes committed on their side of the conflict. "This novel is a kind of message to Armenians living in Karabakh," he said in one interview.[10]

---

9   Shahin Abbasov, "Azerbaijan: Writer Buckling under Strain of Literary Controversy," eurasianet, February 14, 2013, https://eurasianet.org/s/azerbaijan-writer-buckling-under-strain-of-literary-controversy.

10 Daisy Sindelar, "Azeri Author Sends Unpopular Message to Armenians: 'We Can Live Together,'" Radio Liberty's website, February 1, 2013, https://www.rferl.org/a/armenia-azerbaijan-stone-dreams-akram-aylisli/24890815.html.

Don't think that we've forgotten all the bad things we've done to you. We accept that. You have also done bad things to us. It's the job of Armenian writers to write about those bad things, about the Khojaly massacre. . . . Because it's not possible for any people to commit such cruelties and not write about it. Don't politicize these things. If Armenians continue to live in the Karabakh region of Azerbaijan, we have to live side by side. This novel is a message to them. Don't be afraid. It's not the end. We can live together.[11]

But in a development that was as depressing as it was predictable, the release of *Stone Dreams* had an entirely different impact in Armenia. Armenians loved the book: within four years of its publication, no fewer than five translations of the work into Armenian—none authorized by Aylisli—were produced.[12] In 2014, *Stone Dreams* became one of two bestsellers of the year in Armenia.[13]

Armenians loved *Stone Dreams* because it "proved" that Azerbaijanis had been in the wrong. Aylisli's novella was cynically used by nationalist Armenians as evidence that it was Azerbaijanis who had more to apologize for, and his persecution was gleefully portrayed as yet more evidence of Armenians' superiority. Aylisli's call for Armenians to examine their own crimes against Azerbaijanis was ignored; Armenia is no more ready to examine its guilt than is Azerbaijan.

"At this point I don't see any Armenian writer who would take the risks that Akram Aylisli did," said Levon Javakhian, the Armenian writer who had perhaps come closest. He had written a short story, "*Kirve*" [Godfather], that expressed sympathy for Azerbaijanis, and he was criticized (and, he says, surveilled by the state) for it. "We don't have writers as brave as he is. They don't have the courage to write the kind of novel that Aylisli did, but just something as modest as my story '*Kirve*.'"[14] Javakhian also noted, "For me, there is an

---

11 Ibid.

12 Alisa Gevogyan, "Facts Distorted in Azeri Author's Book: Argam Ayvazyan," website of Public Radio of Armenia, May 31, 2016, http://www.armradio.am/en/2016/05/31/facts-distorted-in-azeri-authors-book-argam-ayvazyan/.

13 Alisa Gevogyan, "Azerbaijani Writer Akram Aylisli's 'Stone Dreams' [is] One of the Bestsellers in Armenia," website of Public Radio of Armenia, February 21, 2014, http://www.armradio.am/en/2014/02/21/azerbaijani-writer-akram-aylislis-stone-dreams-one-of-the-bestsellers-in-armenia/.

14 Mikail Mamedov, "The *Stone Dreams* Scandal: the Nagorny Karabakh Conflict and Armenian-Azerbaijani Relations in Contemporary Literature," *Caucasus Survey* 2, no. 1–2 (2014): 42–59.

Azerbaijan of Ramil Safarov and an Azerbaijan of Akram Aylisli. Aylisli's novel elevated Azerbaijan, and didn't let it be stereotyped as a criminal with an axe."[15]

Aylisli has suffered greatly for his courageous stance; "tragedy" and "martyrdom" do not seem hyperbolic descriptions of what has happened to him. What risks getting lost in the political controversy, however, is that Aylisli is an excellent writer, well deserving of the accolades he once received in Azerbaijan. One can only hope that the political intrigue and historical disputes surrounding these novellas will attract readers who, then, are pleasantly surprised to find that his novels are also genuine works of art. This edition is a welcome introduction for an English-language audience to this great humanist and remarkable writer.

Joshua Kucera

---

15 Emil Sanamyan, "Acknowledgement and Praise: Armenian Reactions to Akram Aylisli's Novel Stone Dreams," *Caucasus Survey* 2, no. 1–2 (2014): 60–63.

Translator Acknowledgments

This project is the culmination of over three years' work. I was initially contacted in 2014 by individuals in Russia seeking an English-language translator for Akram Aylisli's *Stone Dreams*, the middle novella of this trilogy. At that time Mr. Aylisli, who had been nominated by supporters in the United States, Russia, and elsewhere for the 2014 Nobel Peace Prize, was already confined by the Azerbaijani government to de facto house arrest, and would subsequently be charged with additional offenses *as a direct result of writing these novellas*. My initial efforts to find an interested publisher to support the translation were unsuccessful—for some the subject matter was too "foreign," for others too "political." There were commercial considerations, as well; on its own *Stone Dreams* was too short a work for most publishers to consider as a stand-alone volume, and the trilogy as a whole was potentially too long.

Even after I was awarded a fellowship to support translation of the entire trilogy, the project was fraught with difficulty; I am a Russian-language translator, and the works themselves were originally written in Azeri. Two of the three novellas (*Yemen* and *Stone Dreams*) had been published commercially in Russia and were available to me in digital copies. However, *A Fantastical Traffic Jam* had only been published in Russian in a fifty-copy limited edition produced in Baku (it has never been published in full in Azeri), and for some months I was unable to obtain a copy. It was eventually sent to me by a colleague in Russia in PDF, which meant the initial work had to be done by hand and then transferred into digital format. With the translation itself fully funded and the Russian-language publications in hand, it still took months of additional effort to find a publisher willing to support this lengthy, linguistically and culturally complex, politically charged project.

The world has changed a great deal since 1991 when *Yemen*, the first novella of the trilogy, was completed. In December of that year the Soviet Union, of which Azerbaijan had been an important constituent republic, collapsed. *Stone Dreams* and *A Fantastical Traffic Jam*, written sixteen and almost twenty years later, respectively, reflect Mr. Aylisli's experience of the post-Soviet world, including some years as a highly honored writer and sometime-member of the Milli Mejlis, Azerbaijan's national assembly. *Farewell, Aylis*, meanwhile, follows Mr. Aylisli's path as a political prisoner and voice of conscience in the aftermath of the publication of *Stone Dreams*. While my best efforts have been made to render into accessible English the personal names, place names, ideas, and ideologies originally conceived in Azeri, Armenian, Persian, Russian, and other languages, cultures, and political environments ranging over this almost thirty-year period—and in the case of *Stone Dreams* extending back into ancient history—infelicities will inevitably remain.

In producing this translated edition of the trilogy and Mr. Aylisli's afterword to it, I was exceedingly fortunate to be able to confer with the author himself in the language we share, Russian. During our consultations, a few minor inconsistencies in the original text, most of them having to do with the timing of events in the novellas, were corrected. The first novella in the trilogy, *Yemen*, was originally translated from Azeri by Mirza Guseinzade and published in Russian in 1994. *Stone Dreams* and *A Fantastical Traffic Jam* were translated from Azeri into Russian by Mr. Aylisli himself (indeed, Mr. Aylisli has said publicly that he prefers the Russian-language version of *Stone Dreams* to the original in Azeri). *Farewell, Aylis*, which was conceived as an afterword to the trilogy and written specifically for this Academic Studies Press edition (and again translated by Mr. Aylisli himself into Russian), has not been published in any edition or language aside from this one. It is a privilege for any translator to work closely with an author—and it is a particular honor for me to have worked with one whose grace under pressure, humanity, courage, and commitment to conscience are not abstract ideals but lived realities.

As I write this at the end of 2017, Mr. Aylisli is about to enter his sixth year of political repression in his homeland of Azerbaijan, where he continues to be confined by the authorities to de facto house arrest. His books have been burned, he himself has been burned in effigy, and in 2013 a politician offered a bounty to anyone who would cut off the writer's ear, a bounty that was eventually rescinded under international pressure. New charges carrying a three-year penalty were filed against him in the spring of 2016, the result of an incident at the Baku airport, where Mr. Aylisli had hoped to catch a flight to address a gathering in Venice (the text of those undelivered remarks can be found here at the end of *Farewell, Aylis*). On December 6, 2017, Mr. Aylisli turned eighty.

Because of the current state of political affairs and Mr. Aylisli's personal situation in Azerbaijan, it is not possible to publicly name all the organizations and individuals who have materially and otherwise supported this project; I am profoundly grateful to them all. Among those who can be named, I am particularly grateful to the National Endowment for the Arts; to Shura Burtin and Natasha Perova in Russia; to Harold Leich at the Library of Congress; to Umair Kazi and the Authors Guild; to Faith Wilson Stein, formerly of Academic Studies Press, for her initial championing of the project; to Series Editor Rebecca Ruth Gould for her wisdom and erudition; to Alex Zucker and Marian Schwartz for sage advice at crucial stages of the project; to Margarit Ordukhanyan for assistance with terms in Armenian; to Mary-Sherman Willis and Patricia Davis for assistance in demystifying horses and riding terminology; to Anne Harding Woodworth for her friendship and warm support of this project; to Lisa Hayden for extraordinary encouragement over the years and for her remarkable insight into the mysteries of translation (including the mysteries of *this* translation); to Liza Prudovskaya, who read every word (sometimes many times over), and without whom this translation could never have been completed; to Daria Pokholkova at Academic Studies Press for carrying the project over the finish line, and to Matthew Charlton and Jenna Colozza for their creativity and determination in spreading the word; and to John Williams and Alexander Young-Williams, whose patience and good humor when duty called have been remarkable.

This translation is dedicated to the memory of Alexander Woronzoff-Dashkoff, teacher.

Katherine E. Young

Yemen

A Story

And it's wasteland here, and wasteland —
All around—is what you see.
The world starts to resemble Yemen,
Endless Yemen, eh, Safaly?

(Being in a superb mood, Ali Ziya, the father of the people, spoke these matchless
lines at the airport of the faraway city of Sana'a.)

Longing as Illness

The idea to describe Safaly *muallim*'s life first came to me two or three years ago. At that time I thought a great deal about the strange life of that strange person. Bead by bead (speaking colorfully in the eastern style) I strung everything that happened to him together on a thread, trying to create a necklace or something resembling a string of prayer beads. But the thing is, the thread kept breaking, scattering beads all over the place, this one in Buzbulag, that one in Yemen. I'm not even talking about Zugulba, Bukhara, or the State of Mississippi—the birthplace of William Faulkner—in the South of the United States of America.

In a sense I was saying goodbye to Safaly *muallim* forever. And honestly, I wasn't particularly distressed by that. In our work these things often happen: you think about someone for months and even years, and then you sit at your desk and see that there's no such person, and no matter how you struggle, you can't write about them. If it had all depended on me, then, clearly, a similar fate awaited Safaly *muallim*. Except everything happened differently. On the twenty-first of July of this year (pay attention: it was the anniversary of the day that the American Neil Armstrong walked on the moon) I descended along Governor's Garden towards the Boulevard, and there Safaly *muallim* again came to mind. And I remembered him not only because the moonwalk by the thirty-eight-year-old American professor had been a big event in Safaly *muallim*'s life and not just because this year at the end of July Baku was hot, the kind of heat they hadn't seen in a long time even in the State of Mississippi in the South of the USA—this heat, I was convinced, would absolutely compel Safaly *muallim* to think about the great American writer William Faulkner and the ninety-six-year-old inhabitant of Buzbulag Khyzyr *kishi*.

I was even planning to begin the life story of Safaly *muallim* with the story of Faulkner and Khyzyr *kishi*. Just imagine, Faulkner and Khyzyr *kishi*: is it possible to find a more interesting opening for a work of literature? It's realistic and at the same time unusual. Its unconventionality is completely understandable all by itself. And its basis in real life is that once, on just such a hot summer day,

Safaly *muallim* made himself comfortable at home in an armchair—bathed in sweat, drinking tea—and suddenly his glance fell on a portrait looking at him from the bookshelf. That portrait was on the dust jacket of a thick book. A black-browed, black-eyed, mustachioed man was looking at Safaly *muallim*. He was around fifty years old. And above the portrait, which was bordered with a black frame, "William Faulkner" was written in bold, white letters.

Safaly *muallim* knew without question that William Faulkner was a great man. Safaly *muallim* had read something of the work of that famous writer. However, Safaly *muallim* had not bought that particular book himself. Safaly *muallim*'s daughter Rena had brought it from Leningrad where she was studying. And the book by Faulkner with the portrait on the dust jacket had been placed on the shelf then, and it stood just as it was standing now. That is, not so much like a book but a portrait. (Who knows, perhaps that black-browed, black-eyed, black-mustachioed person in the portrait reminded Rena not only of the writer Faulkner but of someone else!)

And on that hot summer day when, covered from head to toe in sweat, Safaly *muallim* quenched his thirst with tea, the person in the portrait reminded him of none other than his uncle Khyzyr *kishi*. Moreover, "reminded" is too weak a word—at that moment it seemed to Safaly *muallim* that the person in the portrait was not Faulkner but Khyzyr *kishi* himself. That same Khyzyr *kishi* who was a ninety-six-year-old resident of the village of Buzbulag and the uncle of Safaly *muallim*!

Isn't that an excellent beginning for a story? I'm just afraid you might doubt the truthfulness of it, especially the resemblance of a forty-five- to fifty-year-old intellectual to a simple, ninety-six-year-old peasant! But it was real, I swear by Allah, it was one-hundred-percent real. Because the last time Safaly *muallim* had seen his uncle Khyzyr *kishi* was in 1938. Then Khyzyr *kishi* had been somewhere between forty-five and fifty. And Safaly *muallim* had approximated his uncle's current age himself—in point of fact, Khyzyr *kishi* might have been ninety or ninety-nine. But that's not important. The essential point is that this strange event really did happen to Safaly *muallim* on one of those intensely hot days of the Baku summer and that it absolutely might serve as an interesting beginning for any literary work.

This summer, when I suddenly remembered Safaly *muallim* once again in Governor's Garden (on the anniversary of the day that Armstrong landed on the moon), I also remembered that thing with Faulkner, of course. Now, two years later, it seemed to me for some reason not so funny but more sad. And not because Khyzyr *kishi* was a very unfortunate man compared to Faulkner.

Who can know that? It's not even possible to know whether Khyzyr *kishi* considered himself inferior to other people or not. But there was undoubtedly something sad in comparing those two people living under one sky, one God, if only because by God's allegedly equal graciousness towards all, his ward Khyzyr *kishi* was master of at most a quarter of an acre of land, while Faulkner had used a colored pencil to circle twenty-five hundred square miles on the map of his country and written "William Faulkner, sole heir and master of this earth" and signed his name beneath.

From that same book with the portrait on the dust jacket, Safaly *muallim* knew a few more facts of Faulkner's biography. And Safaly *muallim*'s current knowledge of Khyzyr *kishi* was based on the stories of acquaintances whom he ran into by chance once a month or even once a year at the market or on the street, acquaintances with whom he exchanged a couple of words in passing, and also on his—meaning Safaly *muallim*'s—unrestrained imagination. For example, Safaly *muallim* knew that his uncle's wife Tarlan was still alive. He knew whom Khyzyr *kishi*'s three daughters had married and whom the only son Safar had married. One cow, ten sheep, ten goats, and ten chickens: it seems all that had been at Khyzyr *kishi*'s farm even in old times. However, in those times Khyzyr *kishi* had also had a remarkable, restive black donkey. Safaly *muallim*'s memory preserved many stories connected with that donkey and now, when he'd come face to face with real life, Safaly *muallim* immersed himself in memories of childhood, and it seemed to him that that donkey was still alive.

In this book I'll say a lot about Safaly *muallim*'s childhood, which was spent in the village. I'll certainly make you acquainted with Khyzyr *kishi*, who since that time had remained in Safaly *muallim*'s memory as a person of endless erudition; with Khyzyr *kishi*'s personal plot of a quarter-acre of land; and even with his cow and sheep. It's just, honestly, that I'm not certain whether I'll return to Khyzyr *kishi*'s connection with Faulkner, so I'd like to say a few more words about that.

First of all, I want to say that on that hot summer day when Safaly *muallim* suddenly discovered that a portrait of his uncle Khyzyr *kishi* was staring straight at him from his bookshelf as he drank hot tea, Safaly *muallim* at first rejoiced. But then he was seized by strong unease. Paying no attention to the heat, he headed to the clinic, where he immediately asked them to check his blood pressure, because although that book had been standing on the shelf for more than twenty years, the transformation of Faulkner into Khyzyr *kishi* had taken place in the course of a second or two, which meant, in the language of medicine, that there was an anomaly. "Nostalgia!" was the diagnosis joyously and solemnly revealed to Safaly *muallim* by a young man just recently arrived at Clinic Number Two of the Ministry of Health's Fourth Main Directorate who in a short time had earned the reputation of "a capable doctor"—a young man whose speech and manners clearly showed him to have come from the provinces. But Safaly *muallim* knew that even without the doctor. He even knew that the word was pronounced "noSTALgia" and not "nostalGIa," that is, that the stress fell on the second and not the third syllable. Notwithstanding that, on his return home Safaly *muallim* immediately searched for the meaning of the word in one of the dictionaries and was astonished to read "Nostalgia (Gr. *nostos*, return + *algos*, pain, suffering)—homesickness." In essence, the pain and suffering generated by homesickness, the longing for one's father's home! In Safaly *muallim*'s opinion, there was a staggeringly deep meaning in that, and that meaning was extremely precisely conveyed in the dictionary. But what, exactly, was it: longing or illness? Perhaps it was illness caused by longing? O Lord, may your mercy be a thousand times blessed, it's even possible to become ill from longing!

However that may be, the definition in the dictionary produced the kind of impression on Safaly *muallim* that he hadn't experienced, perhaps, from even the most beautiful, the saddest poetry. At the same time, somewhere in the most secret corner of his heart, that definition made Safaly *muallim* happy. In the first place, if that was the only reason for his illness, then he wasn't seriously ill. And in the second place, if that same nostalgia was in fact an illness, then Safaly *muallim* had long been accustomed to that particular illness—that is, longing for the village where he was born, grew up, with whose springs he was nursed until age seventeen (before he moved to the city), the village that still rose from time to time in his heart as a tormenting pain. Khyzyr *kishi*, into whom William Faulkner had suddenly transformed, was the surprising embodiment of that longing. And no one else but Khyzyr *kishi*! Because Safaly *muallim*'s seventeen years of village life were most of all connected with Khyzyr *kishi*, with his yard, garden, and vegetable garden. Orphaned after the death of his father, Safaly grew up at his uncle's alongside Khyzyr *kishi*'s only son Safar and two daughters whose names rhymed, Naz *khanum* and Gryz *khanum*. Together with his cousins young Safaly tended Khyzyr *kishi*'s livestock on the bank of the stream that ran through their village, drove the cow to join the herd, and sat on that same, restive black donkey and galloped with pleasure around the village from end to end. . . . And so, on that summer day, longing for that unforgettable time appeared to seventy-two-year-old Safaly *muallim* in the person of Khyzyr *kishi*. Here's yet another picture of human loneliness for you. Perhaps it's only a brushstroke, the contour of the sad future of lonely old people. Having retired on a pension and buried, one after the other, his eighty-eight-year-old mother, Seren, and his wife Zarnigyar, Safaly *muallim* uncomplainingly accepted that future with all its torments because his relationship with Rena had broken off long ago. While still studying in Leningrad, Rena had married one of her professors—a Jew with a Georgian last name, a man old enough to be her father—and since then she hadn't returned to Baku.

After his daughter's marriage, Safaly *muallim* had traveled to Leningrad once. Seren *arvad* was still alive then. Seren *arvad* had loved Rena perhaps even more than Zarnigyar did. But on her deathbed she didn't once remember her granddaughter. She continually called her brother: "Khyzyr! Khyzyr!" But Khyzyr wasn't there, of course. Khyzyr could be found among the mountains and gardens of Buzbulag where he was placidly grazing his herd. There was only that same book. It had stood on the shelf for several years during Seren *arvad*'s life: a black-browed, black-eyed, black-mustachioed man. But if that person in the photograph really did look so much like Khyzyr *kishi*, why hadn't Seren *arvad* noticed it even once? In a word, if Khyzyr *kishi* (as he had been fifty years ago when Safaly *muallim* left Buzbulag) to some degree or another did in fact resemble Faulkner, homesickness undoubtedly also played a role in that.

In order to escape that illness for just a little while, Safaly *muallim* had to go to the village after his fifty-year absence. Had to go to meet with his uncle, his uncle's wife, Safar, Naz *khanum* and Gryz *khanum*, with contemporary Buzbulag, and (the most important thing!) with the years of his childhood and youth. And on that day—that is, the twenty-first of July, the anniversary of the day when the spaceship Apollo 11 landed on the moon—as I descended along Governor's Garden to the seaside park and walked around there, I rambled in my thoughts around Buzbulag with Safaly *muallim*. And if I'd sat down on that day to write this book, then I'd have started the first chapter with exactly this episode—Safaly *muallim*'s trip to the village. But I was unfortunate that day because it was hot, extremely hot; my brain was melting from intense heat and stuffiness like pitch in a cauldron. . . .

The other day I went walking in the seaside park again. It was the beginning of September. The heat was already waning. The right time for walks. However, Safaly *muallim*, who after the death of his wife spent practically the whole day in the seaside park, wasn't there that day. Interesting: where could he have gone?

After long thought I came to the conclusion that Safaly *muallim* was most likely in Zugulba at the resort run by the Ministry of Health's Fourth Main Directorate, because even while Zarnigyar was alive he'd gone to that particular resort to relax for a month or two every year.

On the day of his trip to Zugulba Safaly *muallim* had awakened at daybreak.

He was anxious. To some extent happy, even. He forced himself with difficulty to eat a sandwich, washing it down with three or four cups of tea, then went out onto the balcony and greedily smoked a cigarette, but all the same, it was early, very early. If he left home then it was possible that there wouldn't be a crush in the metro, but at the final station where the bus stop was located, he'd undoubtedly encounter chaos: people would be hurrying to work.

He'd already packed his things the previous night. Actually, those things in their entirety consisted of a change of underwear, an extra pair of shoes, soap, and a razor. All of that fit into the little suitcase. Safaly *muallim* packed the hot plate they'd always brought to the health resort when Zarnigyar was alive in a separate basket. More precisely in "Vaska's bag" (Vaska was the cat). That remarkable Siberian breed of animal had been given to Zarnigyar by that same professor with the Georgian last name when Safaly *muallim* for the first and last time in his life had gone to Leningrad to visit Rena. For three or four years—in that very bag—they'd carried Vaska with them to the resort, and the last time, while they were already preparing to return home, Zarnigyar for some reason decided to leave the cat. "Let him stay here," she said. "I swear by Allah, Safaly, I'm just afraid when I see his face. Just you look at the scorn with which he watches us! As if my father owed his father something. He sits, damn him, like the Lord God!"

Zarnigyar was right. Vaska really did look at people as if the human race weren't worth anything besides his scorn. There was so much haughtiness, so much contempt in the cat's glance that it was as if he were the sole intelligent and, moreover, the sole highly cultured being in the world! As if people were created only to be of service to him: to stand for hours in lines to buy him milk and to prepare the requisite, tasty dinner of several foods, served right on time. In short, he was some kind of young nobleman, a hereditary aristocrat. How many times Vaska's divine haughtiness had provoked Safaly *muallim* himself into a rage, driving him out of his mind! But that was all long ago, while Zarnigyar was still alive. Lately Safaly *muallim* had been feeling that he really missed Vaska's tricks, and now, the first time he was planning to go to Zugulba since Zarnigyar's death, he hoped to see the enigmatically haughty Vaska.

Suffering from idleness, Safaly *muallim* turned over everything he was taking with him for the journey in his memory one more time, just in case. However, if he forgot anything, it was no big deal. To return from Zugulba to the city was child's play, something like an hour's trip on the bus. But this time Safaly *muallim* had firmly resolved to himself not to appear in the city until at least the middle of October. He was very much afraid that one of the Buzbulag descendants of Khyzyr *kishi*, one Tariel—the oldest son of Khyzyr *kishi*'s youngest daughter, Bas *khanum* (she'd been born the year the war started)—would suddenly appear in Baku. Tariel, whom Safaly *muallim* had seen in the summer in Buzbulag, had already lived several years in Moscow. There he'd married and, according to rumor, married a general's daughter. That summer when Safaly *muallim* was in Buzbulag, Tariel had suddenly appeared in the village for five days or so but disappeared just as suddenly. And during that time he wasn't able to do much harm to Safaly *muallim*; on the contrary, he gave him an unexpected gift, imported tea in a gilt metal box (Chinese tea in English packaging!). And also various Moscow candies and some wonderful cookies of the sort that Safaly *muallim* had never even seen, although for his whole adult life he'd traveled to Moscow once a year at the very least. A bottle of Scotch whisky that Tariel had given him at their very first meeting now lay in the suitcase—Safaly *muallim* was carrying it with him to Zugulba to give to one of the doctors or to an ordinary Soviet person with whom fate might throw him together.

Of course, it goes without saying that Safaly *muallim* might have harbored suspicion towards that young, thirty-year-old fellow simply because Tariel had given such an expensive present to the first person who came along. However, it seems the unrestrained, all-business character of Tariel frightened Safaly *muallim* still more. Over the several days he'd spent in the village, Tariel was able to roof his own home with colorful sheets of stainless steel. He installed a motor by the river and extended pipes to a height of twenty yards along which a stream, just a little one—about the width of a finger—but all the same a continuous stream of water, flowed into his grandfather Khyzyr *kishi*'s yard. Even in Safaly *muallim*'s father's home, where no one had lived for many years, Tariel managed to leave a trail: he installed a metal tank that was heated by firewood, a faucet, a shower—in short, he built something like a bath. If Safaly *muallim* had agreed, Tariel would even have covered the ancient earthen roof with slate. But Safaly *muallim* could in no way agree to that because Tariel would not take money from him; accordingly, Safaly *muallim* would have been in debt to him, moreover, such great debt that he would never have been able to repay it. Besides, judging from everything, it seemed that Tariel had some kind of hidden plans relating to Safaly *muallim*'s Baku apartment: he repeatedly asked where the apartment was located and how many rooms it had. And if he didn't say it plainly, then the following was clear from his words: Enough hiding from the relatives, now allow us to be closer, to come visit you, you're already old, you've got one foot in the grave, don't let your apartment end up in just anyone's hands after you die. And Tariel had already been able to find out the address and telephone number from Safaly *muallim*. Now he planned to pay a visit to Safaly *muallim* together with the "general's daughter"—his wife—in September. Safaly *muallim* understood that Tariel's long-term plans concerning his apartment were concealed behind this visit, and perhaps he left for Zugulba at this moment most of all so as not to allow that sort of person into his home.

The main story about Buzbulag and its current residents is still ahead. But I consider it necessary to say now that after almost two and a half months of village life (from the sixteenth of June through the twenty-sixth of August), Safaly *muallim*, perhaps as never before in his life, enjoyed the peace in his spacious apartment. Firstly, the domestic amenities: a bath, a shower—hot and cold water when you wanted. Secondly, the market, the stores (with regard to the abundance of food, Baku was a heavenly place, the center of the earth compared to Buzbulag!). And thirdly, if the trip to Buzbulag didn't entirely heal the very deeply rooted nostalgia in Safaly *muallim*'s soul, in any case it still markedly eased the torment that had tortured him for long years. It was as if only now could he fully comprehend and value all the advantages of city life.

In Zugulba Safaly *muallim* wouldn't experience any special difficulty with regard to securing provisions and everyday items. The secluded, two-room apartment was, well, let us say, a room in a health resort. There was hot and cold water, that was the main thing—and at the resort Safaly *muallim* didn't have any special complaints about the food. With regard to the tea required for his heart's content, he could make arrangements—it was for precisely this reason that Safaly *muallim* was carrying the hotplate to Zugulba in "Vaska's bag."

After a couple of hours Safaly *muallim* carried his things to the landing by the elevator, locked the door of the four-room apartment, and knocked at the neighbor's door—Lora the Armenian—so as to give her the key to the mailbox hanging downstairs by the entryway. He'd also given the mailbox key to Lora when he left for Buzbulag in June because he subscribed to many newspapers and magazines, and someone had to collect the mail at least once every two or three days.

The neighbor knew beforehand where Safaly *muallim* was going. And Safaly *muallim* had warned her in advance that if anyone did ask for him, not to tell them he'd gone to Zugulba. But just in case, he now considered it necessary to remind his neighbor one more time.

"One person," (he undoubtedly had Tariel in mind) "I know, will ask about me. Don't tell him I'm in Zugulba. He's a very impudent person. If he pesters you too much, say I went to Leningrad."

And the talkative Lora, who'd seen a great deal in her time and was well past eighty, who spoke Azeri no worse, perhaps, than Safaly *muallim* himself, for some reason answered him in Russian.

"Please! Please! Don't worry. I won't say anything. Not for any reason."

Safaly *muallim* also switched to Russian.

"I'll have to bother you occasionally with a phone call."

"Of course, of course! Call as much as you like. That goes about saying," Lora said this sincerely, and Safaly *muallim* thought to himself that if Lora had known Russian better, she would have said "That goes *without* saying." Musing about that, he pressed the elevator button.

"There are rumors Gorbachev will be removed soon," said Lora unexpectedly.

"Really?" answered Safaly *muallim* with surprise, and suddenly, for some unknown reason, the image of Tariel's father-in-law—the Moscow general whom Safaly *muallim* had never in his life seen—rose clearly before his eyes.

After Safaly *muallim* arrived in Zugulba and settled into his room, more than an hour remained at his disposal until the afternoon snack, and all that time could be used to walk around the resort.

The three- to four-story buildings of the health resort were built in a single line at the same distance from one another, one side facing the sea, and it was precisely from that side that Safaly *muallim* had to begin his walk: all the balconies in those buildings opened to the sea, and if Vaska were still alive, it was quite likely that the cat could be on one of the balconies of the lower floors. Well, and besides that Safaly *muallim* wanted to look at the sea right there, from the resort, because this sea was quite different from the dirty sea covered in spilled oil that splashed at Baku's seaside park. Here the sea water was sometimes clean, like tears.

And the sea was clean now, too. Where the rays of the sun fell, the water sparkled like crystal. And the weather wasn't terribly hot. In any case, after the dry summer in Buzbulag that penetrated a person's body like a knife, the sun of Absheron seemed warm and gentle to Safaly *muallim*.

The best times in Zugulba were July and August. Not just anyone was able to obtain the special voucher required for a stay here during those months.

In the main, the people who came here on vacation with their families in July and August occupied responsible posts: ministers, secretaries of district Party committees, highly placed members of the intelligentsia, and also those who held lesser positions but had money. And it was pleasant for Safaly *muallim* here after they left because nature was able to heal the wounds inflicted on her over the course of the previous two months by those representatives of the most voracious and shit-producing, arrogant, and capricious layers of society. Zugulba was the same as always. The sea in its place, bushes, flowers, trees—everything was as it had been previously. Even the birds: sparrows, hoopoes, Barbary doves. Here and there dogs and cats came into view. But Vaska wasn't in sight. (During the rest of his time at the health resort Safaly *muallim* would look for Vaska many more times.)

After the afternoon snack, Safaly *muallim* intended to nap for an hour or an hour and a half. He planned to make tea when he woke up and only after that undertake the main thing. In the two rooms that he occupied, Safaly *muallim* intended to rearrange the furniture: to move the bed from one room to the other, put the sofa right next to the door that opened onto the balcony, and switch the places of the television and the refrigerator. Only then could Safaly *muallim* feel relatively comfortable. He'd always done this before and had accustomed the "lady of the house," the housekeeper of the health resort, to it because Safaly *muallim*'s life here at the resort necessarily had to differ in some way from the lives of those gluttonous and shit-producing people—otherwise, Safaly *muallim* would have lost respect for himself.

Although it was already fifteen minutes past the appointed time, the cafeteria doors were still shut, and a crowd had gathered for the afternoon snack by the newspaper kiosk just off the entrance to the cafeteria. Safaly *muallim* knew a few of them. But the majority were strangers. And all together there were—at most—fifty to sixty people. It had been that way even in previous years—only in extremely rare instances had Safaly *muallim* seen more vacationers here after the end of the main season.

No one interfered with Safaly *muallim* choosing a place to his liking in the cafeteria, which had been designed for more than five hundred people. On the upper level of the hall there were tables on a glassed-in veranda. That was a place for especially honored guests, and the meals served there weren't prepared in the so-called "general pot." Even now, five or six people sat on the veranda. They seemed to be eating fish *shashlyk*; in any case, a cook in a white cap and white coat kept appearing on the veranda carrying skewers of what looked like sturgeon. And when Safaly *muallim* got up, having finished his *borsch* and meat patties, he couldn't believe his eyes: it seemed to him that among those sitting on the far end of the veranda he spotted Ali Ziya!

In the course of ordinary life Ali Ziya would never have appeared here because, according to rumors, he had his own apartment even in Moscow, and his dacha in Mardakan was considered the best in Absheron. Therefore, Safaly *muallim* decided that Ali Ziya had come here simply to get out, or just to receive foreign guests; after guiding them around the attractions of Absheron, he'd brought them here to eat lunch. However, Safaly *muallim* considered it awkward to look over there another time to see the foreigners Ali Ziya was hosting. He left the cafeteria extraordinarily troubled and, trying to fall asleep, told himself that he'd seen no Ali Ziya here in Zugulba, not at all.

But Ali Ziya wasn't the kind of person it was possible to forget so easily. And in any case, it had been enough for Safaly *muallim* just to see Ali Ziya from a distance to completely lose the pleasure of an afternoon nap. Try as he might, Safaly *muallim* couldn't fall asleep after lunch that day because all of his conscious life, as they say, was connected with Ali Ziya. Together they'd entered "public life." For many years they'd walked through it side by side. And now it had been more than fifteen years since Ali Ziya had lived without Safaly *muallim* in that world they'd entered together. No one there needed Safaly *muallim* anymore, and he suspected Ali Ziya had had something to do with that.

"Safaly. . . ."

"Yes?"

"Do you want to become a *kerbalai*?"

"How?"

"Would you like me to take you to Mecca?"

"Now, really, does someone who goes to Mecca become a *kerbalai*?"

A jerky sound that resembled a cat's cough could be heard through the receiver. Ali Ziya had a strange way of laughing: when he laughed, his voice changed entirely.

"You're a disaster, Safaly, and a pain in the ass, there's no fooling you! Well, alright, then, be a *hajji*. Would you like to become a *hajji*?"

"Not bad for a man over fifty! What, is a delegation going?"

"For now it's just us," announced Ali Ziya genially. "Perhaps one more person from Kiev. We'll go to Yemen, we shouldn't be too picky. They say it's not far from there to Mecca. Minasha just looked on the map. Minasha's a smart girl; I have a very bright daughter."

He was talking about Minaya, his youngest daughter. Safaly *muallim* knew that. But at that time Safaly *muallim* couldn't even have imagined that Ali Ziya spoke about Minasha by design; in fact, it was Ali Ziya's goal to set the girl up at the institute where Safaly *muallim* was rector. And if Ali Ziya hadn't had that goal, Safaly *muallim* would never have seen Yemen.

But he really did see it. And along with Yemen Safaly *muallim* also saw something else new—something he hadn't seen until then—an entirely new face of the world. It's probably possible to write a whole long novel about that bloodless face of the world. You can bet that if Shakespeare had come across that theme, it would have given birth to a tragedy equal to *Hamlet* or *Othello*. But I don't want to write a tragedy now, don't want to become Shakespeare. I'll tell you everything as it was, and you can come to your own philosophical conclusions. In a nutshell.

Yemen

The airplane had left Moscow on the journey to Yemen late at night, around midnight. Besides Ali Ziya and Safaly *muallim*, a thin woman in glasses, Polina Viktorovna—an orientalist and PhD—was also flying to Yemen. And she wasn't from Kiev but from Moscow, a professor at Lomonosov University.

After Simferopol they made a short stop at the Cairo airport during the night and arrived at the Sana'a airfield early in the morning. Safaly *muallim* remembered the airfield's cheerless, grey steppe and the low, bare, grey hills. The landscape resembled Absheron a little, particularly in the areas of Khyzy, Divichi, and Gobustan. Here and there it was possible to note rare lawns and meadows on the hillsides. In any case, Ali Ziya, who was always faithful to the truth of life, hadn't deviated one bit from that basic principle in the improvised poem he'd uttered that morning at the airport.

Ali Ziya had slept the sleep of the dead the whole way from the Moscow airport right up to the landing in Sana'a; that's why, Safaly *muallim* thought, he was in an excellent mood that morning. Polina Viktorovna, who at first glance gave the impression of being a dry and gloomy person, read throughout the flight. It was unlikely that she'd managed to nap, but she also appeared quite refreshed and cheerful at the airfield—in any case not so serious and haughty as in the airplane. And Safaly *muallim*, one may say, hadn't closed his eyes for a minute on the airplane. Over the course of the flight he gazed sometimes at the stars in the sky, sometimes at the lights of the cities and villages, and he glanced sometimes out of the corner of his eye at Ali Ziya and Polina Viktorovna, envying in his soul the deep sleep of the one and the enthusiastic reading of the other. That morning at the airfield, therefore, Safaly *muallim* was feeling something like a sour quince. In comparison to him, Ali Ziya looked like a rosy apple just cut from the tree. He joked, talked loudly, laughed. Almost intoning (as if it were a song), he repeated the short, four-line poem he'd composed right there at the airport with infinite joy and pleasure.

And it's wasteland here, and wasteland
—All around—is what you see.
The world starts to resemble Yemen,
Endless Yemen, eh, Safaly?

It was as if that scholar, thinker, great public figure, novelist, and playwright whom, as they say, every dog knows, rose in his own estimation because of that short verse, fell in love with himself, was delighted with himself. In fact, Safaly *muallim* clearly also liked that little poem very much—otherwise, he wouldn't have remembered it. However, one more detail remained in Safaly *muallim*'s memory in connection with that poem, the recollection of which evoked a strange feeling of shame: Ali Ziya had translated the poem into Russian especially for Polina Viktorovna! Safaly *muallim* shuddered, remembering that. Why he shuddered, he probably didn't even know himself. . . .

Bereft of his customary sleep, Safaly *muallim* was still lying in bed in his room at the health resort in Zugulba remembering everything connected with Ali Ziya when he suddenly noticed some kind of terrible, nauseating smell—it was the smell of bleaching powder mixed with starch that rose from the pillow-case—clean and nasty, like everything in that world. Safaly *muallim* thought it would be a good idea to take off the bed linen and hang it to air out on the balcony. But he didn't get up, he was too lazy. And perhaps his recollections of Yemen kept him from doing it. . . .

A representative of the Soviet embassy had met them at the airfield. With his help, they filled out some forms and, after completing the necessary formalities, passed quickly through customs control and headed into the city in the embassy car, a Volga. But whether the road into the city was too short or whether Safaly *muallim* fell asleep on the road from the airport, in any case, if there'd been anything remarkable on the way to the hotel, anything worthy of a glance, then nothing of it remained in Safaly *muallim*'s memory now. Clay roofs, fences that were also made of clay. Little windows in the houses like our flues. Thin, almost sickly men in shirts of white cotton—the kind of cotton that our women use to sew themselves nightclothes—and each man had a curved, sickle-like dagger hanging from his belt. That's it. I can even say that in the whole city of Sana'a in general, Safaly *muallim* remembered just a couple of similar, insignificant trifles. Not counting, of course, that yard. The yard of the hotel: what a thing that was, O Lord, who transported Buzbulag that day and placed it under the grey Yemen sky!

"WE'LL TAKE SHOWERS, SLEEP A COUPLE OF HOURS. THEN WE'LL MEET DOWNSTAIRS IN THE FOYER. WE'LL EAT HERE AND GO TO THE EMBASSY."

And now in Zugulba, either from the resort building or from the yard, Safaly *muallim* suddenly heard those words anew, words that had been loudly announced at the door of his room in the Yemeni hotel on that long-ago day by Ali Ziya in his capacity as the head of the delegation. And that voice sounded so wearisomely, it worried Safaly *muallim* so much that he couldn't stay in bed one second more. He leaped up and hurriedly began to get dressed. As if he were getting ready to go somewhere. As if he weren't here in Zugulba but back there in Yemen in his room on the third floor of the four-story hotel. As if he'd overslept, and Ali Ziya and Polina Viktorovna had been standing for a long time in the foyer downstairs waiting for him to go to lunch.

From the resort balcony Safaly *muallim* threw a passing glance at the sea and returned to the room; it seems he didn't even see the sea. He poured water into the teapot from the carafe standing on the table. He turned on the hot-plate and put the teapot on it. Now he could attend to rearranging the furniture. Safaly *muallim* stood a little while in a corner looking stupidly at the sofa, nightstand, refrigerator, and television, and for the first time in his life he decided that nothing needed to be rearranged. Moreover, he even came to the extraordinarily thoughtful philosophical conclusion that everything in the world was in its proper place: Khyzyr *kishi*'s place was in Buzbulag, Tariel's was in Moscow, and Ali Ziya's was right there in the enormous resort cafeteria on that part of the veranda where people ate *shashlyk* and other fine foods.

Yes, everything and everyone in this world in its proper place. Perhaps even Rena. And the haughty Vaska had probably found himself a place somewhere and was alive. . . . Then Safaly *muallim* wanted to go out and look around for Vaska until the teapot came to a boil. But he gave up that idea. And Ali Ziya kept his tight hold inside Safaly *muallim*'s head. What Ali Ziya had gotten up to back then in Yemen now, many years later, worried Safaly *muallim* again. Safaly *muallim* wouldn't forget it even in the next world—there was no doubt of that. If only what is called the next world in fact existed and Safaly *muallim* could meet Ali Ziya there! Then he'd say: "Ah, Ali, curse you, what did you do to me back then, why? Were you afraid for your job, honor, and respect, or were you my enemy before that?" And Allah alone knows how much Safaly *muallim* wanted to hear the answer to that question from the lips of Ali Ziya. But not in this world, just in the next one, because life had taught Safaly *muallim* long ago that you won't find answers in this world for many of the questions that arise here.

Safaly *muallim*, my friend, it seems the air smelled of Shakespeare, the same Shakespeare who addressed questions to God that don't have answers in this world, questions that in the end alienated the Lord from the world and from people! Now Shakespeare was probably in some kind of heaven—undoubtedly in a theater—sitting next to the Lord God and gazing at the stage of the Globe Theater as Hamlet beat his breast in an unattractive way repeating, "To be, or not to be" and—along with the Lord God—laughing loudly at the foolishness of the son of man.

Safaly *muallim* was very angry at himself for imagining such a picture, unworthy of either the Lord God or Shakespeare. He got up from the sofa and went out on the balcony. The sea seemed happy; it was calm, contented. Five or six girls swung soundlessly on a swing set built on the beach. A few of the vacationers were swimming. A young man was running somewhere along the very edge of the shore. It seemed to be Garry Kasparov. When Zarnigyar had been alive, Safaly *muallim* had often observed how Kasparov ran along the shore. Once Kasparov had even stopped at the fourth building and stroked Vaska on the head, after which Zarnigyar not only rejoiced all day but for a whole week didn't even complain about her blood pressure.

Besides the beach, it was empty all around—quiet, without people. And it seemed that the ghost of Ali Ziya wandered in this emptiness: his breath could be felt. His playful, artistic voice, which could not be confused with anything else, could be heard in every corner of this world. . . .

"WE'LL TAKE SHOWERS, SLEEP A COUPLE OF HOURS. . . ."

After Ali Ziya had banged the door and disappeared that day in Yemen, Safaly *muallim* also went into his room. He wasn't even going to take a shower. He just washed up hastily so as to sleep longer. He pulled back the sheets, undressed. And then he saw the yard through the window: the trees, the garden beds. Safaly *muallim* froze, staggered, because he'd already seen that yard somewhere before! And not simply seen but run around that yard, played in it. And how many times he'd washed up in the irrigation canal running through that yard! He'd eaten peaches straight from the trees, chucking stones at the tree, romping. O Lord, what was this? Here, right under the fence, grew that very same young tree that also grew by the fence at the same end of Khyzyr *kishi*'s yard and each spring flooded the whole world with green. Even the fence itself, constructed from ordinary river rocks coated with clay, looked like the fence in Khyzyr *kishi*'s yard. The beans here also wound up the supports the way they were planted in Buzbulag. Just as in Buzbulag, the stakes driven into the ground under the bean bushes stuck up. The beans were not yet fully grown; they hadn't extended their runners to the trees. So it was still the beginning of spring here, too. The fruits of the peach had only just appeared. The snow-white flowers of the quince hadn't yet faded.

Safaly *muallim* stood a long time in front of the window in just his underwear and undershirt; forgetting about Yemen, he looked on that piece of Buzbulag anxiously and with longing and then lay down on the bed. But there was no chance of sleep, far from it—instead of falling asleep, Safaly *muallim's* every vein was alive, awake. And while Safaly *muallim* lay sleepless with his eyes closed, it seemed that the leaves of the tree in that yard were continually filling with green, the water of the irrigation canal was becoming even clearer, and the young bean runners were neatly constructing themselves in a row like children in kindergarten holding hands and happily dancing the *Yallı* in the yard. The most terrible thing was that the leaves of the tree, the flowers of the quince, the wall, and the beans all called out in unison to Safaly *muallim*. With a well-known hum that gave him goosebumps, those voices sank into Safaly *muallim*—into every one of his cells, from head to toe—and wouldn't let him sleep.

Realizing finally that he couldn't sleep, Safaly *muallim* got up and dressed. He opened the door cautiously and went out into the corridor. Quietly, almost on tiptoe, he passed the rooms where Ali Ziya and Polina Viktorovna were staying, slowly descending from the third floor.

In the foyer not far from the entrance, a Russian fellow sat in an armchair, the driver who'd brought them from the airport. Loudly banging the tiles, he played dominoes with the hotel doorman, a young, dark-skinned Arab with a saintly face. The embassy's Volga stood right by the entrance, flush with the pavement.

Walking out the door, Safaly *muallim* stopped for a moment and with infinite pleasure heard how that light-haired, yellow-browed Russian fellow spoke Arabic; he even wanted to say something pleasant to the fellow, but he didn't say it, didn't find the occasion, because the driver was extraordinarily carried away and had more important things to think about than Safaly *muallim*.

Experiencing anxiety and fear in his soul, Safaly *muallim* left the hotel. Those feelings were connected both with how well that Russian fellow with the wheat-colored hair spoke Arabic and with the stamp of rare nobility on the dark-skinned face of the Arab, but there was also a third strange, unclear reason. He walked a little in front of the hotel, next to the Volga. And then he looked around and understood that the yard he'd seen from above didn't belong to the hotel—it was a completely isolated plot of land enclosed on all sides by a fence. But there was also an entrance from the hotel yard, a little plywood door that was unlocked. When he'd fearfully opened the door, Safaly *muallim* went into that garden; then not only did he forget his fear, but I would even say, if you believe me, that he even completely forgot that he was a Soviet citizen.

What was that, O Lord: a revelation, an inspiration, an awakening, or just that Safaly *muallim* hadn't noticed that at some point he'd died and now arisen and found himself in that scrap of "Yemeni Buzbulag"? In spite of his sleepless night, Safaly *muallim* felt unprecedented vigor and ease in that garden; it seemed to him that if he wanted to, right now he could fly above the garden like a bird and, in the twinkling of an eye, find himself in Buzbulag and there, in the yard of Khyzyr *kishi*, sit on any tree, on any branch. In that garden, it was as if Safaly *muallim*'s memory and consciousness had awakened from many years' death-like hibernation: he saw his entire half-century's life as if it lay in the palm of his hand—and the very best moments of that life, similar to the strange spring breeze, were affectionately, tenderly seeping into and wandering about his body and blood.

It turns out that a person can rejoice at anything, God willing. For example, at the fact that an Arab and Russian play dominoes; that an Arab and Russian speak Arabic to one another; and that the great writer, great scholar, and great public figure Ali Ziya sleeps like the most ordinary person in the most ordinary hotel, of which there are thousands in the world. But joy number one that filled Safaly *muallim*'s heart that day in that garden was the feeling that the world is simple and compact like home; Safaly *muallim* very much liked that simple and compact world. The earth beneath his feet seemed to be not just any earth but a carpet whose every knot, every pattern was known—and on that carpet where the influence of Khyzyr *kishi* and Tarlan *arvad* could be felt was something of the stamp of nobility on the face of the Arab playing dominoes in the foyer. Looking around in delight at the trees, peaches, quince, and beans in the garden, Safaly *muallim*'s attention was sometimes attracted to unknown grasses, bushes, and fruits—but, strangely enough, those bushes and grasses that he'd never before seen also seemed terribly familiar to Safaly *muallim*. And perhaps he'd seen them sometime and somewhere. Perhaps Safaly *muallim* himself hadn't seen them any time in this life but his distant forefathers had, and the fact that those grasses and bushes seemed familiar to him now was a manifestation of genetic memory. In any case, as he wandered in that garden that day, the present of this world was mixed with its past and future in Safaly *muallim*'s thoughts—and from that simple and enchanted harmony, the two clear eyes of Buzbulag looked calmly and gently on Safaly *muallim*.

In a word, that day Safaly *muallim* opened a direct route from the Yemeni garden where he himself was standing to the yard of his uncle Khyzyr *kishi* in Buzbulag without having obtained permission from any government or from the United Nations itself; without a war, without any weapons, he'd amalgamated the world. Now he was a Yemeni to the same degree that he was a native of Buzbulag. In other words, Safaly *muallim* was a citizen of the world. How wonderful that turned out to be, being a citizen of the world!

And how incredibly enormous was that Buzbulag if it was scattered over the whole earth, over all the space from West to East! Wherever Safaly *muallim* had been previously, the Lord had always and everywhere revealed to him a little piece of Buzbulag, whether it was mountains or a valley; all around, if only in the shade of a tree, if only beneath a bird's nest, it had been possible to sense the breath of his motherland.

But this time, it seems, more than the shadow of a tree or nest was revealed to Safaly *muallim*. Buzbulag, with all its gardens and meadows, burst in on Safaly *muallim*'s soul, entered his flesh. The bright, multicolored memories of childhood escaped into freedom; the world around shone with clear, clean light. From a distance, the red, white, and yellow voices of the flowers of the pomegranate, peach, quince, and cornelian cherry reached him from Khyzyr *kishi*'s yard. And the black brood hen that Tarlan *arvad* loved perhaps more than she loved Naz *khanum* and Gryz *khanum*, striking up an old song with new passion, went into the henhouse to lay eggs, and that cackling sounded like a hymn of peace and plenty to Safaly *muallim*; it provided Safaly *muallim* with a strange delight that didn't yield to any logic in the world, a delight similar to that he'd experienced listening as the Russian fellow spoke Arabic. The voice of the black hen reminded Safaly *muallim* of the story with Khyzyr *kishi*'s black donkey: Buzbulag, cherry season, early in the morning. That morning Khyzyr *kishi*, the black donkey, and twelve-year-old Safaly had set out on a long journey. By unfamiliar roads that Safaly was seeing for the first time in his life, through unfamiliar irrigation canals, near trees belonging to strangers, they were going towards the place called Train Station. The donkey carried a load on his back—two sacks of dried apricots, mulberries, and quince. Khyzyr *kishi* was carrying them to sell somewhere in the place called Valley. And having sold them, he planned to bring back a lot of wheat and oats in exchange. And also—sunflowers! When *Daijany* Tarlan roasted sunflower seeds in a skillet some fine day, Safaly would get the biggest portion. Even more than Safar got, because Safar was lazy, clumsy, and slow-witted; that was the reason Khyzyr *kishi* took Safaly to the train station instead of him. At the train station Khyzyr *kishi* would load the sacks into the car, seat himself, and travel to that same Valley. And Safaly would sit on the donkey and return to the village "in comfort." All Safaly was required to do was sit firmly on the donkey, and the donkey would do the rest himself.

That return trip to the village on the donkey was one of the most miraculous events not only of his childhood years but perhaps of all Safaly *muallim's* life. The world never again seemed to him so wonderful, so immense, so alive, and no car or airplane gave Safaly *muallim* so much delight as that return trip on the donkey from the train station to Buzbulag. To travel that long path in the soft saddle of Khyzyr *kishi's* black donkey that was famous throughout the village (the equal of any horse in strength, beauty, and dexterity), to feel himself its master and sovereign—any young boy in Buzbulag would undoubtedly have been in seventh heaven with that kind of good fortune. And when Safaly *muallim* remembered that day, that road, it seemed to him that all of that had happened in a completely different universe, because in this universe a person wouldn't have been able to view the world from such a great height. That day, for the first (and last) time in his life, Safaly watched the stones, the earth, the grasses from an amazing height—of course it wasn't the height of the donkey's saddle! The saddle was possibly soft, comfortable, but it bore no relation to the cliffs or meadows. Why were the cliffs' stones so soft that day, why was the wormwood, the grass, the clover of the meadows so green, so tender?

In the Yemeni garden Safaly *muallim* now heard the voices of the clover and the grasses as if anew. He delighted in conversing with the leaves of the trees, the flowers of the quince, the water of the irrigation canal. Now, when feelings overwhelmed him, especially when he felt himself with new strength to be a citizen of the world, Safaly *muallim* even wanted to say something to a few people. And although those words were addressed to Nukhbala Nukhievich, who'd been hurriedly named by the Central Committee as vice-rector of the institute Safaly *muallim* had directed for ten years, those words (in my opinion!) pertained more or less generally to the intelligentsia of the republic: "Rogues, thieves, sons of bitches! What are you divvying up in this little world? You learned to read and write, you finished three or four books, and that's already enough for you to distribute the blessings of the world: this is my portion, that's yours, we'll deal this way with one people and that way with another. And you aren't ashamed to divide this unfortunate, small people into those from Baku, those from Karabakh, those from Nakhchivan. It's just because you thirst for glory, titles. Not even having become fully formed people, you want everyone to consider you as such, to bow down to you, idolize you. Without removing your peasant slippers, you dream of becoming heroes of the people. As if this world were really so grand! What's so big about it if you can make your way around it in a single night? How big a world can it be if they plant beans in Yemen just as they do in Buzbulag? Yes, it's small, this world—for those with human blood in their veins! But an animal must display its savage essence: attack, bring down, destroy, tear to pieces. What difference does it make to an animal whether the world is great or small, so long as its stomach is full? As long as it's sitting in a car and there's a medal on its chest?"

That day in the Yemeni garden Safaly *muallim*, having made full use of the possibilities and rights of a citizen of the world, even found time for a passing glance at Bukhara. And he'd traveled there once—with Ali Ziya—to take part in some kind of cultural event. It had been just the beginning of June, but there was such intense heat in Bukhara that it seemed as though earth and sky were ablaze with flame. People steamed all day in the conference hall as if it were a Finnish bath. But it was nice at night; they took the guests outside the city in cars. And there they arranged remarkable refreshments for participants in the event. As a matter of fact, it was precisely there that Safaly *muallim* for the first time saw a most impressive copy of one of the scenes of the Buzbulag that had absorbed the whole world in itself from East to West: the river bank, fruit garden, and green lawn. How closely they resembled one another, the rivers, gardens, lawns! Things got to the point that, having drunk a couple of shots of Moskovskaya vodka on top of a splendid Uzbek *plov*, Safaly *muallim* beheld Khyzyr *kishi* completing his prayers on the bank under the bushes! But it wasn't that forty-five- to fifty-year-old Khyzyr *kishi* who looked like William Faulkner. This Khyzyr *kishi* was old, very old—three-hundred-and-thirty-one to three-hundred-and-thirty-two. Apparently, Safaly *muallim* was extraordinarily shocked and worried by the fact that Khyzyr *kishi* turned out to be so old. He sat down right there on the river bank and wept, sobbing loudly; at the time, Ali Ziya, who was now sleeping sweetly in his room on the third floor of the hotel in the city of Sana'a, had had to expend a good deal of his fruitful labor and valuable time to quiet Safaly *muallim*.

BUT, OH MY LORD GOD, **THAT** DAY IN **THAT** HOTEL, IT TURNS OUT THAT ALI ZIYA WASN'T ASLEEP EITHER. . . .

Ali Ziya just couldn't close his eyes; he tossed and turned in bed for a long time until, resorting to the simplest logic, he came to the conclusion that there were bedbugs in the hotel. He got up and thoroughly inspected the bed but didn't find a single insect. However, he didn't have the slightest desire to lie down on that bed again. For a little while he wandered around the room, and then he went out into the corridor in just his pajamas and saw that the door to Safaly *muallim*'s room was slightly ajar.

Ali Ziya carefully pushed his head through the door and discovered that Safaly *muallim*'s bed was empty. He went into the room, glanced in the open bath and the toilet, and after that, as Safaly *muallim* wasn't there either, an entirely crazy thought came into Ali Ziya's head: that Safaly *muallim* could only be in the adjacent room with the tightly closed door—the room where he must now be abandoning himself to carnal pleasure and debauchery with Polina Viktorovna! Even if that kind of outcome to some degree affected Ali Ziya's honor as leader of the delegation, however, he tried as best he could to maintain his dignity, and for that reason he decided to immediately take cover in his own room. But he hadn't yet reached the door of his room when another thought disturbed everything in his head in a single instant and forced him to turn away from his noble intention. Ali Ziya headed resolutely for Polina Viktorovna's room and, extraordinarily politely, knocked quietly at the door. The door flew open immediately. Polina Viktorovna appeared in the doorway in a little grey bathrobe; she had already been able to take a shower and had therefore become prettier. Ali Ziya was finally satisfied that Safaly was not in Polina Viktorovna's room, and then the thought that had unpleasantly pricked him before hit Ali Ziya in the head with such a powerful electric shock that even his bones ached: "He's run away!" Deathly white, Ali Ziya said these words unsteadily, with shaking lips. Leaving Polina Viktorovna to repeat "Who ran away? Where did he go?" in bewilderment and understanding nothing himself, he darted into his room to get dressed.

By the time he'd dressed and was tearing downstairs, taking almost three steps with each stride, Ali Ziya didn't doubt that Safaly *muallim* had run away and hidden in the American embassy. He was rushing downstairs, therefore, with a single goal—to show up at his own embassy as quickly as possible to bring everything to the knowledge of the Soviet ambassador and by so doing remove even just a small share of the responsibility from himself as head of the delegation. Having asked downstairs and satisfied himself that even the driver hadn't noticed whether Safaly *muallim* had left the hotel, Ali Ziya was even more convinced of the soundness of his suspicions. "The bastard ran away. He stole out quietly and slipped away!" Ali Ziya thought to himself and, without asking the permission of the driver, got into the car.

"Come on—let's go—there—to the embassy—" Ali Ziya was close to madness.

And soon after that, all the telephones of the Soviet embassy in Yemen were busy, including even the telephone of the ambassador. And the same thing was repeated on each and every one: "They lost someone." Some said this seriously, some with a mocking smile—as if they were joking with Ali Ziya. And even the ambassador himself (a little later) received Ali Ziya in his office entirely calmly.

"Where will he run to? There's nowhere for him to run," said the ambassador very confidently, smiling. "Go, rest. They'll bring you here after lunch. We've already arranged an itinerary for you. Tomorrow you'll proceed to al-Hudaydah. We have a joint venture there. You'll meet with our people; you'll also go swimming in the Red Sea then."

After meeting with the ambassador, Ali Ziya's mood improved. His heart became calmer, and the color returned to his cheeks. But at the same time, he was as certain as he'd been before, one-hundred-percent certain, that Safaly *muallim* had run away from the hotel and could be found nowhere else but the American embassy, where he'd asked for political asylum. Returning from the Soviet embassy and—still sitting in the car—seeing Safaly *muallim* strolling by the hotel entrance, Ali Ziya considered it another brilliant victory of Soviet intelligence: Safaly, he said, really did run away from the hotel, and the fact that he was now humbly strolling in front of it was the real-life result of an operation conducted magnificently by the intelligence organs.

"Safaly?! Curse you, I've been run off my feet searching for you!" He said these words in a shaking voice in the dialect spoken in Sabirabad, which he'd left at age five and where he'd never again returned. Here's still another of the wonders of the universe for you: in moments of agitation, Ali Ziya always spoke in the dialect of his village.

"And why are you looking for me?" After his journey to Buzbulag, Safaly *muallim* hadn't yet managed to leave his childhood behind, and he asked his question gently, with a childlike smile.

"Did I really not tell you that we'd meet downstairs?"

"No, you said we'd sleep a couple of hours," Safaly *muallim* looked at his watch. "It hasn't even been an hour," he added.

Ali Ziya's lips shook, and he spoke unsteadily.

"And you. . . ." He wanted to say "Didn't you run away to the American embassy?" but instead of that he said, "And where were you all this time?"

"Over there," Safaly *muallim* pointed to the fence. "I was walking around the garden."

"And where's that woman, Polina Viktorovna?" In asking Safaly *muallim* that question, of course, Ali Ziya just wanted to change the subject so as to play for time.

"How should I know where she is? She's probably sitting by herself in her room curling her whiskers," answered Safaly *muallim* with a laugh. However, Safaly *muallim* had put in "whiskers" on purpose just to irritate Ali Ziya. Sitting in the airplane last night in Moscow, he'd already noticed Polina Viktorovna's whiskers. Not even whiskers, strictly speaking, but a few strands of hair. And the most remarkable thing was that those hairs were neither white nor black in color but a very strange shade of violet. Furthermore, in the morning—before getting off the airplane—Safaly *muallim* had noticed Polina Viktorovna gently smoothing her whiskers with the tip of her little finger.

"What, you're mocking me?!" growled Ali Ziya, finally losing control of himself at Safaly's light-hearted laugh. "You run right now, call her, tell her to come down immediately!"

Here the spell of childhood cast over Safaly *muallim* by Buzbulag and Bukhara, the spell still wandering across his face, finally disappeared. Of course, almost anything could be expected from Ali Ziya, but not this: Ali Ziya had openly spoken to him like a little boy!

It was a good thing Polina Viktorovna appeared at that moment. It turned out she'd been sitting in an armchair in the foyer, waiting. Hearing her name, she rose before them in a white dress with a big white handbag on her shoulder, coquettish as a fifteen-year-old girl. With an artificially thin, girlish voice she cooed (in Russian, of course), "I'm here."

And then in the large, deserted restaurant laid out on the first floor of the hotel, Ali Ziya conveyed all of his completely made-up story in such a way, with such an expression on his face, that Safaly *muallim* understood from the very beginning that he'd landed in a great deal of trouble. Safaly *muallim*'s appetite disappeared immediately because in that—at first glance—amusing story there was, in fact, nothing amusing. And there was amazing vileness and treachery worthy of the pen of Shakespeare.

A person could only dream something like that and only in a nightmare! On what basis might Ali Ziya to such a degree doubt Safaly *muallim*'s political trustworthiness? Indeed, Safaly *muallim* hadn't once cursed Soviet authority in the presence of Ali Ziya, hadn't once praised America. Moreover, Ali Ziya had always surpassed Safaly *muallim* in anti-Soviet conversations. Wasn't it Ali Ziya, for example, who'd chatted with the taxi driver the whole way from the Peking Hotel to the airport telling repulsive anecdotes about Brezhnev? And perhaps Ali Ziya had planned to do Safaly *muallim* a dirty trick for a long time, otherwise why did his eyes burn with such an evil light? Even now, remembering that gleam in Ali Ziya's eyes and the expression on his face, Safaly *muallim* wanted more than anything to spit in the face of this world. Until that day Safaly *muallim* had never seen a face wear such an expression; afterwards, for Safaly *muallim* the face of Ali Ziya in the restaurant that day turned into a symbol, probably, of the face of our whole world.

That day in the restaurant Safaly *muallim* had been surprised to see the shaggy-haired devil with a tail romping in the depths of Ali Ziya's eyes. Strange, gloomy thoughts that had never before occurred to him crowded into his head, and Safaly *muallim* almost believed some of those thoughts. Safaly *muallim* almost believed, for example, that Ali Ziya didn't fully value the dose of praise in Safaly *muallim*'s critical articles about his novels *Glorious Victory* (dedicated to collectivization) and *Synthetic Rubber* (about industrialization), or that Ali Ziya remembered that Safaly *muallim* had promised but didn't in fact write an article about his last novel, *Where Are You, Mama?* (dedicated to the unmasking of serious mistakes made in the period of collectivization and industrialization), bitterness harbored since that time by Ali Ziya, who'd nurtured and fostered that devil in his eyes and brought him all the way to Yemen. Of course, in order to remember things like these, to take revenge on someone for them, it was necessary to possess the malice of a camel, because Safaly *muallim* had written those articles long ago—they were affairs of the 1940s and 1950s. And by the time Ali Ziya's novel *Where Are You, Mama?* appeared, Safaly *muallim* had already been occupied for seven or eight years solely with fundamental questions of literary studies and didn't play any part in the current literary scene. The idea of "vengeance" wasn't very convincing, but it would have been hard to think up a different explanation for Ali Ziya's behavior; perhaps Shakespeare himself would have passed when presented with that sort of task.

In a word, it was tragicomedy in its most classic form. It would have been one thing with Ali Ziya and his completely devilish face, but it was another that Polina Viktorovna—who looked like a cockroach—was prepared to declare Safaly *muallim* crazy for no reason at all. The old tart, making herself out to be a young girl! In front of Ali Ziya she preened and flirted, and as she looked in the direction of Safaly *muallim* she made a wry face, the bitch, turning herself into Shemr or Yazid; it was as if by strolling an hour in that garden Safaly *muallim* had set back the international achievements of Soviet oriental studies by a hundred years at the very least! And then that stupid question from the ambassador: "And where's your old guy, the alcoholic?" When the ambassador asked that question Ali Ziya had nodded in the direction of Safaly *muallim*, and the devil hiding in the depths of his eyes again appeared. In fact, Safaly *muallim* hadn't had a drop of alcohol for probably about five years—after the two shots of Moskovskaya vodka in Bukhara, it seems he'd drunk an additional small glass of Gek-gel brandy in Leningrad at the birthday party of Rena's child.

Alarmed, Safaly *muallim* couldn't fall asleep at the hotel that night either, and tossing and turning in bed, he decided to have it out with Ali Ziya once and for all. He got up and headed towards Ali Ziya's room. But just short of the slightly open door he was stupefied by what he saw: a half-empty bottle of Gek-gel brandy! By the round table in the middle of the room on which the brandy stood, Polina Viktorovna had both arms twined around Ali Ziya's shoulders, and he was exchanging long-drawn-out kisses with her lips (and with the whiskers!) with delight. After that scene, Safaly *muallim*'s attitude towards Polina Viktorovna's violet whiskers changed significantly (for the better!). But it was already too late, clearly: the damage had been done. Throughout the rest of the trip, the old tart demonstratively did not notice Safaly *muallim*, looking straight through him. The only reason Safaly *muallim* could see for that was the violet whiskers; clearly, that vile woman had felt while still at the airport in Moscow that Safaly *muallim* didn't like her whiskers, and she was taking complete, one-hundred-percent revenge on him for it. Indeed, it couldn't have been anything else—for what other reason could that woman have treated Safaly *muallim* in such a way? Did she, perhaps, think that Safaly *muallim* had really wanted to run away and ask for asylum in the American embassy and that the vigilant agents of the KGB, having shown the greatest courage, had returned him again to the hotel? Whatever it was, that woman played a large role in the fact that Safaly *muallim*'s trip to Yemen turned out to be so ill-starred. Otherwise, on remembering the Red Sea—remembering how Ali Ziya and Polina Viktorovna had romped in the sea—Safaly *muallim* wouldn't have experienced repulsive nausea to this very day.

But that was just the beginning: Safaly *muallim* expected worse would come. He was still in Yemen, but the intelligence service of Nukhbala Nukhievich in Baku was already working diligently. And when Safaly *muallim* returned to Baku, his unsuccessful "attempt to request political asylum in the embassy of the United States of America" was known not only to everyone at the institute, but had even become the subject of lively discussion at weddings and funeral feasts. It seemed that the porters, the cleaning ladies, the teachers, and the students of the institute where Safaly *muallim* had been rector for more than ten years had only now begun to find out what kind of person he was; they looked at him so attentively—sideways—that it was as if they were seeing the person of that name and appearance for the first time. Some walked past Safaly *muallim* with haughty looks. Each day fewer people greeted him. And, strangely, Safaly *muallim* didn't receive any more invitations to Party activities or events.

In the end Safaly *muallim* decided to write a letter of resignation himself and leave the post of rector with his good name unsullied. And it turns out that the higher-ups were just waiting for that. Within a day that same Nukhbala Nukhievich—who only three months ago had been an instructor at the Central Committee and was then named vice rector of the institute—was named in his place. Thus, Safaly *muallim*'s influence was no longer needed for Minasha, Ali Ziya's daughter, to enter the institute.

But there were still five years until Safaly *muallim* could retire on a pension. And in order to somehow hold out for those five years, Safaly *muallim* had to cross the threshold of the institute at least once a week. Safaly *muallim* was prepared to ask for political asylum even in Mozambique if only he didn't have to cross that threshold any more, didn't have to see how the institute that over ten years—at the cost of unbelievable labor—he'd turned into a relatively decent educational institution was now being ruined before his eyes by Nukhbala. Already there were no worthy teachers or students there. The students smoked in the corridors, gnawed sunflower seeds. And already girls ran shamelessly after fellows, right there in the institute. And the rector was busy with his own affairs; he got around, enjoyed himself. The whole institute was talking about Nukhbala's dacha in Pirshagy. According to rumor, Nukhbala's brokers met there each year on the eve of the entrance examinations and set up shop in earnest. A verse about that even went around the institute:

> Look for Nukhbala upstairs,
> And look for Nukhbala downstairs,
> When it's time to take exams,
> Nukhbala's in Pirshagy.

At the Zugulba health resort now, turning over line after line of that verse in his tired memory, Safaly *muallim* for some reason remembered yet another repulsive picture: Ali Ziya and Polina Viktorovna romping in the Red Sea. He got up and went out on the balcony to spit. Then he returned to the room and was just about to pull the plug of the rapidly boiling teapot out of the socket when suddenly there was a knock on the door. From the corridor he heard the voice of Ali Ziya.

"Safaly, are you asleep? It's me, Ali—your old friend!"

At the sound of that voice, Safaly *muallim*'s mood changed sharply. And because his mood changed, it's not a bad idea if we start a new chapter.

Ali Ziya

"Hey, Safaly, listen, where've you been? Well, give me your hand, let's shake. How many years it's been since we last shook hands!" For some reason Ali Ziya only grasped two of Safaly *muallim*'s five fingers, shook his hand for a long time in the air like a fan, and then sat on the sofa, panting. "I called you three times from below. What, you've started to lose your hearing, or you simply didn't want to answer me?" Ali Ziya tried to force a smile.

"I didn't hear," answered Safaly *muallim* and thought that the voice he'd heard after he left the cafeteria had, in fact, been Ali Ziya's voice and not the noise of the sea. Not looking at Ali Ziya, Safaly *muallim* asked, "And when was it you saw me on the balcony?"

"Oh, a little while ago—about an hour ago. I saw you didn't answer and decided to go nap a little and then come by. It seems you've got tea? And sugar, too? Do you have one glass or two?"

Besides the teacup and saucer that Safaly *muallim* had brought from home, there was a tall glass standing on the table. Safaly *muallim* nodded at it and said, "It's fine, I'll drink from that. Sit down, I'll make the tea."

"Make it, for heaven's sake. Make some good tea, we'll drink. My mouth is all dry. I've got diabetes, Safaly. . . . And rinse out that teacup thoroughly with boiling water. There's infection everywhere now."

While Safaly *muallim*'s tea was brewing, Ali Ziya, as always, walked around on the balcony, Napoleon-style. It turned out that that morning—before the journey—the sugar had been forgotten.

"What a shame, I forgot the sugar!" Safaly *muallim* said these words almost crying.

Ali Ziya took five caramels in red wrappers from his pocket and laid them on the table.

"If it were just sugar that we're short of, Safaly!" he said. "Take these. Candy from the reserves of the period of stagnation. Three for you, two for me. How well did I share? I wasn't too stingy, was I?"

Safaly *muallim* took a single candy.

"That's enough for me," he answered. "You know, back at home before I left, I felt it. I knew I'd forgotten something. Turns out it was the sugar."

Ali Ziya drew the teacup and saucer closer. "You arrived recently?"

"This morning. I had lunch here, in the cafeteria." Safaly *muallim* wanted to say, "And I saw you there," but didn't.

"Really? So you were in the cafeteria? I also had lunch there. I sat in the upper area, you know, where there are fewer people. Rasim came with friends— our Minaya's husband. I ate a couple of pieces of fish *shashlyk*, that's it. It's all thanks to Rasim, he comes here often. They respect him a great deal here. He works in trade, you know, in the ministry. That's why all the employees tiptoe around him."

Safaly *muallim* thought it would be interesting to know what had happened—why wasn't Ali Ziya relaxing at his wonderful dacha in Mardakan? What was he doing in Zugulba at this time of year?

It was as if Ali Ziya had read Safaly *muallim*'s mind.

"We've got a real mess, Safaly. I swear by Allah, it's complete and utter misfortune. A man doesn't get a minute of peace, even at the dacha. They stir up the people and, on the other hand, they've got the intelligentsia by the throat— 'Go, answer to the people.' And you see yourself, the people are just looking for someone to hiss offstage. I've been here ten days already, somehow or other I've come to myself. I've rested a little. I was supposed to leave today. Well, I thought, I'll stay here one more night. These days, one quiet night—that's also a great blessing. And it's a good thing I stayed. I swear by Allah, Safaly, I really wanted to see you."

Ali Ziya poured tea into the saucer, blew on it, drank with pleasure, and strange though it may be, that delight poured balm into Safaly *muallim*'s heart. It seems his heart was beginning to burn anew with longing for old friendship, or else the memories of childhood were waking up again in Safaly *muallim*'s heart, because ever since the day of his birth he'd seen how his uncle Kyzyr *kishi* drank tea exactly the same way—pouring it into the saucer and blowing on it.

"And how is Rena, is she still there in Leningrad? Are you able at least sometimes to visit her there? I wasn't here when Aunt Seren died. And I heard about the death of Zarnigyar *baji* too late. I didn't want to come too late, reopen your wound. . . ." Ali Ziya fumbled for a long time in the pockets of his pants and jacket and finally pulled out a handkerchief. He wiped the sweat from his brow. "How well this tea turned out!" he said and fell silent for a long time. He was silent until tears appeared in his eyes, and wiping them, he continued, "And Farakh *baji* died last year. Like a candle melting before my eyes. And my joy and happiness died with her, Safaly! I can't complain about my daughters. Both my daughters and my sons-in-law take care of me. But things didn't turn out well with my son, may Allah punish him. He drinks. A lot. Drunk every day."

And here for some reason the misfortunes of Yemen rose again before Safaly *muallim*'s eyes: night, the hotel, the bottle of brandy, the muddy Red Sea whose water smelled of salt, and the younger-looking Polina Viktorovna who had been transformed in a single night—undoubtedly with the active participation of Ali Ziya—shamelessly romping in the sea with Ali Ziya. . . . And that candle. That melting, failing, slender, tiny candle with a tired smile frozen on her face: thin, short, sickly Farakh *baji*. But Safaly *muallim*, marveling at the whims of fate, wasn't supposed to remember all that—perhaps then Ali Ziya wouldn't have started talking about Yemen, and Safaly *muallim* wouldn't have driven away the bird of friendship just now alighting near them.

"Not too bad, the way we wriggled out of things back then, eh, Safaly? I mean that business in Yemen. If it had been 1937, they'd have jailed you for that kind of thing," said Ali Ziya, pacing up and down the room with his hands in his pockets.

"For what kind of thing?" The booming echo of his own voice sounded for a long time in Safaly *muallim*'s ears, and then—while the echo died down—it was as if the world had begun to contract, to grow smaller. And in that shrinking world Vaska suddenly arose: it seemed that Vaska was meowing plaintively somewhere. And immediately, only Allah knows how much, Safaly *muallim* wanted to leap up, ransack the whole resort, and find Vaska.

"If you didn't run away, then in any case you really wanted to, Safaly! Well, tell me, for the love of God, did you or didn't you want to?" Ali Ziya's laugh still sounded like a cat's cough.

Safaly *muallim* didn't answer. He was happy that Ali Ziya was leaving tomorrow, and at the same time, he'd finally resolved for himself the question that had been tormenting him for a long time: if he were fated to meet him in the other world, Safaly *muallim* wouldn't ask Ali Ziya anything.

"You still teach at the institute?" asked Ali Ziya, now in an entirely different voice; evidently, he felt the rising awkwardness and understood that he shouldn't have stirred up the past.

"I don't teach." Safaly *muallim* looked warily at Ali Ziya because he didn't want to see the devil he'd once seen in Ali Ziya's eyes again. "What's the use of teaching where that Nukhbala is in charge?"

"What Nukhbala?" Ali Ziya sat down on the sofa and looked innocently at Safaly *muallim* with distressed, bewildered eyes. "Heydar made short work of Nukhbala a long time ago, what, you didn't know?"[1]

"No-o-o!" said Safaly *muallim* with great surprise and now looked at Ali Ziya without any fear; it seemed he was prepared to forgive Ali Ziya because of that news alone. "And who's in Nukhbala's place now?" Safaly *muallim*'s eyes suddenly brightened. As if—after all these years—he wanted to go once again to the institute where he'd been rector.

"You truly didn't know?"

"I swear by Allah, I didn't hear anything."

"Ah, Safaly, you slept through it all!" Ali Ziya exclaimed loudly, with feigned friendliness. "Now Shakhbala's there—the youngest uncle of our Rasim. And he's been there a while, almost ten years."

Here Safaly *muallim* lost himself in deep reverie. There was nothing surprising in the fact that some Shakhbala had now taken the place of Nukhbala; however, such firm adherence to the principle of rhyme seemed to Safaly *muallim* to be a new trend in questions of personnel selection. Evidently, the comrades higher up had recently been able to arrange closer connections with the Writers Union.

"And where did he work before, that Shakhbala?" Safaly *muallim* inquired indifferently, letting the gleam in his eye go out for good.

"What do you mean, where? How quickly you've forgotten—he was responsible for communications in the KGB. You know Shakhbala very well—he once treated us to an excellent feast at Uzeir's kebab place on the Shemakhinsky Highway."

Safaly *muallim* rooted around in his memory for a long time but couldn't dig up either Shakhbala's face or Uzeir's kebab place; he was only able to remember the place called Shemakhinsky Pass, which he'd travelled through once or twice.

"How nice!" he said. "If he's from the KGB, then things got even better."

"What, you're offended by the KGB? Hee, hee, hee!" That really wasn't a laugh but a cat's cough.

"No, why would. . .?" Safaly *muallim* lifted his head but didn't dare look in Ali Ziya's eyes because that devil, it seems, had come to life again.

"Maybe I'm saying you're also complaining about the KGB. It's fashionable to scoff at them now."

Safaly *muallim* was silent. Ali Ziya got up from the sofa again and began to pace around the table and then sat down and asked unexpectedly, "Is your neighbor still alive? That grey-eyed Armenian fox? Ah, Safaly, what a looker she was when she was young!"

Although Ali Ziya's nasty laugh again irritated Safaly *muallim*, he thought it was a good idea to answer a joke with a joke.

"She's not too shabby now," he said and for some reason remembered the violet whiskers of Polina Viktorovna.

"And what do you think of this Armenian business, Safaly?" It seemed Ali Ziya himself wasn't asking the question, but that same old devil that had appeared in the depths of his eyes.

"What Armenian business?" answered Safaly *muallim* as sharply and coldly as he could, and it seemed to him that Vaska's voice was now reaching him from some very cold place; Safaly *muallim* suddenly felt the chill and put on his jacket.

"I have the Karabakh problem in mind. The problem of Nagorno-Karabakh. They just won't leave it alone, the sons of bitches. They've incited the whole world against us."

"They aren't leaving it alone—so, give it to them. What's there? Just a scrap of earth." Safaly *muallim* said this specifically to annoy Ali Ziya because the violet whiskers of Polina Viktorovna were getting on his nerves again.

Ali Ziya stretched his neck, which looked like a withered, yellowing cucumber.

"I don't like your words, Safaly!" he said. "I know you were joking, but don't joke like that anywhere else. Margaret Thatcher says the same thing, but she has an Armenian grandmother. And Bush has Armenian blood in him. And that damned Sakharov, you know yourself, married the daughter of an Alikhanyan. The same Alikhanyan who in Wrangel's army tormented the Komsomol fellows for ten years. . . . You can't give Armenians even an inch of Karabakh because if you give them Karabakh, they'll demand Nakhchivan. And then they'll say, 'Baku is ours, and it isn't called Baku but Bakuravan. Ganje is Kanza,' they'll say, 'and it belongs to us. Qazakh is Katsakh, and Ordubad,' they'll say, 'is Urduvar.' And there'll be nothing to say about Salyany—it ends in '-yan.' What'll we have left then? The depths of the Caspian! Safaly, one should never, ever yield to Armenians. They're a very impudent people!"

And here Safaly *muallim* suddenly exclaimed enthusiastically, "Yes, we're a sovereign republic! And not a souvenir one!" He said this so passionately that it was as if he was remembering his long-ago Young Pioneer days. And Safaly *muallim* agreed wholeheartedly with Ali Ziya's original thought—that Armenians are a very impudent people—because as a youth he himself had once experienced the impudence of an old Karchevan Armenian who distilled vodka from dried mulberries. The Armenian had exchanged half a sack of excellent dried mulberries—which Safaly had brought with a thousand torments from Buzbulag to the market of the Karchevan collective farm—for fifteen pounds of rotten potatoes. Safaly, who up until that time hadn't liked to swear, spent the whole return trip from Karchevan muttering about the grave of that Armenian's father. Nevertheless, if it were up to Safaly *muallim*, he would now have cut off the conversation about Armenians. But it turned out that Ali Ziya had something more to say on that subject.

"Scoundrels, vile bastards! This is their eternal way of doing things—make a commotion for the whole world. Who needs these conversations about land now? They could've just lived there, nobody would've bothered them. But, no, they started skipping away like monkeys because of the Soviet authorities, who gave them a free ride. They think Karabakh is halva for them—they catch it and swallow it. There it is, their much-vaunted ancient culture! Their own brains aren't worth a kopek, and still they drag us into it. There's no peace at home, none at the dacha. Every day some gang of rascals stirs up the people at the House of Unions. They yell at the top of their lungs. They don't recognize their elders, they care nothing for the government. And no one can be found to go out and shut them up." Ali Ziya pulled out his handkerchief and for a long time angrily wiped the foam from his lips. "Many terrible things might happen, Safaly! I don't know how it is for you, but what's coming really worries me. I'm afraid they'll pull down the statue of Lenin—that would be a great misfortune!"

"What, do misfortunes only happen in places where there are no statues of Lenin?" asked Safaly *muallim* angrily; clearly, his memory was still offended by the rotten potatoes of the old Armenian maker of homebrew.

This irrelevant question from Safaly *muallim* deeply wounded Ali Ziya.

"Don't argue with me!" he exclaimed. "You know what I'm talking about."

Safaly *muallim* wanted to say, "Ali, I swear by Allah, I don't know what you're talking about," but he was silent. Evidently he was frightened by Ali Ziya, or else the thought that had suddenly struck Safaly *muallim* negatively affected his eloquence. And the new thought that occurred to Safaly *muallim* was not, of course, such a deep one. He suddenly understood: that which was called Soviet authority was also Ali Ziya—and so what if he drank tea, pouring it into the saucer and blowing on it like Khyzyr *kishi*? And if Safaly *muallim* hadn't remembered right there about Nukhbala, then perhaps after that idea he might have generally fallen silent, silent as a clam. But Nukhbala again spoiled everything. More precisely, Safaly *muallim* suddenly lost his temper because he knew

Nukhbala's biography extremely well—starting with the Komsomol—and that led him, without any connection at all to the preceding conversation (and at that moment, when Ali Ziya certainly didn't expect it!), to suddenly, angrily lash out at the Komsomol.

"If Gorbachev had even a lick of sense, he would first of all have liquidated the Komsomol," he said, and he looked so expressively at the foam at Ali Ziya's mouth that it was as if that foam were the sole material evidence in the world of the existence of the Komsomol. "First of all, what is the Komsomol? It's the refuge and support of cunning careerists who don't want to do anything useful in life, hundreds of rascals who, having barely torn themselves from their mothers' breasts, dream of money, glory, offices, and easy income. Seventy-seven percent of those doing deals at their dachas and organizing brothels at their offices came from the Komsomol. It's right there that scoundrels learn the basics: how to bow down, lick someone's boots, serve important people, crawl into someone else's pocket, to sell and be sold. Now, let's see, who goes on from there to get a higher education, that is, to clamber further up the career ladder? Of course: those who learned those things well, those who got an 'A+' in those 'basics.' The ones who learned best and mastered the science of making connections." (It seems that Safaly *muallim* was moving by degrees from Nukhbala to Shakhbala.) "And that's your Komsomol! And that Alikhanyan was right to join Wrangel's army, he did an excellent thing, what does it matter that he was Armenian? Precisely as a result of the glorious doings of those Komsomol kids, the people of a rich, sovereign republic are prepared to pluck out Marx's beard because of a lack of souvenirs. Yes, respected comra—"

Safaly *muallim* was so fired up that he almost said "respected comrade deputies." To hell with Nukhbala, but when Safaly *muallim* had ascertained that even Shakhbala was from those "Komsomol cadres," the pain in his heart for the years when he was rector of the institute woke up again—and along with it the hope to regain those years, to be rector of the institute, and that hope had carried him away on its wings and delivered him straight to a session of the Supreme Soviet. . . . It's a good thing Safaly *muallim* quickly came to his senses. And coming to his senses, he glanced at the sofa where Ali Ziya was sitting. But Ali Ziya wasn't there; he stood in the doorway on the opposite side of the room. Flinging open the flaps of his jacket, he stuck his hands in the pockets like a monument and stretched his yellowing neck that looked like a withered cucumber. It seems he was going to object to what Safaly *muallim* had said.

"Brilliant! Brilliant!" he said. "Good job, you gave an excellent speech, professor! Yes, the oratorical gift is buried in you! How did we not know that until now? So well done—you gave it to the collective farm!" (Allah alone knows why Ali Ziya said "collective farm" in place of "Komsomol.") "And you stuck it to Marx!" Ali Ziya passed his hand over his face, meaning that at some time he, too, had had a beard. "Now, listen to what I tell you. Pay attention, listen carefully: you won't make a good extremist, Safaly, be reasonable! Doing that, attacking the collective farm—" (again the collective farm!) "you must know that even Gorbachev grew up under the collective farm, and even if you didn't know that, criticizing the Komsomol" (and now—the Komsomol!) "is at least politically ignorant, I won't even call it a political adventure." Ali Ziya licked the foam from his lips and thought for a minute. "You had dirty, vague ideas of that kind even before. Do you remember your article about *Glorious Victory*? In that article you openly tried to place a donkey—a typical remnant of feudalism— higher than that great development of socialism, the tractor. You tried, yes, yes, you tried! But at the time I considered that I ought not lose you, that you needed to be taught, returned to the true path. That's why I brought you back from the American embassy then. I was sorry for you. I didn't want you to leave and rot amid the vileness of capitalism. And now I want to hope again that sooner or later you'll free yourself from these pro-Armenian" (aha, now it's already "pro-Armenian," save me, Lord!) "sentiments. That you'll find your-self a worthy place in the ranks of the supporters of *perestroika*. That's all, until later!" Ali Ziya took his hands out of his pockets and buttoned his jacket. "We'll continue our educational conversation over dinner in the cafeteria tonight."

And Ali Ziya suddenly vanished, as if into thin air. Safaly *muallim* looked at the doorway for a long time in surprise. Then he got up, walked onto the bal-cony, and looked at the sea. The sun had just gone down. The air was clear. The sea looked like the sky, the sky like the sea. In a word, everything in the world remained in its proper place.

That evening Safaly *muallim* didn't go to eat dinner in the cafeteria. Only when Ali Ziya's spirit had fully dissipated from the room did he come to himself a little. He vented his rage by washing the teacup from which his "old friend" had drunk several times with soap and hot water. But Safaly *muallim* didn't refrain from going to dinner because he didn't want to see Ali Ziya's blessed countenance any more. The most terrible thing was that it seems Safaly *muallim* himself gradually began to believe that sometime, somewhere, he'd asked for political asylum at the American embassy! Perhaps that had really happened, only not in Yemen but in some other country. Or perhaps it had been right there in that four-story hotel in the city of Sana'a—but not inside the hotel and not outside—somewhere, let us suppose, on the fifth floor of that four-story hotel!

In the end, Safaly *muallim* began to believe that a four-story building might have a fifth story and that anything you liked could happen on that floor, from a request for political asylum in the American embassy to pro-Armenian sentiments. . . . Therefore, instead of eating dinner in the cafeteria, Safaly *muallim* decided to take a shower so as to fully wash himself clean of Ali Ziya. However, just then the supply of hot water was turned off.

Abandoning the thought of a shower, Safaly *muallim* settled himself more comfortably on the balcony and—filling his chest with the sea air—decided to replace the missing hot water with hot remembrances of Buzbulag. And while our main character was looking right at Buzbulag from that balcony, we made use of the occasion to find a name and think up the contents of a new chapter of our amusing story.

So, then.

Buzbulag, Khyzyr Kishi, De Gaulle, Neil Armstrong, and So Forth

W hen Safaly *muallim* got out of the train car at that same train station from which at one time he'd seen Khyzyr *kishi* off to the place called Valley, the hot rays of the sun pieced his body like knives, although it was still two hours until noon.

For five rubles, a man who happened to be passing by drove him to Buzbulag in his red Moskvich. It was cooler in Buzbulag than at the train station. But there was no one to be seen in the streets, other than some kids. And with the noisy accompaniment of these kids—both in front and behind—Safaly *muallim* came to Khyzyr *kishi*'s yard, not even having stopped on the threshold of his father's home.

The gate was half-open, but out of politeness Safaly *muallim* considered it necessary to knock, a gesture celebrated with a unanimous "hurrah" and applause by the Buzbulag youngsters. The kids' voices hadn't yet died out when the voice of Khyzyr *kishi* could be heard from the yard.

"Who's there? Come in, it's open." And hearing that voice, the kids dispersed immediately, as if they considered their mission fulfilled.

Tarlan *arvad* was sitting in the yard by the brazier and roasting seeds in a large basin; Khyzyr *kishi* sat on a stack of firewood not far from his wife.

"Hey, Tarlan, isn't that Safaly? It is him! And what's this, nephew? Is this any way for a person to come see his uncle?" Khyzyr *kishi* said these words in such a tone that it was as if they'd last seen one another all of a week ago, said goodbye at one of Buzbulag's crossroads, and over the course of that week Safaly *muallim* hadn't found time to drop by to visit.

Khyzyr *kishi*'s enormous, dry palm that resembled a threshing board shook the small, soft-as-cotton hand of Safaly *muallim*. Having fidgeted and seated herself more comfortably, Tarlan *arvad* also expressed joy and gratitude at Safaly *muallim*'s arrival.

"Bring over the *sloot*, let our nephew sit," said Tarlan *arvad* to Khyzyr *kishi*. "I feel sorry for him, what a journey he's had from Baku. In a minute I'll get up and heat up the *simavar*. I've already had mine, there's a little tea left. I don't want to put out the brazier, it would be a waste." While Khyzyr *kishi* went to fetch the stool, Tarlan *arvad* stirred the coals in the brazier and then, energetically stirring the seeds, spoke in her same, long-remembered tone, a tone so homey and familiar to him that Safaly *muallim*'s heart trembled: "Ah, Safaly, that Gogan, the orphan, really torments us! We just don't know what to do with him!"

"It's your own fault!" growled Khyzyr *kishi* from afar, bringing the stool. "The child wants money—give him big money, three whole rubles, so what? But, no, your *daijany* preaches that everyone must earn it through his labor. She sits almost every day covered in sweat in front of that brazier, and for what? So that whelp Gogan can sell seeds and earn his own three-ruble note! And if he were an ordinary child, that would half-fix the problem. But this is torment, absolute punishment. He's not yet fifteen, but you can't save enough money for his cigarettes. He smokes two packs a day, the son of a bitch. What's worse, the expensive ones."

"You make him quit, if you can," said Tarlan *arvad*, getting to her feet with difficulty. "Yes, sonny, your uncle isn't what he once was, either. Your uncle has gotten old. Gotten stupid. No one listens to him. And what am I supposed to do, I see the boy adores it, he smokes that filth, so make him work a little bit for it. Let him know money doesn't grow on trees. This morning I spent a whole hour hammering it into him until he got it. Our yellow cow didn't calve since last year, so he needed to take her to Goturder to the buffalo. He'll show up soon and grab me by the throat, 'Money, Grandma! Money, Grandma!' Here's money for you! Go sell these—buy yourself what you want. These are seeds, we grew them ourselves, they weren't bought at the market."

Barely dragging her feet, the entirely stooped Tarlan *arvad* went to stir up the samovar. And it seemed to the tired Safaly *muallim* sitting in the yard on the old stool that he wasn't in Buzbulag at all, not in Khyzyr *kishi*'s yard that he'd dreamed of almost a thousand times; it seemed that he was still riding on the train and that the "train" was even rocking gently. And the stone fence at the far end of the yard was rocking gently along with the "train," and also the trees and the bushes growing not far from the fence, and even the shadow cast by the trees, and the hens swarming in that shadow. But these weren't the same colorful hens of various breeds that Tarlan *arvad* had once raised—all these were white, of a single breed engineered in a laboratory.

"Well, you heard, she says she's training the child for work," Khyzyr *kishi* laughed hoarsely like an old man. "You'd think the father of that scoundrel had earned something through honest work! For more than twenty years he was the district policeman, wore a pistol on his ass, and in the end they shot him down with that very same pistol. Shot him in the heart at night, in the road, right in front of the district Party committee. And they never found the killer. In his old age he made a big effort, became a father at age fifty-eight, and the child—from age three or four he was an orphan. And his wife, nephew, was much younger than he was. So, not a year after the death of her husband, she threw the child on us, got mixed up with someone, and ran away, we don't know where. And now for more than ten years already your *daijany* and I have been tormented by that child. . . . And his name is some kind of imported one, maybe Dogul or Digul—since childhood we've been calling him Gogan, that's how it is. She also overdid it then out of joy. As if there weren't enough names to give a child. I said to her, 'If you can't think up a name, then how about your grandfather's name— Hamza—no one's named a son that yet.' And she says to me: 'You don't understand anything. It's an excellent name. That's what they named the France-land tsar.' And she starts telling me what a great tsar he was. How many wonderful deeds he did. That we'd give the boy his name so it wouldn't be lost on the earth. If only you knew how your *daijany* has been tormented now because of that 'smart' France-land tsar. He hasn't left her anything in her trunk, poor thing—he stole everything, sold it. If his father, may his grave be open wide, had known what that fellow would get up to with us, perhaps he wouldn't have tried so hard to make his wife's belly swell!"

"I still haven't told you, Khyzyr!" Tarlan *arvad* said from the samovar, which was beginning to smoke. "Last night I counted, there were eleven eggs in the henhouse. I look this morning: not one is left. Either he ate them raw out of malice or he carried them off and sold them to someone and bought cigarettes."

De Gaulle . . . Dogul . . . Digul . . . Gogan, Gogan, Gogan. . . . The shadow from the trees again rippled lightly over the earth, and the hens that swarmed in the shadow also moved along with it, swaying. O Lord, why weren't those hens cackling? Why was there no cheeping of chicks to be heard? At one time it had taken just the cackling of the black hen to bring the whole yard to life, to compel even the lifeless stones to answer. From behind the bright green branches of the two apricot trees growing a little way from one another there, where the hens swarmed, sometimes the red heights of a mountain peeked out, as if frightened. Or perhaps it was Safaly *muallim* himself who feared the mountain. Feared what the mountain would say, that it would say terrible words—words he didn't want to hear for anything—

would say, for example, "You came here in vain, Safaly *muallim*, the Buzbulag you seek isn't here. That Buzbulag," it would say, "doesn't exist in this world. Enough inventing your own world."

And the mountain would say that even the black hen was a lie, and that her cackling that you, Safaly *muallim*, once called the hymn of fertility was also an empty invention, a legend—there never was and never could have been such a hymn on earth. With regard to the black donkey, that was also, undoubtedly, a stupid invention, a whim. It would say that, I swear by Allah, would say that, for when a mountain actually speaks—that's a bad sign!

It seems that Safaly *muallim* had gotten completely drunk on the fresh air; otherwise, a person couldn't have been so stunned after a night on the train. If he'd been himself, it wouldn't have taken any work at all to find the likeness between this yard and that Yemeni garden. Perhaps he'd have found the likeness between that three-hundred-and-thirty-three-year-old Khyzyr *kishi* (who'd never prayed in his life) performing his prayers on the river bank in Bukhara and the Khyzyr *kishi* right here, and then that reddish mountain would probably have taken pity on Safaly *muallim* and not started saying those red-hot words to him.

Only after the second glass of tea did Safaly *muallim* understand, with difficulty, that the policeman killed one night with his own pistol on the road in front of the district Party committee was in fact that person of his own age, his childhood friend Safar. And that the complicated personality called Gogan— the one who'd swiped eggs from the henhouse this morning and was now busy in Goturder breeding a yellow cow with a bull—was the orphan son of that Safar. A little later (after the third glass), Safaly *muallim*'s mind cleared to such a degree that he found an ancient—at least three-hundred-and-thirty-three-year-old—explanation for why his uncle, in speaking of Safar, hadn't once called him by name. It meant that Khyzyr *kishi* was certain his son Safar was now in the best of worlds leading a calmer and more prosperous life there than on this earth, and he didn't call his son by name because it would have been unworthy of a man to disturb his spirit.

And not yet having gotten to his fourth glass, Safaly *muallim* came to the firm conclusion that Gogan was a fine crook. With the stories of the trunk and the eggs alone, Gogan couldn't have impressed Safaly *muallim* as being a particularly original personality. More exactly, Gogan couldn't have appeared to Safaly *muallim*'s eyes as the most remarkable phenomenon from the last fifty years of Buzbulag's existence. Giving children imported names had been locally fashionable even fifty years before; to this day Safaly *muallim* remembered children with the names of Marx, Engels, Thälmann, Voroshil, CollectiveFarm, October, November, Aggregate, Delegate, and Deputy playing in the village lanes. There was even a fellow by the name of Molkogan, that is, Molotov-Kaganovich. But it still seemed strange to Safaly *muallim* that Safar had named his son De Gaulle. And the pistol and police service as well. No matter how Safaly *muallim* tried, he couldn't imagine Safar in a police uniform. And suddenly a dream accidentally came to mind that forced Safaly *muallim* once again to be astounded at the affairs of this world. Moreover, it was a dream that Safaly *muallim* had had while still in Yemen—but not in Sana'a, in al-Hudaydah. During the night of that day when Ali Ziya and Polina Viktorovna had romped in the Red Sea, in the room of the al-Hudaydah hotel that was stuffy as a bathhouse, Safaly *muallim* dreamed of a strange village yard. Summer, strong heat: he was romping happily with Safar on grass that had turned yellow from the heat. Then they had quarreled for some reason, Safar extended his hand, and at the same moment a strange, black pistol was in it. Laughing loudly, Safar squeezed the trigger of the pistol. The bullet struck Safaly right in the heart. Safaly felt the warm blood flowing from his heart, but he wasn't a bit distressed, rather the reverse—he rejoiced, rejoiced with all his heart, because the dead yellow grass where he fell suddenly began to turn into yellow flowers, and next to Safaly *muallim* in the yellow flowers lay that same black hen that had sung the hymn of fertility all her life.... How could Safaly *muallim* not be astounded now at the strangeness of the world, if at the time of the dream he hadn't known and hadn't heard from anyone that Safar had become a policeman and carried a pistol?! Perhaps they'd killed Safar in front of the district Party committee on exactly that same night, at that same moment, at that very instant! Perhaps the shot heard near the district Party committee woke Safaly *muallim* that very night in the stuffy room of the hotel; the difference was only that Safar hadn't shot but had been shot, and also that the bullet had landed not in Safaly *muallim*'s heart but in that of his cousin, his childhood friend. . . . Waiting for Tarlan *arvad* to pour the fourth glass of tea, the astounded Safaly *muallim* reflected on (probably from the old habit of being a literary critic) and somewhere in the depths of his soul rejoiced that that subject hadn't yet come into the head of a single Azerbaijani Soviet writer; Safaly *muallim* was convinced that if some third-rate Ali Ziya had come across such a subject, he would have turned it into a thick novel and named it something short and sweet (so it would have been easier for the Baku critics to praise it), *Death*, or (to cut a dash in the eyes of Moscow publishers with a dose of national character and national color) *Death of the Black Hen*.

But Tarlan *arvad* didn't pour a fourth glass of tea. (Clearly, it was not done to give more than three cups to one who'd left Buzbulag at eighteen and returned at seventy-two). Instead, she considered it necessary to communicate a whole string of important pieces of information (not less interesting than the theft of eleven eggs from the henhouse by Mr. De Gaulle).

"And your female cousins were too picky to marry fellows from our village. Gryz *khanum* is in Chykhnagiul, on the other side of Delidag. She has five daughters and three sons. She gave away the youngest—Durdane—last fall. And at the same time, Naz *khanum* married a drunkard, a veterinarian, and went with him to Chukhakend. And they haven't come back here since then. Only Bas *khanum* stayed here, but even she had bad luck with her son Tariel: he went to Moscow, married a Russian woman. Now they say he's got a fine son from that Russian woman. I'd curse that son of a bitch Tariel to ease my soul, but I don't have the heart for it. He's very affectionate, Safaly. Loves his relatives so much. If he hears you're here, he'll come tearing back from Moscow."

Khyzyr *kishi* sat with his head lowered. Occasionally he glanced sideways at Safaly *muallim*'s suitcase leaning against the post of the veranda, as if considering something to himself.

"Have you come for long?" Khyzyr *kishi* asked, not taking his glance from the suitcase.

"Yes, I think I'll stay here a little while."

"Will you stay with us or at your own place?"

"I think it would be better if I lived at my place."

"As you like. This is your home, too, you know: we're family. But that boy won't give you any peace. He'll swipe and sell everything you've got, disgrace us for nothing, for nothing at all."

"That's right, he'll do it, he will. You can bet that rogue will do anything!" added Tarlan *arvad*.

Khyzyr *kishi* lost himself in reverie.

"Go see which of the girls is there—have one go and put things in order a little. Bas *khanum* can't go herself, she has a hernia, you can't ask her to do that kind of work. And your *daijany*, you see yourself, can barely get to the door. There must be all kinds of dishes there, tea—if that scoundrel Gogan, the son of a scoundrel, hasn't stolen and drunk everything away. Soon your *daijany* will get together sheets for the bed. Gogan will bring them to you. Don't worry, it's more peaceful there than here. When I work in the yard I sometimes sleep there, too. And there's water once a week, Gogan goes to water things. This year I planted a lot of cucumbers there. And a couple of beds of beans.

There's cabbage there, potatoes—everything's there. And as much as I'm able, I've always looked after the house. The roof is still strong, but the beams are already old, they're rotting, little by little. . . . WELL, NOW, LET'S DO IT, OPEN YOUR SUITCASE, GIVE YOUR UNCLE THE SUIT OR WHATEVER YOU BROUGHT HIM!"

If another person had been in Safaly *muallim*'s place, perhaps that person wouldn't have been flummoxed by his uncle's words. But Safaly *muallim* was to such a degree struck dumb that not only could he not find a couple of polite words to answer Khyzyr *kishi* but, even worse, such stupid, such inappropriate words for the occasion burst from his lips (parched even after three glasses of tea) that anyone hearing them would have considered Safaly *muallim* mad:

"Faulkner! Faulkner! William Faulkner!"

However, no one besides Safaly *muallim* heard these words, for which Safaly *muallim* was very glad, and that gladness helped him come to himself a little.

"No," he said, "I didn't bring anything. I'll buy whatever it is here. They probably sell suits here, too."

"They sell them, why wouldn't they? Only why do I need a suit you've bought here? Look, if you'd brought one from there, that would have been a suit. It would have been clear you respected your uncle." Khyzyr *kishi* turned his stool and now sat with his back to the suitcase.

Tarlan *arvad* was puttering around a little way away, but it turned out she'd heard everything.

"Listen, why do you need a suit? Is there nothing else left for the moths to gobble up? The suit Tariel brought you last year from Moscow is still lying packed up in the trunk."

"Are we really talking about a suit? I'm talking about something else entirely."

Safaly *muallim* nearly repeated those inappropriate words that had burst from him earlier, but he controlled himself. At that moment the black-browed, black-eyed, black-mustachioed man from the photograph on the cover of the book in Baku stood clearly before his eyes once more, and for the first time in his life, Safaly *muallim* had to accept an (entirely debatable) idea—probably Faulkner himself was one of the greatest smart alecks on earth.

Khyzyr *kishi* sat sullenly, not wanting to change his antagonistic relationship towards Safaly *muallim*'s suitcase. Tarlan *arvad* was still puttering with the hens under the apricot trees. But Safaly *muallim* didn't want to look in that direction because there was a red mountain there, visible between two apricot trees, and it seemed to him that if he looked over there, the mountain would say something unpleasant to him.

"So you buried my poor sister there—among the Baku *kafirs*." After a long, dissatisfied silence, Khyzyr *kishi* at last lifted his head.

"No. Why among *kafirs*? I buried her in the Muslim cemetery," answered Safaly *muallim*, rejoicing like a child.

"And are infidels really found only among Russians or Armenians? A *kafir*, nephew, isn't distinguished by nationality, it comes from the essence of a person. And the people of Baku are a very bad people. Even their language is impossible to understand. We have a *tellervision*. Sometimes I watch it at night. There are all kinds of concerts there—I understand them, but what they say, I can't understand a word of. When you listen to Iran or Turkey on the radio, at least it's possible to understand something. I even understand Gorbachev very well, so what if he speaks Russian?"

Having said the last words, Khyzyr *kishi* rose sharply and turned again to Safaly *muallim*'s suitcase. But now he looked at the suitcase differently. In that glance one could clearly read: The conversation is over, you can take your suitcase and clear out, and if you come back not in fifty but even in one hundred years, we have nothing more to say to one another about anything. And his next words convinced Safaly *muallim* that he'd interpreted the glance cast on the suitcase correctly.

"When Gogan gets here, he'll bring you bedding right away. There's a folding bed on the veranda. I covered it with a goat skin—if you get tired, lie down, rest. Gogan will also bring a bowl of *qatıq* for you to eat. If we make anything for dinner, we'll send it to you."

Safaly *muallim* didn't remember very well how he and his suitcase got from his uncle's to his father's house. But if he lived still another seventy-two years, he wouldn't forget how he opened the gate with the ring (through which a stick as thick as his hand passed) and how, going into the yard, he saw the withered, yellow grass. It was really that same grass, Lord! It was on exactly that grass that he'd struggled with Safar in his dream! And besides, there was that Gogan-De Gaulle. He imagined Gogan much more clearly, more fully than Tariel. . . . Gogan ran in about five or ten minutes after Safaly *muallim*. He threw down the bedding wrapped in a shawl and immediately made for the cucumber beds. Stuffing the inside of his shirt with cucumbers, he went up to Safaly *muallim*, tossing the very biggest one in his hands.

"Uncle, give me ten rubles, eh? And I'll buy Grandfather cookies in the store." He said this so casually that it was as if he'd lived with Safaly *muallim* his whole life, damn him! And having received the ten rubles, he added slyly: "Don't be afraid, Uncle, I won't stay in your debt—I'll go to the mountain and bring you some quail eggs."

The first night of his arrival in Buzbulag, Safaly *muallim* dreamed of his mother, Seren *arvad*. Moreover, not in Buzbulag but in the Baku suburb of Buzovny. This is what happened: having entered the institute in Baku, Safaly *muallim* began to look for suitable work in September. With the help of one of his classmates he found work in Buzovny, in the cashier's office at the train station where tickets were sold for the suburban trains. From five in the evening until twelve at night he sat in that office; he both sold tickets and calmly prepared for his lessons. And if he wanted, from time to time he locked the office for a half-hour and went to pay his compliments to Sima, who worked as a snack bar assistant in a restaurant along the road to the beach. Her real name was Samaya, but she called herself Sima, and that name suited her very well. Safaly liked Samaya very much, and apparently the girl wasn't indifferent to him, either. Once they agreed to meet at the Sabuchinsky railroad station; for one thing, it was calmer there, and few of their acquaintances might see them in the city. For another thing, Sima lived in the city; she came to Buzovny every day on the *elektrichka*. But Sima didn't come to the rendevous. Having waited for her for a full three hours at the train station, Safaly sat on the *elektrichka* and returned to Buzovny with nothing to show for his trouble. With that, the affair came to an end. It's true that even after his marriage Safaly *muallim*'s heart skipped a beat on meeting Sima, but it was probably good that things had turned out the way they had: what kind of wife would a snack bar assistant in a restaurant have been for Safaly *muallim*?

Having found work in the cashier's office, Safaly rented a room in an apartment from a Buzovny resident, Azizaga, who worked in the same office on the first shift. The salary wasn't bad—in the old money he received about eleven hundred rubles each month in hand. Besides that, he collected thirty to thirty-five rubles each day in change left behind by ticket buyers. Thinking everything over, Safaly then decided that Seren *arvad* should no longer stay in Buzbulag—with a living son, it was unseemly for her to live under her brother's wing. Moreover, Azizaga *kishi* also fully approved of his decision; he was even prepared to give up the big room after the arrival of Safaly's mother and move himself to the small one occupied by Safaly. In sum, having entered the institute, Safaly brought his mother from Buzbulag before the start of winter. Seren *arvad* very quickly found a common language and made friends with that same Azizaga *kishi* and with his wife Melek *khanum* and their daughters Kheiransa and Zarnigyar. And after a little time had passed, half of Buzovny idolized Seren *arvad*.

But there was an unpleasant side to all this: Azizaga *kishi* wanted to marry off his older daughter, Kheiransa, before Zarnigyar. And in character and appearance Kheiransa was better, more beautiful, but she had one defect: one arm was shorter than the other. More precisely, it seemed that one of Kheiransa's arms ended at the elbow.

Although Safaly had long before decided for himself to marry Zarnigyar, he didn't want to offend either Azizaga *kishi* or Melek *khanum* or Kheiransa, and therefore he might have, perhaps, agreed to marry Kheiransa. But Seren *arvad* was sharply opposed: "Kheiransa will find a cripple like herself and marry him. If we're going to take a girl, we should choose one of full value; why do we need a girl with half an arm? Well, okay, but she has a big birthmark under her breast the size of a quail's egg, a black, hairy, creepy thing—I saw it with my own eyes in the bathhouse."

The dream Safaly *muallim* dreamed that night in Buzbulag had a connection—it's true, a very distant connection—with the story about the "quail's egg." More precisely, with Kheiransa, because Safaly *muallim* dreamed that Azizaga *kishi*, having planned it with Melek *khanum*, had put Kheiransa in bed with him on the wedding night in place of Zarnigyar. Carefully hiding one arm under her shawl, Kheiransa stood in the middle of the room and looked meekly at Safaly, and Safaly didn't know what he should do: get up and leave the room, remain there and wait for morning or, submitting to fate, take Kheiransa in place of Zarnigyar? Seren *arvad* saved Safaly from this desperate situation; first she shoved Zarnigyar into the room, and then she seized Kheiransa by the hand and led her out of the room, Hoarsely, like Khyzyr *kishi*, she said, "I understand that Gorbachev extremely well. But I can't understand anything that these *kafir*-Muslims get up to." And she left, slamming the door.

Safaly *muallim* started and woke up. Everything all around was bathed in milky-white moonlight. The thirty-six-ounce container of *qatıq* that Gogan had brought was rolling around on the floor, and at the window where the container had been resting sat a black cat who appeared to be quite distressed by what had happened.

Awakened, Safaly *muallim* just could not get back to sleep. On the one hand there was the radiant, white moonlight flooding over the whole world, and on the other there was the radiant countenance of Seren *arvad*, who didn't resemble anyone else. Seren *arvad* had said and done many things of the sort that one couldn't forget. But one of her deeds was worthy of including in history: she'd made a fiery speech at the grave of the highly venerated Etaga in Shuveliany. That was an old story; it had happened more than five or six years after Safaly *muallim* received an apartment and moved with all his family to

Baku. Rena was still little and studying in school. One Sunday all of them had gone together to Buzovny to visit Azizaga *kishi*. On the walk back, Zarnigyar suggested that they stroll around a little before returning to the city. So they walked along the bank to Shuveliany towards Etaga's grave. Women were crowding around the grave. They compelled everyone to kiss the gravestone and make a monetary donation. It turned out that Rena was also supposed to kiss the gravestone. But when the little girl leaned over and wanted to touch the stone with her lips, Seren *arvad* placed her hand beneath, and instead of kissing the gravestone, Rena kissed her grandmother's hand. That was enough for the women. They attacked Seren *arvad* and began to accuse her of unbelief, of following the Babi sect. And then Seren *arvad* exploded: "Oh, you *matyshki*, swine-eaters! What are the saints, the prophets, to you! What do you understand of them? You gathered here posing as mullahs—but can a woman really be a mullah? The Prophet forbade eating fish without bones, but you eat them, gobble them up, and then shamelessly lick your fingers! Why must my little girl kiss that stone? A hundred people kiss it during the day—do you want her to catch something from kissing it? And who would study in her place? Just the other day they gave her a 'C' in geometry, so she cried until morning. Do you even know what geometry is? You don't read newspapers or books, so at least listen to the radio. Has anyone said even once on the radio, 'Go to the cemetery, kiss a gravestone, then let diarrhea seize hold of your guts so you can shit all over town?' Where do they say such a thing, where do they write it? Your minds aren't worth a kopek, but you take it on yourselves to teach those who are smarter than you. First you should learn to speak properly, unfortunate ones," she said, "and then you can teach people. What language are you speaking? Whose language is that? Bah, a rabble of mullahs! Just look at you: you don't even look like people, you're the spitting image of jackals, kites!" In a word, Seren *arvad* taught those women such a "geometry" lesson that ten minutes later they still looked blank.

Seren *arvad* hated two things more than anything in the world: mullahs and the Soviet authorities. And before her death she demanded: "Not a single mullah should be at my funeral feast. Take me to Buzovny and bury me next to Azizaga and Melek *khanum*. The people of Buzovny are good people, real, because how" (Seren *arvad*, who her whole life didn't recognize any dialect other than that of Buzbulag, undoubtedly said this "because how" commonly used by the people of Buzovny as a sign of her respect and gratitude to them) "because how they" (that is, the people of Buzovny) "don't submit to those authorities."

During the month and a half that Safaly *muallim* spent in Buzbulag, he dreamed many dreams and thought over many things; during that time, it was as if he in full measure drained both the woe and the sweetness of his seventy-two-year, not-having-begun, ending life. And in the end he came to the conclusion that if you don't count childhood and early youth, nothing of this life remains in a person's memory. And if you remember something, then it's the kind of thing that stretches its threads back to childhood. For example, American professor Neil Armstrong's flight to the moon. That event was one of the landmarks of the seventy-two years of his life because in the old days Seren *arvad* had told Safaly *muallim* the most wonderful stories in the world about the moon. In those stories, which Safaly *muallim* heard from Seren *arvad* starting in his very early years, the crescent moon was a handsome youth and the sun was a fine girl like an angel, and everything on earth—from the grasses and bushes to the highest plane trees—was born from the love of these two. The bright yellow sunflower was their first-born, that's why it always looked at the sky. And the scarlet mountain poppy was also the child of that heavenly love, which is why the scarlet mountain poppy closes its boll at night and opens it in the morning—you see, it was only in the morning that Mother Sun fed the poppy with her milk. Later Safaly grew up, went to school and, of course, found out that the crescent moon wasn't a youth. But how could the spirit, light, and radiance of those stories disappear, stories he'd absorbed with his mother's milk? And the fairytale reveries ingrained in him along with the bright yellow sunflower and the scarlet mountain poppy later turned the crescent moon youth into the moon-world. And for the rest of his life, for Safaly *muallim* the cleanest rivers in the world flowed through the moon, the greenest grass grew there, the tallest trees, and the best people in the world wandered in green glades under tall trees.

Remembering when Apollo 11 flew to the moon and the day Neil Armstrong took his first steps, Safaly *muallim* was angry most of all at himself. Because if on that same day—July 21, 1969, to be exact—Safaly *muallim*, who was then living near Baksovet, hadn't left home and set out along Governor's Garden to walk along the seaside boulevard, perhaps he'd never have seen that horror with his own eyes. And if he hadn't seen it with his own eyes, then possibly doubt would have only, as they say, glanced off Safaly *muallim*'s life and passed painlessly by. Of course, it's better to see something once than read or hear about it a thousand times. That day in Governor's Garden, sitting in the tearoom laid out right beside the wall of the fortress, Safaly *muallim* saw on the television screen with his own eyes that there's absolutely nothing on the moon except black dust. Wearing a protective suit, Neil Armstrong was stirring around in that dust, and up above him Apollo 11 circled like a helicopter. Safaly *muallim* looked at that black dust and remembered the ashes his mother Seren *arvad* had poured out of the chimney flue each summer in Buzbulag; it seemed someone had collected all the ashes burned by the people of Buzbulag since the time of Noah and poured them out every summer on the moon.

From that very day the world had begun to lose all its mystery for Safaly *muallim*. The world became very poor, pitiful; moreover, it was as if hope for a different world beyond the grave had withered, gone out. Even his former life (when he was living actively—working in philology, leading the institute, etc.) had suddenly begun to seem horribly grey and boring to him. With the disappearance of the moon of his childhood, all the mystery of the world also disappeared, and along with it, the very brightest colors of his whole life faded from memory. In Safaly *muallim*'s soul, his former faith not only in the infinite extent of the heavens and the enchanted beauty of the galaxy but even (to tell the truth) in the wisdom of Seren *arvad* and in the maternal virtue of Zarnigyar had been shaken. And then: that story in Yemen, Nukhbala, Rena's marriage in Leningrad to an old Jew with a Georgian last name. In Safaly *muallim*'s imagination those were links in a single chain, and one end of that chain extended straight towards the day of July 21. Every time he looked at the moon, Safaly *muallim* became accustomed to remembering—besides the black dust, the black ashes—that devil in the depths of Ali Ziya's eyes; Nukhbala, who looked like that devil; and his beloved only daughter, Rena. And when the moon rose in Buzbulag, it wasn't even necessary to lift one's head to see it. There the moon was everywhere—in the house, in the yard— and it found a person on its own. It merged together the trees and cliffs, the earth and sky, and called them to converse. At night when moonlight ran riot, even the birds were unable to fall asleep peacefully in their nests. How many times during such nights did Safaly *muallim* shudder and wake up because of the cawing of the old crow who'd made herself a nest at the top of the tree in their yard? On the other hand, Safaly *muallim* lived peacefully in Buzbulag. Only Tariel disturbed that peace for five or ten days. One night Khyzyr *kishi* listened to the speech of People's Deputy of the USSR Sheikh-ul-Islam Allahshukur Pashazadeh on the *tellervision*, a speech that was dedicated to unmasking the slanderous conjectures of imperialist circles about Islamic fundamentalism; the next day—before the first cock crow—he came to Safaly *muallim* and made a fiery speech about the pitiful condition of the government of the republic, which also conveyed some unease to his (that is, to

Safaly *muallim*'s) soul. And sometimes even that swindler Gogan, who put forward more and more economic demands—having decided to bankrupt Safaly *muallim* once and for all—periodically declared a strike and didn't appear to water the garden. Then Safaly *muallim* took the shovel on his shoulder and set to work on the land himself, pursued by the teasing of the women passing by: "Why do you hold the shovel handle that way, Safaly *muallim*, are you afraid it will eat you?" "Why don't you take off your Panama hat, is it that you don't want to tan your face?" "Tighten your trousers, Safaly *muallim*, you don't want your 'little swallow' to fly out of the nest!" And that was payback not only for the fact that Safaly *muallim* had lived fifty years in Baku, worked ten years as a rector and been a professor for twenty years, but also for the fact that he'd once been a friend of the famous writer and prominent public figure Ali Ziya, flown on the same plane with him, and lived in the same hotel. But that only happened once a week or every couple of weeks when by long-standing custom his turn came to use the water. The rest of the time no one bothered Safaly *muallim*; he spent the days stretched out in the yard, reading newspapers and books. At night he admired the stars, the moon on the veranda. And when he was especially overcome by boredom, he had pleasant conversations with Professor Neil Armstrong.

"Good evening, Mr. Professor!"

"Good evening, Professor! How are you?" (Neil Armstrong knew that Safaly *muallim* was also a professor).

"How are you, Neil? How is America after your return from the moon?"

"Fine, fine!" Neil Armstrong was seated in a soft armchair, stretching out his legs on the desk, a glass of whisky in front of him.

"Neil, Mr. Neil, sir! Do you know, to this day I don't believe the moon is made that way!"

"Believe it, believe it, Comrade Safaly. There's no life on the moon. There's nothing on the moon except sand and dust!"

"Surely some kind of grass grows! No bushes, not even a little flower?"

"No, Professor, not even a weed."

"They say there are mountains there?"

"Yes. Many mountains. The surface of the moon consists mostly of mountains."

"So many mountains: is it possible that not a single little poppy flower has grown, Neil?"

Neil Armstrong lifted the glass of whisky to his lips and put it down again.

"It's possible," he said. "And such things happen. Once you doubted that a four-story hotel could have a fifth floor. And weren't you convinced later that such a thing exists?"

"I was convinced," said Safaly *muallim*, almost crying. "So convinced, Neil. And I wouldn't wish being convinced that way on my worst enemies."

Neil Armstrong didn't like Safaly *muallim*'s plaintive tone.

"I don't see grounds here for great misfortune, Comrade Safaly," he answered. "It's necessary to go through everything in life. You should know that even I have occasion to be on the one-hundred-and-eleventh floor of the one-hundred-and-ten-floor World Trade Center in New York, and several times I've even played pool with Mr. Rockefeller there."

"It happens, it happens," Safaly *muallim* answered in a shaking voice. "For a person who's been to the moon, it's not a big deal to play pool on the one-hundred-and-eleventh floor. And what's Earth like from there, Neil?"

"From where? From the one-hundred-and-eleventh floor?"

"No. From the moon. From that celestial body."

"Forgive me," said Neil Armstrong with truly professorial politeness, although his legs were stretched out on the desk as before. "I didn't have a chance to look at Earth from the moon. Time was limited. But three years before the moon flight I went for a ride on a near-earth orbit in that rattletrap Gemini 8, and then I often looked at Earth. At that time your country was especially visible from the cosmos."

"When? In 1966?" asked Safaly *muallim* with infinite interest, because that was the year of his journey to Yemen. "It would be interesting to know how our country looks from the cosmos now."

"Bad! Very bad!" Neil's mood was suddenly spoiled. He lowered one leg to the floor and in English, Persian, and poor Russian loudly repeated: "Bad! *Bəd!* Nyet good, so nyet good."

"Why, Neil? Why did this suddenly happen with this country? You have to know, you must know these kinds of things very well because, no matter what, you flew to another celestial body."

"In order to know that, Professor, it's not necessary to fly to another celestial body!" This time Neil's answer sounded very sharp, moreover, he once again put both feet on the desk—he always did that when the capitalist in him spoke. "Leaders of a new type have come to power in your country, and they are much more farsighted than your previous leaders. That's obviously why this sort of situation arose for you."

Safaly *muallim* sulked like a child and hung his head in distress because he didn't agree with unanimous world opinion, particularly on the farsightedness of the new leadership.

"You call the tears of hundreds of thousands of innocent people, the moans of grey-haired old men, old women, and children 'farsightedness'! Robbery, arson, murder—the bloody bonfires of the Inquisition of the Middle Ages at the end of the twentieth century! No, Neil, here you and I cannot agree. I can't possibly believe in the farsightedness of politicians of the new type, under whom prices in the country have risen at the very least tenfold in just five years, and only human life has depreciated! Even earlier we were running into that kind of Komsomol 'farsightedness.'"

The astronaut was dismayed. It seems that after the hot, fiery words of Safaly *muallim*, Neil was prepared to reconsider his earlier view on farsightedness and humanism. After long thought he said, "I completely agree with you. It goes without saying that the farsightedness of your current leadership is on the one hand connected with the Pioneer-Komsomol movement. Therefore, a great many of your emigrants to America still consider this reform with considerable doubt. Even that bearded guy, Solzhenitsyn. . . . Ninety percent of the intellectuals who believed in the bright future of Russia are now in deep depression. Don't pay much attention to the superficial prognoses of Margaret Thatcher."

Safaly *muallim* rejoiced greatly because he was in full agreement with what the famous astronaut said about the Komsomol.

"You're right. I know that Nukhb—that Komsomol very well. They have only one goal, Neil: today a person must forget who he was yesterday. Last name, first name, father's name, even what he ate yesterday. For example, in Brezhnev's time no one ever bought frozen meat. Fresh beef cost two rubles, lamb a ruble-ninety. Who remembers now that those kinds of interesting things were in our Soviet stores? Maybe a dozen veterans. And now, not five years since this new type of leader came to power, people are forgetting, for example, what color wieners are. If not today, then tomorrow people really might even forget about cheese, fish, strawberry preserves, eggplant caviar. . . . If you can believe it, Neil, at one time people in our country didn't concern themselves with the nationality of a person before shaking hands! Who remembers that now? Again, probably, a dozen veterans. I believe, Neil. I believe that this country won't always be this way. A time will come when they'll sell wieners, cheese, strawberry preserves, and eggplant caviar in the stores again. And a person won't care about another person's nationality when saying hello, just like it was in the period of stagnation!

But to whom will those wieners and greetings be attributed, which wise and farsighted politician will take credit for that brilliant victory? Gorbachev and *perestroika*, of course. But no one will answer for the hundreds of thousands of pitiful refugees who've been deprived of shelter, who've lost the graves of their fathers, their motherland, their nest, or for those who were cut to pieces before the eyes of their children. Neil! Look at the games memory plays, Neil! Now do you understand what Komsomol farsightedness means?"

"Orwell. George Orwell!" The American professor leaped up from his armchair, his cry signifying, apparently, that he also agreed with Safaly *muallim*'s second monologue. "Lenin! NEP! Cultural revolution! The collective farm! Wieners! Nukhbala! Sumgait!"[2] Neil Armstrong seized the glass; this time he didn't take a sip but drained it in a single gulp and wiped his lips with the back of his hand, Russian-style. Then he sat in his place again and made a wry face, as if he were now gathering himself to give a lecture to all the students of the university in Cincinnati forthwith.

But Safaly *muallim* didn't allow his colleague to give that lecture.

"Mr. Neil! Professor, sir!" he said. "I most humbly ask you: do not say the word 'Sumgait' ever, anywhere. Talk about wieners, about Nukhbala, but not about that."

Here the blue eyes of Neil Armstrong looked at Safaly *muallim* with the same malice that Vaska once looked at Zarnigyar. "What do you mean by that, Comrade Safaly?"

"I swear by Allah, Mr. Neil, I don't mean anything. Only the comrades in charge could share their objective thoughts with you about that. But one of our especially conscientious comrades becomes very nervous on hearing that word. Now conversations about Sumgait cause him a fit of bile. It's necessary to protect the health of that comrade, he's a person the country needs very much. A whole string of essential articles about the friendship of peoples has come from his pen. When he was a bigwig in the Central Committee of the Communist Party, everyone thought he was the godfather of our renowned Azerbaijani internationalism. And not long ago he was seen in the dacha-bordello of Nukhbala Nukhievich. He sat on the veranda and bawled in a drunken voice, 'Death to all Armenians! Long live glorious Azerbaijan!'"

"I know him very well," answered Neil Armstrong. "He's a cannibal from the tribe of cultural cannibals."

"A cannibal?" Safaly *muallim* couldn't believe what he'd heard. "Professor, you probably mean to say 'a canny pol'?"

"No! A cannibal is it, exactly."

Safaly *muallim* decided not to get into an argument with the famous astronaut. He fell silent, thoughtfully imagining to himself all the area from wherever cannibals rule to our new socialist settlement of Shuveliany—probably half the world—and suddenly his face (that is, Safaly *muallim's* face) lit up so much that it was as if a bright sunbeam had fallen on it.

"Neil! Ah, if only Seren *arvad* were alive, I'm telling you, Neil! Cannibals, canny pols—she would have gathered them all in one cemetery and taught them an excellent lesson in geometry just like she taught those illiterate *matushki* gobbling up boneless fish!"

And the all-knowing jokester, witty Neil Armstrong, understood perfectly what Safaly *muallim* wanted to say this time.

"Yes? Yes!" he answered. "Seren *arvad*! Khorosho, so, so khorosho!"

With that, of course, the conversation could have concluded. But it was still a long time until morning. Therefore, Safaly *muallim* considered it necessary to open a new subject for discussion.

"And a few words about Ali Ziya, Neil. What can you say about the biological and psychological characteristics of that individual?"

"That's a bad individual!" Neil Armstrong turned his head as if he wanted to spit. And then he said in an enigmatic voice: "This conversation must stay between us. Flying to the moon, I dropped in briefly on Mars and Jupiter. There are such individuals there. Comparatively few on Mars, but on Jupiter. . . ."

"Oh, Lord! Lord!" It seems Safaly *muallim* was again drawn to complain.

Neil Armstrong noticed this in time and prevented the possibility. "But at the present moment we don't have a single individual of that sort in North America. Gus Hall was the last one, and we pensioned him off recently. Do you have any more questions, Professor?"

"I do! I do!" Suddenly Safaly *muallim* was seized with wild trembling; it probably seemed to him that his partner in conversation was getting ready to go. But as a matter of fact, he didn't have anything more to ask; he himself was ready to stop the argument for today.

"With regard to that Georgian last name, I've already stated my firm opinion about that. This is the issue, Comrade Safaly: not one Muslim man in the world, beginning with the Prophet Mohammed and ending with the new hope of the East, Saddam Hussein, has ever taken such care of, ever cherished his wife as much at that person! He gets up at night when the baby cries?"

"He gets up, Neil, I won't lie."

"He washes diapers?"

"Yes, he washes them. And even irons them!" added Safaly *muallim* with special pride.

"Has he ever once allowed the hand of his wife to touch baby poop?"

"No! Not once has he allowed it!"

"Then why are you still hung up on his last name?!" Neil Armstrong was extraordinarily stirred up.

Safaly *muallim* couldn't find anything to answer. He looked at the moon until tears came to his eyes and remembered his Leningrad granddaughter. But Safaly *muallim* wouldn't have been Safaly *muallim* if he'd allowed Neil Armstrong to escape so simply with remarks about diapers and poop; he again led the conversation to the moon.

"Neil! Mr. Neil! Perhaps you accidentally ended up on the wrong part of the moon! Perhaps there are other places on the moon with poppies, sunflowers, and violets?"

In the blue eyes of the famous astronaut, which looked like shining celestial stars, the well-known, clean, mysterious smile of the universe broke out anew.

"There are!" answered Neil Armstrong. "There are! The cleanest rivers and springs in the galaxy are on the moon. But what should we do, Comrade Safaly? For now we need to hide that genuine truth from the world. That's the opinion of our president. Orwell! Seren *arvad*! It's a problem of individuals, do you understand, Professor?"

"I understand. I absolutely understand!" Finally Safaly *muallim* calmed down and sighed with relief, because he hadn't been able to satisfy himself at all that the moon was really just an assemblage of dust. Safaly *muallim*, citizen of the world, very much wanted rivers to flow, ships to sail, and sunflowers, poppies, and violets to grow on the moon. He wanted there to be life on the moon, people, and for the people on the moon to live more happily than earthlings.

But (the devil take it!) at that point Safaly *muallim* suddenly shivered, and it was as if he had awakened from a sweet sleep. And Safaly *muallim* saw that the moon in the sky wasn't the same moon as in Buzbulag and that he wasn't sitting on the veranda in Buzbulag but on the balcony in Zugulba. He returned to the room and looked at the clock: it was eight-thirty, so the cafeteria was long closed. Perhaps, thought Safaly *muallim*, he'd go out, walk around the cafeteria, look for Vaska. But he didn't go out; clearly, he was wary of meeting Ali Ziya there. And (again, the devil take it!) stepping out once more on the balcony, Safaly *muallim* saw Ali Ziya walking about importantly below. Ali Ziya wasn't walking on the comfortable asphalt paths laid out beneath the balconies now but much further off—the great thinker had probably decided that if he walked along those alleys, Safaly *muallim* couldn't throw a teapot, a hotplate, or anything heavy at his head.

After that Safaly *muallim* never again saw Ali Ziya anywhere. Later he heard from one of the regulars on the seaside boulevard that somewhere, at some entirely honorary celebratory meal, Ali Ziya had raised a toast in his honor. "Let's drink," he said, "to Safaly's health! I love him very much," he said, "but he (that is, Safaly *muallim*) is a stubborn person, an egoist, a maximalist, he never wants to understand me." And after those words, it seems, he drained his glass, sat down, and began to sob.

Yes, such strange things do go on in the world. What a coincidence that at about that time I met Safaly *muallim* on the Boulevard. He'd just heard that story about the "toast" and was in such a state then that, as they say, though cut with a knife, not a drop of blood spilled out. Safaly *muallim*'s state upset me very much. I was tormented all night, and in the morning I wasn't even able to think up a name for the next chapter of this story. Well, what of it—I have enough troubles of my own, why should I be tormented by the troubles of others?

Okay, fine, whatever. . . .

Unnamed

Exactly one week after his arrival in Zugulba, towards evening Safaly *muallim* telephoned Baku from the pay phone next to the cafeteria. The first thing he heard from Lora rattled him so much that he didn't show any interest in the remaining news from the city, about which his neighbor told him in a voice that shook.

Tariel had arrived. He was in Baku. And although Lora had told him at least ten times that Safaly *muallim* had gone to visit his daughter in Leningrad, all the same he hung around near her door. Three times a day—morning, noon, and evening—he rang at Lora's door wanting to know if Safaly *muallim* had come back.

"Oy, oy, how horrible it is, Safaly! Come back, don't stay there. The city is dying. The things going on here, Safaly! Horrible! Horrible! Oh, Lord, how horrible!" Lora's wails resounded from the telephone receiver. But Safaly *muallim* wasn't able to properly clarify for himself the reason for these wails because protests had been taking place in Baku on the square at the House of Unions even before his trip to Zugulba. What in the world could have happened in the city over the course of just a week?

"So what happened, Lora? What's going on in the city? Did they pull down the monument?" This time Safaly *muallim*'s rich imagination for some reason did not extend further than the monument standing in front of the House of Unions.

"No, Shaumian is still there in his place. But they say yesterday a big dog was tied to him. Right to his leg. Ah, the bastards, what bastards our Yerevan nationalists are! They, they are responsible for all this. . . ."

"I'm not talking about that monument, Lora! I'm talking about the other one, the one near the House of Unions." Safaly *muallim* didn't want to say the name of the leader on the telephone.

And because of that, probably, Lora wasn't able to give a full reply to his question. "About which one? No. . . . I don't know. I haven't heard. . . . To hell with the monument, Safaly. It's miserable for living people."

"That's true. But there's no need to fret, Lora. Everything will be fine, don't be afraid," said Safaly *muallim* with sincere belief. "And that, what's his. . .did he bring his wife?"

"No. I haven't seen her. . . . Seems he didn't bring her."

Even before he'd hung up the receiver, Safaly *muallim* made a firm resolution not to leave Zugulba for anywhere in the near future and not to even telephone the city for at least a week. Tariel's appearance in Baku was half the problem, but there wasn't anything in Lora's mournful voice to induce Safaly *muallim* to return to Baku, either.

But after three days or so a strong north wind rose in Zugulba. In five minutes the hurricane gusts mixed together clouds, dust, sea, and trees. And in those same five minutes Safaly *muallim* lost his peace of mind—his mood was spoiled. In stormy, gusting winds Safaly *muallim* made it to the telephone with difficulty and dialed Lora's number with shaking hands.

"Hello? *Who this is? Speak up, why you quiet?*!"

The voice was a man's, and it's impossible to say that it was a voice less well known to Safaly *muallim* than Lora's; however, it's also safe to say that it wasn't the most beloved voice in the world: Tariel!

Safaly *muallim* hung up the receiver. He didn't think it was anything bad. He simply decided that over a short period of time Tariel had probably been able to solve his problems efficiently; he'd found an opening with Lora, wormed his way into her trust, tasted her excellent lunches, and in the end settled in with Lora and now—waiting for Safaly *muallim*'s return from Leningrad—was living the good life, from time to time even answering the telephone. It came into Safaly *muallim*'s head to dial the number again—Lora would surely answer it herself. But he didn't call again. He glanced around, looked at the sea, at the clouds mixed with dust in the sky and, suddenly, finally, understood that it didn't make sense to stay longer in Zugulba. He set out for his room, hurriedly packed his things, and under gusty storm winds headed for the bus stop.

Safaly *muallim* reached home very late; it was already around two a.m. Coming out of the elevator, he rang first at Lora's door (he knew she went to bed late). But no one answered. Safaly *muallim* opened his own door, went in, turned on the light in the hallway, and his heart stood still.

In the hallway—next to the telephone—was a pile of newspapers and magazines! There were two envelopes, one sealed and one unsealed. But who had put them there? Because in departing for Zugulba, Safaly *muallim* had left only the mailbox key with his neighbor. . . .

The thunderstruck Safaly *muallim* walked around the rooms; he didn't notice any change. He went out into the stairwell and rang at Lora's door another time, and again no one answered. Returning to the apartment, Safaly *muallim* picked up the envelopes lying on top of the pile of newspapers and magazines. The sealed letter was from Leningrad, from Rena; on the unsealed envelope, "To Safaly *muallim* from Lora" was written in violet ink. Inside was a sheet of graph paper folded in two. Safaly *muallim* was just going to pull the paper out of the envelope when he heard the sound of the lock turning. The door swung open, and in came Tariel.

"You're back, Uncle? *Welcome you come!*" said Tariel in broken Russian, puckering his lips, but he wasn't able to kiss his uncle on the cheek, so he kissed him right in the middle of his head where there was a circular bald patch the color of an egg yolk. Tariel was much taller than Safaly *muallim*, and moreover, when he'd bent down for a kiss, Safaly *muallim* had adroitly lowered his head.

"Where did you get my key?" Safaly *muallim* stood by the telephone clutching the pile of newpapers to his chest and panting as he said it, as if every word weighed forty pounds.

"I just ordered it, Uncle, is it really so difficult to order keys? I didn't change the lock. I'm thinking: what if you suddenly come back, and I'm not home, and you're standing there in front of the door?" Tariel glanced surreptitiously at Safaly *muallim*, and there was something in his uncle's face that compelled Tariel to become slightly thoughtful. "What is it, Uncle? Did I do something wrong? You know, Uncle, I was frightened. Anything could happen. Suddenly, I'm thinking, God forbid, maybe you came back from Leningrad, got sick, and no one knew. . .how that would shame all our people! You know very well, of course, these days our enemies would happily spend a million for that news. A stinking corpse turns up in an apartment, so they shout it all over the world that the whole Azerbaijani nation is decomposing!"

"So now are you convinced that I'm not dead?" It seems Safaly *muallim* was going to put the question point blank.

"Well, of course! If you only knew how much I rejoiced that day when I came into the house and saw you were in Leningrad."

"Thank you," said Safaly *muallim*. "And now, please, give me that key."

"Why do you need it? You've already got your own key!" Tariel's eyes were round with amazement.

They went into the room and sat on the antiquated old sofa.

"I bought that apartment, Uncle, you can congratulate me!" said Tariel, indicating the wall that divided the apartments of Lora and Safaly *muallim*.

"Don't be afraid, your neighbor was satisfied. She moved to Moscow. She has an elderly sister living there, eighty-five years old. She says she's also alone, it's better for the two of them to be together. I arranged the ticket for her myself—you can't get a ticket to Moscow now for less than three hundred rubles." Tariel pulled an oblong piece of paper from his pocket. "Here it is, Uncle, the title! Today the chair of the district executive committee signed it with his own hand and presented it to me. He's also one of us. I put it in the names of Grandma Tarlan and De Gaulle so that enemies won't be able to find any fault with it later."

"Extraordinary! Excellent! Glory to everyone who loves us!" exclaimed Safaly *muallim* with absolute sincerity. However, it's unclear to whom, exactly, these words were addressed: to De Gaulle, Grandma Tarlan, or the person who'd signed the title.

Tariel admired the title and then hid it again in his pocket. He threw a sidelong glance at Safaly *muallim* and then once again turned a glance full of love on the opposite wall.

"What do you think, Uncle—maybe we should completely get rid of that wall sometime soon? It would be excellent, spacious. Space is a good thing, isn't it, Uncle?"

"Yes! Yes! Indeed it is! Space is a good thing. An excellent thing—space." It seems that Safaly *muallim* did say these words, but in some kind of alien voice. It was the voice of Tariel, Gogan, Tarlan *arvad*, or (still further) Ali Ziya—because after Safaly *muallim* had seen the title, it was simply impossible for him to remain himself, to speak in his own voice. After that, the rest of his seventy-two-year-old life could not possibly be considered a human one.

Tariel got up.

"I'll go get you something to eat, Uncle. There's everything in the refrigerator. What should I bring you?" To all appearances, Tariel was satisfied with Safaly *muallim*'s words about space.

"Thank you, I'm full," said Safaly *muallim* barely audibly, and he laid the stack of newspapers—which to that moment he'd been clutching protectively to his chest like a child—onto the sofa next to him.

"Please forgive me, Uncle, I had a bit to drink today. I really didn't expect that you were coming. If I'd known, I'd have met you at the airport. . . . I don't particularly like drinking, Uncle. It just that today the beys, real men, got together, and therefore I had to drink."

"What beys?" asked Safaly *muallim*, looking not at Tariel but at the ceiling.

"Why, the beys!" Tariel, astonished at his uncle's lack of comprehension, also fixed his gaze on that spot on the blue ceiling where Safaly *muallim* was looking. "The best sons of our people, Uncle! The majority of them are academics. A couple of poets, writers."

"Allah! Allah!" Safaly *muallim* sighed deeply, continuing to look at the ceiling. And it's a good thing he sighed so deeply; if not, Tariel would have fluttered around him still longer.

Feeling he couldn't stand even one more such sigh from his uncle, Tariel headed slowly towards the door and had already gathered himself to slip out, but he stopped on hearing some kind of noise. Behind him stood Safaly *muallim*, the bottle of Scotch in his hand.

"Take this. I've got no use for it. Give it to one of those mustachioed beys."

"How about a bearded one?" It turns out that Tariel wasn't entirely devoid of a sense of humor.

"Give it to one with a moustache!" Safaly *muallim*'s voice sounded stern, commanding. "Could a person with a beard really appreciate whisky?" And tightly slamming the door behind Tariel, he said the most highly abstract curse: "Vile filth!"

He returned to the room and sat on the sofa. He wanted to read Lora's letter first, but then he reconsidered, laid it down, and picked up the sealed enveloped sent from Leningrad.

Rena wrote to the dictation of her young daughter, in Russian.

"Grandpa, my sweet Grandfather, my unforgettable swallow! You've already completely forgotten about me, you don't even write any letters. You did promise to come here this summer, but you went to some village. I miss you very much. Mama-Rena also misses you. And our Papa went to London not long ago. He brought you a very good electric razor, but Mama-Rena doesn't know whether to mail it to you or wait until you get here. She's afraid it will get lost. Nowadays they say it's a complete zoo at the post office, too. Grandfather, you should really try. . . ."

Safaly *muallim* didn't have enough patience to finish the letter. Having read the signature at the end, "Your granddaughter, Sonechka," he hid the letter again in the envelope and got down to Lora's letter.

"Dear, deeply respected Safaly! I'm sorry I wasn't able to wait for you. Everything happened very quickly, but I'm happy that I'm moving. I'm going to my sister in Moscow. You know my sister, she visited me once. Remember, she argued with you about Silva Kaputikyan. Dear Safaly, you can't imagine how terrible it's been for me during these days without you. I didn't sleep entire nights. I was sitting and waiting for bandits to break down the door, come into the apartment, and cut my throat. What's happening in the city these days is a horror. To hell with that Nagorno-Karabakh and its healing mountain air! That Karabakh will still cause many calamities. But I, dear Safaly, am not offended at your nation. To this day I haven't seen anything bad from Azerbaijanis. How well we lived, dear Safaly, and we would have lived that way until the end of our days, probably, without that person with a black, toad-like birthmark on his head.[3] Recently, his buffalo-like equanimity has practically smothered me! The country is just going to pieces; only screamers without a conscience are flourishing around here, even a schoolchild understands this isn't a state anymore, it's a slaughterhouse, a hellish inferno. And he walks around as if nothing's happened! He's even picked up a suitable smile, like an American president. Oh, horrors, Safaly, and what can one say, only a bumpkin from Stavropol could act that way with people. And your nephew, dear Safaly, turns out to be not as bad as I imagined him to myself. For my two rooms he gave me a whole fortune, a whole seven thousand. That money will last me my whole life. He also got my plane ticket. And he even ordered a container so I could send some of my things to Moscow. I'm very satisfied with your nephew, God grant him good health. And he'll bring you your mail. I'm sorry I couldn't wait for you. Farewell, dear, deeply respected Safaly. It's late now, and my plane leaves early tomorrow morning. Thank you for everything. Lora, your neighbor."

Safaly *muallim* didn't throw the letter away but laid it down carefully and decided to save it, because that sheet from a notebook of graph paper was the sole reminder left of the person with whom he'd lived as neighbors for twenty years.

That night was very difficult for Safaly *muallim*, and that very night he dreamed the most terrible dream of his life: on the surface of the moon was a reddish-grey crater that resembled the depths of a dried-up sea. Here and there were black mountains and heights made out of dust and ash. And Neil Armstrong—aged, fatigued, shaggy, with a long beard like a priest or a dervish—was using the Soviet lunar rover, which resembled a hand cart or baby carriage, to move corpses somewhere. Sometimes the astronaut got tired, sat down to rest, pulled bottles of Agdam from the pockets of his threadbare pants and jacket smeared with black lunar dust, took a gulp from each bottle, and again set to work, because there were many corpses in that hollow resembling the depths of a dried-up sea. It was as if those corpses tormented Neil Armstrong, and the consciousness of the impossibility of transporting all those bodies made his appearance tired and hopeless.

Probably anyone who'd dreamed such a nightmarish dream would look on the future with great sadness. But here (Allah rest her soul!) Seren *arvad* came to Safaly *muallim*'s rescue. "My son," she said, "when you see a beard in a dream, that's a good omen. And death means peace, good fortune. A person who sees a dead person in a dream will live an additional ten years, my son!" she said. His mother's voice calmed Safaly *muallim*, who'd awakened in a cold sweat in the middle of the night. All the same, he could in no way make sense of that terrible picture, especially the Soviet apparatus—resembling something like a hand cart, something like a baby carriage, on which "USSR" was written in black letters—wandering around the moon. Who knows, perhaps sometime that kind of misfortune might even befall the world: the depths of the sea dried up and countless human corpses! Safaly *muallim* didn't want to believe in that. But then he remembered that many of the things in which he hadn't wanted to believe had come true, and the horror of the dream swiftly spread over Safaly *muallim*'s body, chaining it, depriving him of life.

Perhaps predicting this or that event in the world in and of itself isn't such a big accomplishment. But it really depends on where, when, and in what country. Didn't Khyzyr *kishi* foretell back in the 1920s what that undertaking with collective farms would lead to? He predicted it, predicted it in full exactitude! Why did Seren *arvad* relate with such distrust to the various activities of the Soviet authorities? Undoubtedly because she had the ability to foresee everything; she knew that sooner or later that authority might end with the complete triumph of the mullahs! But who in this world listened to Khyzyr *kishi* or Seren *arvad*, and who cared if Safaly *muallim* had nightmares now?

In order to finally drive the traces of the night's visions from the room, Safaly *muallim* decided to turn on the light. He got up but didn't turn on the light; he thought Tariel might see it and put in an appearance.

He quietly opened the door and went out on the balcony. It was amazing: the wind had completely quieted down. It was just beginning to get light. Something grey, dead, woven from the merging of night and day—something resembling fog or haze—hung over the city. Safaly *muallim* couldn't make out even the House of Unions from the balcony, although he lived quite close to it. From time to time something made its way to Safaly *muallim* from the giant square in front of the House of Unions, something distinctly resembling a sigh, or the moan of a thousand people. Those people had been there even before his trip to Zugulba; at night they bravely guarded the square where demonstrations took place during the day. Children of their native soil whose hearts were full of the thirst for freedom. . . . Now, early in the morning, there was no strength left in those people exhausted by sleepless nights to chant loudly, no strength even for quiet conversation. Only their breathing was audible.

It sometimes seemed that the dead thing resembling fog or haze woven from the merging of night and day shuddered and swayed from that breath, and then a feeling of horror arose. . . .

Safaly *muallim* left the balcony, and in the half-light of the room his glance fell on the book with the portrait on the cover that stood on the shelf. He looked for a long time at the black-browed, black-eyed, black-mustachioed man, and he came to the conclusion that William Faulkner, one of the greatest writers in the world, very much resembled not only Khyzyr *kishi* from Buzbulag but also Azizaga *kishi*, who had lived in Buzovny. And here Safaly *muallim* for some reason very much wanted to curse.

"Vile filth! Vile filth!" That abstract curse helped Safaly *muallim* ease his soul for the second time in a day. Then he resolutely took the book from the shelf. Because at that moment he firmly resolved that the book, brought sometime from Leningrad by Rena, must without fail be sent back today.

Vaska Appears

B ut Safaly *muallim* didn't go to the post office that day to send the book back. And for whatever it's worth, it wasn't because the book had been a gift from Rena or because Safaly *muallim* had become so accustomed to it that he wasn't able to part with it. It was simply because after the nightmare with the moon and Neil Armstrong—on that very same morning—when it was just beginning to grow light, a thought came into Safaly *muallim's* head that he had to carry out before he could attend to anything else in life.

The city was dying. There were strikes everywhere. Almost all the residents of Baku had collected in front of the House of Unions and were demonstrating there from morning to night. The House of Unions resembled Moscow's Butyrka prison, the Central Committee resembled a giant market, and the Council of Ministers resembled the bathhouse in Sheki. Baksovet, the city hall, had been transformed into revolutionary Smolny. And for several hours already Safaly *muallim*, lost, had tramped along the long, half-lit corridors of the Baksovet that had turned into Smolny.

One of the comrades in charge telephoned to summon his secretary.

"Are there many people in the reception area?" he asked.

"No. Just that person. That CRAZY person. The one who wants to exchange his four-room apartment for a one-room one."

The comrade in charge sighed deeply.

"Ah, life, life!" he said. "Curse you, fate!" With all his strength he banged his fist on the desk and added bitterly, "It's we who are the crazy ones, babe, not he. If you only knew what a person he is! He taught me at the institute. It's a good thing he didn't remember me. He's a great scholar. A diamond in the rough. The conscience of the nation!" he exclaimed in Russian and again switched to Azeri. "To exchange a four-room apartment for a one-room apartment isn't difficult; moreover, one in the center of town in a prestigious neighborhood. Anybody else would've made that exchange happen in an hour and put a hundred thousand in his pocket. And this person, you see, doesn't want to do it that way. He wants everything to be done according to law." He switched again to Russian. "According to law, according to conscience, according to fairness, do you understand that? No, of course, you don't understand. Well, you don't need to!" The comrade in charge rubbed his forehead in agitation. "Listen, you know where we're meeting this Sunday? In Pirshagy. At Nukhbala Nukhievich's dacha. It seems I already told you about that."

"No. You haven't said anything to me," answered the secretary in Russian.

"Look, you see, babe, because of all these demonstrations, pickets, strikes, sclerosis is quietly setting in. . . . So you, Seva, Roza, and also call Ainurka: if she gets difficult, bring Toma. There'll be two beys and one from Moscow. A young major, a handsome fellow, Ainurka's never seen one like him. He's a person from *There*. From the Moscow embankment. Dzerzhinsky Square, KGB head-quarters, is that clear, babe? But he's not Russian, he's a full-blooded Muslim. And his name is Tariel. Shota Rustaveli's *The Knight in Panther Skin*. Did you go through that in school? His father-in-law is a very influential general. Quite a youngster, babe, but an operator. You know what kind of operator: the kind that calls dollars 'spare change.'" The comrade in charge slipped his hand into the inner pocket of his jacket as if he wanted to take something out of it. But he didn't take anything out; he quickly dragged his hand out of his pocket and responsibly scratched his head.

"'Spare change'! Oy, how interesting! I'll go phone Ainurka." The secre-tary hurriedly headed for the door.

"Wait," said the comrade in charge. "I beg you, babe: when you go there, don't spray on Finnish deodorant. It smells like Vietnamese ointment. I have an allergy to that crap." He fell silent and quietly added, "Look, if that person is still there, tell him reception hours are already over for today. Tomorrow, please God, he won't come. And if he does come, you'll say I'm not here. I'm in Moscow, out of the country, dancing with the devil—in a word, I'm not here!"

But Safaly *muallim* was already gone. Having lost hope of being received today by the comrade in charge, Safaly *muallim* slowly climbed down along Governor's Garden towards the Boulevard.

The weather wasn't especially overcast, but it wasn't clear, either. The plants and factories were closed, and therefore the slightly sour smell of the sea was in the air.

All around Governor's Garden was the spirit of *perestroika*. A few women, the eyes of whom—both within and without—burned with a holy thirst for freedom and the wish to beat up First Secretary Abdurakhman Vezirov, were walking along the opposite side of the street towards the building of the Central Committee to take up their places in the picketing. A burly hulk of about twenty-five or thirty with the neck of an ox—which no ax would have been able to chop off—and powerful muscles enthusiastically toppled the stone figures in Governor's Garden to the ground with infinite joy and pride. In the lower end of the garden, a group of masters of the pen, brush, and plectrum zealously tried—on the basis of a recently adopted joint resolution of the presidium of the Writers Union of Azerbaijan and the board of the Ministry of Culture—to saw off an ornamental oak at the root, the highest branches of which joined together in an extremely indecent cruciform shape.

Only when going out onto the Boulevard and finding himself by the network of canals that Baku residents call Venice did Safaly *muallim* finally calm down and breathe with his whole chest. It was a remarkable thing: not a soul was on the seaside boulevard. On a bench in the shaded alley in front of Venice, an old woman sat alone; either she was knitting or she was drawing—in any case, she was busy with something. Safaly *muallim* looked attentively once more in her direction, and at first he didn't believe his eyes, because next to the woman on the bench sat a cat, and that cat very much resembled Vaska!

Here Safaly *muallim* grew agitated. Hearing clearly the beating of his own heart, he slowly walked up to the bench and there recognized the woman who was sitting there: Sima! Samaya! O Allah, Allah! It was as if Samaya hadn't changed a bit.

"Hello! Is it you?" Safaly *muallim* was able force out of himself after long torment.

Just think—Samaya recognized him, too. "Safaly! Oh, what a long, long time it's been! Do you see how quickly I recognized you, Safaly?"

"I recognized you first," smiled Safaly *muallim* and cast his glance on the cat. "Yours? What a beautiful cat." Safaly *muallim* extended his hand as if to pet the cat on his little head. "Vaska, good Vaska!" he almost moaned. But the cat shrank away, arched his back, bared his teeth, and looked at Safaly *muallim* so maliciously that he regretted his intention. And in addition to his entirely indecent behavior, Vaska grimaced and gave a long, drawn-out meow. "Get out of here," that meow said, "I know you very well. If you knew how to value cats, you wouldn't have thrown me to the whim of fate in that Zugulba desert."

"Vaska! Shame on you!" said Sima angrily, who was becoming a little embarrassed on account of the cat. But she immediately said gently, "How long it is that we haven't seen one another?"

"We ran into each other once. Ten or fifteen years ago. By the Nizami movie theater—do you remember? It seems you were still working in Buzovny then."

"Yes, I always worked there. And about five years ago, now, I worked for a year in Zugulba as a nurse-housekeeper in a Ministry of Health resort. And then I retired."

"Really? Interesting. So, in a Ministry of Health resort," Safaly *muallim* glanced warily at Vaska. "Five years ago. . . . Yes, I wasn't there at the time. . . . But your cat, it seems, is already old."

"Yes, old. Absolutely decrepit." Samaya petted the cat on the head. "Poor devil, if he doesn't die today, he will tomorrow."

Vaska looked scornfully at Samaya and meowed evilly. "You die yourself," the meow said, "but I'm not planning to go anywhere."

"I'm also retired," said Safaly *muallim* in a shaky voice.

"You probably have children, grandchildren," said Sima plaintively, and her entirely unchanged large, gentle eyes suddenly filled with tears.

"I do," answered Safaly *muallim*. "I have one daughter and one grand-daughter. But they don't live with me. They're in Leningrad."

At the word "Leningrad," Vaska started as if scalded. At first, having bared his teeth, he looked at Safaly *muallim* and snarled. And then, completely losing control, he began bitterly scratching the bench.

Samaya folded her knitting—a stocking or something else—and packed it along with her knitting needles and yarn in her bag.

"Back then I took so long choosing a groom that I ended up with this one," Samaya pointed at Vaska and, seeing that he was in a rage, was surprised. "Oy, what in the world is the matter with him? Come on, Vaska, come on, stop it! This is something new for him today."

But Safaly *muallim*, knowing perfectly well what a malicious being that Vaska was, of course understood the reason for the cat's fury. Therefore, nothing remained for him to do except hurriedly say goodbye to Sima. And although Safaly *muallim* absolutely did not want to part with either Vaska or Sima, he had to get as far away as possible. Safaly *muallim* quickly left the alley and headed along the bank towards home.

Above—from the direction of the Central Committee—the hum of voices reached him. Those same women with flashing eyes who had just been rushing around Governor's Garden were shouting. To all appearances, the women thirsting for freedom still hadn't achieved it, and Abdurakhman Vezirov still hadn't been beaten up, because the hum gradually increased, and so the people's struggle for freedom continued still. . . . And still the square in front of the House of Unions hummed. The hum would swell and then die down. It was as if a wounded dragon were stretched out on the earth breathing heavy, dying breaths.

Forgotten by everyone, the sea seemed concentrated, pensive, solitary, and pitiful. By the Pearl Café some old Russian woman was feeding seagulls fresh, still-warm bread probably just bought at the store. The old woman's lips moved quickly. It was as if she was arguing with herself, arguing heatedly, and by her hurried whisper it was evident she wanted to finish that fight before the bread was gone. . . . . A little way away from the café, under a wall by bushes whose leaves had fallen, a dark-skinned, elegant Azerbaijani girl of fifteen or sixteen embraced a young, well-built Russian soldier, entwining her arms around his slim waist above the belt. Anyone seeing that picture would have said that nothing could separate Azerbaijan and Russia and that to try to do so would be cruel. . . .

Safaly *muallim* walked, and he thought that if he were young again, he wouldn't have married Zarnigyar but Samaya. How good, he thought, that not everyone had gotten involved all at once in the revolutionary transformation of *perestroika*, that there still remained people who owned cats, knitted stockings, fed seagulls, embraced by the bushes. . . .

The closer Safaly *muallim* got to home, the more the hum on the square in front of the House of Unions strengthened and intensified. But it didn't bother Safaly *muallim* at all. Only the voice of Ali Ziya occasionally interrupted his thoughts: a faded, weakened, fatty, sticky voice.

And from somewhere—far or near—the voice quietly, smoothly whispered that four-line verse to Safaly *muallim* again:

> And it's wasteland here, and wasteland
> —All around—is what you see.
> The world starts to resemble Yemen,
> Endless Yemen, eh, Safaly?

It was the beginning of the fall of 1989 in Baku. . . .

May–June 1991

Stone Dreams

A Novel-Requiem

*Dedicated to the memory of
my fellow countrymen, who
left us their unwept pain.*

The Curious Death of an Old Coat Check Girl, the Deadly Dangerous Joke of a Famous Artist, and the Party Card-Pistol

The condition of the patient just delivered to the trauma department of one of the major Baku hospitals was very serious.

They took the patient, who was lying unconscious on the gurney, along the very middle of the half-lit hospital corridor that stretched the length of the whole floor to the operating room, which was located in the other wing of the building. There were two women in white lab coats and two men, also in lab coats. The surgeon himself walked beside the gurney, a spare, silver-haired man of middling height, distinguished from his colleagues by his reserve, the compelling sternness of his face, and the particular cleanliness of his lab coat.

If there was anything unusual or seemingly incongruous in this ordinary scene of hospital life, it was the tragic humor in the appearance and behavior of the person who'd brought the patient to the clinic. That small, fidgety man of fifty-five to sixty whose small face was not at all in harmony with his enormous, round belly ran around the doctor constantly repeating the same thing over and over.

"Doctor, my dear Doctor, they killed him! Such a man, in broad daylight, they beat him, destroyed him. It's those *yerazy*, Doctor, *yerazy*. Five or six of those *yerazy*-boys who fled from Armenia! Those sons of bitches, those refugees simply don't respect people, Doctor, my dear Doctor. They don't recognize artists or poets or writers. Just call someone an Armenian—and that's it! Then they slam him to the ground and trample him like wild animals.

They tear him to pieces, and no one dares get involved. I told them: 'Don't beat him,' I said, 'That man's not Armenian, he's one of us, a son of our people, the pride and conscience of the nation.' But who listens? They didn't even let me tell them my name. They kicked me so hard in the side that I almost died there, too. Right here, Doctor, in the right side. It still hurts badly now."

The doctor didn't really understand what the man who'd brought the patient was saying. Maybe he didn't want to understand. Maybe he wasn't even listening to what that fussy, funny man who'd knotted a yellow tie over a brown checked shirt was babbling without pause. However, an observant person might have noticed that the doctor from time to time smiled into his moustache. And not because every word, every gesture of the man who'd brought the patient rose to comedy. But, rather, because the light-haired man lying on the gurney was slender and remarkably tall. And it's possible that the contrast in appearance between these two reminded the doctor of the very saddest pages of the story of Don Quixote and Sancho Panza.

When they reached the doors of the operating room, one of the men wearing a white lab coat blocked the path of the funny man in the yellow tie.

"Let him in," said the doctor. "It seems he has something to say. Let him have his say."

Although the operating room was considerably smaller than the corridor, all the same it turned out to be a spacious room with a high ceiling and gigantic windows. The operating table standing directly in the center resembled the linen-covered gurney on which they conveyed the patient. The two men in white lab coats delivering the gurney that bore the patient lifted him, laid him on the table, glanced at the doctor for permission, and silently left the operating room.

"Peroxide!" said the surgeon loudly to the nurses, rolling up the sleeves of his lab coat. "Bring it here, wipe off his face." Looking at the patient covered in blood, he muttered an oath, and turning to the man's companion, he asked, "Who did this to him?"

"I already told you, Doctor: *yerazy*. Those bastard refugees arriving from Armenia. It wasn't enough to smash his face. They also knocked him to the ground like wild animals and began beating him in the stomach. It's a good thing, Doctor, that I arrived in time. I went out this morning to get some air in the city. I'm coming down from that cursed place they call the Parapet when I see five or six mustachioed scoundrels beating up a man at the edge of the fountain. And people just standing by and watching in silence. . . ." Then he suddenly hesitated. His lips continued to move, but the words, it seems, died in his throat.

"There's no more peroxide, Doctor," said one of the nurses in an apologetic voice, as quietly as possible. (One of them was elderly, the other quite young.)

"There should be some alcohol," said the surgeon, without hope.

"No, Doctor. Everything we had was used up yesterday."

"Fine, clean him with water. Don't use too much manganese." The doctor washed his hands with soap at the sink standing in the corner of the room and then went up and stood in front of the operating table. "Take everything off of him. Leave only his underwear."

The patient—his face, nose, chin, the collar of his orange wool shirt, the lapels of his bluish jacket covered in scarlet blood—was lying so calmly on the operating table that it was as if his most evil enemy rather than he himself had been beaten up in the aforementioned Parapet Square. He was sleeping deeply, although frequent, harsh moans escaped from his chest. Not only did he sleep but, apparently, also dreamed, and it seemed that his dreams gave him great satisfaction.

While the women washed the dried blood off the patient's face, the doctor checked his pulse. When the nurses had stripped the patient, he began to examine him attentively, as if compiling a report for himself or dictating to someone.

"Put two stitches in his lower lip. No fractures noted in the area of the jaw. Two dislocations in the left hand at the elbow and wrist. Two fingers dislocated on the right hand: the thumb and middle finger. Severe muscle trauma in the left leg. A fractured kneecap in the right leg. No serious anomalies noted in the back, rib cage, or spine. No skull fractures observed." The doctor fell silent and again cursed angrily. "A concussion!" He said this loudly for some reason and in Russian, then pulled a handkerchief from the pocket of his trousers, slowly wiped the sweat from his brow, and added in Russian, "A brutal beating!"

After every word the doctor said, the face of the man who'd brought the patient reflected all his feelings, all his pain and suffering. With difficulty, he held himself together, so as not to burst out sobbing. When the doctor had finished his exam, the man's self-possession was also at an end. He wept violently, like an aggrieved child.

The eyes of one of the women in the white lab coats standing beside the operating table (the younger one) filled with tears. The elderly nurse was also upset and shook her head woefully. And the doctor was very sorry for the man. He began to calm him.

"There, there, this isn't good. . . . It's nothing terrible. In fifteen days your friend will be like new, I'll make a beauty out of him." Lowering his head, he thought a bit and then again lifted his head and asked cautiously, "So, you say this man is Armenian?"

The eyes of our comic hero bulged in surprise.

"Really, you don't know him?! You don't know Sadai Sadygly? The pride of Azerbaijani theater! Our number one artist! You really don't know this great master, Doctor? You haven't even seen him on television? You've even seen me on television more than once, Doctor. Maybe you just don't remember— Nuvarish Karabakhly, a well-known actor of comic roles. Maybe you don't know me. I'm not offended by that. But there's no one who doesn't know Sadai Sadygly. You see, no one else in the world has played Hamlet, Othello, Aidyn, and Kefli Iskender like he has."

"I recognized you immediately," said the young nurse with unconcealed pride.

"I've often seen the two of you on television," said her elderly colleague, for some reason a bit coquettishly. "But Dr. Farzani isn't to blame. He lived more than thirty years in Moscow, and it hasn't been three years since he returned to Baku."

Understanding now why the doctor didn't recognize him or Sadai Sadygly, the artist calmed down at once. And that the nurses, having recognized them immediately, hadn't let on, Nuvarish Karabakhly put down to the fact that they'd certainly feared the information would have been poorly received by the doctor.

Nuvarish Karabakhly guessed that all his words had gone in one of the doctor's ears and out the other. Either the doctor had been too immersed in his thoughts or else he, Nuvarish Karabakhly, had been unable to find the necessary words in his nervous state. Therefore, he tried to focus as much as possible and resolved to recount everything that had happened on the Parapet again, more simply and basically.

"It was like this, Doctor: today I was walking around the city. What time it was, I can't say exactly—maybe ten, maybe eleven. On the Parapet there's a place with a fountain—you've probably seen it. And suddenly a terrible shriek came from there. As if someone was howling. It turns out it was an old Armenian. He'd gone out to buy bread, and there he fell into the hands of the *yerazy*. Right in his housecoat! And slippers. When I got to the place, the unfortunate man was already dead and had been thrown into the pool. But his eyes were open, Doctor, and he was looking straight at me. I personally didn't see how they killed him. But people who were there earlier said that at first they threw the Armenian into the pool, right into the frozen water. He was an old man, he couldn't stay in the water. He wanted to climb out. And those guys were standing at the edge of the pool, kicking him, until they kicked him to death. And Sadai Sadygly, God help him, always has trouble circling around his head. Otherwise, how could he have been the one to show up at that moment in that cursed place? He couldn't hold back, that's what happened! He's an artist, a humane person. His heart couldn't bear it. He ran to help. And how could those *yerazy* know who and what he is? They've just arrived, they're not from here. So they took him for an Armenian and attacked like wild animals. If I'd been just a minute later, they'd have sent him to join the old Armenian. But God spared him—he remained alive. I beg you, Doctor, save him. The life of that great person is now in your hands." With these pathetic words, the artist finished his speech.

The doctor hurried to start the operation. But it seemed that some necessary item was missing.

Besides, the story of the artist had apparently shaken him. He didn't see anything particularly unusual in the fact that the Hamlet-Othello-Kefli-Iskender lying unconscious on the operating table had been trying to save an old Armenian. In the doctor's opinion, anyone who considered himself a human being would have behaved the same way. However, the inhabitants of the city, as if they'd come to an understanding about it, were trying to steer clear of what's called humaneness. It seemed it was no longer even worth their while to pretend to be human beings.

Just ten or fifteen days previously in that same operating room, Dr. Farzani had performed a very complicated operation on an Armenian girl of fourteen or fifteen who, by God knows what miracle, had been brought to the hospital.

In the metro, where it's always full of people, a few Azerbaijani women had attacked her and, watched by hundreds of people, inflicted savage punishment. And just a few days before that, some poet-degenerate had burst into the hospital and beaten up a doctor who'd worked in the cardiology department for forty years, driving him out of his office just because he'd had the misfortune to be born Armenian. After that, not a single Armenian remained at the hospital—neither doctors nor members of the supporting staff. Some had hidden at home, some had left Baku forever.

"Numaish *muallim*, it's as the Persians say: *mesele melum est*, the issue is clear," the doctor said in a cheerful voice that was not at all in concert with his obvious bad mood, shifting his surgical instruments.

Nuvarish Karabakhly wasn't offended that the doctor had mangled his name (a person who'd lived more than thirty years in Moscow had full right to do that), but he didn't fail to correct him:

"Who is Nuvarish Karabakhly, Doctor?" he said. "An ordinary actor. Hundreds of Nuvarish Karabakhlys aren't worth the little finger of Sadai Sadygly. It would have been better if those scoundrels had beaten me in his stead."

"Is he also from Karabakh?" asked the doctor, checking the patient's pulse again.

"No, of course not, Doctor. I'm not from Karabakh either. Karabakhly is just my stage name—I'm originally from Kiurdamir. And Sadai Sadygly was born in Nakhchivan, a place in the Ordubad region, the village of Aylis. A very ancient village, Doctor, although I've never been there myself. They say at one time many Armenians lived there. It seems seven or eight of their churches are standing there to this day. Apparently, those Armenians were very smart, good people. And Sadai Sadygly is the kind of person, Doctor, that even if the world turned upside down, he wouldn't call white black. He's suffered for his outspokenness many times already, but he hasn't learned anything. In a couple of months he'll turn fifty, but he remains a ten-year-old boy. He says what's on his mind. He can't even occasionally be silent, even in such dangerous times. He says it's not the Armenians but we ourselves who are bad. And he isn't afraid. He says it everywhere, all the time, in the theater and in the tearooms."

Dr. Farzani, his eyes widening, looked in the patient's face, this time with a kind of special interest. It was as if he'd just now seen him for the first time. The women, who'd been preserving a dead silence, suddenly began whispering in a lively way about something. Farzani took Nuvarish Karabakhly firmly by the arm and, leading him to the door, said:

"Well, young man, there's nothing more for you to do here. Go sit in the corridor, rest. And if you want, go home, drink a shot of vodka as needed, and topple into bed. Then come back if you want to. This isn't cutting out an appendix, my friend. A full overhaul is necessary here, which will take three or four hours. Don't worry. Your friend will live. I'll make such an Othello of him that Desdemona will faint with joy."

With those words, the doctor escorted the artist into the corridor and closed the door behind him.

When the double doors of the operating room closed, Nuvarish Karabakhly suddenly felt acutely alone, as if the whole world remained there behind those closed doors.

The melancholy of the cemetery wafted over the long, half-lit corridor. The lights were off. There was no one around. The giant, double windows on the opposite wall of the corridor were veiled in gloom, not admitting light; either they were extremely dusty, or it was already dark outside.

In only one place—not far from the glassed-in balcony by the doors—was a bench visible. There was nowhere else in the corridor to sit. Nuvarish Karabakhly walked slowly along to the bench, feeling dizziness and approaching nausea. He'd been wanting a smoke for a long time, but he didn't even have the strength to shove his hand into his pocket and pull out the pack of cigarettes.

Approaching the bench, he saw two plaques attached, one above the other, on the wall by the door. On the upper one, "DEPARTMENT OF TRAUMA AND SURGERY" was written in big, black letters, and on the lower one, in smaller letters, "Farid Gasanovich Farzani, Surgeon, Head of Dept." The door to Dr. Farzani's office was open.

No matter how worn out Nuvarish Karabakhly was, no matter how much he wanted to sit down, he didn't seat himself on the bench by the door. It seemed that if he sat down now, he'd never be able to get up. He peered cautiously through the open door into the office: a desk, two old chairs, a sofa, a safe, a refrigerator, an old television, an electric tea kettle, a sink. He pulled his cigarettes out of his pocket, but again he couldn't make up his mind to smoke. Feeling nausea approaching even more strongly, he moved towards the window and, before reaching it, saw that a similar long corridor stretched out on the other side of the operating room. In contrast to this empty one where Dr. Farzani's office was located by the entrance, the other corridor had an abundance of windows, and the bluish doors of the rooms strung out along the corridor looked out on opaque, ash-colored windows.

A man with his leg in a cast was smoking by one of these windows, leaning on crutches. Near the open door of the farthest room stood an old woman with a bandaged hand. Besides these two, there was not another soul in the corridor.

Nuvarish Karabakhly lit the cigarette he'd been holding in his hand all this time, but at the first drag darkness fell on his eyes. Afraid he'd fall down, holding onto the wall, he forced himself along to the bench and sat there a long time while the mist that had been obscuring his eyes gradually dissipated.

The mist didn't disturb Nuvarish Karabakhly. He was used to it.

The thing he was most concerned about now was how to inform Sadai Sadygly's wife, Azada *khanum*, about what had happened.

Nuvarish had often been in Sadai Sadygly's home. And he knew where Sadai's wife worked. Azada *khanum* was probably still at work. But to stand up and get himself to where Azada *khanum* worked was almost impossible for Nuvarish at that moment. He was still considering how to tell her about everything. The best thing was to stay here and wait until the operation had concluded. Then, when the operation was over, the wounded Sadai bandaged and conscious again, it would be much easier to tell Azada *khanum* what had happened. (He'd forgotten that today was Sunday, and she wasn't at work.)

Nuvarish Karabakhly had been married three times, but on that night not a single person in the whole city waited for him.

He'd undertaken his first attempt to create a family when he was nineteen or twenty; he'd simply seated his beloved in a taxi and, without an engagement, without a wedding, and without a dowry conveyed her to his father's home. The lack of a wedding would have been acceptable, but Nuvarish's mother could in no way forgive the bride for having arrived at her husband's home without a dowry. After a month-and-a-half war with her mother-in-law, the young woman collected her things and left the house, never to return.

Also during Nuvarish's youth, when he still played only cameo roles at the theater, the living conditions of one of the most senior theater employees had been "bettered." The senior employee's damp basement apartment in Baku's Montina Village district was given to Nuvarish, where he'd lived for only nine months with his second wife, who died of lung cancer. Nuvarish Karabakhly's third wife, Julietta, had been a worn-down, thirty-six-year-old virgin, the daughter of one of the most eminent actors of the theater. For about five years they had no children. Then a son had been born. But when the child was not yet three months old, Julietta had once fallen sound asleep during his night feeding, and waking up, she found the baby had turned blue, suffocated between her breasts. Julietta couldn't forgive herself: the dead baby wouldn't be quiet, he cried and begged for milk. And the mother stopped eating, drinking, and sleeping. The poor thing didn't live even ten days after the death of her baby. She wasted away, burned out like a candle, and disappeared like a shadow—as if she'd never been.

For more than ten years now, Nuvarish had had a wonderful, two-bedroom apartment in the center of the city. Up until February of that year, he'd led a somewhat lonely but, compared to the present, calm, maybe even too-happy and comfortable life in it. And then fate played a trick on him—now Nuvarish Karabakhly tried to make use of his apartment only at night, and mainly because there was nowhere else to go. In his own home he knew not a minute of calm or sleep or rest. The reason was that one of the employees of Baksovet, the city hall, someone who worked in a minor but very lucrative post—a hefty, paunchy hulk of a man—had seized the next-door apartment of an old theater employee, the coat check girl Greta Sarkisovna Minasova. Greta Sarkisovna had received that apartment on the tenth floor, the highest floor of their building, the same day Nuvarish received his. And now that hulk had turned it into a real, actual brothel. All day noises and crashing resounded through the wall. The animal laughter and shrieks of experienced prostitutes and girls who were still young (just getting into the profession) and their authentic and feigned moans of pleasure drove him out of his mind, giving the artist no peace during the day and disturbing his sleep at night.

According to rumor, the hulk had been one of the richest people of Shusha. He'd appeared in Baku not long before, found work at Baksovet, and bought a four-bedroom apartment in a cooperative building next to Nuvarish's building. The man was shaped like a block. The amazing width of his back exceeded any standard frame. He had thick, raven-black hair; thick, black brows of the same color; a wide, generous moustache; and the bulging, empty, expressionless eyes of a crocodile. Even the first and last names of that man expressed cruelty and ungodliness to Nuvarish Karabakhly: Shakhgajar Armaganov. A curse on whomever had given that animal a name!

One morning when it had just turned light, noise rose from the courtyard: they said, "Listen, people, some Armenian woman threw herself off a balcony." The tiny, old woman's body of Greta Sarkisovna was just expiring in a large pool of blood, but the strange news was already going around the city that the Armenian woman who'd thrown herself off the balcony had left a letter of repentance before her death: "I hate myself for the crimes Armenians have committed. I despise my own people and therefore don't want to live in the world anymore. Karabakh belongs to Azerbaijan. Long live Azerbaijan!"

Neither then nor now did Nuvarish have any doubt that the "suicide" was the handiwork of that Shusha hulk. It was fully possible that Shakhgajar Armaganov himself had thrown Greta Sarkisovna off the balcony. The times were like that now. Go ahead, throw even a hundred Armenians a day off a balcony! And Muslims along with them. It's possible to easily erase any person from the face of the earth if there's no one standing behind him. And with each day, the artist became more afraid of the man from Shusha. There weren't any laws, now, no courts—one fine day he could easily take Nuvarish himself and throw him off a balcony and call it suicide. Who'd find it worthwhile to investigate his crime, who'd prove that that cold-blooded, ungodly, and ruthless Baksovet functionary was also a real-life criminal?

The cold, grey shock of the stress he'd experienced still hadn't left his soul, but the delicate, emotional insides of the artist were already blazing with hatred and anger. But how many times a day can you reiterate the same thing to a district policeman—be a man, have a conscience, close that brothel because soon the whole city will turn into one endless whorehouse—? For that reason, the artist had been more than once to see the head of the police, and he'd sent so many telegrams and letters to the district Party committee, the Central Committee, even Baksovet, that in the end he resolved that either there was no authority in the country, or else those people in authority were all on the same side as the executioner Shakhgajar Armaganov. And at the theater, he told everyone what had recently been going on in Greta Sarkisovna's apartment. Except he never said a single word to Sadai Sadygly about it. He considered that to be pointless because the man lived in his own world, his head stuck in the clouds. Besides, Nuvarish Karabakhly didn't want to drag a man in whose genius he believed with his whole soul into that filth.

Now, even during the hottest summer days, the artist closed all his doors and windows tightly, and God alone knows how many torments he endured each night while waiting for morning. During one of those terrible nights, he even made a resolution, no matter what it took, to equip himself with a pistol. With that request, he approached numerous acquaintances who worked in the police and the military enlistment offices.

However, his request elicited nothing but laughter from people who were accustomed to laughing just at the sight of him. And when the artist had already completely lost hope of arming himself and finding even some sort of peace in his own home, a well-known writer who'd had three plays presented in their theater had showed him (only two days ago) the simplest way. According to the writer, nowadays every member of the Popular Front had one or even several pistols. And with the help of those "guys," it was possible to buy not only a Makarov or Kalashnikov but even a real machine gun. And again, according to the credible writer, for such a famous artist as Nuvarish Karabakhly, it would be enough to simply go to the office of the Popular Front and whisper two words in the ear of the Head Bey.

He'd known the Bey for a long time and quite well. They'd drunk tea hundreds of times in various Baku tearooms on the Boulevard, in Molokansky Garden, on Azneft Square, and even when he'd had almost nothing in his pocket, he always tried to pay for tea himself.

And thus, on coming out of his apartment building today at noon, the artist had headed straight for the office of the Popular Front. The Bey hadn't yet arrived. The artist stood around for about an hour near the office entrance waiting for him. Then he left to eat some breakfast in a café near the movie theater Araz; he drank a shot and a half of vodka and ate two servings of wieners. And when, coming out of the café, he again headed for the office of the Popular Front, there—near the pool with the fountain—he'd found himself involved in this terrible story.

Now, sitting on the bench in the hospital corridor and waiting for the end of the operation, Nuvarish Karabakhly dreamed up a wonderful scene in anticipation of his still-unrealized meeting with the Head Bey.

"Hello, Nuvarish Bey! I'm infinitely delighted to see you!" Thus (in the artist's fancy) the Head Bey affectionately and amiably greeted his longtime friend from the tearoom. "How are you, my dear fellow? What's new in the theater? Whose play are you staging? Just yesterday I was asking the guys about you. 'Something's up,' I said, 'he's not around. Find out where he is, why our master of the stage isn't around. Maybe he's in need of something?'"

Hearing "in need," the artist began laying out his request for the desired pistol. He was also intending to tell the Bey about the actively functioning brothel in the neighboring apartment, but the Bey, with the great sensitivity inherent in great people, already understood exactly what had led his old friend to the office of the Popular Front and generously delivered him from discomfort.

"It's really nothing, Nuvarish Bey!" Here, the Head Bey lightly stroked his beard. Then he announced loudly and enthusiastically, "It's our responsibility to protect people who are needed by the nation." After that, he lifted his telephone receiver and ordered someone, "Bring the artist a new pistol. This is my friend. Our great artist. Yes, times are tough, it's a dangerous period. As much as possible, we must protect our best people." The Head Bey (in the artist's fancy) pronounced exactly these words and, smiling affectionately at Nuvarish, quietly added into the receiver, "Throw in some extra ammo."

Finally believing that he'd soon receive a pistol from the Head Bey himself, Nuvarish Karabakhly remembered sadly how only a year and a half ago the two of them had long and pleasantly sat in various tearooms. He remembered May of 1979, when the then-First Person of all Azerbaijan had suddenly visited the theater and just as suddenly allotted him an apartment in the center of the city. He remembered how, back at the end of the 1960s, he'd once been plastered and, heading to the bus stop completely drunk, had met the person whom the people called the Master on the corner of Zevin Street. At that time Nuvarish Karabakhly still lived in his father's house and had just begun to go on stage at the theater in cameo roles. However (there are indeed miracles in the world!), it turned out that the then-Master had seen these minor roles of Nuvarish. And not just seen, but vividly remembered.

That night the Master was also returning, it seems, from some kind of party and was in excellent spirits. (There were two strong men walking right beside him—bodyguards.)

"Oh, Artist, wait up, brother," he said. "Well, you've been drinking! Where did you get so sloshed?" He winked at one of the men standing next to him. "I've been drinking, too. Only, look, the earth isn't wobbling on its axis."

At that time Nuvarish wasn't formally acquainted with the First Person in the Republic, naturally, and if the First Person hadn't stretched out his hand and said, "Pleased to meet you," he probably wouldn't have remembered whom he'd run into that night on the corner of Zevin Street.

"Pleased to meet you," said the First Person, giving his name. "And you I know, you're an artist. And play good roles in the theater. And where are you going now?"

Nuvarish, stumbling over his tongue, stammered faintly, "To Khy-Khy-Khyrdalan. I'm taking the bus."

The man with the slightly oblong face scanned the artist from head to toe.

"Well, go!" he commanded with frightening disdain. "It's already late. At a march! And don't drink so much again."

"Do you still live in Khyrdalan?" Those words, spoken years later in the theater by the First Person, sounded so alive now in the ears of the artist that it seemed even the lifeless walls of the hospital corridor heard them clearly.

"Now I live in Montina Village—one floor underground," the artist had joked boldly with his longtime acquaintance.

"From tomorrow, you'll live in the center of the city—on the tenth floor above ground," the First Person said firmly, answering the joke with a joke.

That night, having performed Akhundov's *Monsieur Jordan*, the whole creative collective of the theater gathered in the office of director Maupassant Miralamov. In the show Nuvarish played the dervish Mastali Shakh, and his performance, to all appearances, was pleasing to the First Person himself. "You also play Sheik Akhmed in *Corpses* extremely well," he said. "I've seen it twice on television. Play those kinds of roles more."

It was clear that day that while getting ready for the theater, the Master had planned in advance to bestow apartments on several employees, among the lucky number of whom necessarily must have been Greta Sarkisovna Minasova. "There was one elderly employee here—Minasova. Does she still work in the theater?" the Master had asked the director for the sake of form, knowing, of course, that she never left the theater for anything. And Greta Sarkisovna, losing her head after the unexpected invitation, had walked into Maupassant's office whiter than a corpse, but came out crying from happiness and repeating over and over, "Thank you, my son! Thank you so much!!!"

To this day, Greta Sarkisovna's face on that night stood before the eyes of the artist. Maybe it was even more alive now than then, still more expressive. And also Sadai Sadygly's face turning grey, his eyes reddening, his glances full of fury and anger.

For some reason, he hadn't hit it off with the First Person from the very beginning. However, in Nuvarish's opinion the fault lay not with the First Person but in the stubbornness and pride of Sadai Sadygly. "He makes friends by dishing out delicacies from the common pot—our common pot—as if it were his own. He gives everyone something, taking away the most important thing in a man—his dignity. He castrates the soul of the people so as to make everyone quiet and obedient." Sadai Sadygly wasn't afraid to pronounce similar terrible words even in the presence of the theater bosses.

"So, are you in need of anything, Mr. Sadygly?" Speaking in a constrained and uncertain voice that didn't sound like his own, the First Person had then turned to Sadai, and it seems his voice even shook a little with those words. But open sarcasm and even hidden anger sounded in the word "Mr." Of course, the "mindset" of Sadai Sadygly was well known to the First Person. "I don't need anything!" Sadai Sadygly answered, loudly and loftily. When speaking with the First Person, everyone always rose. But Sadygly didn't even stir. "When he doesn't have anything better to do, he comes here to have some fun. He gives out apartments to everyone with such largesse—apartments owned by the state!—it's as if all the buildings in the city had been left to him by his late father," he said angrily in front of everyone at the end of the gathering, not afraid of anyone. The next day everyone in the theater was saying with regret that if Sadai Sadygly had behaved himself a little more "decently" in the presence of the Master, then he, too, would have been given an apartment in the center of the city, in the very best building, whose apartments were not even accorded to some of the ministers.

After that, just try saying that the tongue isn't the most despicable enemy of man.

Finding room for himself in a corner of the bench and curling up into a ball, Nuvarish Karabakhly fell asleep, and the artist dreamed what was, perhaps, the most nightmarish dream of his life.

It was a strange, greyish place. Dampness penetrated to the bone. There were no buildings, no trees, no one and nothing in the world except a black puddle of blood. Like a small turtle just hatched from the egg and hurrying towards water, Greta Sarkisovna crept out of the pool of her own blood. Her naked body with its raw skin, dead and at the same time living, was so ugly and terrible that perhaps no one since the creation of the world had seen such a terrible sight. Greta Sarkisovna crawled and crawled across the earth, wriggling like a snake. However, this wasn't the asphalt courtyard of the building where Nuvarish now lived. This place resembled the naked earth in Nuvarish's Khyrdalan courtyard, and Greta Sarkisovna crawled across that earth, trying, it seems, to crawl to her death. But that death never came to her, exactly as if it had been stolen and teasingly hidden away by someone. Sometimes, lifting her head, she murmured, "Thank you, my son! Thank you so much!" and in unbearable pain and torment again continued the journey towards her death. And Nuvarish suddenly realized that Greta Sarkisovna was crawling straight towards him. As if her death were in the power of Nuvarish himself.

And Greta Sarkisovna wanted to receive death from him, so as to forever rid her raw body of torment and suffering. The closer Greta Sarkisovna crawled, the greater the fear and horror that enveloped Nuvarish. The artist tried to run from the dead woman who was unable to die. However, he wasn't able to do anything—he couldn't move a single inch. It was as if his whole body had been bathed in molten lead.

Unable to bear the nightmare, the artist opened his eyes and—happy— came to himself in the cold and damp corridor. The lights were already on, and the operating room doors at the other end of the corridor stood wide open.

When Nuvarish Karabakhly, not yet fully recovered from the dream, entered the office of Dr. Farzani, the doctor immediately understood he was in no shape even to talk.

Farzani had just left the operating room. He stood at the sink with his face to the wall and washed his hands.

"Come in, sit down, Mubariz *muallim*," he said. "Don't worry. Things are going well. Your friend's in a room. Fast asleep. His constitution is strong. Made of iron, really. Just between us, he certainly doesn't look like much of a drinker."

In his state, the artist didn't even notice that the doctor had called him Mubariz and not Nuvarish.

"What do you mean, Doctor? What do you mean 'asleep'? He's conscious now?"

"Not yet," answered the doctor calmly, wiping his hands. "Don't be in a hurry, everything in its own good time. If not tonight, then tomorrow morning, for sure, he'll come to himself. I assigned an excellent nurse to his room. She'll be in constant attendance on the patient until morning." The doctor hung the towel on a nail and sat down in his place. "And you, obviously, fell fast asleep, although you look pretty beat up. What, did you have a bad dream?"

"Indeed I did, Doctor, how did you guess? I've never had such a nightmare in my life!" The artist fell silent. Then, suddenly, he sobbed loudly, and through tears he began entreating the doctor, "For the love of God, Doctor, give me some rubbing alcohol, just one swallow! I'm suffocating, I swear to God. My head is just splitting. It's as if rats and mice are running around inside my skull."

"No, my friend, that won't do it," the doctor said gently, sincerely pitying the artist. He spread out an old newspaper on the desk. He locked the office door. From the refrigerator he took a small carafe that was misted over and contained some kind of transparent liquid, clear as a tear, and stood it on the desk. On the newspaper he spread out a bit of sausage. A couple of pickled cucumbers. The salty curd cheese called *shor*. Lavash baked on a *saj*. A bunch of cilantro, picked over and washed. He poured cornelian cherry vodka into two pear-shaped tea glasses. At just the sight of the vodka, the artist's eyes began to shine.

"You're a really good person, Doctor. As soon as I saw you, I understood that." The artist stretched his hand towards the glass, but he didn't touch it because the doctor hadn't lifted his glass. Dr. Farzani's glance was directed towards the sink. And the artist understood what the doctor meant by that. He washed his hands with soap, came back, and sat down.

"Shall we drink?" said the doctor with a smile and drank his vodka. He took a piece of lavash, picked up a bit of *shor* with it, and directed it towards his mouth.

"To your health, Doctor!" Nuvarish drank standing, winced, and sat down.

"Chase it down with sausage. Eat up," the doctor commanded his guest. However, he himself didn't touch the sausage. He took a pair of cilantro sprigs and slowly began to chew. "Does he have family?"

"He has a family, Doctor. He's got a terrific wife, Azada *khanum*. She's a splendid dentist and a good person. She's the daughter of Dr. Abasaliev, the well-known psychiatrist. Maybe you've heard of him?"

Now Dr. Farzani was completely surprised.

"Who doesn't know Dr. Abasaliev?" he said. "Is he still alive?"

"He's alive, Doctor. And doing quite well!" answered Nuvarish inspiredly, having come to himself after the vodka. "He's still sound, just like an ice ax. It's already been a year since he moved, and he's been living at the dacha in Mardakan. 'I,' says he, 'won't concern myself with crazy people any more. Now there are too many of them spread all over the place.'"

"So our friend is the son-in-law of Dr. Abasaliev?" asked the doctor, pouring vodka into the glasses again.

Nuvarish Karabakhly went into raptures because the doctor was pouring vodka and because he had now said not "your friend" but "our friend."

"Yes, yes, his son-in-law. Moreover, they're great friends. They simply adore one another. For more than thirty years they've been living together. Well, who else does Dr. Abasaliev have? His wife is gone. Only the one daughter remains. Thus, he treats Sadai Sadygly like a son."

"That's how it is. . ." said the doctor, thinking of something else. "And it seems that they're from the same place, is that right? As far as I know, Dr. Abasaliev must be from Nakhchivan. . . . Well, let's drink." He lifted his glass, drank, and again chased it down with some lavash.

"Exactly! They're from Nakhchivan!" confirmed Nuvarish, tossed back the vodka, took a piece of sausage, and swallowed, almost without chewing. "They're from the same village, both from Aylis. And both of them love their village like crazy people. No matter when or where they get together, they only talk about Aylis. Once, they say, there were many Armenians there. And it turns out they—meaning the Armenians—lived with our Muslims in great friendship. Dr. Abasaliev praises those Armenians very highly. He says that kind of cultured, honest, hard-working people can't be found anywhere else in the world. I've often heard their conversations. When father-in-law and son-in-law start talking about Aylis, you want to move and spend the rest of your days there."

Dr. Farzani listened to the artist, continuing to think about his own concerns.

"So that means Dr. Abasaliev is in Mardakan now," muttered the surgeon as if to himself, then thought for a moment and asked, "Does he live there alone?"

"Of course, whom does he have left? But Azada *khanum* visits him often. Every Sunday morning she goes out there to him. She stays the night, and in the morning she goes straight from there to work. You're right, it's difficult for an old man to live at the dacha. However, he doesn't have much free time in which to get bored. In the apartment here he had over thirty thousand books. Poor Azada *khanum* has been dragging them from Baku to Mardakan for a whole year already. And Dr. Abasaliev just sits in the dacha and reads those books. They even say he has begun to write himself."

"And they don't have any children?"

"No, Doctor. On the one hand, of course, it's a good thing such a person as Sadai Sadygly doesn't have children. Honestly, this is a person who's not of this world. He's always somewhere up in the clouds. And his character is entirely childlike. When he was still little, out there in the village someone shot a fox cub in front of him. So, he remembers that cub to this day. He's told me about it many times. And every time he has tears in his eyes, that's the kind of person he is!"

"So, you say he's a good artist?" the doctor threw out, obviously for the sake of keeping the conversation going.

Here Nuvarish Karabakhly arrived at the highest state of excitement.

"He's a genius, Doctor, I swear to God! This is a great artist on the level of Abbas Mirza and Ulvi Rajab. And well educated, exactly like a scholar. What books he's read! But stubborn as the devil in his character. Indeed, he sorely loves to dig in his heels. He could've received the title People's Artist ten or twenty years ago. But to this day he remains, like me, an Honored Artist. Because he can't hold his tongue. In 'seventy-nine he and two other of our artists were recommended for the rank of People's Artist. The day before, everyone was congratulating him. But in the newspapers the next day they printed only the names of the other two, and there was nothing about him. It turns out that the night before he'd been drinking heavily with someone and again let his tongue run loose: says he, 'I don't need any rank of the kind that your generous Master gives out left and right—let me earn my rank in the eyes of the people.'"

The artist rummaged a long time in his pocket. Then, clearly, having willed himself to it, he extracted a single cigarette from the pack and looked imploringly at Farzani.

"Doctor, allow me just a single drag. Don't fuss at me, for the love of God. I desperately want to smoke."

The doctor took a small glass ashtray from the desk drawer and placed it in front of the artist.

"Smoke as much as you want. I smoked for exactly forty years, starting at age twenty-five. But I gave it up five years ago." He poured vodka from the carafe again. "Well, let's drink one more glass—and that's enough. A good thing, the purest thing, something that never did harm.

"I have an acquaintance from Qazakh. And he has an interesting name— they call him Aftandil. Once his car rolled over, he broke all his ribs. And I had to give him a thorough overhaul. Every time he comes here, he brings me a couple of bottles of vodka." The doctor opened the window a little, took his glass and, right there by the window, drained the cornelian cherry vodka. "So, then, you said he doesn't need any rank given out by the authorities? And who reported that to the Master in the middle of the night?"

"Someone obviously did, Doctor. Otherwise, why would they cross out just his name of the three?" Having smoked half his cigarette, the artist put out the stub in the ashtray. "For some reason, he hated the Soviet authorities from the very beginning. Believe me, he couldn't bear them. I think it was in 'sixty-eight. One of our shows was in the running for the State Prize. Five performers received it, but Sadai Sadygly was left out again. But you know, he played the lead role. Then, too, he simply couldn't reign in his tongue. He blurted out to one of the members of the Central Committee, right to his face, he says, 'That thing you've got in your pocket, it's not a Communist Party membership card, it's a pistol. You frighten people with your pistol—you control them with fear so you yourselves can live without fear.'"

Not yet having drunk his third shot, Nuvarish was already in such spirits, he was experiencing so much lightness and happiness in himself, that if it had been solely up to him, he would have burst into a jig. On the one hand, the vodka he'd drunk was affecting him but, on the other, there was the happiness that he was sitting and talking with such a great surgeon as Farzani. And all the torments he'd experienced over the course of the day, even the nightmare he'd had not long ago, were forgotten. Even that son of a bitch Shakhgajar

Armaganov himself now seemed not quite so frightening to the artist. And Dr. Farzani was pleased with the refreshed, restored look of his artist guest.

"Come on, drink," the doctor ordered in a friendly manner. "So, a Party card-pistol! Well said. Bullseye! If you're not trying to scare someone, why does any of us need a Party card?"

Nuvarish drank the vodka, and this time he also decided to chase it down with lavash and *shor*.

"But why even bring up a pistol, Doctor? Sometimes he comes out with these things, I tell you, you wouldn't believe. Once, during a banquet in Nardaran, that village where they're so pious, they beat him up very badly—he found himself there at a circumcision celebration. And during that kind of banquet, you know, there are certain rules: if you're asked to speak, you have to speak according to those rules. And what should one say when celebrating a circumcision? That it's a thing pleasing to God, how important it is for hygiene and health. Talk about the saints and imams. About the teachings of the Prophet, where this rite is considered one of the most important for Muslims, about His great wisdom. . . . And at the very height of the banquet, Sadai Sadygly is asked to speak as an honored guest. And yet again something comes over him. He starts to mock the rite. Then he gets completely worked up, forgive me, Lord, he begins to insult the Prophet himself. 'Is it possible,' he says, 'that your Prophet is smarter than God? If there were something unnecessary in the body of a person, would God really be so blind as not to see it? How could it be that the Lord, not having made a single mistake in creating the face, eyes, nose, and ears and having done everything else correctly, suddenly, the devil knows how, came to this part where he up and made a mistake like a schoolboy? Who commanded your Prophet to correct God's mistake?'

"Never in their lives had the Nardaranians heard such a thing. And what happened next! The village elders bestowed every kind of curse there is on Sadai. Even the women, who didn't sit at the table, yelled from behind the fence, 'A curse on you!' In the end, when the banquet was finished, the youth of Nardaran thrashed him soundly. They beat him so badly, poor devil, that he was then unable to go on stage for three whole months. They say that Sheikh Allahshukur Pashazadeh, the head of all the Muslims of the Caucasus, personally visited Sadai in the hospital to persuade him to publicly apologize before all the Nardaranians. Because the offended Nardaranians might easily have killed him afterwards."

The artist recounted this tragicomic story with delight and even, of course, with a little embellishment. Suddenly he looked at the doctor, noticed the expression of his face had entirely changed, and was frightened that it had been too much for him. It seemed to the artist that the doctor had disliked his story very much. Therefore, he hurriedly and uneasily added:

"How should I know, maybe none of that even happened. Maybe some idiot like me, a clown worse than me, just made it up." And he fell silent, deeply upset and evidently having decided that the deadly dangerous joke of Sadai on the God-fearing Nardaranians had also offended the religious feelings of Dr. Farzani.

But Farid Farzani wasn't a fanatical Muslim. The doctor didn't observe the fasts, didn't perform the prayers. However, living in Moscow he'd tried as much as possible to follow the rules and laws established by his religion and the Prophet.

And the faithfulness to his religion that had remained more or less intact in him was precisely the main reason for Farid Farzani's sudden move from Moscow to Baku. If, just three years ago in Moscow, someone had told him that the artist now lying unconscious in his hospital room had once slandered the Prophet, it would have required a great deal of strength for the doctor to listen to that. However, what he'd seen during three years in Baku had sharply changed his attitude towards religion and towards his motherland and towards the Prophet himself. The doctor had been especially struck by the brutality of the Muslim population of the city towards Armenians, possibly because he personally had never seen similar brutality on the part of the Armenians.

"Is the sheikh also from Nakhchivan?" the doctor asked thoughtfully, obviously preoccupied and dispirited.

The question surprised the artist.

"Of course not, why? The sheikh's from Lankaran, he's an ethnic Talysh. And he seems to be a good person, gentle." The artist was silent a while, seeking the right words. "To tell the truth, I'm uncomfortable asking. But you yourself, Doctor, who are you by birth? Your last name seems to be Iranian."

"And I'm Iranian." The doctor sighed deeply. "My father once did something foolish and brought me here. And I myself did something even more foolish—I moved here from Moscow. I worked as a surgeon for fifteen years in the Sklifosovsky Hospital." The doctor pronounced the last few words with special pride, again poured a little vodka in the glasses, and added, "Let's drink to the health of our atheist. Let's hope he won't fall into the hands of savages again." And for the first time, the doctor clinked his glass with Nuvarish.

The artist increasingly felt a liking on the part of the surgeon and like a child rejoiced wildly at that.

"Yes, yet, let's drink to it, Doctor, let's hope he doesn't fall into the clutches of savages like those unfeeling *yerazy* again. But, Doctor, his wife had a presentiment of this long ago. She knew something like this would happen to him someday. And she tried to arrange it so that her husband never went out in the street. And he didn't go out. Except he went to the theater for a couple of hours last night. I myself phoned him from the director's office and just barely convinced him to come. Because he also grew tired of the theater. He didn't come even to pick up his salary. God alone knows why he happened to be in the city today."

"Smoke, go ahead, smoke." Doctor Farzani decided to deliver the artist, who'd again been rummaging in his pocket, from torment. He went up to the half-open window and flung it wide open. "Such a person can hardly continue to live in this city," he said with a shaking voice and, hunching his shoulders, lost himself in thought.

Yes, the artist had observed correctly: the mood of Dr. Farzani had really changed unexpectedly. And not because weariness had suddenly fallen on him or because for some reason he hadn't liked the artist's story. The fact is that at one time the doctor himself had heard the words spoken by the artist at the celebration of the circumcision from his own wife: "Your Prophet is wiser than God, is he?" At the time, they'd rocked Farid Farzani. And because of them his wonderful family in Moscow had fallen apart. Those exact, offensive words that had deeply wounded him were the reason for his present single and joyless life in this essentially foreign city.

At times fate brings astonishing gifts: married to a Russian woman, not having experienced the slightest psychological discord during many years in Moscow, the happy father of an only daughter, Farid Farzani all of a sudden began to lose his peace of mind after the birth of his son. When the son was still a baby, the question of circumcision had already turned into a real problem for the father. And that problem grew in proportion to the son's growth. Persistent unease led the doctor to start having nightmares, something that had never happened to him before. One morning when the son turned twelve, Farid Farzani expressed his firm resolution to his wife: "Such law is decreed by the Prophet. I don't have the right to break it."

And on hearing "Your Prophet is wiser than God, is he?" from his wife, he could have beaten his head against the wall from fury.

That very same morning, after his wife had gone to work and his daughter to school, having easily persuaded his son, in just ten or fifteen minutes Dr. Farzani completed that which the Prophet considered the primary responsibility of every Muslim before Allah. Who would have thought that for an experienced surgeon of the Sklifosovsky Hospital that very simple operation could result in complications? However, whether from fright or some other reason, towards evening the boy's temperature spiked to 104 degrees. And the mother who, on returning from work, found her son in that condition lost the gift of speech in her stupefaction. She didn't say a word to her husband, didn't attempt to lower her son's temperature—just looked at the child in horror. Then she threw herself into the bathroom, taking shelter inside, and for a long time her weeping and sobbing could be heard from behind the locked door.

It turns out that the love of Russian women can very easily redirect itself into hatred. Although the boy got up the next morning and wandered calmly around the house, Farzani's wife broke off her relationship with her husband forever. She immediately filed for divorce and exchanged their three-room apartment in the center of the city for two two-room apartments in outlying districts. Having lived for several years without his family, in 1986 Farid Farzani traded apartments with a Russian in Baku, moved to Baku, and understood on the first day what an inexcusable mistake he'd made.

Now Farzani's son was nineteen. But in his father's memory, he remained a twelve-year-old. And for many years the innocent, bewildered eyes of the boy cruelly followed the doctor. The full horror lay in the fact that the boy, not having made a sound during the operation, later, when the doctor had finished what he was doing, looked at his father with such murderous contempt that it was impossible to forget that look. Farzani read in the boy's eyes that he would never forgive him for that operation. Only much later did the doctor begin to understand where the essence of his sin lay. It would have been all the same to the boy whether a piece of his foreskin or an entire finger had been cut off, because for a child brought up in Moscow circles, it was incomprehensible in whose name his father had acted thus. The boy perceived it as physical violence done to him on the part of his father, as utterly senseless cruelty and savagery. That morning the doctor clearly read in the eyes of the son spoiled and loved beyond all measure that he'd become a stranger to him.

And he comforted himself in vain with the idea that time would pass and the estrangement disappear. The father didn't have the strength to overcome it, and the son didn't even make the attempt. During the time Dr. Farzani had lived in Baku, his daughter had come to visit him twice. And now she phoned at least once a week, asked about his health, asked how he was doing. The son hadn't visited Baku once and didn't once phone.

Yes, the son was Dr. Farzani's weak spot. The story of the artist, apparently, had touched precisely that weak string, reopened the wound, and rubbed salt in it. He fell into a mystically melancholy mood completely uncharacteristic of him and tried in every way possible to come out of it.

"Yes, he's a born Don Quixote!" Farzani exclaimed with forced gaiety. "Don Quixote, that's a real role for him. When he recovers, I'll tell him that. What do you think, will he be offended?"

The artist looked at the doctor with surprise because he knew *Don Quixote* was Sadai Sadygly's favorite work of art.

"Tell him, why not." Agitated again, the artist once more stuck his hand into his pocket in search of a cigarette. "He's read *Don Quixote* a hundred times. Cervantes is his favorite writer. And among our authors he values Mirza Fatali Akhundov most of all. And among the living he has one idol, his father-in-law Dr. Abasaliev, and also some woman from his village, an Armenian named Aikanush, he always speaks of her with love." Nuvarish Karabakhly blurted out all this in a single breath and, dragging his hand from his pocket, looked meekly at the doctor.

Doctor Farzani had read *Don Quixote* at least two times and knew something about Mirza Fatali Akhundov, but about that Armenian woman Aikanush, of course, he couldn't know anything. On the other hand, he was well acquainted with Dr. Abasaliev. They'd met many times at various medical symposia in Moscow, Leningrad, Prague, Warsaw. . . .

"And where does Dr. Abasaliev's daughter work?"

"At first she worked at the medical commission. But now a new dental clinic has opened on Neftianikov Prospekt, and Azada *khanum* works there." The artist looked at his watch. "Only she's not at work now. She's probably already home."

"But you said that on Sundays she goes to her father in Mardakan."

"Yes, she does. . . ." Suddenly, it was as if a light had come on in the artist's head. "It's really Sunday today, Doctor, right?! My stupid brain forgot again, and all this time I've been tormented about how I'm going to go and tell Azada *khanum* about all of this. This is just great, Doctor. For the time being, let Azada *khanum* suspect nothing. But tomorrow, God willing, he'll be better, regain consciousness, and it won't be so difficult for Azada *khanum* to see her husband. They love one another so much. They don't have children, so they give one another the love they would have spent on children." Having said this, he looked at the desk from the corner of his eye. "Will you allow me to clear up?"

"Don't worry, they'll clean it up without you." The doctor carried the half-empty carafe to the refrigerator. "Do you have Azada *khanum*'s telephone number?"

"Her work number, no, but I know their home number."

"Then write it down for me. Dr. Abasaliev probably has a phone at the dacha?"

"There's a phone there, but I don't know the number."

Dr. Farzani shook the artist's hand.

"Well, off you go, have a good rest tonight. But I have many things left to do."

"Doctor!" exclaimed Nuvarish Karabakhly, and he looked so mournfully at Farzani that he understood without a word what the artist wanted to say.

"We won't go into the room," he declared. "That's pointless. But don't you worry, everything's in order there. I gave him an excellent room, later you'll see for yourself and be sure of it. With a phone, a television—not a room but a khan's palace." Dr. Farzani looked at the paper with the telephone number that the artist had written for him. "And I'll get in touch with his family," he added, "Don't you worry about anything."

It was night, a cold December night in 1989. Nuvarish Karabakhly was very much afraid to go home. And it was precisely that fear that gave birth to a feeling of powerlessness and hopelessness in his soul.

If he'd been able to bring himself to do it, he'd have gone back to the hospital and asked for shelter for himself there, if only for one night; just a hospital bed in any old run-down room. The further he got from the hospital, the artist felt how an almost-physically experienced pain of loneliness was growing in him, and because of that, the evening he'd spent with Dr. Farzani had already turned into a distant, no longer attainable, pleasant recollection in his memory.

Dr. Farzani had charged one of those nurses who assisted him during the operation to sit by the bed of Sadai Sadygly—the seventy-year-old, experienced, long-serving Munavver *khanum*. The old hospital hands called Munavver *khanum*, who'd worked there more than fifty years, simply Mira *khanum*. A few called her Mina *khanum*. As for Dr. Farzani, what he called that experienced nurse who knew her business depended on his mood. In an ordinary mood, he called the grey-haired woman of approximately his own age simply Munavver or, familiarly, Sister. In a good mood, that indispensable colleague of the trauma department and surgery was always Minasha for him. And that special nickname gave Munavver *khanum* great joy every time she heard it.

It was the unwavering habit of Dr. Farzani to lock himself in his office and drink a couple of shots of vodka after every operation. When there wasn't an operation, the surgeon locked himself in his office towards evening all the same and for some time cut himself off completely from hospital life. He always drank in solitude; today was the first time he hadn't been alone in his office. For that reason, the nurse was quite worried. On the one hand, she was afraid that this time he'd drink more than his customary amount, and on the other, she was simply jealous; ordinarily, the doctor shared his solitude only with her.

And the meticulous and rule-following Munavver *khanum* was also worried that Dr. Farzani had given the order to place the patient in a room designated for those who were highest in the *nomenklatura*—a room that was under the personal control of the head doctor—and that perhaps the order had been given without the head doctor's approval.

"Here I am, Minasha!" That's how Dr. Farzani greeted the old nurse, coming into the room with his white lab coat thrown across his shoulders. The warmth of that address, as always, was balm poured into Munavver *khanum*'s heart. Probably, she thought, Masha had phoned from Moscow, because only after a phone call from his daughter was Dr. Farzani so cheerful and happy.

"So, our artist isn't planning to return from the dead?" asked the doctor, taking the patient's pulse. "What a heart he has, Minasha. Beaten black and blue, and his heart works like a clock."

"Ah, Farid Gasanovich, if only you knew how he looked in his best years!" responded the nurse anxiously and sadly. "There were times when people went to the theater in droves just to see him on the stage. If only you knew how he played the role of Aidyn! It was so wonderful that even the men in the audience wept." The nurse, deeply moved, barely held back tears. "Do you see the kind of radiance that emanates from his face? And that's after so much torment! I just sit here, looking at him, I don't get tired of looking."

"Yes, a strong fellow," agreed the doctor, who left the bed of the patient and stood a little while by the window. Then he returned and sat in the armchair beside Munavver *khanum*.

"Only, Doctor," the nurse lowered her voice. "You should tell the head doctor that we put the new patient in this room. Just because that's the way it's done."

"I let him know," the doctor answered unwillingly and, getting up from the armchair, again went to the window.

It was as if a weight had lifted from the shoulders of the nurse. She quickly rose and moved towards the door at a brisk clip.

"I'll go clean up things in your office," she said, leaving, and then glanced again into the room. "Shall I bring you tea here?"

"Bring it here. Only don't forget to ask permission of the head doctor," answered the doctor, laughing.

After the departure of the nurse, the doctor again went to the window. He'd recently acquired this habit of standing by the window at night and looking at the deserted streets. It was strange that for several months already, not just at night but even during the day, it had been impossible to see people walking on the streets of Baku either alone or in pairs. Now people walked in crowds, herds. And the sovereign right to speak, shout, and extol was given only to these crowds. And it was stranger still that the quantity of words these beings cried out was probably equal to the quantity of words used when primitive people were on the hunt:

Free-dom!
Re-sign!
Ka-ra-bakh!

In recent days, these people had enlarged their stock of words with two more phrases:

Death to Armenians!
There you are!
There you are!

"There you are! There you are!" muttered Dr. Farzani to himself and walked away from the window.

On the yellowish face of the patient, he noted the clear trail of a tear that had rolled down one cheek.

O Almighty Lord,
Be So Kind, Tell Me:
Did You Create My Aylis
or Did My Aylis Create You?

O Lord, what is this place?

Can this world of steps stretching from the steep bank of the river up along the slope of the mountain really have existed in Aylis? What on earth was that Aylis, where a single narrow gorge suddenly became enormous, like the world? Is it really possible that Aylis grew so great, or did someone collect all the steps carved of stone and all the ledges of the world and arrange them as far as the eye could see in that same narrow gorge of Aylis?

What is this place, O my God?

Perhaps it's the mouth of Babylon's Ishtar Gate in Mesopotamia. Or the Acropolis. Perhaps these steps and ledges lead straight up to the Parthenon. And why do these curved steps remind one so much of the stone seats in the theater of Dionysus?

Perhaps this stone world in the higher part of Aylis named Vuragyrd can be called Harmony. But for the moment it's impossible to say. Because from the stone ledge on which Sadai Sadygly stands, not a single stone of the church located in Vuragyrd can yet be seen. Besides, he'd come to this mysteriously wonderful world specifically in search of harmony, and if what the artist beheld was indeed harmony, then doesn't his entire path beyond lose all meaning? In order to catch even a distant glimpse of that place towards which the artist was striving, he'd have to clamber up the stone steps for a long time still. But his legs refused to go, his hands wouldn't obey, and the heaviness in his head interfered with the movement of his body. As soon as the artist managed to climb just one step, then and there his strength deserted him. Then Sadai Sadygly would lie on the cold ledge, recover a bit, and again begin to move towards the majestic church built from hewn red stone that still wasn't visible. And each time he began to move, the ledges towering over him started to move, too. In this stone world made up of steps stretching from the bank of the river to the very heavens, the earth quaked, the ledges began to rock and shake, and along with that shaking and rocking stone world, Sadai Sadygly once more completely forgot where he was and what he was looking for, plunging into the absolute darkness of Nothing and Nowhere.

From the minute he'd lost consciousness, the artist had been in just this world.

When he'd left home that morning between eleven and twelve o'clock and headed towards the Parapet, a certain secret power had once more attracted the thoughts of Sadai Sadygly and again carried him to Echmiadzin, the ancient cathedral of the Armenian Apostolic Church. Sadai Sadygly had never been to Echmiadzin. However, recently almost every night in his dreams he'd walked towards it among steep rocks and cliffs, and in every one of those dreams, he wandered exactly halfway towards the Vuragyrd Church among the countless stone steps and ledges about which he'd read a great deal in books and seen in films.

The desire to set out for Echmiadzin—to accept Christianity with the blessing of the Catholicos himself, to remain there forever as a monk and beseech God to forgive Muslims for the evil they'd done to the Armenians—arose unexpectedly in Sadai Sadygly's soul on one of the nights after the events in Sumgait. And later Sadai Sadygly was unable to understand whether that wish had come to him in a dream or in waking life. However, on that morning he awoke filled with joy, washed, ate breakfast with gusto, drank tea with pleasure and, unable to hold back, excitedly shared this new, fantastic idea with his wife. Even without that, Azada *khanum* had recently been experiencing serious unease about the psychological state of her husband; she felt worried that day at work, and that evening she phoned Mardakan and, almost crying, told her father everything.

Dr. Abasaliev, having bid medicine farewell for good and having passionately collected all kinds of facts about the history of Aylis from various sources almost since his student days, supplied a diagnosis for his son-in-law without particular difficulty. "Manic-depressive syndrome," he said and, as if ashamed of the seriousness of his words, tried to turn it all into a joke. "He's, what, going there to circumcise the Catholicos? Let him go, don't stop him. Best case, he makes it to Vuragyrd."

And then, abruptly changing the subject, he began with youthful fervor to talk about his new enthusiasm. "Azia, yesterday I found the diary of a certain Armenian merchant in one of the books. That Zakary wasn't a very educated man, but he was an excellent merchant. And he kept a diary just so that merchants after him would know the main methods of trade. Azia, how that man loved Aylis! I'm simply astounded—do you know what Aylis represents for an Armenian? Why did they have to construct that heavenly corner among mountains overflowing with jackals and snakes, where there are a million times more stones than water and earth? Were there really so few places on earth for Armenians? I can't say why Echmiadzin is so widely renowned. In fact, I was there three or four times. However, now, in my old age, I understand that the true house of God is Aylis. In comparison with Aylis, that Echmiadzin is simply a sniveling youth. You tell Sadai that the Catholicos of Echmiadzin won't suit him in the role of teacher. Let him come here to his own teacher, who's more knowledgeable in the affairs of God," laughingly added Dr. Abasaliev.

"Stop it, Papa! You turn everything into a joke," said Azada *khanum* in a slightly irritated voice. "He experiences the fate of every Baku Armenian painfully, as if he alone is obliged to protect them from every attack. Each and every Armenian has become dearer to him than he himself. As if they're all heavenly angels, and we're just butchers thirsting for their blood. He thinks only of those Armenians of Aylis and just can't understand that today's Armenians aren't much better than our own brainless screamers. He simply can't forget the slaughter the Turks conducted in Aylis that he himself didn't see. It's you, Papa, who made him this way."

"No, my daughter, I've got almost nothing to do with this. From birth he was an honest, conscientious, and vulnerable person. And what today's Armenians are like is beside the point—the point is what we're like now. Sadai isn't interested in Armenians, past or present. He's only thinking about the ethnicity we share. Of course, you know how sincerely he loves his people—that's what distinguishes him from the ill-assorted, brainless screamers who've now multiplied around the world like mushrooms after rain." The doctor paused for a long time. Then he started speaking in the warm and tender voice his daughter knew exquisitely well. "You've read *Majnun and Layla*, my daughter.[1] Remember what Majnun does when the army of his tribe goes to the last assault against the army of the tribe of Layla's father. You know that war was started to punish Layla's cruel father, who didn't want to give his daughter to a person from another tribe. And Majnun, blinded by love for his Layla, pitying her father, at the decisive moment throws himself into helping the enemy army.

Because that's what true love is. True love doesn't know any boundaries. You can love a woman that way, and also a motherland. That kind of love is a clear mirror, my daughter—only goodness and mercy are reflected in it. It doesn't come from life, but from God. That's what ails him, our Majnun. And how wonderful, my little girl, that the medicine to treat that illness still hasn't been found," concluded Dr. Abasaliev with tears in his voice, acknowledging his powerlessness in the situation.

Then Dr. Abasaliev lectured his daughter about Aylis for almost an hour on the phone. And that phone conversation not only didn't soothe Azada *khanum*, but increased her alarm still further. She was in utter dismay; it seemed to her that all the men around her were beginning bit by bit to lose their minds.

"Our church here in Vang is an exact copy of the one in Echmiadzin." Dr. Abasaliev had spoken those words at one time to his future son-in-law in the yard of the Vang Church. But how did the artist know that one of the many roads leading to Echmiadzin runs right through the Vang Church? In any case, length by length, inch by inch, he'd already surmounted that agonizing stone world consisting of steps and ledges that resembled Vuragyrd.

Oh, Lord, this is the one—the Vang Church. A yellow-rose sunbeam making its way through the crown of a cherry tree as high as a finely chiseled poplar fell on the very center of the stone cupola of the church and shone past it—not changing color or strength—on the crest of the mountain standing beyond. Once Sadai Sadygly, being in a fine disposition of spirits, had compared that light—first appearing, then slowly fading and disappearing from the church cupola and the crest of the mountain—to the smile of God and the radiance of the Almighty's eyes. God himself had sent that light. Without His blessing, how could Sadai Sadygly, currently unconscious in a Baku hospital, so closely, so distinctly see the Vang Church in Aylis, the yellow-rose light on its cupola, its yard, garden, and that same tall cherry tree disappearing as if it were a poplar into the height of the sky?

It was the start of the summer season. June 1952. The willows had already lost their bloom. Clusters of flowers still hung from the branches of the silver berry trees, from the jasmine and acacia. And there was also the pathway of mixed, multicolored flowers planted in front of the church by Aniko, whom everyone in Aylis called Anykh. And filling the heart with radiance, there was also the freshness of just barely blossoming sunflowers planted in the church-yard by Mirali *kishi*, who lived not far from the church and had turned God's home into his own private storehouse for firewood, hay, and straw.

It seemed as if the yellow-rose light on the high cupola spoke with the mountains—that were as high as it was—about the existence here, at one time, of the purity, sublimity, expanse, and beauty of the world. And Lyusik was present again in the yard of the most beautiful of the churches, the Vang Church: the artist Lyusik, granddaughter of Aikanush, a girl of thirteen or fourteen. That summer Lyusik had come from Yerevan for the first time to spend the summer holidays in Aylis, and from the very first day she didn't leave the churchyard from morning until night. But just how many times was it possible to draw one and the same church? Perhaps the church was just a pretext. Perhaps Lyusik also saw God's smile in the yellow-rose light that appeared morning and night on the cupola and believed she could draw it; perhaps she settled firmly in the churchyard, drawing exactly the same thing day after day, for that reason. And perhaps she already knew then that the church was an "exact copy" of the one in Echmiadzin. But for Sadai that knowledge lay ahead.

At that time, Sadai had never even heard the name of his future father-in-law.

It was a big event when, after many long years, Dr. Abasaliev appeared in Aylis with his daughter at the beginning of the 1960s. Sadai was studying at the institute in Baku.

At one time *Hajji* Hasan, the father of Zulfi—Zulfi, who became Dr. Abasaliev—had traded in Iran, Iraq, and Anatolia, and in Aylis he maintained his land, farm, cattle, and other property. *Hajji* Hasan heard about the Armenian-Azerbaijani hostilities in Isfahan, and returning to Aylis, he collected the most valuable possessions from his enormous holdings and moved his family to Baku for good.

When Dr. Abasaliev appeared in Aylis after many years, the upper story of their two-story house in the Muslim quarter had been almost completely destroyed. Only two rooms on the first floor were relatively well preserved. Putting one of them in order, Dr. Abasaliev began living there with his daughter, and at the same time he began to build a small, one-room house with a modest entry hallway for himself at the other end of the yard. With the active help of his fellow villagers, construction was finished in less than a month; he even managed to cover the roof with slate, which at that time was not found on any other roof in Aylis.

While engaged in the construction of his new home, Dr. Abasaliev didn't forget about relaxation. Every morning before dawn he went for a long walk to the Vang Church. There, in the spring that sputtered in the churchyard, he washed himself in the water clear as a tear, drank a glass of that water on an empty stomach, and filled up the big thermos he'd brought from Baku to use at home.

The whole Abasaliev family was highly respected in Aylis. And Dr. Abasaliev felt that respect at every step, a fact that, undoubtedly, made him very happy. The honor and respect shown him only increased the pleasure of those summer days spent in the village, strengthened the feeling of tranquility and freedom, and simplified and eased the relationship between the people of Aylis and their famous fellow villager.

Dr. Abasaliev was able to comfortably enter any home and converse with the owner. He familiarly scolded the women who didn't sweep their plots by the wicket gate or polluted the river bank with garbage. He supported the sick and helped the poor as much as he was able. And having spoken all of one time with Mirali *kishi*, who'd turned the church into his personal storehouse, he forever put to rest the war that the Armenian Aniko had waged for long years with that willful old man; on that same day, the old man not only cleared out the church but also thoroughly cleaned and washed everything there and with his own hands presented the keys to Aniko.

According to the stories of Dr. Abasaliev, at one time there had been a full twelve churches in Aylis. Sadai Sadygly knew where eight of them had been. The whereabouts of the remaining four ruins were unknown even to Dr. Abasaliev. Strictly speaking, it was incorrect even to call the eight churches "churches" because only the pitiful rubble of them now remained.

The most ancient of them was called Istazyn by the people of Aylis. Even now, it's almost impossible to convince anyone in Aylis that the correct name isn't Istazyn but Astvatsadun, which means "God's house" in Armenian, and that those ruins, of which only two walls and two basements have been preserved whole, were formerly Mecca and Medina for Armenians.

The surviving basements of that Armenian Mecca, standing a considerable distance from the village at the foot of the naked mountains where not one sapling grew; where there was not a scrap of shade; where on hot days the earth, stones, and gravel were all scorching hot like a tandoor oven and blazed with heat—those basements now served as shelter for herdsmen and livestock, and the destroyed walls stood as if just to remind people that everything on earth is transient, even if it's the home of God himself.

The other three churches (no one in Aylis remembered when they'd been destroyed) were the White Church (Ag Kilse), the Orphan Church (Etim Kilse), and the Church on the Square (Meidan Kilsesi). And the remaining churches—in Vuragyrd and Vang, the Stone Church, and Dop—although they'd been left without God and untended, all the same hadn't wholly lost their past grandeur. How those four churches were constructed—in such a way that behind each stood, in the literal sense of the word, a single mountain—the Muslim population of Aylis, naturally, never saw. However, there was no need to be Armenian or know the ABCs of history to see the harmonious unity that those churches created with the mountains standing behind them. Each church was the exact same color as the mountain next to it—as if it had been cut out whole from that mountain and placed there, where it was easy and comfortable for God to contemplate it. And each individual church, it seemed, was the natural child of that mountain at whose foot it had been built.

It was from Dr. Abasaliev that Sadai Sadygly learned that summer that the word Vang means "monastery" in Armenian. And it was precisely there, in the yard of the Vang Church, that Sadai saw his future father-in-law for the first time. There they exchanged their first words, began a conversation, and from then on they felt mutual goodwill and over time became friends.

That summer they wandered a great deal around Aylis (sometime as a twosome and sometimes with Azada accompanying them), making the rounds of its gardens, springs, and churches. They climbed up the mountains and hills. On other days, when the weather was a bit cooler, they crossed over the nearest mountain together and walked around the neighboring villages.

Often, having made arrangements in the evening, they met the next morning in an agreed-upon place. Sometimes Dr. Abasaliev himself even came to Sadai early in the morning and hurried him along: "Hurry up, young man, soon it'll be dawn." From then on Dr. Abasaliev called Sadai "young man."

For many years, every one of those summer days spent with Dr. Abasaliev in Aylis was imprinted in the memory of Sadai Sadygly as a real holiday, not only because of the interesting stories about Aylis but also for the pleasant, dry warmth of the weather and its fresh greenness, the taste of the water of the various springs, and the special affability of people.

One night they agreed to meet the next day and set out together on a far path—much further than Vuragyrd—to the summer pasture of the Aylis shepherds. Earlier, arriving in the village for the summer holidays, Sadai had dreamed about seeing those summer pastures just once. Sadai's childhood friend Jamal, who'd studied with him in the same class for seven years, had joined an elderly herdsman after the seventh grade and tended the collective farm herd in the mountains with him. From then on it was impossible to find Jamal in the village in summer. But it was difficult for Sadai to set out on his own to search for his friend in the mountains.

First they walked along the level road to the Vang Church. From there they descended to the river and entered the path leading upward. At that time there was no more water in the little mountain river of Aylis than in an ordinary spring. And it wasn't the kind of cold water that could quench a thirst as spring water could. But when they were growing especially hot on their long journey, that water came to their aid. All the same, they were only able to go as far as the weir. Understanding that without guides and horses or donkeys they wouldn't reach their goal, they somehow got back using the narrow paths built by herdsmen, and near noon they found themselves by the Vuragyrd Church, standing on the slope of the mountain—at the very highest point of Aylis.

Sadai had known that church from childhood. A great number of pigeons lived there, and for that reason its nickname among the people was "the Pigeon Bazaar." When they entered the church, the pigeons weren't there—they'd flown out among the gardens and fields, where there were grain and water in abundance. And because of that, a special atmosphere having nothing in common with the real world now reigned within the high, thick walls of the church—a special world of stillness and silence, a world without people and outside of time.

Even the air inside the church was somehow unearthly—not of this world, not of these parts. And the long, rectangular beams of light that had fallen from the narrow windows in the cupola didn't seem as if they were the light of Aylis—it seemed that light emanated from other far-off and unknown worlds. Even the light seeping through the crack that had formed not long before just below the cupola created the mystic feeling of another world inside the church.

Since childhood, Sadai had often dreamed of the stone steps leading from the channel of the river up towards the church, dreamed of the square paved with stones beneath those steps and of the narrow little street paved with those same stones running from there down towards the steep bank of the river. However, on that day when he and Dr. Abasaliev were returning from their unsuccessful journey, it seemed to Sadai that he was seeing the church; the little stone roads leading to it; its stone walls; and that strange, ancient, solitary street in Vuragyrd for the first time in his life. Something resembling a dream or a fairy tale was present in the landscape of the far-off Vuragyrd Quarter of Aylis that Sadai saw then—and Pessimist Gulu, well-known in Aylis, who was pacing by the gate of his house and loudly conversing with himself, only intensified the mystic mood that corresponded to that landscape in Sadai's soul.

Gulu hadn't changed in the least. When his fits began he always left his house, circled around in front of the gate, and for whole days passionately, loudly, and without ceasing conversed with himself from morning till night.

He said that someone was pouring poison every day into the irrigation canal that ran into his yard. Gulu heaped the choicest abuse on the heads of those "saboteurs." He rained down terrible curses on the heads of the children who'd thrown stones in his yard or climbed onto his roof. From afar, he threatened the young people who for a long time had supposedly wanted passionately to seduce his hunchbacked wife and aged, sick daughters.

Dr. Abasaliev pulled a banknote from his pocket and thrust it into the pocket of Gulu. Gulu fell silent and looked at Dr. Abasaliev for a long time in surprise.

"Well, Gulu, don't you recognize me?" asked the doctor.

Pessimist Gulu thought for a little while, and then he suddenly clapped the doctor on the shoulder and said, "You're Zulfi, isn't that so? And I recognized your companion immediately. Even when he was a little boy, he hung around here every day, doing nothing." Gulu shook the doctor firmly by the shoulder. "Listen, Zulfi, how'd you end up here?"

"Ah, well, I came to see how you're getting along with your jinns," answered Dr. Abasaliev, winking discreetly at Sadai. "Well, Pessimist, what are they whispering to you this time? Do they come only at night, or do they torment you during the day, too?"

"That's what you came to say to me?!" said the outraged Gulu. "And you call yourself a doctor."

"So, then, you're finished with jinns? And did you plant anything in your yard this year?"

"Of course I planted something, why wouldn't I?!" Pessimist Gulu announced loudly, but he immediately changed the subject. "But do those scoundrels allow anything to be harvested from what's sown?"

"But you say the jinns have left you alone."

"Of course they leave me alone! Everyone who lives here is a hundred times more terrible than jinns." Pessimist Gulu kicked open the gate. "Just look for yourself. See, those scoundrels poured poison in my water—and all my trees started to wither."

Sadai looked into the yard; the trees were mainly apricot trees, with a few apple, pear, hazelnut, and peach trees. A goat whose udder hung down below her knees was tied to a cherry tree. A few hens with chicks scratched between the branches of a barberry growing by the wall. Nothing had been planted in the yard. But not one of the trees looked like it had withered.

"You know he's an old nut case, young man," Dr. Abasaliev said after they walked away from Gulu's gate. Heading down the little paved street and not taking his eyes off the surrounding houses, he began to tell Sadai an entirely unexpected, terrible, and strange story.

"I'll tell you something, young man, only I'm afraid you'll think I'm a nut case, too. Here in Aylis there really are a lot of jinns. Now, by jinns, I mean ghosts. Do you know in whose home Gulu lives? At one time an Armenian, a cross-eyed stonemason by the name of Minas, lived there. And his ancestors were stonemasons from ancient times. The stones of many of the churches are the work of Minas' ancestors. And Minas worked with stone from the day he was born; he produced gravestones, mortars, millstones, and many other things. . . . The grandfather of that nut case Gulu, Abdulla, was exactly the sort of loafer and nitwit his grandson is. He worked as a porter in the bazaar, carried water from the stream to the tearoom, and earned a few pitiful coins with which he made do. And what do you know, when Adif Bey ordered the extermination of the Armenians in Aylis, that jackal Abdulla suddenly plucked up his courage. He ran home, snatched up an ax, and burst into Minas' house. Minas was quietly sitting and working a stone. That scoundrel Abdulla attacked him with the ax and chopped off his head, and then he spared neither the poor man's wife nor children. If you would be so good, please explain to me how that Gulu can now live tranquilly in Minas' house? He can't, I swear to God! The ghost of the tormented Minas will never give him peace. God is not so forgetful as to forgive such monstrous villany."

Evidently, the mystic landscape of Vuragyrd strongly affected Dr. Abasaliev then, too. He stopped often, surveying the river stones polished over a thousand years with which the road beneath their feet was paved. With unceasing surprise he looked at the ruined and falling-down old houses, unable to tear his eyes from the yards and trees. And perhaps it was on exactly that day after the conversation with Pessimist Gulu that, with the genuine passion of a psychologist, he decided to research and substantiate the vexing ideas that suddenly took up residence in his own consciousness.

"In every Aylis family," he began irritably, in a somewhat-odd voice, "that seized an Armenian home, there are mentally ill people; I say that to you as a doctor. Did you ever once see peace in any of those homes? Let's list all the homes below Vuragyrd if you doubt it. We'll start with the home of Myryg Muzaffar standing next to the Stone Church. Neither he himself nor his wife was distinguished by mental deviations. Because the houses in which they were born and grew up weren't seized at the time of the pogroms. But look at their children: all mentally ill. Moreover, with a classic form of schizophrenia. In my time at the hospital, I treated two of Muzaffar's daughters. And treated them properly.

Now you can meet those girls on the street, at the spring. They have the look of sick sheep. They don't say hello to anyone, don't talk with anyone. Because it's an incurable illness.

"I think it's not even an illness but a punishment. Punishment sent by God to man for his unforgivable conduct. . . . A little below Myryg Muzaffar stands the house of Wild Man Gulam. You see the state his grandson is in? He climbs on the fence and throws stones at passersby. Now, look at what's happening in the other houses seized at the time of the pogroms. Gafil, the son of the old woman Beyaz, is outwardly a normal person. But he's also cuckoo. The other day he stopped me in the street and talked for a good hour about how Mohammed flew up Mount Sinai on a black horse for a meeting with Allah.

"Well, that's enough, we'll leave the mentally ill. Not one person in Aylis who at that time tried to improve his own life through violence against the Armenians knows peace to this day. You yourself hear how the two sons of Gazanfar who seized the house from *Mugdisi* Alekhsan bawl and curse every night. Those brothers are prepared to gnaw one another's throats. That's how children bear the punishment for a sin committed by parents. The ghosts of those we've tormented won't give us peace. Look at Mamedaga the butcher, who hacked the daughter of Mkrtych the priest to death in the street with his dagger. I didn't see him in his old age. But those who traveled to Baku said he kicked the bucket like a dog. First he went completely blind, then he suffered a stroke—his mouth was twisted up towards his ears. Besides, the scoundrel suffered dreadfully from constipation. When he strained in the bathroom, his moans carried all the way to Zangezur. Even today, people are ready to spit on his grave. In a word, young man, I no longer believe that sometime better times will arrive here. And I see that the people of Aylis don't believe it themselves."

Moving a little further from Gulu's house, Dr. Abasaliev opened the first wicket gate he came to and went into the yard.

Old Nubar, the mistress of the house, sat on the veranda sorting wool and talking loudly to herself. Seeing guests, she rejoiced with all her soul.

"Come in, come in," she greeted them. "Welcome! How is it that you suddenly remembered about me, Mr. Doctor? They say you've been here a month already, and I'm just seeing you for the first time."

"And whose fault is that? Do you ever leave your home so people can see you?" Dr. Abasaliev looked around the yard. "Thank God, you have a beautiful yard. And an abundance of water, it seems."

"May the Lord gladden you with all things in abundance, Zulfi *gardash*. So long as I have the strength, I'll look after my household. And to our good fortune, this year there's enough water. Much better than in previous years. And now I'll light the samovar and make you tea."

"Not to worry, we're leaving now. I just dropped in for a minute to find out how you're doing. You're all by yourself, still?"

"By myself, Mr. Doctor, by myself," old Nubar uttered mournfully. "I lost one of my daughters when she was just a girl. She fell in love with some rascal and stupidly doused herself in kerosene and burned to death. I married off two girls who went away. And my son left and married a Russian, so he doesn't show his face here anymore."

"And do you remember the Armenian who lived in this house?"

Old Nubar was surprised.

"That was Arakel, you yourself know better than I do. And it's as if it happened just yesterday—his wife Eskhi threw herself off the cliff. How beautiful she was! Do you remember how she sang at weddings? At both their Armenian weddings and our Muslim ones. . . . A curse on that Adif Bey! When his army came into Aylis, poor Eskhi lost her mind. You remember it—every day just as the sun set, she was already up on Khyshkeshen Mountain, where she climbed on the cliff and wept while she loudly sang:

Adif Bey, don't slay us, don't slay us,
We're the flowers of Aylis, have mercy, spare us."

"And who killed Arakel in this house?" Dr. Abasaliev asked uncertainly.

"But you know Arakel wasn't killed at home, Mr. Doctor!" old Nubar answered, astonished. "The son of the snake catcher Abdulali killed Arakel on his plot of land. I know what you're getting at, but no one's blood was spilled in this house."

The doctor thought seriously.

"That may be," he said, "Yes, perhaps I was mistaken. And to whom were you talking when we entered the yard?"

"Well, who's left for me to talk to?" Tears appeared in old Nubar's eyes. "I just talk to myself."

Old Nubar's tears clearly moved the doctor.

"And do you believe in ghosts, Nubar?" he asked in a shaken voice.

"I believe in them, Mr. Doctor, exactly as I believe in Allah and the Prophet! You know it was those ghosts who led us to such a life, Zulfi, may your grief pass on to me. Do you remember that Iranian from Maragheh? Do you remember what he said on his last visit—long before the slaughter of the

Armenians—that Maragheh merchant who often came through here selling all kinds of spices, persimmons, chewing gum, ginger, and cinnamon? 'Leave this place before it's too late,' he said, 'A person can't live in a place where there are so many cemeteries without knowing woe.'" Old Nubar smiled through her tears and suddenly sighed so painfully and deeply that a long wheeze burst from her ancient chest. "But honestly, Zulfi *gardash*, even if they lived a thousand years, the Muslims of Aylis would never have done evil to their longtime neighbors. It was after the command of that cursed Adif Bey that greed enveloped our people. If your father *Hajji* Hasan had been here then, perhaps people would have felt ashamed before him, and they wouldn't have robbed the Armenians. Five or six villains who'd long hankered after Armenian property stained their hands with blood because of their greed."

Dr. Abasaliev heard the story of old Nubar with great attention, as if it were news to him. Although only a few days earlier he'd told Sadai that story himself, moveover, with almost the same details. Nubar was part of the older generation of inhabitants of Aylis. However, at the time there were still more than a few middle-aged people in Aylis who'd seen the unprecedented slaughter of the Armenians of Aylis with their own eyes.

Everyone told of that slaughter in their own way, coming from their own understanding of man and humanity. Nevertheless, none of the witnesses of those events hid what they'd seen. The exact same facts were reliably present in the stories of different people. In terms of how everything began and ended, the opinions of people fully agreed.

This is what happened. So that the Armenian population of Aylis wouldn't suspect anything beforehand, thirty to forty Turkish horsemen of Adif Bey had been riding around all the houses—both Armenian and Muslim—since early morning and announcing that on that day a truce would be declared, and therefore everyone needed to gather immediately in the yard of a certain Armenian. After that, as people assembled in the appointed place, the Turkish soldiers divided Muslims from Armenians and stood them in rows on opposite sides of the yard. Suddenly, a loud command rang out from somewhere: "Fire!" The Turkish soldiers surrounding the yard on all sides rained down a hail of bullets on the Armenians. Many perished immediately. Those who survived had their throats cut with daggers or were stabbed to death by bayonets, to the very last person. Digging a ditch, they buried those they could bury right there in the yard and the garden. They threw those for whom there wasn't space in the yard and garden into the stables and cellars of the nearest homes and burned them. The Muslim women who on that day didn't even dare leave their homes later described events this way: "The water in all the irrigation canals was red with blood for an entire week." And this: "Adif Bey had a horse that was black like a crow. Adif sat on him by the gates of the house. Shouting 'Fire!' he lashed his horse with his crop and galloped off. And immediately the rain of bullets began to flow; it seemed as if the sky had fallen, ash rained down from above. A cry went up such as no one had heard since the creation of the world. All the dogs in the yards began barking all at once. All the crows in the trees began cawing. The frightened magpies and pigeons disappeared instantly from the village; they flew off to hide beyond the mountains. It seemed as if hell had opened up, as if the sun were just about to crash down to earth!'"

Not once had Sadai Sadygly ever heard anyone remember that slaughter in Aylis without horror and sympathy. And all Sadai's knowledge of his hometown was closely connected with those tragic events.

Only after his acquaintance with Dr. Abasaliev did the artist in full measure begin to understand the true worth of that small geographic expanse called Aylis that—thanks, perhaps, to its being well built, and to the cleanliness and neatness of its streets that staggered the imagination—had once been nicknamed "Little Paris" or "Little Istanbul." Only then did he grasp the significance of the unparalleled culture created there through the work and intelligence of people who believed deeply in God. Dr. Abasaliev, according to his own words, was not only "an Aylis fanatic"; he was its historian and psychologist and even a sort of philosopher. Only from Dr. Abasaliev did Sadai Sadygly learn that the famous monk Mesrop Mashtots had invented the Armenian alphabet right there in Aylis and that the well-known writer Raffi had taught at the local school in his time. "Aylis, young man, that's divine perfection!" Dr. Abasaliev exclaimed to Sadai many times. "And for what we did to it, we'll be called to answer before God on Judgment Day."

According to Dr. Abasaliev, a certain Armenian girl who'd been saved from the slaughter in 1919 cultivated a new flower in France that she called Agulis, that is, Aylis. And the artist Gayane Khachaturian, who from age nine or ten drew just the Aylis churches for the rest of her life, lived in Tbilisi. In sum, from the stories of Dr. Abasaliev it turned out that Aylis was indeed one of the thousand-and-one names of God. And possibly his love for Aylis had absolutely no connection to Armenians or to Muslims. More likely, it was one more distinctive and truly noble manifestation of man's faithfulness to Truth.

———————

"That Nubar was extremely intelligent from childhood. At that time she still went to Mirza Vahab, who'd studied in Istanbul, to learn to read and write." Dr. Abasaliev pronounced those words when they'd already walked far away from Nubar's house. It seems he was upset by their visit to her—shaken either by her utter sincerity or for some other reason. And if they hadn't met Zohra *arvad* a little later, then probably he would have returned home in a bad mood.

Having flung open one half of the gate, apparently so as to see people passing in the street, Zohra *arvad* had settled herself comfortably on the steps leading to the veranda and was drinking steaming tea. The entire yard, from the wicket gate to those same steps up to the veranda, was swept clean and sprinkled with water. A narrow little stream of water flowed through the whole yard along the long pathway planted with various flowers. Zohra *arvad*'s yard pleased the eye in every sense of the word. Shapely lemon trees grown in special large pots—so they could be carried indoors during winter— stood near the stream in front of the veranda, giving the yard a particular charm.

Those potted lemon trees had formerly belonged to Aikanush; Sadai had known them long and well. But the strangest thing was that even Dr. Abasiliev recognized Aikanush's lemons at first glance.

"Listen, why did you drag Aikanush's lemons here?" he'd asked from the wicket gate, not yet entering the yard.

"What? You see a lemon, and already your mouth is watering? And again you fail to notice such a beauty as I am?"

"And what's left of your beauty? All unraveled, eh, Zohra, my soul!"

Between them, evidently, lay a long, friendly relationship that allowed them to joke with one another.

"And what's with you? Here you are—all of you, like a piece of candy." Zohra *arvad* brought three old stools from the veranda and set them under the lemons near the little stream. "Come in, sit down. Now I'll give you some excellent tea—tea from India-land. Where are you coming from in all this heat?" Zohra *arvad* brought two glasses, stood them on one of the stools, picked a ripe lemon from the branch and, slicing it, asked, "And why didn't you bring your wife?"

"She didn't want to come." Dr. Abasaliev poured tea into the saucer and, blowing on it, sipped it with pleasure. "Something's not right with her heart, Zohra. She's afraid to travel very far."

"And they say your daughter's going to be a dentist? So be it, God willing. What use do I have for a doctor like you? Maybe your daughter can give me new teeth," said Zohra *arvad*, stroking her toothless gums.

Dr. Abasaliev's mood gradually improved.

"And what did you do with the unfortunate Khankishi? You dispatched him to the other world, did you?"

"If only an unlucky snake would bite that Khankishi, Zulfi! Did that son of a bitch really live with me? Three years he had his way with me, lived it up day and night. And then ran away from me like a tomcat on the prowl. You see, he had no need of a barren wife. After me, that jackal got married two more times, but he remained childless like before. And he finally figured out that it wasn't me but his seed that was barren." Zohra *arvad* gently stroked Dr. Abasaliev's back. "But what was I to do, you didn't marry me, you went off, found yourself a city girl."

And here Dr. Abasaliev's well-known, ordinarily sharp wit failed him. He suddenly turned deep red and, so as to somehow get out of the situation, quickly changed the subject.

"So your greatest girlfriend really deserted you? Somehow these lemons are painfully familiar to me."

"Of course they're her lemons. Who else in the village had such lemons as Aikanush?" said Zohra *arvad*, pouring tea into the glasses. "Yes, Mr. Doctor, Aikanush moved away. Last fall she collected her things and moved to Yerevan to her son Zhora. If it had been up to her, I doubt she'd have moved there. Zhora absolutely insisted. If you'd seen how she was when she was leaving! She simply couldn't part with her house, her yard. She circled around her trees like a crazy woman. She kissed and embraced even the rotten beams on her veranda. And just before she left, she came here, stood and wept in front of these lemons as if she weren't leaving lemons here but seven of her own children. And since then I've looked after her house. This year the lemons ripened well—I collected a whole big bucket and sent them to her. Our people carry goods to Yerevan from here year-round; I asked them, and they took the lemons." Zohra *arvad* picked two lemons, bright yellow among the green leaves, and laid them on the stool. "Here's one for each of you. Drink tea at home. I left three or four on each tree for just such dear guests as you."

Relaxing after tea, Dr. Abasaliev sat and smiled sadly, looking at the lemons. And then he asked, simply to keep up the conversation, "And Aikanush hasn't invited you to Yerevan?"

"She has invited me. She's asked a number of times through our Aylis people working in the Yerevan bazaar: 'Please tell my sister that she should come, stay here with me for ten or fifteen days.'" Zohra *arvad* laughed and winked at the doctor. "Well, what do you say? Should I go, so that in my old age I can lose what little is left of being Muslim there, in an Armenian home?"

"As if this home of yours isn't Armenian!"

"Look at this old rogue!" exclaimed Zohra *arvad*, addressing Sadai. "And from where would Mr. Doctor get the brains to treat crazy people?" Then, half-laughing, half-serious, she shook her finger at the doctor. "My father Meshdali bought this house from Uncle Arutiun-Samvel for fifteen gold *tomans*. As if you didn't know!"

"I know. I didn't mean it that way."

Zohra *arvad* fell silent, considering something to herself, then seriously and anxiously whispered, "I'm not offended, even if you speak ill of my father. Only, for the love of God, Zulfi, don't ever mention the name of the executioner Mamedaga. His foul spawn is worse than the man himself. I mean that Jinn-Eye Shaban, Zulfi. They say he even did you a dirty trick. Don't get involved with them, you can't expect anything good from that tribe."

"And how did you find out about that?" he asked with infinite surprise, fidgeting noticeably.

"As if anything could be concealed in this village. The women were gossiping about it the other day at the spring. They say he dug up an old skull somewhere and threw it across the fence into your yard, and that he stuck a note into the skull: 'Here I am, Mkrtych the priest, cousin of the Armenian spy Zulfi Abasaliev.'"

Seeing that the doctor was upset, Zohra *arvad* fell silent.

Sadai was hearing the story of the skull for the first time, although he'd long known that it was hardly possible to find a person more despicable and spiteful than Jinn-Eye Shaban, son of the butcher Mamedaga who'd killed the daughter of the priest Mkrtych. That Jinn-Eye Shaban, five or six years older than Sadai, was the very same Shaban who since the age of ten or eleven had carried a butcher knife in his pocket and a hunting rifle over his shoulder. It was with that same rifle that Shaban once shot a tiny, black, and beautiful fox cub on the fence of the Stone Church, a cub that for some unknown reason had turned up that spring in Aylis. And although at the time Sadai had been four or five, he never forgot that event and many times leapt up at night from the sound of that fateful shot. Rain and snow had long since washed the blood of the dead cub from the fence; however, in Sadai's mind a scarlet spot of blood remained on the wall of the fence forever.

That same hellraiser Shaban was probably spreading rumors about the skull thrown over the fence and the words written on the note around Aylis now. However, Dr. Abasaliev never again mentioned the foul escapade of Mamedaga's spawn.

Aikanush, the former mistress of the lemon trees, was one of two Armenian women whom Sadai had often seen and known more or less well in childhood. In Aylis there were also a few more Armenian women. However, they didn't differ at all from the Azerbaijani women and for that reason weren't preserved in Sadai's childhood memories.

The first summer when Sadai came home for summer break after studying in Baku, Aikanush was still living in Aylis. She was already stooped from old age and eternally working the earth, but she still had the ability to manage her household. With her own hands she hoed the earth in the little yard right by the river, growing her own beans, potatoes, cucumbers, tomatoes, and greens there. She herself tended her lemon trees, the fame of which spread throughout Aylis. She even sent pears, peaches, dried fruit, and *sujug*—fruit sausage stuffed with nuts—to her son Zhora in Yerevan. On Armenian holy days she walked around the Vang Church, prayed for hours, and made the sign of the cross over herself. Tired out from work, she sat by her gates and conversed with her closest neighbor and longtime friend, Zohra *arvad*.

Aikanush's house stood a good distance from the Vang Church in a low-lying area on the bank of the river closer to the Muslim part of the village. In spite of that, the church became a second home for old Aikanush. Coming through the high, strong gates that no cannon had ever breached, each time she saw the church it was as if she'd lost her reason. Like a crazy person, she began making circles around the church. Then she kissed its stone walls almost stone by stone, making the sign of the cross over herself. Finally old Aikanush went up to the doors and stopped before them. There she crossed herself several times before the stone image of the woman holding a baby whom the Aylis Muslims nicknamed "Turbaned Woman with a Babe in Arms." With that, she ended her pilgrimage, which looked like an amusing performance when seen from a distance.

As a child Sadai saw Aikanush's son Zhora—who lived in Yerevan—several times in Aylis. And when Zhora's daughter Lyusik came from Yerevan to Aylis, Sadai was already eleven or twelve and was one of three inseparable schoolmate-friends: Sary (Light-Haired) Sadai, Bomb Babash, and Jambul Jamal.

They were always together when they went to collect stray spikelets of grain from the field after the grain harvest. Together they clambered over the mountains and cliffs in search of partridge eggs. And when there was no school, no work on the threshing floor, and they were tired of playing *babki* in the street, they started in on the churches. Using river stones heavy from moisture, they tried to break off a nose or ear of the marble statues in the yard of the Stone Church and smash the stone crosses carved on the Vang walls. They climbed onto the high Vuragyrd roof and loudly cat-called the village from above. They ran roughshod over the peas, beans, and corn planted by Mirali *kishi* in the yard of the Vang Church and the bright flowers planted by Anykh-Aniko. Or else they inscribed their names on the walls of the church with the sharp-edged stones found at the bottom of the river, which they always carried in their pockets: Sary Sadai! Bomb Babash! Jambul Jamal!

Light-colored hair had been passed to "Sary" Sadai as the legacy of his ancestors—their family members were all blonds. Babash had received the nickname "Bomb" because of his proud disposition, endless agility, and his iron health and strength. The nickname that Jamal bore, "Jambul," had a special and sad history.

They belonged to the prewar generation, having been born a couple of years before the start of the war that took away their fathers. However, three or four years after the end of the war, news suddenly arrived that Jamal's father Bony Safi was alive. His wife Dilruba received a letter from Safi in which he simply announced that he hadn't perished in the war, that he was alive and healthy and lived now in a land called Kazakhstan in the city of Jambul. He wrote that he'd married again and that his new wife had given birth to a son. He announced that he'd never come back to Aylis, but if his son Jamal wanted, he could come join him in the city of Jambul.

After that ill-starred letter, the wailing of Jamal's grandmother Azra brought the whole village to their feet in the dead of night: her daughter Dilruba had poured a can of kerosene over her head and tried to burn herself to death.

After that, Jamal's mother simply couldn't right herself. She didn't eat or drink, didn't sleep at night, stopped doing the simplest tasks, and completely abandoned the house. Finally losing possession of her wits, she tramped around the mountains at night like a wild animal; she was searching for her husband to punish him, but she didn't know the road to Jambul. They found the body of Jamal's mother at the edge of the highway some twenty to twenty-five miles from Aylis. That's how that idiotic nickname stuck to Jamal—"Jambul."

Living in Baku, Sadai remembered Jamal almost every day. And each time he remembered Jamal, he also remembered the Vang Church: its yard, the tall and shapely cherry tree, and old Aikanush with a shawl invariably hanging down her back. Sleeves rolled up above her elbows, almost crying from stupefaction, she was diligently washing Jamal's lice-ridden head.

That morning the three of them had climbed the tall cherry tree in the churchyard. That year the weather had already been very hot for a long time, but all the same Jamal hadn't taken off the dirty cloth cap for which he'd been made to sit all winter at the last desk in class. Right up until the summer holidays, their faculty advisor Myleila *muallima* had dedicated the majority of the lessons to discussing that cap. As if she didn't know that after Grandmother Azra had gone blind during the winter, no one had washed Jamal's hair once, and Jamal himself, depressed by the sudden death of his mother, hadn't found the strength to wash even once.

It turns out that old Aikanush knew this better than any of the others. Moreover, somehow old Aikanush found out that on that morning Jambul Jamal was going to be there in the churchyard. While the boys sat in the tree, she started a fire right under the cherry tree; heated water in a large copper pot; and brought soap, a towel, a pitcher, and some sort of mud-like mass—black, like tar, with which she planned to grease Jamal's head afterwards—in a pint-sized jar from home.

Hardly had old Aikanush removed the cap from Jamal's head than Babash vomited up the cherries they'd been stuffing into their stomachs. Sadai simply closed his eyes and turned away. Aikanush shrieked "*Vai!*" as if she'd been stung and grabbed her head with both hands. There were as many lice on Jamal's head as ants in an anthill.

Old Aikanush sat Jamal by the fire on a flat river rock. Sadai filled the pitcher with warm water and poured it on Jamal's head, and Aikanush rubbed that lice-ridden head with soap, combing with her fingernails until it bled. Then she again soaped and washed it, saying in a quiet, mournful voice, "My child. Poor boy. Poor orphan!"

And lying unconscious now on a bed in the Baku hospital, Sadai Sadygly heard that voice so clearly, so close by, that even if old Aikanush had turned out to be right next to him in the room, that mournful voice wouldn't have sounded so distinctly.

And Sadai Sadygly heard equally clearly the shouts of the women hurrying from their homes to the churchyard when old Aikanush, having already washed and smeared Jamal's head with medicine, bandaged his head with gauze.

"We call ourselves Muslims and yet didn't have enough sense to wash the boy's head."

"Look, she washed it, so what if she's not Muslim. You know Aikanush didn't fall from the sky! She's also from our village."

"May God be with you in times of trouble, Aikanush *baji*! You've always been known by your kindness towards us Muslims."

"Who wouldn't wash the head of an orphan? How were we to know that the poor boy had lice?"

"What, you didn't see that he never took the cap off his head? If he didn't have lice, would he have gone around in a cap in this heat?"

"May Allah protect your only son in Yerevan, Aikanush. You're the most merciful of our Aylis women."

"You, Aikanush, love Allah, so what if you're Armenian!"

After washing her hands thoroughly with soap and rubbing the small of her back draped with the shawl, Aikanush could barely manage to straighten up. One by one the women dispersed. And as soon as their voices ceased, Aikanush stretched out her hands and moved towards the church with such fervor that it seemed that small, frail woman would now clasp that whole, huge stone thing to her breast like a baby.

When old Aikanush made the sign of the cross before the "Tubaned Woman," Jamal, white gauze on his head, sat silently by the wall in front of the entrance to the church. And Lyusik, who up until now had squeezed herself into a corner of the gate, observing with fear and horror how her grandmother washed Jamal's head, now stood up, leaning against the trunk of the cherry tree and, it seemed, crying quietly. And tears also shone in Jamal's eyes. He gazed with amazement on the world, as if he were seeing it for the first time. Babash stood next to him, hanging his head low; he was embarrassed that he hadn't been able to control himself just now and thrown up so shamefully.

And Aikanush, as usual, stood by the church entrance and prayed furiously. What kind of miracle took place on earth that day so that Sadai, who until that moment hadn't understood a single word of Armenian, suddenly began to understand every word that Aikanush was whispering very quietly, almost to herself? Is it possible he dreamed it? Or did that mystic, spiritual-heavenly gift of the great Creator descend on Sadai—the Creator who at least once in life shows a miracle to every one of his creations whom he named people? And who knows, did that "Turbaned Woman" gazing forever on the world with dead stone eyes really just forget that she was carved of stone to suddenly, gently, smile at Sadai? And the baby she held in her arms suddenly came to life, began to turn his neck, to move his arms and legs. With his own eyes, Sadai saw how the infant, opening his eyes wide, winked happily at someone. And—why is it, O Creator—why were the eyes of the infant at the same time the eyes of Jamal? Let's say all this was a hallucination—a dream or a vision—but from where, then, did that voice sound, the voice of Lame Chimnaz, the deformed daughter of Jinni Sakina, who lived next to the church?

"Look, people! Sadai Sadygly is crossing himself like an Armenian!"

And that disgusting "specimen of folklore" that the idiot Chimnaz sang loudly after that in her disgusting voice?

> *The Armenian, hey, the Armenian*
> *In the mountains threshes grain.*
> *He's got a son and a daughter,*
> *Up his ass is a buffalo horn.*[2]

And also that unearthly light?!

How did it happen that on the day when Sadai suddenly understood the prayer of old Aikanush and for the first time in his life unconsciously crossed himself, the yellow-rose light of the eyes of the Almighty—which usually shone gently on the church cupola and the top of the mountain alone—spilled over everywhere? Never again did Sadai Sadygly see the earth so lit up with unimaginably bright light, but he never stopped believing that in Aylis there exists some other light that belongs only to Aylis. Sadai was deeply convinced that it really must be so—you see, in both length and breadth Upper Aylis probably encompassed no more than three or four miles. And if the people who at some time raised twelve churches on that tiny scrap of earth and created a heavenly corner near each of them had *not* left just a little of their light after themselves, then for what reason does a person need God?

And had anyone besides Sadai seen how that yellow-rose radiance spilled over all of Aylis that day? And why hadn't he dared to ask anyone about it on that same day, there in the churchyard? Now, in Baku there was only Babash to ask about it. But how? Which Babash? To ask today's Babash Ziyadov about that day and that radiance would be as laughable as asking the head of the housing office the address of the Lord God.

That summer Bomb Babash, beginning to act like Majnun, had circled continuously around Lyusik, Aikanush's granddaughter from Yerevan, trying out every kind of pitiful trick. First he climbed up to the top of the tallest trees, crowing like a rooster and cawing like a crow; then, hiding in the bushes, he emitted the cries of a partridge. He bleated like a ram and howled like a wolf. Several times a day he walked on his hands with his feet in the air, making a circle around the church. "*Iski sarumis! Iski sarumis!*" he yelled, first from behind the fence, then from the roof of the church, mistakenly thinking he was declaring his love to Lyusik in Armenian.

However, thin and dark like her grandma, Lyusik patiently bore all these tricks; she didn't pay any attention to Babash, didn't notice him at all. Not seeing anything or anyone around her, Lyusik busied herself whole days in the churchyard with her brushes and paints.

Naturally, old Aikanush, who was responsible for every day her twelve-year-old granddaughter spent in the village, looked in at the church once a day without fail, bringing her tea in a thermos and hot lunch in a pan. But Lyusik never told her about Babash's escapades. Over time Aikanush herself somehow found out about his pranks and went to the Ziyadov house and complained to Babash's grandfather about his grandson's mischief. After that, Babash seemed to stay away from Lyusik. However, it turned out that the main scandal was yet to come.

It happened during those same summer holidays. One day a rumor went around the village that someone had climbed into Aikanush's yard during the night and picked a single lemon from each of her trees. Of course, it wasn't a serious theft, someone had simply wanted to offend the person to whom the lemons belonged. Aikanush, who suspected Babash more than anyone, all the same didn't complain to anyone. But two days later someone again climbed into Aikanush's yard at night and this time pulled down Lyusik's underwear, which had been hanging on the clothesline. The next morning was the last of their many years of unbreakable friendship and perhaps the end of all their light-filled, sunny childhood.

That morning, on the small square in front of the mosque where the Aylis kids usually played, even Sadai himself didn't understand how he felled Babash—considered the strongest of the boys—and was extremely surprised that Babash collapsed to the ground at his blow. Then he snatched the underwear Babash had been brandishing from his hands, displayed it to the kids, and yelled with all his might:

"This isn't Lyusik's, it belongs to Babash's sister, Rasima! So, who wants Rasima's underwear? I'm selling, come and get it!"

After that, although they sat in the same class for a year or a year and a half, they didn't speak to one another, not even in greeting. Later they sort of made up.

However, the coolness between them always remained. Even after they'd moved to Baku to study, they didn't once make the attempt to find one another. Later Sadai found out that Babash, while still a student, had found work in the central committee of the Komsomol and was successfully making a career. And each time he heard about Babash's appointment to the next, more important post up the ladder, Sadai involuntarily remembered the church, Lyusik, Aikanush's lemons, the square in front of the mosque, and Babash brandishing Lyusik's underwear.

The next day Aikanush settled her granddaughter on the train at the Ordubad station and sent her back to Yerevan. After that, Lyusik didn't come to Aylis once.

The second prominent and colorful Armenian woman in Aylis was Aniko, whom everyone called Anykh. She was a courageous woman, proud and determined. She was able to do everything, knew everything, and could give useful advice to forest beekeepers about beekeeping and to silk worm breeders about the cultivation of silk worms. She treated the ailing and the sick in the village without having a medical education; only Allah knows how there was so much passion and strength in that woman! Aniko was a witness to how, on that black fall day in 1919, Turkish soldiers—after exterminating people with bullets and hacking them to pieces with sabers—drowned everyone great and small in a lake of blood. Among the dead were her parents, brothers, and sisters. All Aylis knew the ten-year-old Aniko had hidden then in a tandoor oven and survived only by accident; she stayed there three or four days without food or drink until Mirza Vahab's mother Zahra *arvad* discovered her. Mirza Vahab, who'd been educated in Istanbul and according to Dr. Abasaliev was considered the most learned Muslim in Aylis, was then about thirty years old. He hid Aniko in his house, raised her, and—of course forcibly—made her his wife. If not the greatest miracle in the world, what, then, should one consider the care and tenderness Aniko showed her husband, who was twenty years older than she was? She always spoke of him with pride and boasted of his learning, knowledge, and nobility. Aniko gave Mirza Vahab two sons and a daughter; the name of her husband was always on her lips.

Here, there, and everywhere she talked loudly about the fact that she'd converted to the Muslim faith.

And just as passionately, not afraid of anyone, about the fact that a time would certainly come when Armenians would return to Aylis, and it would again become a heavenly place.

During the days of mourning for the imams, the self-described Muslim Aniko didn't forget to sit in someone's home along with other women in the chador, loudly bewailing the cruelly murdered grandsons of the Prophet Mohammed; nevertheless, early almost every morning she went to the Vang Church. There she swept the churchyard, tended the beautiful, bright flowers she herself had sowed, and didn't let slip a chance to fearlessly rain down a stream of abuse on the head of all the ancestors of Mirali *kishi* who, turning the church into his personal storehouse, had hung locks on all the doors.

And Aniko's home itself on all sides resembled a celebratory exhibition of never-fading flowers, one that could be found nowhere else in Aylis. Mirza Vahab had settled in that house after the Armenian slaughter in 1919. They even said that the house, one of the most beautiful in Aylis, had personally been given to Mirza Vahab (who'd received his education in Istanbul) by Adif Bey, the leader of the Turks. How could one not believe, after that, that it was only miracle guiding all of Aniko's actions if, precisely in the location where the most bloody massacre caused by Adif Bey had taken place, she'd turned the yard into a veritable flower bed? Of course Aniko must have known. Perhaps, cultivating her flowers, she pursued a fixed goal—perhaps she wanted to immortalize the memory of each of her murdered fellow-tribesmen. To show that after every murdered Armenian a flower remained on the earth. And that she wanted every single Muslim in Aylis to understand that. It's possible that the blood once spilled in that yard still seethed in Aniko's memory and that the only way to soothe the blood-soaked memory was for her to adorn her yard and all the pathways of the Vang Church with flowers.

Aniko remained in Sadai's memory not only as a fine person and woman but also as a particular kind of voice, happy and ringing. A voice that encompassed in itself all of Aylis—with its homes, churches, mountains, roads, trees, streams, and springs—and a ringing herald of approaching morning. Because Aniko always woke at dawn and loudly sang on her high veranda, as if she wanted to announce to all the Muslims of Aylis that an Armenian voice still lived and sounded in Aylis.

In contrast to Aikanush, she always went to the Vang Church noisily, walking along the old coach road in the mountain and talking loudly. She recalled Eskhi, who'd thrown herself from the cliff, and cursed Adif Bey for all to hear, and from a distance began scolding Mirali *kishi*, who'd turned the most beautiful Aylis church into his own pathetic storeroom. The voice of Aniko, who never forgot to mention she'd converted to Islam and become the wife of such a noble and learned man as Mirza Vahab, it seemed, had nothing in common with the voice of the little Armenian orphan girl saved by a miracle from a Turkish bayonet. This, beyond all doubt, was the voice of the true mistress of Aylis, reaching from the depths of time. In a word, it was the morning voice of Aylis!

Living in Baku, Sadai Sadygly often heard it in his Aylis dreams, and many Baku mornings began for the artist with that exact same voice.

At the very same time when the dirty, corrupt mug of the old world, like an old whore, was just beginning to show signs of the fiendishly unavoidable clash of Muslim and Armenian on itself, Sadai Sadygly dreamed of a strange church. The strange thing was that it didn't look like any of the Aylis churches. And at the same time, there was something of each of them in its frightening, mystical look.

In the dream it was impossible to tell the time of year. It was early morning in Aylis: dawn had just commenced, the village was dragging itself with difficulty out of the dark of night. In the mountains, on the shady side, snow still lay in little islands. Above them were rare, fleecy white clouds. And still there was that cosmic, mystical light, both alien and to the highest degree native, familiar!

The high, white walls of the church that appeared to Sadai in the dream had cracked from the inside, and that light could be seen filtering into the church through the cracks that had formed. A sound resembling the hum of a swarm of bees streamed without stopping, a sound bringing horror with it, pouring directly into the church as if from some entirely different world and from there—through the cracked walls—hurrying with diabolical passion to spread the terrible news it brought around the world.

And from that time that strange, unearthly sound followed Sadai without stopping. From the radio—from the television screen—from the revolutionary, religious, and various patriotic leaflets stuck here and there on the walls of entryways and telephone poles—from the headlines of articles black with large letters on the front pages of newspapers and journals—from everywhere the artist heard that lightsound sowing unprecedented horror around the world. It was incomprehensible to him why, at just the moment when it would seem that no one was afraid of anything, he had to live with the continual sensation of fear. Why, in every word read in the newspaper and heard on the radio, on the television, from the lips of the orators on the squares and the women in the streets, did he hear a portent of tragedy? Why did his heart darken at the sight of pregnant women or young couples walking in the parks and on the Boulevard? Was it possible that it fell only to him to fear for the future of all people? What had so frightened him once that he now walked in horror at the thought that that roar of the streets and squares sooner or later would bring a new Master to power? Why, exactly, was he, Sadai Sadygly, fated to experience the pain and suffering of inevitable bloodshed now, before it had happened?

Not finding answers to the questions tormenting him, Sadai Sadygly saw Aylis every night in his dreams. Because Aylis was the unhealed wound of his heart. And Sadai, who in any case was inclined to fall into a depressive-melancholy state from time to time, began to shun the world and people more and more each day. He often raved in his sleep, moaned. In his incoherent monologues he mentioned the names of Aikanush, Aniko, Jamal, Lyusik, Babash, and many other people known and unknown to Azada *khanum*. Once, when Azada *khanum* saw that Sadai, waking up in the middle of the night, crossed himself, she couldn't recover her composure for quite some time.

In one of those nightmare-filled nights, her husband brought up the Aylis fox cub long forgotten by everyone else in his incoherent monologues. Her husband moaned so much in his sleep that Azada *khanum*, who often hid Sadai's ailments from her father, couldn't avoid sharing her anxiety with Dr. Abasaliev the next day.

"Maybe you can talk with him, Papa? Find out what torments him?"

Dr. Abasaliev, who understood quite well that such psychological conditions are not at all a medical problem, tried to calm his daughter.

"It's cryptomnesia," he said. "It's found in all emotional people; as they age, they 'fall into childhood.' Don't be alarmed. One way or another, everyone lives his life."

But the sad thing was precisely that Sadai Sadygly wasn't living his life now. It was strange: Sadai Sadygly, in whose family there was no one with a drop of Armenian blood (one of his grandfathers had made a pilgrimage to Karbala, the other to Mecca), for some time had apparently carried within himself a kind of nameless Armenian. More precisely, hadn't carried but hidden. And with every Armenian beaten, offended, and killed in that giant city, it was as if he himself had been beaten, offended, and killed. Since the beginning of autumn he probably hadn't smiled once, and he'd walked around dispirited and gloomy. He completely forgot the theater, where earlier he'd gone at least twice a week.

Even rallies, which at one time he gladly attended, lost all interest for him now. He felt restless in town and didn't know any peace at home.

On one of those windy, rainy evenings he came home in such a state that Azada *khanum* almost shrieked in horror. It was as if someone had plunged him into a pool—all his clothes were wet, and water was pouring from his hair and his chin and from the pockets of his raincoat. His pants were smeared with filth; the buttons on his jacket and shirt collar had been torn off.

Weeping, Azada *khanum* undressed her husband and sat him in a bath of warm water. She gave him a shot of brandy and brought tea. And only when Sadai came to himself did she set about questioning him.

"Where did you fight?"

"I didn't fight."

"Then who did this to you?"

Sadai didn't say anything. But after a long silence he wept so bitterly that Azada *khanum* regretted her question.

"Azia, they set a young woman on fire at the train station! They poured gasoline on her and burned her alive."

"Who set her on fire?" asked Azada *khanum*, wiping away tears.

"Women, Azia. A crowd of street traders. As if they weren't people but a horde of actual jinns."

"Women did this to you?"

The artist was surprised because he really hadn't noticed the state he'd come home in.

"I don't know. I wasn't able to understand anything. When those she-devils set that Armenian on fire and immediately disappeared, I saw that I was standing in the train station alone."

And then he began to relate another thing so upsetting that Azada *khanum* felt very uneasy.

"Last night I dreamed they gave money to some Armenian to kill me."

"Who? Who's planning to kill you?!" cried Azada *khanum*, unable to control herself, in a voice that wasn't her own.

"Our people gave money to that Armenian, the ones in authority now."

"Wake up! There hasn't been any kind of authority here for a long time. And if there is any authority, then it's what's sowing the seeds of enmity every-where. Do you think the people arranged that hellish nightmare in Sumgait? No, my dear, no! It was arranged by the KGB or possibly the remnants of the authorities who've now separated into the various mafia groups. I'll never believe, Sadai, that Azerbaijanis could come to such senseless wildness without a real, live organizer."

"How can you say such a thing? You were in Aylis, too," said the artist, glancing piercingly, sadly at his wife, and immediately he hung his head, like a child.

"Yes, I was in Aylis, and I know the Turks dealt brutally and cruelly with innocent people there. But you've also been in those places from which *Armenians* drove out thousands of unfortunate *Azerbaijanis*. Have you thought even once about how it is for those unfortunate people, those Azerbaijanis, homeless now and living without the slightest hope for the future? Do our Azerbaijani instigators, the ones who stirred up this bloody trouble, really think about them, the Azerbaijanis whom the unfortunate Armenians themselves now curse? I mean both the Karabakh Armenians and the local Baku Armenians who don't care about us because, according to their thinking, we're also Turks? If the Turks slaughtered your people, go ahead, fight it out with them, why are we Azerbaijanis even involved? In what way are those Armenian screamers better than our home-grown ones? Why don't you think about that, my dear?

Since all this began, you haven't been yourself. Do you know how emaciated you've become, sweetheart? If you won't take pity on yourself, then at least take pity on me. This is not acceptable, Sadai, understand? You won't change anything in this world, just thoroughly destroy yourself. You say you went to the train station? And what did you do there, sweetheart?"

"I wanted. . . . I wanted. . . . I want to die, Azia," he uttered, with difficulty.

Azada *khanum*, understanding that her husband was on the edge of madness, fell silent.

Sadai Sadygly, retreating into himself for good, was now fully estranged from both his wife and from all earthly things in general. Azada *khanum* understood why her husband went to the train station. For entire days Sadai hung around there just to meet and see off the Baku-Yerevan train known to him since childhood. On that train, which passed through his native Ordubad, he traveled every day in his thoughts, cherishing a crazy new dream about Echmiadzin, where he planned to go to convert to the Christian faith.

The Young Author of a Play in Which Sadai Sadygly Will Never Perform Accuses the Former Master of the Country of Ethical-Moral Genocide against His Own People

Perhaps Sadai Sadygly had again been dreaming of those wonderful summer days spent in Aylis with Dr. Abasaliev. Or perhaps the voice of his father-in-law, which he'd heard the previous night on the telephone from Mardakan, still sounded in the artist's ears. In any case, just as soon as Sadai awoke that morning, it seemed to him that the whole world was filled with the ringing, bright voice of Professor Abasaliev. And continuing to hear that bright, ringing voice, Sadai felt more cheerful and peaceful than he'd ever felt before; it seemed it was easier for him to bear his pain in a world where the voice of Dr. Abasaliev could still be heard.

It was the next-to-last Saturday in 1989. About an hour had passed since Azada *khanum* had gone to work, and hardly had she left the house than the phone began to ring. For more than an hour it rang at five- to ten-minute intervals, but Sadai didn't pick up the receiver.

In the pauses between the rings, the artist heard a cloyingly sweet voice in his ears, and before his eyes stood the well-known figure of Maupassant Miralamov, the director of the theater, from whose lips floated lines by a well-known poet of the people:

We greet the Great Master,
The Equal of Eternity![3]

For more than a week now, the director had phoned Sadai Sadygly every day and, instead of greeting him, each time repeated those lines—disgusting in their triteness—that evoked an almost physical nausea in him.

Finally, Sadai had to pick up the receiver.

This time it wasn't Maupassant Miralamov but Nuvarish Karabakhly.

"Brother, why don't you pick up the phone?" he asked in his quiet, wheezy voice. "I've already called you fifty times. I'm sick with worry—I keep thinking something's happened. Your fellow villager arrived here, someone from your hometown—your childhood friend Jamal."

"He arrived where?" Sadai asked this with such amazement that he was frightened by his own voice.

"He's here, in the theater. Come quickly, he's waiting for you." Nuvarish Karabakhly paused for a second and added, "He's in Maupassant *muallim*'s office."

If Nuvarish Karabakhly said "Maupassant *muallim*," then he really was phoning from the director's office. Otherwise, he would have called the director something different: behind the director's back, everyone called him Uncle Moposh.

"I'm coming," answered Sadai Sadygly. However, he lacked the strength to move from where he was.

Since the time Jamal had become a shepherd after the seventh grade, Sadai hadn't seen him once. But he always remembered him. Moreover, recently he'd been obsessed with the idea of going to the village to find Jamal there in the mountains, no matter what it took, and finally asking him: on that day after Aikanush washed his head in the churchyard, had the whole world really been lit up with such a velvety-soft, yellow-rose light or had it seemed that way to Sadai alone? But now that the real possibility of seeing Jamal had appeared, it turned into a heavy burden.

When he finally left the house and was already getting into a taxi, the thought suddenly entered his head that Jamal's arrival might not be a fact but a clever trick of the sharp Maupassant Miralamov. In fact, for a long time the director had been trying to lure him to the theater by various ruses and absolutely force him to read a play he'd already lavished praise on for many days over the phone. It was indeed possible that Moposh wasn't making this up, that the lead role in the play had, in fact, been specially written for him, Sadai. And it was fully possible that the eternal optimist, the businesslike, quick-witted Maupassant hoped that Sadai Sadygly playing the lead role would put the dying theater back on its feet. That was his character; if he undertook something, he was bound to carry it through to the end. And to discover that Sadai had once had a childhood friend named Jamal wouldn't have presented great difficulty for Moposh—the director might have heard about it from Sadai himself and remembered. In any case, this was the truth: the artist now riding in the taxi didn't have any particular desire to meet with Jamal.

However, it turned out that Jamal really had arrived.

Looking serious, dressed in a cheap, new suit and wearing an expensive Bukhara *papakha* on his head, he'd made himself comfortable in the warm and cozy office of Maupassant Miralamov. His face had been tanned a shade of copper in the mountains, and his large, hazel eyes shone from the agitation and excitement elicited by unfamiliar conditions.

Sadai didn't see Nuvarish Karabakhly in the office. He'd probably gone to rehearsal, Sadai decided, or to shoot something somewhere in the television studio. (Sadai didn't know that for a long time now Nuvarish, being preoccupied with the search for a pistol, had been sitting around waiting in vain in various reception rooms of important people.)

Seeing Sadai, Maupassant Miralamov leaped up from his armchair with unexpected agility for his age, threw himself on the artist, embraced him right at the door, and clasped him firmly to his bosom. He was even able to squeeze a tear from his eye in an attempt to demonstrate how happy he was to see him.

Jamal puckered his lips naïvely, like a child, clearly preparing to kiss his classmate warmly. Sadai clasped the head of his friend to his bosom, along with the stylish *papakha*. For several seconds they looked at one another in silence. And those short seconds were enough for Jamal to collect his thoughts, decide how to start the conversation, and even to become a little emotional at first and then burst into tears—loudly, with sobs.

"I'm in a terrible mess, brother!" he said. "I came to ask for your help. My son has been arrested and put in jail. There's not a single office in the district on whose door I haven't knocked. No one wants to hear me out. So I came here, maybe I can find help here."

"And why did they arrest your son?" the artist asked irritably; clearly, he didn't like the fact that Jamal was crying like a woman.

Jamal didn't answer. Pulling a handkerchief from his pocket, he painstakingly wiped away the tears and sweat that had appeared on his brow. Then, finally coming to himself, he began to tell the story in a now-quiet and calm voice.

"It's Divine punishment for my stupidity, Sary. What a fool I was to take the granddaughter of that butcher Mamedaga as a daughter-in-law, to mix my blood with the blood of that rotten breed. And I'm suffering now. She just rides roughshod over me, and she attacks her mother-in-law like a mad dog. She only knows how to growl, quarrel, and put a curse on things.

"She's disgraced us before the whole village. And then she caught up a sharp cleaver and hit herself in the head: what a bitch! And at the instigation of her father, Jinn-Eye Shaban, she rushed to town, to the hospital, she says, 'Look, people, my husband wanted to kill me!' She slandered the boy and had him arrested. And for twenty days now, I've left no stone unturned. I've been to everyone in the district; no one wants to even listen. I've lost every hope. All my hope is on you, Sadai. You can help me. After all, you're a well-known person." Jamal fell silent, fastening his gaze full of mildness on Sadai.

Sadai began to pity Jamal. At the same time, he experienced tremendous sympathy for himself and for Aylis, even for that crazy, quarrelsome daughter of Jinn-Eye Shaban. Aylis was grey this season, the mountains were grey. Freezing, hardly breathing from the cold, the stones, streets, and houses were waiting for the arrival of spring. The Stone Church. That same *qanat* spring, the most powerful in Aylis, flowing out from beneath its stone walls, its water running now under the icy irrigation canals and turning a little bit black, mixing with some nameless fear; that same miraculous black fox cub—God's little creation. And also that scarlet spot of blood, stiffening forever on the stone fence by the spring there, where Jinn-Eye Shaban had shot it. Looking into the grey and pitiful face of Aylis, the artist was suddenly ashamed with his whole heart that he'd ever wanted to ask Jamal about the yellow-rose light.

"We'll see. We'll think up something," Sadai Sadygly answered uncertainly, without any hope, and added, a bit louder, "Well, tell me, what's new in Aylis?"

"What could possibly be new in Aylis? Everything's exactly the way you saw it," Jamal replied, with extreme reluctance.

"Do you know how many years it's been since I was in Aylis?"

"Say it's been a hundred. If you didn't come to Aylis for a hundred years, nothing would change," answered Jamal, and for some reason he smiled pitifully at just Maupassant. Then, apparently deciding that he had to tell Sadai something or other about Aylis, he said unwillingly, "This year Mirali *kishi* died at the end of winter, you probably heard about that. And the other day Anykh also gave her unclean soul to Azrail. And there was so much anger in that old woman—she remained an Armenian even on the threshold of death. When our old women went to say goodbye to her, she announced to them, she said, 'I didn't even think about changing my faith, and I never renounced my God.

That means that to this very minute I was actually pulling the wool over your eyes, to put it in polite terms.' How vile these Armenians are!" Jamal comically wrinkled up his face, and again he looked meekly and warily at Maupassant Miralamov. Then he turned his gaze on Sadai and in some kind of strange confusion hung his head.

"So now it's fashionable in Aylis for people to spread lunacy about Armenians?" asked Sadai in a constrained voice that could barely be heard. He tried to imagine Aniko, the last Armenian of Aylis, on her death bed, surrounded by the Aylis Muslim women in the hour of her death.

But he wasn't able to imagine the scene of her death. He could see the big, two-story house, the best in Aylis. The tall veranda filled with flowers of all different kinds. The solid stone steps leading up to it, pleasing the eye with their irreproachable cleanliness and neatness. In Sadai's eyes, the world was made much brighter by Aniko's multicolored flowers, grown by her in the yard of the Vang Church and cared for by her year round. Glancing at Jamal's expensive *papakha*, the artist remembered his dirty, lice-ridden cap that Aikanush had once taken from his head in fear.

"If you had a God, you wouldn't have betrayed him, either!" he said loudly and pitilessly. And immediately thereafter (either from regret about what he'd said, or for some other reason), he felt a terrible emptiness in his soul—some sort of boundless, hopeless ruin, without life and without air. In the brief moment of silence arising after his words, he was able to see a suspiciously reproachful, cold smile in the eyes of Maupassant Miralamov; the clean-shaven, well-fed face of the director had suddenly turned grey. However—just think!—Sadai's angry words didn't offend Jamal in the least.

"You're absolutely right," he answered. "Armenians are always in harmony with their God."

The words seemed painfully familiar to Sadai. The artist heard them not just as words but as some forgotten sound, as a gentle, kind light that had existed at one time in this world and then disappeared without a trace. In some miraculous way, Sadai Sadygly found peace and consolation for himself in those words. He was prepared to rifle his entire memory to recall from whom, when, and where he'd first heard them. He wanted to embrace, to press all Aylis to his bosom like one communal house, to rock it like a small sapling, to gather it in his cupped hand and drink it like a swallow of water so that he could remember from whom in Aylis he might first have heard that most simple—and at the same time, unbelievably profound—phrase spoken just now by Jamal.

Your secrets are inscrutable, Lord—couldn't those words really once have been spoken by True Majesty Itself, inscrutable Aylis? "Armenians are always in harmony with their God."

Rejoicing sincerely, Sadai embraced Jamal about the shoulders.

"Ah, you're still Jambul—Jambul! Look how honest you turned out to be. You didn't take offense. After all, I insulted you."

"An honest man is never offended by honest words!" said Jamal, enunciating every word grandly. "It is said: Better to be the slave of an honest word than the lord of a lie."

"This is your first time in Baku?"

"No, I've been a couple of times. And one of my daughters got married and moved here."

"To whom have you left the mountains while you're away?" Sadai asked, joking.

"Who could threaten the Master of the mountains?" Jamal answered seriously, meaning God, of course.

"You don't look after sheep anymore?"

"I do, why wouldn't I? I have tons of grandsons in Aylis. They can certainly manage the place without me."

Sadai stood up and began to pace around the office. "So, what should we do?"

"About what?"

"About jail, what should we do about that?"

As if he'd been waiting for just that moment, Maupassant Miralamov stood up.

"What's so complicated? You'll write a nice little note to the district public prosecutor, and our brother will give it to him. The public prosecutor won't refuse you. They'll release the boy, and that's the end of it." The director winked stealthily at Sadai Sadygly and held out paper and pen towards him, already prepared. "What right does a prosecutor have to not listen to the word of a famous People's Artist?" (In unofficial situations he always called Sadai Sadygly a People's Artist.) "Moreover, nobody's killed anyone. So, something happened, they fought, they quarreled. So, they'll reconcile, that's it." The director again winked surreptitiously, slyly at Sadai, and only now did the artist understand that Moposh simply wanted to get rid of Jamal as quickly as possible.

"No, that won't do. What will my letter matter to the prosecutor if he can get some money out of someone else?" The artist resolutely crumpled up the paper that had been extended to him, giving the director to understand that he didn't agree with his charade. And glancing at Jamal's sad, worried face, he saw dim, sunless, dismal, dead, dreary Aylis once more in the depths of his heart. Aylis, which had lost the greatness of its mountains and of its churches, which were just as great. The grey streets with no people. The dead yards that lay bare after autumn. The lifeless trees left without a single leaf, the ruined mountains—without shepherds and without sheep. Only grey crows flew in the grey, dead sky over the grey Muslim cemetery. Feeling a terrible hopelessness, after long deliberation Sadai said, "Maybe we should track down Babash?"

Jamal cheered up and instantly came to life.

"Yes!" he exclaimed excitedly. "Let's find him! He'll surely help me. He has an important job, honor, respect—Babash has it all." He leaped up from the desk. "You just lead me to him. I'll take care of the rest."

Sadai Sadygly had heard plenty about Babash's big career achievements. After a short stint in the central committee of the Komsomol, he'd immediately gotten a job as chair of the district executive committee of one of the large districts in Baku. He was the first secretary of the district Party committee and for a long time even occupied a minister's chair. Recently Babash had been head of a department of the Central Committee, and only two months ago a new organization had been created, the Society of Those Who Are Dedicated to the People, whose president Babash Ziyadov had become.

Having avoided contact with Babash for many years, Sadai was now prepared to do anything for Jamal. However, he didn't know exactly where the organization led by Babash was located. In spite of this, he decided without hesitation to throw himself into the search. Concerned by this decisiveness, the director began bustling about and ran out from behind the desk, not letting them leave the office.

"Where are you going?" exclaimed Moposh, blocking the exit. "Do you mean your fellow villager Babash Ziyadov? Then wait a minute. Let's phone, inquire. Maybe he's out."

On the director's desk sat three telephones, not outwardly distinguishable from one another: an internal line, a local line, and a third line for just three-digit numbers—a private government line. The fact that Moposh picked up the receiver of that third line was reflected on his face, which all of a sudden became detached and serious. Cleary demonstrating his own importance, he dialed three numbers. However, hearing the voice of Babash Ziyadov, he couldn't hide his confusion.

"Hello, Babash Bilalovich! This is Miralamov. . . . Yes, from the theater. . . . Yes, and God grant you the same. . . . Endlessly grateful. . . . There will be. We have a fantastic play. . . . He himself? Yes, of course, He knows. Yes, yes, He's aware. . . . He acquainted himself personally with the play. . . . He liked it. Liked it a lot. . . . Yes, the subject is extremely topical. . . . His image? It is, it is. Yes, the whole play's about the shameful excesses he committed here for thirty years. . . . In the lead role? Yes, yes, it is he. Your fellow villager, our pride and joy. Actually, the author wrote that role specifically for Sadai *muallim*. And He himself said He'd like to see Sadai Sadygly in that role. Yes, yes, He himself."

Sadai Sadygly knew that with the rise of the new First Person to power, a campaign was unfolding everywhere to unmask the former, already disgraced leader. By the way the director suddenly sprang from his chair and began to thank Babash, the artist understood that Babash Ziyadov had promised the theater something. Undoubtedly, Babash had guessed that Sadai was now in the director's office. However, true to bureaucratic etiquette, Maupassant was waiting until Ziyadov himself expressed the wish to speak with the artist. And finally that long-awaited moment arrived.

"Yes, he's here, right next to me, wants to say hello to you." And Moposh, almost dancing from happiness, handed the receiver to Sadai.

After greeting Babash, the artist immediately got down to business.

"Jamal's arrived," he said drily. "He has business with you."

"Is it really that difficult a thing?" Babash tried to joke.

"Not difficult for you."

"Then why is it difficult for you, great artist? Is it possible people respect you less than they respect us?"

"If I were able to help, I wouldn't have bothered to phone you." Sadai tried to be as friendly as possible. "So, will you see him?"

Apparently, Babash Ziyadov had quickly understood that joking with the artist wouldn't lead to anything good, and after a short pause, he answered in a now-serious tone.

"Fine, send him over, I'll see him." Then he was silent again and, with ill-disguised injury in his voice, added, "I thought you phoned to congratulate me."

With those words Babash hung up the phone, while the artist stood with the receiver in his hand, looking uncomprehendingly at Maupassant Miralamov.

"Did you hear? He says, 'You didn't congratulate me.' What was I supposed to congratulate him for?"

"I don't know. . ." muttered the director thoughtfully, not lifting his eyes from the telephone. "A big article came out in yesterday's *Kommunist*. Probably he's thinking of that."

"He's also become a writer?!" growled the artist, and he headed towards the door after Jamal, who was leaving the office.

"Where are you going?!" yelled Maupassant with unexpected rudeness.

"To show him the way—he won't find it on his own."

"Sit down. My driver will take him." Practically shoving Jamal out of the office, Miralamov seized hold of Sadai's arm, led him over, and sat him in an armchair. "Listen, what's going on with you?" he said in a sorrowful voice, clearly pitying the artist.

"What do you mean?"

"For a whole month I haven't been able to drag you out of your house."

"Don't exaggerate, it hasn't been a month," responded Sadai Sadygly.

"When were you last here? If you remember, I owe you a good *khash*."

"Honestly, Moposh, I'm tired, everything is repulsive to me," confessed the artist sincerely.

"Why are you so tired? Who repulses you? When did anyone here treat you badly? But you lock yourself up and sit at home. I don't understand, what can you possibly do at home for days on end?"

Miralamov took a key from the pocket of his jacket and unhurriedly began to open the little door of an ancient locker masked as a safe—in the theater they called it Moposh's hidey hole. From there he extracted a bottle of French cognac reserved for the most important visitors, a box of Moscow bonbons, and two crystal shot glasses and stood them on the desk.

"Well, let's sit down," he said, pouring cognac into the shot glasses. "Let's sit a while, relax."

Sadai Sadygly hadn't drunk a drop of alcohol in many months. He'd somehow convinced himself that if he drank, he'd surely cause some kind of trouble. Moreover, some kind of terrible trouble. However, the cognac he was drinking freed him here and now from that fear. A pleasant, aromatic warmth spread over his body, penetrated his soul, was absorbed in his blood. And everything around him unexpectedly became wider, freer, kinder.

And why, my God, in an Aylis long forgotten by You, did all Your mountains and stones come to life again? And, Lord, how was the voice of Aniko, gone now into non-being, able to create one more bright, living, and sonorous Aylis morning out of nothing? And why, Creator, did Sadai suddenly want so badly to praise and glorify Aniko in front of Maupassant Miralamov—to speak about the love of hard work and uprightness of the last Armenian woman to inhabit Aylis?

The passionate wish to say some lofty words to the theater director about the Aylis Armenians in general, about their marvelously creative love of hard work and never-ending faith in God, rose in the artist. However, he didn't do that. He understood there was no point in talking about any one of the Aylis Armenians to a person not born in Aylis, a person who had no conception of the ringing of bells from the twelve Aylis churches when it sounded all at once; who hadn't heard anything about the black horse of Adif Bey or the sharp dagger of Mamedaga the butcher; who hadn't once seen that yellow-rose light shining mysteriously on the high cupola of the church that might to this very day bewitch the soul of some young Aylis boy.

No, he didn't say a single word to Maupassant Miralamov about Aylis. Instead, he praised Moposh's cognac and said nice things about the bonbons. And in his soul he thought there was no purpose in persistently avoiding people. Loneliness, he thought, is death, and possibly even worse than death. And he also thought that, in any event, it was good to drink a little now and then; otherwise, it was possible to leave this life without having escaped its sticky melancholy.

After a shot of French cognac, Maupassant Miralamov's mood also visibly improved. His face cleared, and his eyes shone. But "Uncle Moposh," who was impatient to talk about the new play, didn't hurry at all to get to business. Perhaps he wished first (according to plan) to improve the artist's mood, so as to persuade him more easily later. But perhaps he dragged his feet for fear of hearing a refusal from Sadai Sadygly, whose character he knew very well. Or else the director himself wasn't certain of the artistic merits of the play sent to the theater from the Central Committee, and therefore now, under friendly conditions, it was hard for him to lavish praise on it as convincingly as he'd done more than once in phone conversations with the artist.

Maupassant Miralamov again poured cognac into the shot glasses. Sipping in small mouthfalls, he smiled, shining all over from happiness.

"Look, Master, how well everything has turned out! It seems God is favorably inclined towards me, too, although I'm not nearly the saint my best friend Sadai Sadygly is. God did all this. And Allah himself sent your shepherd here today. If he hadn't come, I might not have been able to lure you from home for another month. And how excellently things turned out with Ziyadov. What reason would I have had to phone Ziyadov if your childhood friend hadn't showed up here in the flesh? You heard how I charmed him with the name of the new First Person? Ziyadov is already prepared to finance three or four showings of our next play. And he will finance it, I'm one-hundred-percent sure of it. He's back on the horse now. He made friends with the new First Person when he worked in the Komsomol."

"But wasn't Babash a person of the former First Person?" Sadai Sadygly asked artlessly, all his thoughts focused on Jamal.

"Drink," proposed the director, nodding at the shot glass standing in front of Sadai. "It's real balm. I have excellent tea, we'll make some now." He got up, filled the electric samovar with water, and plugged it into the socket. "Stop it, for the love of God! Did the former First Person ever really want to see another living person as his equal? Who would have dared say 'I'm also a person, the son of such-and-such a man or such-and-such a woman' in front of him? With his gendarme methods he could turn anybody—if there was anything human left in that person—into any kind of beast, so long as that person humbly served him. He compelled everyone, without exception, to wear a mask on his face. How can we say now which of those people were his people and which weren't?"

Sadai Sadygly remembered how Moposh himself had bowed and scraped in front of the former First Person some ten years ago in this very office and barely stopped himself from uttering a colorful oath. He drained the cognac and stood the shot glass on the desk.

"Stop, stop, have you no shame?" he exclaimed. "You're saying this to me?!"

The artist's sudden outburst plunged Maupassant into confusion, took him down a peg.

"If not to you, then with whom can I share this now, my brother?" he said in a plaintive voice. "I'm telling the truth, isn't that so? If all of those had really been his people, then at least someone among them would have gone to visit him now at least once. But they say no one goes near him. He sits by himself in the dacha and moans and groans from loneliness."

"Of course he moans and groans, who wouldn't moan and groan?" Getting up from his seat, the artist began pacing around the room. "Those people in whose faces he spat—with the spittle still fresh—have already lined up to lick the butt of the new First Person, as you pompously name him, either from 'love' or from 'fear.'"

Maupassant wasn't able to hide his embarrassment; all the same, he collected himself and found something to answer.

"Yes, that's so, you're absolutely right. And we are like that, both I and that Babash Ziyadov. But that's really his legacy, brother mine. You know, for thirteen years we watched him convert servility into a way of life for the whole country. Can a new First Person really change anything in a couple of years?"

Maupassant even turned red from agitation. "But everything will be put to rights, you'll see, step by step everything will change."

"No, nothing will change," said Sadai Sadygly feverishly, excitedly. "And you won't do anything to hurt the former Master, as they call him to this day among the people, even if you revile him still more loudly. Now you plan to pile all the guilt for your own servile obedience on him so as to get out of that shit with clean hands. You crave a little bloodletting and are in a terrible hurry for it because you want everything immediately, and more of it, and—most importantly—without expending energy or intelligence. But, look, he reached such heights thanks to his own intelligence. And an innate passion for power supplied his energy. Yes, he composed servile hymns, but didn't you sing them in unison? And now, at the very height of corruption, when not a drop of conscience or shame remains in people, when insult and malice suffocate everyone, when lies have become so widespread it's difficult not to lose your bearings, you've found the 'boldness' in yourself to present the bill to the disgraced Master." Having fallen aloofly silent, he then continued, harshly and adamantly, as before, "But he deserves respect, if only because he had a clear life's goal, even if it was a police-strongman's goal. He was a person of living, flexible intelligence and unbelievable quickness. A person who always knew precisely what he needed. And he was damnably strong, to boot." The artist spoke loudly, and he'd already ceased being angry; on the contrary, he exulted in a restrained way.

Maupassant Miralamov sat without moving. Having known the artist well for a long time, he'd probably assumed in advance that Sadai Sadygly wouldn't go against the disgraced former Leader, wouldn't stand for singing in one choir with his new-minted opponents—that would have been against his character. But what the artist said alarmed him.

"Look at this, look at this," he muttered, dismayed. "To tell the truth, I thought as much. I knew you wouldn't swim with the current." Maupassant spoke gently and amicably, trying to appear respectable. "You endured much evil from him, but you don't want to answer evil with evil. At the same time, such scrupulousness would do you honor if we were talking now about an ordinary person who'd been undeservedly offended. But we're talking about a state official. Therefore I'm inclined to think you've succumbed to your emotions. You know you didn't think this way just two or three months ago when we were meeting a minimum of once a week in the theater."

"Yes, we were meeting," answered Sadai Sadygly, screwing up his eyes in suffering, eyes that were red from excitement. "But I had more than enough in those two to three months to clearly imagine where all this *perestroika* yapping and all this political stirring are leading the country. I'm convinced that only supremely untalented people could so talentlessly ruin the country. Do you really not see that there's no clear thinking in any one of their actions? And all of their *perestroika* is nothing more than a new weapon in the struggle for power. The people are in complete confusion, and no one believes he's master of his own fate. Everything's going to pieces and being ruined. The country's becoming a stinking swamp. A pack of quarreling dogs intoxicated with cheap freedom, competing day and night in empty, pointless chatter. A lot of water will have to go under the bridge for these insatiable talkers to want to even hear one another." The artist spoke passionately, as if he were onstage wishing to be heard in the last row. "And instead of considering and comprehending the meaning of what's happened, your new First Person and his friend from the Komsomol are hurrying to kick the former First Person in the teeth just for the trite and banal reason that when he was in power, they trudged along at the tail of power for a long time, although they received even that power from his hand." The artist again grew irritable, and excitement caught in his throat. "Yes, he collected toadies around himself and periodically mocked them publicly. But as I now understand, he did it because he knew for sure: in the depths of his soul, every toady is a potential tyrant. And in every such petty tyrant he saw a pitiful parody of himself. But all that was yesterday. And is today any better? They've turned the country into an enormous insane asylum. Even the Kremlin resembles a fly-by-night operation without a guard where self-described political wunderkinds got carried away with their schemes, driving the country into a dead end. They test the people, promising them some kind of illusory *perestroika* miracles, and what really happens? Everybody runs wild. Fires blaze all around, and a handful of sharp thugs with dull consciences irresponsibly summon people to still greater social activism. Compared to these political shits, I'm prepared to place the former First Person on the level of the greats."

Maupassant Miralamov, who knew dozens of Sadai Sadygly's monologues by heart—monologues spoken from the stage under an avalanche of applause—listened to this one, fascinated, like an experienced theatergoer. Even before this he'd known Sadai Sadygly had long outgrown being an artist, but now he was becoming a bit scared. He wasn't planning to argue with Sadai, but suddenly, it was as if he'd been stung. Gloatingly rubbing his hands, he unexpectedly interrupted the actor.

"Stop, stop! You don't think He himself planned Sumgait to get back at the Kremlin?"

"No, there was no thought of that," Sadai answered without hesitation. "Moreover, I'm absolutely certain that when the people who'd lost their heads from cheap liberty did their black deeds in Sumgait, he was sitting in front of the television at the dacha and weeping bitter tears, horrified at what third-rate politics was doing in this once-exemplary Soviet Socialist Republic."

"Well, just listen to you, my God! As if you've already forgotten what an insufferable person he was. You were just outraged in front of your fellow villager that now anyone who wants to can spread lunacy about Armenians. But you know very well the Armenians turned away from us as the result of his cunning and treacherous politics. And now you pretend none of that happened. You praise him, having decided a debt of honor and decency demands it. And you know he hated you ferociously, everyone knew it."

The artist was stunned by the insincerity of Maupassant's belated boldness.

"O Lord, save me, save me!" he exclaimed loudly. "You're lying again, Moposh—sometimes he was even in sympathy with me. He always had his own interests, I don't deny that. But he never squandered those whom the people valued and respected.

"And as far as how the former First Person related to me personally, he was guilty to exactly the same degree that I was. I lived and breathed hatred towards the system of state security organs then. I wanted to save the honor of Azeri theater all by myself —that's what kind of fool I was! It seems to me now that he somehow sensed and understood my quixotism. Because he himself was quite talented, Moposh!" The artist thought for a minute, annoyed at his fit of temper, then continued in a more restrained way. "He forbade me formal prosperity and cheap glory. He pushed me to mutiny against himself. And I very much liked the role he assigned me in that good-natured tragicomedy. You know, I've always thought it's necessary to periodically spoil one's relationship with authority in order to preserve the feeling of freedom in oneself.

In that regard, I'm prepared to consider him as my godfather."

"Aren't you aware, my dear man, that you unceasingly contradict yourself?" asked Maupassant quietly.

Lit with an inner flame, Sadai Sadygly either didn't hear his retort or else decided to let it go in one ear and out the other.

"But that was then, when I was able to find the strength in myself to get up after any blow. Now I don't have that strength. I don't understand anything now, Moposh, I swear on the grave of my mother. I confess to you, Moposh: I'm afraid. I'm constantly having nightmares, each one more terrible than the last. For a long time I've tried to not have any connection with the external world. And when I collide with it, I'm astounded at what goes on in it. People have changed to the point of being unrecognizable. It's so terrible, Moposh, that there didn't turn out to be a single spiritual authority in the whole country who was able tell people the truth, who was unafraid for his own skin. Where is our humane nation? Where is our celebrated intelligentsia? I've felt that for a long time, Moposh, and I thought about it earlier, too: even without him, the noose our former 'Dear Father' tightened around the throats of the unruly should have at some point strangled our unfortunate intelligentsia." The artist fell silent, experiencing a terrifying devastation within himself.

Maupassant excitedly leaped up from his armchair and exclaimed, "Brother, you're a genius, I swear by Allah! What a terrific monologue you've given. Only, my dear man, am I really arguing? After all, I'm saying the exact same thing."

"No, you're saying: Let's ally ourselves with yet another power-loving Master of the country. So that when he's got nothing better to do, he can come here and amuse himself with us. And you do indeed see that the place of the former Master is empty. All the people have now fastened their gaze on that empty place and with diabolical unease in their souls secretly long for the former First Person. That's where his strength lies. He left such a hole after himself that no one but he can fill it."

This time he himself poured cognac into the shot glasses with shaking hands and, hardly having swallowed, grasped the reason for his unease, which had lodged in some corner of his brain.

"I've been meaning to ask, but I forgot. You said Babash Ziyadov wrote an article. What did he write in it? Is it possible that he, too, is denouncing the former First Person?" he asked sarcastically.

"No, it seems it's not about the former First Person. On the other hand, your fellow villager really sticks it to the Armenians." Maupassant forced himself to smile. "I'll have a look now, it must be here somewhere." He got up and easily pulled the newspaper from a thick pile.

It was a long article, occupying a whole page of the newspaper *Kommunist*.

In the center was a headline composed of giant black letters: "The Vile Armenian Trail," and at the end stood the name of the author—"Babakhan Ziyadkhanly."

Even without his glasses, Sadai Sadygly could make out the phrases "ungrateful people," "treacherous people," and "dangerous enemy" highlighted in thick type and scattered generously throughout the article. He was ready to set the paper aside when his glance came across the word "Istazyn," and then, putting on his glasses, he began to read the whole article.

Before this, the artist had encountered similar appalling vulgarity only, perhaps, in trashy, pseudopopulist articles by newly minted historians and hack writers who'd fallen into full senility. It was clearly apparent from the article that Babash had read an abundance of those kinds of compositions.

According to Babash Ziyadov, the word Istazyn originally meant *usta ozan* ("master" or "preacher"), and Armenians had deliberately distorted it in converting it to their own language, allegedly to erase the traces of the indigenous inhabitants on that land from history. Those same *usta ozans*, he said, had migrated from mountainous Aylis to the land between the Tigris and Euphrates rivers three thousand year before our era—that is, the plains, the *sum er*—and created a state there that was called *Sumer* in their language, thus giving birth to an ancient civilization, now well-known under the name Sumerian.

According to "Babakhan Ziyadkhanly," the word Aylis was formed from the word *ailaj*, meaning "place of settlement." It was as if Armenians had never lived in Aylis and all the churches and the cemeteries had earlier been named *giur od* (wild flame) in the mythical "Odar" language so revered by pan-Turkists—in short, that these had been the lands of ancient Turkic peoples better known as Albanians.[4] The author argued heatedly that our "ungrateful neighbors" had altered the toponymy of the territory of Azerbaijan for the duration of all recorded history, giving it their own names. For example, they named Oderman "Girdiman," Giursa "Goris," Gurbag "Karabakh," and Elvend "Yerevan," giving out that these lands had historically belonged to them. The land called Gapuagyz (entry, gate) in the "Odar" language that subsequently acquired the name "Caucasus" in its Russified form was the land of the ancient "Ermens"—courageous Turkic men. However (he said), our neighbors took their name precisely from that word, which is how the heretofore non-existent Armenian people arose here in the Caucasus.

Babash concluded his lengthy article with lines from the poet Ulurukh Turanmekan (whose name means "the supreme being of the Turan lands"), lines well known to all and already becoming the hymn of a new time:

> *Dearer than blood, dearer than life:*
> *Azerbaijan—our home—is that pearl.*
> *Only a coward, an out-and-out scoundrel*
> *Wouldn't give blood or life for her.*

Reading Babash's nonsense, the artist's mind wandered around Aylis, street after little street, house after house, from Istazyn (Astvatsadun) to Vuragyrd, and having finished the article, for some reason he suddenly thought he'd never see Aylis again, never pass through its gardens and streets.

Before his eyes rose the solitary grave of his mother in the Muslim cemetery of Aylis. During the last week his mother had come to Sadai every night in a dream. She sat near his bed trying to speak with him, but each time she rose silently and left. Why was she silent, with what was she displeased? Sadai didn't dare ask her about it. More precisely, he couldn't—he was struck dumb before his mother. And each time he woke up, he thought that perhaps his mother was displeased and worried precisely because in his soul he so thirsted for Echmiadzin. He couldn't imagine any other reason for his mother's displeasure.

And suddenly it seemed to him that Aylis itself had never existed in the world. There had never been a Babash or a Jamal or a Lyusik. There had never been that church or that yellow-rose light that reminded him of the smile of the Almighty. And swallowing the lump in his throat, he thought that maybe even God was an invention, a lie. That He doesn't exist and had never been.

"Since when has our Babash Ziyadov become 'Babakhan Ziyadkhanly'?" he asked, his face dark. "In Aylis, one of his grandfathers was a half-educated mullah, and the other was a clown who ran a tearoom."

Maupassant smirked, looking around himself in confusion.

"Look how that scumbag has taken off," Sadai Sadygly continued. "No conscience and no shame. What the insatiable thirst for power can do to a person! That Asskhan Pussykhanly has found himself a whole arsenal of choice lies to slander his hometown, but he hasn't found one word of compassion for his very own godfather. And you know, God didn't make that Asskhan out of clay, Moposh, it was actually our Leader who made him." He sat down, devastated, enveloped in despair and despondency. "And now, be so good as to tell me: who authorized Babash Ziyadov to publish such stinking shit in the official Party newspaper, and why did he sign that shit not as Babash Ziyadov but 'Babakhan Ziyadkhanly'? What khan did he descend from? There's never been a bey or khan in the lineage of that mongrel."

"What can I say?" Moposh forced himself to say after an extended pause. "Probably they advised him to sign it that way. So they decided to do it that way."

"Who decided?"

"Oh, those at the top. Where else are those questions decided?"

"What, up there at the top they're planning to start a war? If Babash is their person why, in his article—if one may call it an article—did he so unthinkingly, like an irresponsible 'rally patriot,' pour oil on the fire?"

The director decided that the moment had obviously arrived to demonstrate his intelligence and statesmanship to the artist.

"Your naïveté kills me, to be honest! Do you really not see what these conjurers, these 'front line soldiers' screaming 'Karabakh, Karabakh!' everywhere are up to? They don't give a damn about Karabakh. Their goal is to topple the authorities and take power in their own hands.

"And now the mob on the street only listens to those who curse Armenians. What's the government supposed to do in such a situation? They also need to play the Armenian card for their own ends. That's politics, Master. And politics is a multifaceted thing." And Maupassant smiled, clearly proud of his own intelligence.

"Yes, yes, really important politics. Dear God, it's simply genius! So, the mobs got lucky again—look at all those opportunities opened up for baseness. It's possible to do any dirty trick, the Armenians will be guilty in the end, all the same." The artist walked right up to the director and looked him straight in the eye. "Now, Moposh, let's talk, man to man: if your play is dedicated to such 'political ingenuity,' then you can consider it already decided that I refuse to do it. I'm not of an age to propagandize that kind of nonsense and vulgarity from the stage."

If Maupassant Miralamov could have seen anyone else in the lead role of the play on whose success he'd pinned such great hopes, then perhaps he might have disregarded the author's request and even the wish of the leadership and fired this overly fastidious person on the spot. But the fact of the matter was that he himself could only see Sadai Sadygly in that role.

"You say strange things," he said. "Does it really become me to use cunning with you in these matters?" He dragged a folder from a drawer of the desk and held it out to the artist. "Here's the play *We Called Hell Heaven*. It's perfectly clear from the name what it's about. You yourself at one time told us all this, only we didn't have the intelligence to understand. And now, a young author has appeared, having written a play about it. In it, he creates a negative portrait of the Leader as quite a political adventurist." The director fell silent and thought for a little while. "Such a great artist as you has never received the title of People's Artist. Why? Because you always spoke the truth. You never bowed down before that political dragon. And now, a thousand times glory to Allah, everything is gradually changing. And the new First Person knows you well.

He knows you're one of the few in the intelligentsia who didn't sing dithyrambs to the Leader. So, immediately after the premier you'll receive the title you earned long ago. It's all arranged."

It seemed Maupassant Miralamov wanted to cast a spell over Sadai Sadygly. And anyone watching them might have thought the director was succeeding. Because the artist, it appeared, listened submissively and meekly to Maupassant in silence. In fact, Sadai Sadygly was just tired. Now there was no difference at all for him between the former First Person and the new First Person, Moposh and Babash, Jambul Jamal and Jinn-Eye Shaban, between fact and fiction, the truth and a lie. It seemed to him that everything around him was steeped in falsehood and corruption. And still, some kind of feeling of shame and regret that refused to be explained pitilessly pursued the artist. What did he regret so painfully? Perhaps that he'd talked too much with Moposh who, even after everything that had happened, hadn't learned anything and as of old, tried to be a lifeless backdrop of the court-party theater. Or perhaps Jamal had left that bottomless emptiness of soul in his wake—such a pathetic and practical person, not having anything in common with that yellow-rose church light and their shared childhood in Aylis. Or was he feeling so grieved and anxious because in his mind he'd seen the new face of Eternal Evil, which had acquired a new name—Babakhan Ziyadkhanly?

One way or another, after his wearisome, hours-long conversation with Maupassant Miralamov the day before that tragic Sunday of December 1989, Sadai Sadygly found himself in humiliating emptiness. And the very worst thing was that in that emptiness, even the holy altar of the Echmiadzin Church seemed to Sadai Sadygly just as dreary as the stage of their theater.

He left the theater with a dulled heart and a shriveled mind.

Dr. Abasaliev Claims That If a Single Candle Were Lit for Every Armenian Killed, the Radiance of Those Candles Would Be Brighter Than the Light of the Moon

A thick fog, enveloping the world entirely. . . .

But the world can't consist of fog alone. There's bound to be something behind it. What's hidden in fog is bound to appear soon. Sadai Sadygly knew that, and in his unconscious state he was waiting for just that.

By degrees the fog really did begin to disperse; however, the artist still was unable to understand where he was. And suddenly he found himself on cold stone pavement. And it seemed to him that he was in Aylis, sitting right there in the middle of the little paved stone street leading to the Vuragyrd Church. However, from where he sat the church wasn't visible—not even the high mountain behind the church was visible—and the artist, stricken with anxiety and fear, again attempted to understand where he was: if this were really the little paved Vuragyrd street of Aylis, then where had the church and the mountain gone?

And then, with sweet hope, the artist believed that he was already a long way from mountain and church and the Vuragyrd street and was already approaching Echmiadzin. This new happiness gripped him in precisely that moment when they wheeled him from the operating room to his room, pouring balm into his heart. Although his mind now lacked the strength to understand what was happening, Sadai Sadygly had experienced the change of place with some organ of the senses.

Only on the fourth day, close to evening, did the patient's condition become somewhat better. He wasn't yet able to speak, but it seemed he heard voices and even understood what was being said. For three days Azada *khanum* had been constantly beside her husband. Munavver *khanum* also spent the better part of the day in Sadai Sadygly's room.

And it seemed that Dr. Farzani had found a long-lost kindred spirit in the person of Azada *khanum*. He spent all his spare time in the room. Alternating between Russian and Azeri, they talked to one another on various subjects. The room where Dr. Farzani had placed the artist only four days ago had changed from a hospital space into a home where a friendly family lived.

Azada *khanum* still hadn't brought herself to tell her father about the grave condition of her husband. And while the patient was still in a coma, she asked Dr. Farzani not to disclose the full truth in telephone conversations with her father, as she was afraid it might agitate him.

Dr. Farzani didn't allow anyone except Nuvarish Karabakhly to see the patient. If it had been up to Munavver *khanum*, she wouldn't have allowed Nuvarish, either; she didn't like the fact that Nuvarish always left the room with tears in his eyes. In the nurse's opinion, his tragic pose at the patient's bedside was suggestive of mourning for someone already dead.

On the fourth day of Sadai Sadygly's stay in the hospital, significant changes in his condition began to take place. He moved his tongue, trying to lick his lips. His right hand was in constant movement. The artist was straining every nerve trying to lift it, and Azada *khanum* very much feared this; it seemed to her that he wanted to lift his hand to make the sign of the cross.

Munavver *khanum* fed the patient meat bouillon from a spoon. Dr. Farzani was pacing noiselessly around the room, sometimes stopping and, not taking his eyes off the television, thinking seriously about something. The volume of the television had been turned down; on the screen was some fleshy, round-faced man with a thick beard who'd often been onscreen recently, talking about something heatedly and waving his hands.

As a matter of fact, it was the poet formerly known as Khalilullakh Khalilov who, thanks to his verses about the Party and Lenin, had occupied a place in school readers for more than thirty years. However, in a single year those verses had been erased from people's memories along with the name of their author. Today the poet was called Ulurukh Turanmekan, and hundreds of thousands of people—not only in rallies on Lenin Square but at weddings and funeral feasts in the remotest villages—inspiredly recited his poem "Karabakh—you're my *chyrakh*" from memory. It goes without saying that Dr. Farzani knew absolutely nothing about either Khalilullakh Khalilov or Ulurukh Turanmekan. It's possible that as a doctor, he simply wanted to understand from which sources that person drew his irrepressible energy. In the end, however, he came to the conclusion that there was nothing that needed special understanding here. And two lines addressed to Armenians nudged him towards that conclusion, two lines that the poet pronounced loudly and with special pathos in concluding his performance:

> *Don't you covet my homeland,* hai,
> *We don't share land like a piece of pie.*

"Well, wonderful!" Dr. Farzani waved his hand and, walking away from the television, began pacing around the room again. "That baby with a beard probably isn't even afraid of Azrail. He thinks the day won't arrive when they'll measure out his piece of earth, too. Six feet and a half, at most, and not more than two feet wide. Then again, no," laughed the doctor, "his portion will probably be a bit bigger—his beard is exceedingly wide."

Thus, in an excellent mood, the doctor went up to the patient. He cautiously lifted the eyelids, looking attentively into the pupils.

"For now, the same treatment plan" he said. "We'll wait until he begins to recognize people and speak. We have to do everything to prevent a stroke. If he's able to avoid a stroke, with God's help he'll recover from all the other injuries. For the time being, he's far away. He'll come back when he wants to see us. And if he doesn't want to. . . ." The doctor sighed and smiled. "No, God willing, he'll want to."

Sadai Sadygly really was far away. Very far away from the doctor, his wife, the room in which he lay, and even from the trauma to his brain and the wounds to his body. In Aylis. Yes, yes, undoubtedly, he was in Aylis. However, this Aylis wasn't the one that really existed in the world but a living memory of the world Sadai had known when he was four or five, where one spring a beautiful black fox cub had come running from somewhere. Sadai saw him once on the fence of their yard. The black fox cub sprang from the fence to a tree, began to jump from branch to branch, and was lost among the green leaves. And a few days later, Sadai saw how Jinn-Eye Shaban shot that fox cub on the fence in front of the Stone Church near the spring. Since that time, Sadai had dreamed of the fox cub almost every night.

And look, now that fox cub was alive again! Springing from the fences to the trees, from the trees to the fences, he moved from one end of Aylis to the other. And God alone knows how long the little boy of four or five followed the trail of that beautiful black fox cub. He'd never seen a more beautiful animal. And there'd never been a better spring, and there'd never in the world been an Aylis more wonderful than this one. Light. Light all around. On the mountains, sunlight. On the trees, the light of cherries. The first young leaves had just appeared on the willows. The lilacs had just bloomed. What was it about that year, what kind of season was that spring? Because cherries don't ripen at the same time that lilacs flower!

And it also seemed that the fences on which that playful fox cub jumped weren't made of stone but of yellow-rose light, and that light was spilling from the walls onto the streets, the roads. All the yards that the little boy saw in Aylis were neatly cleaned and planted with flowers, and the streets were as clean as freshly cleaned glass.

Colored with that light, water was flowing in the irrigation canals, along the sides of which grew violets and iris. Rejoicing and playing, the handsome fox cub was jumping along the fences, higher, towards the Stone Church, whose cupola was turning gold under the sun's rays. The bright-green leaves of the nut tree, the cherry plum, the apricots growing along the fences and the edges of the irrigation canals were rejoicing and quivering with him. Sometimes the fox cub disappeared from view among the bright-green leaves and then appeared again. And it was in these moments—between the appearance and disappearance of the fox cub—that Sadai Sadygly, lying in the hospital bed, experienced the most painful torment.

In a nutshell, Dr. Farzani's assessment that the patient was now far away was exactly right. And the doctor was also right when he said that now it depended only on the patient himself as to whether he'd continue to live or not. If he wanted to, he'd return; if he didn't want to, he'd remain where he was. . . .

For the time being, the patient didn't want to return. The fantastical, wonderful chase after the fox cub continued. And the little boy's sole desire was to catch him, clasp him to his breast, kiss him, and stroke the head and tail of that wonderful creature. While that fox cub was jumping along the fences flooded with light and able to hide among the green leaves—alive and healthy—our artist Sadai Sadygly was also alive.

———————

On the last day of the year, the first thing Munavver *khanum* did on coming to work was to remove the patient's bandages. She joyfully told the doctor that the dislocations on two fingers, the left elbow, and the wrist had fully healed. Then Munavver *khanum* and Azada *khanum*, working together, wiped the artist's body with alcohol. Now the broken right leg encased in a cast was the only remaining physical problem. As far as the patient's consciousness, no special changes had been observed; it was still impossible to know whether he was responding to the conversations of those around him.

Azada *khanum* had earlier planned to arrange a New Year's feast in the room. She also invited her father to come from Mardakan and spend the evening with them. Because neither Dr. Farzani nor Munavver *khanum* had anyone with whom to greet the New Year.

However, although he'd promised earlier in the day to come to the city towards evening, Dr. Abasaliev later reconsidered. Long before evening arrived, he phoned and said, "I'm afraid to leave the dacha unguarded on such a day. They've turned the country into a den of bandits. I can't even count on the Mardakanians anymore."

For the first time in her life, Azada *khanum* greeted the New Year without her father. Munavver *khanum*, who lived not far from the hospital, celebrated the New Year along with Azada *khanum* and then went home. Dr. Farzani glanced into the room for a few minutes before Munavver *khanum* left and then sat in his office to wait for a call from his daughter in Moscow. Azada *khanum* remained alone with her husband and, wanting to rouse him, spoke words to him that she'd hidden for long years in the deepest corners of her heart; now, with these words, she caressed her husband like a child. But Sadai Sadygly didn't say a single word that night. Only the eyes of the artist spoke. At times it seemed those eyes laughed, at times it seemed they wept. But most often they were fixed on some endless distance—as if he were looking right at the face of the Almighty.

Early on the morning of the tenth day after Sadai Sadygly had landed in the hospital, Dr. Abasaliev unexpectedly threw open the door and entered the room. When the old psychiatrist appeared on the threshold in a sweater, dressed in a thick jacket, briefcase in hand, Dr. Farzani was washing his hands in the far corner of the room, having just finished his morning rounds. Munavver *khanum* had prepared breakfast for the doctor and laid it out on the little round table. Azada *khanum* was standing at the window and looking at the door thinking about her father, whom she hadn't been able to visit the previous week. And the patient was lying as before, smiling like a little boy of four or five, however, with melancholy reflected in his eyes. . . . The day was clear and sunny in spite of a strong wind. A stranger looking in from the outside might have thought that the patient rejoiced more than anyone else at the sunlight now pouring into the room.

Not even removing his jacket, Dr. Abasaliev threw himself on his son-in-law, kissing him. Then he went up to Dr. Farzani and heartily shook his hand, and he familiarly stroked the grey hair of Munavver *khanum*. And only after that did he remove his jacket, throw it on one of the chairs, kiss his daughter on the forehead, and sit in an armchair next to the bed.

Dr. Farzani was astounded; either he was staggered by the liveliness and dash of an acquaintance no longer young, or else it had occurred to him how psychologically healthy the professor was in allowing himself to behave so expressively in the presence of a very ill patient. However, Professor Abasaliev didn't give the doctor the chance to say a word and didn't try to understand the meaning of the secret anxiety in his daughter's eyes. With hands that shook from excitement, the great patriot of Aylis opened the briefcase resting on his knees, pulled a single page from a stack of papers covered in writing and, waving it like a flag, said with unprecedented enthusiasm, "Young man, I've brought you the wonderful Aylis of three hundred and forty years ago! And don't think these are fairy tales. Everything that's written here is one-hundred-percent true.

"At one time I told you that a certain Aylis merchant kept a diary. I saw it at Mirza Vahab's some time before the Turks destroyed Aylis. And after the Second World War, my friend from Yerevan sent me a Russian translation of that diary. I'd forgotten where I hid it, and I looked for it a long time. And think, just recently I found it among some old books. In Russian it's called *The Diary of Zakary Akulissky*.[5] But it seems to me that his name shouldn't be Akulissky but Agulissky. Because in many old books the ancient name of our town is written not as Akulis with a *k* but Agulis with a *g*. Maybe the Russians changed the *g* to *k* later. And in Aylis, you know yourself, to this day they remember that man as Zakary Aylisli. And Mirza Vahab always pronounced the name that way. And my late father knew a lot about him." Dr. Abasaliev transferred his gaze from the patient to Farzani. "Farid, he was so well respected in Aylis that even Muslims name their children in his honor!" He turned again to his son-in-law. "Young man, did you ever, in any other place, see Muslims who gave their sons the name Zakary? And in Aylis you encountered our fellow villager Zakary more often than I did. Do you remember, when we were there, how he went and bought himself a gramophone? He had all of one recording—Khan Shushinsky.

He sang 'Who Will Caress You, My Dear, Who Will Caress You, My Dear?' from morning to night."

Seeing that Dr. Farzani was getting ready to leave the room, the professor broke off for a minute. "Where are you going? Sit, listen!" And when the surgeon sat down, he continued, "He wrote in the diary that he was born in 1630. See, that Aylis Armenian recorded everything with German precision, including the day and hour of his birth *on Sunday, the day of St. Gevorg, in the second half of the day.*" He pulled still another sheet from his briefcase. "And here's how he began to trade: on March 5, 1647, at age seventeen, he left Aylis with a bale of silk. *Today I, Zakary, am leaving Aylis. Holy Spirit, help me! If I see anything interesting anywhere, I'll write it in my notebook. And if anyone beholds lies in my writing, may the Holy Spirit enlighten his reason.*

"Notice he doesn't say 'give him reason' but 'enlighten his reason.' How noble that man was! Now, pay attention to the route his travels took: Yerevan, Kars, Erzurum, Tokat, Bursa, Izmir, and later Stambul. And he always writes not 'Stambul' but 'Stambol.' His first journey lasted ten months; at the end of December, he returns to Aylis. After that, where didn't he go? Greece, Venice, Spain, Portugal, Germany, Poland, Holland. . . ."

Azada *khanum* poured her father a little hot tea in place of the cold.

"Drink just a glass of tea," she said. "Your Armenian merchant isn't running off anywhere."

"I already had tea. You know I only drink tea once a day," Dr. Abasaliev answered his daughter angrily, and in that same angry tone he continued, "Do you know how much misery those sheikhs, khans, and sultans brought Aylis?! Here, listen, I'll read: *July 10, 1653, Aylis. Today Aga Liatif, the deputy of Sheikh Abbas, arrived in Aylis. He wrote down the names of sixteen young boys and girls on a paper but didn't take anyone with him. This time God spared us.*

"And how many misfortunes Sheikh Suleiman, the successor of Sheikh Abbas, rained down on Aylis! *Someone by the name of Gagaiyz Bey arrived in Aylis today from Yerevan on the order of Safikuli Khan. He led thirty horsemen with him. By order of the sheikh, they had to collect one thousand tomans from the inhabitants of Aylis. There was no limit to the bribe taking, oppression, and violence. They subjected more than one hundred people to torture and hung thirty-five people. But even after all that suffering, the people could only collect 350 tomans in all.*"

Not only had Dr. Abasaliev translated the diary from Russian into Azeri— the diary of that Armenian merchant who'd been born three hundred and forty years earlier in Aylis and who'd traveled the whole world—but it seemed he'd learned the whole text by heart. The extraordinary memory of this person who was already more than eighty years old struck Dr. Farzani. He followed his colleague attentively and heard him with growing interest.

"*Today Khosrov Aga arrived in Aylis and announced to the people that he'd been named ruler of Gokhtan. He led many people from Merga, Shorut, Legram—* that's what they called Negram earlier. *How they mocked the rich Aylis land-owner Ovanes. They sat the poor fellow on a donkey and had him carried all around to the sound of the zurna. Then they took one hundred tomans from him and let him go.*"

Dr. Abasaliev sorted through the papers in his briefcase for a short while. "Just think, young man," he said. "Can you imagine, on July 22, 1669, snow fell in Aylis! And in 1677 there was not a drop of rain from the third of June through the end of August. And in May of 1680 such a downpour broke out that it washed away all the houses by the river. And later there was such a drought that nowhere from Nakhchivan to Tabriz was there water, not even to drink. In 1667 more than two hundred children perished from smallpox in Aylis. In 1679 there was such a strong earthquake in Yerevan that walls cracked in the houses and churches even in Aylis. Zakary Agulissky lists all the churches in Aylis. The Vang Church is the church of Saint Foma. You know that. Vuragyrd is a corrupted form of the word Vardakert, and the Vuragyrd Church where you and I walked is the Church of Saint Christopher. And the church we call the Stone Church is the Church of Saint Ovanes—it seems it was built during Zakary Agulissky's time. Or else it was restored during that time and reopened on November 5, 1665. That's what it says in the diary."

Again Dr. Abasaliev rummaged for a while among his papers. "*January 4, 1668. Today there was an earthquake in Aylis. . . . February 26, 1668. Today a comet appeared over Aylis in the western half of the sky. It foretells misfortune for our sins. . . . December 21, 1668. Archimandrite Petros, head of the Monastery of Saint Foma, commanded that the monastery be enclosed on all sides with a tall fence. They are using river stone and baked brick to construct the cupolas and bell tower. Master builders arrived from Kurdistan—*at that time the Turkish regions of Van, Bitlis, and Diyarbakır were called Kurdistan. *The interior walls are being faced with stone. Water is being conveyed to the monastery. God grant strength to all the builders.*"

Dr. Abasaliev was no longer looking at the patient; one after the other, he pulled pages covered with writing from his briefcase and read them with strange passion, as if for himself.

Understanding that this might go on for some time, Munavver *khanum* tried to interrupt. "But, Doctor, people are writing all over the place that those churches aren't Armenian but Albanian. They say the Armenians claimed them later. Perhaps your Zakary wasn't Armenian but Albanian?"

It seems that Dr. Abasaliev didn't want to take even a second to raise his head and look at the nurse. Not lifting his eyes from the paper, he exclaimed, "You're talking complete nonsense! If someone calls himself an Armenian, how can I say: 'No, you're not Armenian? You're an Albanian or a Lezgin, a Talysh, a Multanets.' It's true that the language of the Aylis Armenians differs a little bit from the language of the Yerevan Armenians. And a difference is noticeable in the writing. But you know, in our Ordubad every Muslim village speaks its own dialect. You'd never confuse people from Shaki with those from Baku—there's so much difference in language, character, and customs. It's the same way with Armenians. I don't know who those Albanians were or where they lived. But I do know that the people in Aylis were Armenians. Moreover, the very best kind of Armenians.

"Yes," said the doctor, again addressing Farid Farzani, "after the Arab invasion—from the eighth through the thirteenth centuries—there were Turkish and Tatar-Mongolian invasions and the Oghuz and Seljuks. Then, for almost three centuries that land was the arena for bloody wars between Iran and Turkey. One group arrives, kills, then the other arrives, kills. If a single candle were lit for every Armenian killed violently, the radiance of those candles would be brighter than the light of the moon. The Armenians endured it all, but they never agreed to change their faith. Those people were worn out and tormented by violence, but they never stopped building their churches, writing their books, and raising their hands to the heavens, calling on their God."

"And what else can a people who lack land do? Just stay put, call on the heavens!" answered Farid Farzani, chuckling quietly.

Dr. Abasaliev pulled out yet another sheet from his stack. "*October 7, 1651. Tabriz. I arrived in Tabriz with my brother Simon. The ruler of Tabriz, Aligulu Khan, wanted Simon to convert to the Muslim faith. Only God saved us from that great misfortune.* That's how piously our Agulis natives believed in their God, Farid. You know, Aligulu Khan was prepared to shower Simon with gold if he'd agree to accept the Muslim religion." He looked at the patient, who was smiling continuously, smiled broadly and heartily himself, and continued speaking with his earlier fervor. "The Armenians had a wild poet—Yegishe Charents—who was purged in 1937. They say that restless merrymaker and great lover of strong mulberry vodka once joked quite wittily, 'We didn't let them cut one pitiful piece of unnecessary skin from a certain place, and it gave them a remarkably slick excuse to cut an entire nation to pieces.'"

There still remained a half-hour until the patient was administered his regular round of medicine. However, Azada *khanum*, recognizing that her father was going to continue reading the diaries, walked towards the bed and began to make signs to him; she meant, It's time to leave the patient in peace. And once again, the doctor paid no attention to his daughter's worry. He pulled a new page from his briefcase and, waving it, said, "And what's written here, young man! Look, on November 10, 1676, Zakary Agulissky writes: *I, Zakary, planted a large, spreading plane tree in the yard of the Church of Saint Ovanes today.* It seems to me there wasn't any plane tree there by the Stone Church. But maybe one does grow there, I've forgotten: you know better than I do."

And at that moment Sadai Sadygly's eyes suddenly opened unbelievably wide, and he muttered with shaking lips:

"Chesh-me-se-din! Ech-ma-echmaz-za!"

Those were the first sounds resembling a word that he'd spoken the whole time he'd spent in the hospital bed. But only Azada *khanum* was able to understand that they meant "Echmiadzin." And understanding that, she couldn't help herself: sobbing loudly, she burst piteously into tears.

"Papa! Papa!" she said through sobs. "He still can't speak, Papa! He doesn't know anyone. And you talk, talk, talk without stopping."

Dr. Abasaliev instantly turned white. As if he were a person who'd been suddenly awakened and was trying hard to understand where he was, he looked at the patient and then in turn at Farzani, at Munavver *khanum*, and at his only daughter weeping uncontrollably.

"But he said something just now," said the professor, looking with piteous inquiry at Farzani.

"Yes, it seems he produced some sounds. He should have spoken long ago. But for some reason, it's taking a long time."

"Clearly, he has a heavy kind of amnesia. Why didn't you say anything to me earlier?"

"Well, you didn't let us open our mouths," answered Dr. Farzani with a bit of friendly reproach. "You were far away, you ran off to Aylis three hundred years ago and didn't even notice us!" Dr. Farzani laughed and then asked in a more serious tone, "Doctor, were all those people really in Aylis?"

"Of course they were! In those times people lived in Aylis who were the equals of gods. They channeled water, planted gardens, hewed stones. Those Armenians, both artisans and traders, went around and visited hundreds of strange cities and villages, earning money bit by bit just so they could turn every shred of earth of their little Agulis into a heavenly place. Ever since the

Turks departed at the end of 1919, leaving Aylis in ruins, to this day the Muslim population looks for gold in the ruins of Armenian homes. Even when they plow the earth to sow crops, they hope for—look, look!—pure gold to turn up under their feet. The same gold that helped the Armenians extract water from under the earth and hew carriage highways from all directions in the mountains. They built a weir. Along the banks of the river, they erected a parapet from hewn river stones. They paved all the streets with choice river cobblestones. Over time, twelve majestic churches were also built in Aylis with that gold. Perhaps a ton of gold was spent on each of them."

From his faraway world, the patient gazed at Dr. Abasaliev with unceasing astonishment. This person seemed to Sadai Sadygly like someone he knew, and the artist was trying with all his might to remember who he was. The women waited impatiently for the end of the conversation about churches, monks, and Aylis.

Munavver *khanum* spoke about the patient's condition. "His wounds healed quickly, Doctor," she said, addressing Abasaliev. "There was a dislocation in one arm, several fingers were dislocated in several places, but over four or five days everything healed. And the knee fracture isn't dangerous. He moves his toes easily. His system is still young and will mend quickly, God willing. There could have been complications after a concussion. You know that better than anyone. And ten days is a long time, Doctor. In that amount of time, the patient should at least have been able to speak. Perhaps he should be sent to Moscow before it's too late. Farid Gasanovich and Azada *khanum* think so, too."

"It's amnesia in the form of confabulation. In psychiatry we also call this Korsakoff's syndrome. Did you conduct an angiogram?" Abasaliev asked Dr. Farzani.

"A craniography was done yesterday. We don't have angiography equipment." Dr. Farzani was silent a little while and added, "Munavver *khanum* is right, it would be better to send him to Moscow."

"And what did the craniography show?"

"Nothing good," answered Dr. Farzani, and after a little thought he added, "I noticed a small tumor in his brain. Perhaps it's an old tumor, it's hard to say now. At the moment it's very dangerous to move the patient; it's necessary to wait a little while. However, I don't think we'll be able to manage this without Moscow." Glancing at Azada *khanum*, he hung his head guiltily.

For a little while, no one uttered a sound. Dr. Abasaliev broke the silence, communicating one more piece of unpleasant news.

"Azia, did you hear what that Nuvarish did?"

"No, what did he do?"

"They say he threw himself off a balcony."

"Who says that?" whispered Azada, her voice shaking.

"Women were talking in the bakery in Mardakan. And I myself heard about his death three or four days ago on the radio. But I didn't know he killed himself."

"So that's why he stopped coming here," said Dr. Farzani.

"Allah rest his soul," muttered Munavver *khanum*, her whole body rocking sorrowfully.

Dr. Abasaliev, who that morning had appeared in the room inspired, left the hospital completely changed around noon and went home to Mardakan.

And Sadai existed as before in his faraway world. Now the little boy following the beautiful black fox cub was at the top of the hill that divided the upper and lower quarters of the village and not far from the Stone Church nestled up to the slope of the mountain that was a little rose-colored in the rays of the sun. The air was full of the thick, bitter aroma of the leaves of the nut trees mixed with cool water, because the green branches of the walnut trees from all around leaned towards the height where he stood. The sound of the water seething in the stone reservoir beneath the Stone Church resounded far and wide.

And the beautiful black fox cub kept jumping between the green branches. The little boy was afraid to lose sight of him, but at the same time he wanted a drink. His brain was burning with thirst. And the cool water running loudly in the ditch laid of stone and coursing into the little stone pool was attracting him to itself like a magnet. But fear of losing the fox cub wouldn't let him go near it.

Then he saw the fox cub spring from a tree to the stone fence and continue his journey. The little boy rejoiced: now he could come closer to the ringing water. He put his palm under its resilient stream. However, not a single drop of water landed in the little boy's palm. He didn't feel the slightest coolness, quite the opposite—he was enveloped in nauseatingly hot air. The little boy thrust his head into the ditch to cool his burning brain. But here, too, nothing happened—even that energetic water couldn't cool a brain engulfed in flame. At precisely that moment, fear enveloped the little boy, fear he'd lose sight of the black fox cub forever. And just then a shot rang out. The whistle of the flying bullet burst like molten lead in the artist's ears. Trying to understand where the shot had come from, he gathered all his strength, and lifting his head, in place of the stone fences woven of light he saw the ordinary, grey fence molded of clay of today's Aylis and the scarlet blood of the wonderful, furry, coal-black fox cub of his childhood flowing across it.

Blood was still flowing across the fence when the hum that had for a long time roamed like a swarm of bees through the chinks of the cracked walls of the Aylis churches rose like a black cloud in the sky, mixing with the sound of the shot.

Before closing his eyes forever, high, high under Heaven, on the slope of the tallest mountain of Aylis, he suddenly saw the Vuragyrd Church clearly—the "Pigeon Bazaar." And he finally understood that there was nowhere further for him to go.

On Friday, January 12, 1990, evening approached.

Crying out frightening slogans about freedom, independence, and Karabakh, Ulurukh Turanmekan had led a neurasthenic crowd of unmarried women through the streets all day. Now, towards evening, he conducted yet another rally by the Armenian church located next to the Parapet. Khalilullakh's assistants had already been trying for more than an hour to set it on fire. However, the church simply didn't want to burn, and it was this circumstance that especially enraged the unmarried women-patriots surrounding the poet.

In the hospital car, Azada *khanum* and Munavver *khanum* conveyed Sadai Sadygly's body to the mosque for the ritual of washing.

Not having been able to save the patient from stroke, the sad and miserable Dr. Farzani sat in his office, for the first time feeling himself alien and transitory there. Mentally bidding a final farewell to Baku, that evening he waited for the call from his Moscow daughter with especially thrilling hope and especially anxious worry.

The clouds of black smoke coming from the windows of the church near the Parapet became thicker and thicker, mixing with the black night of January 13, 1990, which smelled of blood.

At home in Mardakan, Dr. Abasaliev knew nothing about any of it yet.

And the pigeons spending the night in the Aylis churches still slept peacefully and dreamed pigeon dreams.

Aylis, July 2006
Baku, June 2007

A Fantastical Traffic Jam

A Novel-Requiem

*I dedicate this to my seventy-fifth birthday,
which has not coincided with the best of
times for my fate as a writer.*

*No matter in whose hands power lies, my human right to look at it with a critical
eye remains.*

—Maksim Gorky

This work is not about SOMEONE but about SOMETHING. To be precise, about glutinous regimes that devour themselves.

In a theoretical country that we'll call Allahabad, the highest authority of that kind of regime is embodied by fictitious personages who do not have proto-types in real life.

PART ONE

inexplicably frightening

In this chapter we'll ask the reader to pay special attention to the words "progress" and "pluralism," which entered the lexicon of my Allahabadians after the word "AIDS," and which for all leaders-for-life of rich, oil-bearing countries became even more terrible than AIDS itself.

I

Was he dreaming or not? The situation in which Elbey found himself was so unexpected and unbelievable that he couldn't decide that simple question for himself. It seemed that the air around him had disappeared, and its place was taken by fear: enormous, thick, and dark, like a swamp of hopelessness. Until now, Elbey had experienced something similar only in the sort of dream people call *garabasma*: a black vision, a nightmare! And it really was as if he were submerged in unrelieved darkness—the darkness of fear, or the fear of darkness. And as if it were the sensation of hopelessness that before had seized him only in dreams, an echo of older—but not yet healed—wounds of memory now came to him, mixed either with the fear of that darkness or with the darkness of that fear. And it seemed to Elbey that everlasting time had frozen for all eternity: died, gone missing, vanished in the mysteries of an infinite black nightmare.

Perhaps even God himself didn't know how long Elbey fidgeted in front of the door to his own office—the office of the chief of Operations Headquarters, which took up the whole seventh floor, the serpentine corridor of which ran exactly eleven hundred yards long. That seventh floor was located, strangely enough, in the luxurious Seat of Power, which had only six floors; that fact didn't surprise anyone, however, just as no one was interested in the long name of that invisible, enigmatic organization, which from afar gave off the aroma of a splendid bouquet of lies: Operations Headquarters for the Restoration of Fountains and Waterfalls in the Name of Progress and Pluralism.

Elbey had absented himself all of two hours on business, after which time, as usual, he'd taken one of the seven elevators of Operations HQ to the seventh floor of the six-floor building and had already paced here for eleven minutes now. During this time, pulling a heavy bunch of keys—it weighed over two pounds—from the pocket of his black leather coat, he'd put the key to his own office into the lock a great many times. And after every unsuccessful attempt to unlock the door, his understanding dulled, his brain refused to obey him: it wasn't possible that he could confuse the key of his own office with some other one if every day for eleven years, several times a day, he'd opened the door with exactly that key!

Although he didn't think for a second that the lock might have broken all by itself, he checked to see that it was undamaged, just in case. And the next second he tried to convince himself that during the two hours of his absence it wouldn't have occurred to anyone to change the lock. Finding a little consolation in that thought, Elbey looked up and discovered that *not a single light* shone along the whole, eleven-hundred-yard corridor of Operations HQ. At that instant the black, cold breath of the grave that was wafting along the floor touched Elbey's face. He experienced all of this as if in delirium. Rooted to the ground in horror and sinking still further into the mysteries of the unknown, he stood by the door of his own office as if struck by lightning. The limit of his self-delusion appeared to have been exhausted. Elbey felt like a hunted fox. Breaking loose from its hiding place—where it had been concealed up till now—fear materialized with lightning speed and demonstrated its palpability, turning into a certain, terrifying person. At that precise instant, Elbey finally understood that none of this was a dream. "My grandmother Gushver, these are *his* tricks," he muttered, wiping the sweat from his face with his sleeve. "Mother Eizengiul, my little son Anar, my little son Elgiun, my little daughter Giunel, you should know: it looks like a certain person has gotten even to me."

It's possible that Elbey, by mentioning his nearest and dearest in that terrible moment in a voice trembling from fear, was trying to convince himself that he wasn't alone in the world. That's why there's no need to search for anything mystical here. He'd seen his grandmother Gushver and mother Eizengiul for the last time a minimum of forty years ago. During that period he'd sometimes remembered his grandmother, but only when he was pursued by humiliating fear did he remember his mother. And at those times, she always appeared in his memory in the exact same place, in the exact same way, in the same red dress, with that same resigned, guilty face. . . . It had been hot, the very hottest summer day in the world. And Elbey's mother—

young, beautiful, grey-eyed Eizengiul—looked at Elbey shyly from that hot day with that infinitely sad smile on her face. The *Rais* was also there. Naked to the waist, he stood next to the young, beautiful, grey-eyed mother of the young Elbey and toweled off his sweat with a large bath towel. That day, Elbey had left the sheep in the field and run home to drink *ayran*. "I also dropped by to drink some *ayran*," said the *Rais*, putting on his shirt. Elbey both believed and didn't believe his words. He drank some *ayran* and left his mother turning pink—stunned either from the heat or because of something else, looking timid, as if begging pardon for something—and ran off. (Well, we'll also stop the reminiscing at that and continue our story.)

When fear, finding human form, looked at him with the impassive eyes of one raised from the dead, Elbey came to himself a bit and realized that he was in his own workplace—but at the same time, he realized it was no longer his workplace. However, he didn't rush to leave. Maybe he was trying then and there to ascertain whether the Chief intended to give the order for his arrest. Although if he'd been in a condition to think straight, it wouldn't have been difficult for him to understand that the Master of Fear was not intending—in any case, not yet—to arrest him. By sending Elbey off on an assignment, the Chief, with his characteristic caution and cunning, had undoubtedly decided to erect a new order in the Headquarters for Restoration of Fountains without any unnecessary fuss: "Drive out there, get the Old Dacha in shape. Take a look at how things are there. Pay attention to cleanliness, the furniture. If anything's lacking, come and tell me. Don't hurry, I'll give you two hours. If need be, take longer." Had Elbey been just a little more quick-witted, he'd already have understood from the senselessness of the assignment that black clouds were thickening above his head. Really, what did the Old Dacha matter to the Chief? Last year they'd fully renovated the place, and they'd changed the furniture already this spring. Last summer the King of Fear and Treachery had planned to spend a whole ten days there during the very hottest weather; however, he didn't spend even a full day there before returning to the New Dacha. For what reason, now, in the cold December days, would he remember about the Old Dacha? And why, in receiving such a senseless assignment, had Elbey not dared to question it?

He heard the voice of his wife Giulara—it echoed painfully in his brain—and Elbey, his whole body shaking, began swearing to himself. Lately it had only taken one sound of that voice to spoil Elbey's mood for the entire day. And now it suddenly seemed to him that it was precisely his wife's voice asking, "Listen, where are you?" that had been the beginning of misfortune. With exactly that question she'd begun all her telephone calls with him, even twenty and thirty years ago. She never said hello, that bitch, never asked about his health. "Listen, where are you? That drunk has disappeared again! If only he'd arrive just once at the agreed-on time to teach the child. Find him, send him here! Do you hear? Fine, make it quick!"

Not once—from the very first night of their marriage—had they ever conversed normally, like people; there'd never been normal family relations between them. Not ordinarily suffering from masculine weakness, Elbey had been unable to satisfy Giulara's passion on their first night. And with that night, the primacy of his wife was confirmed. For forty years of wedlock—not in bed, not in the bath, not in the kitchen, not in the garden behind the bushes, not in the forest behind thick trees—driving Elbey to exhaustion, Giulara had never attained satisfaction with him.

And now, for more than a year, they'd each lived on their own. He had dachas in Sosnovka and Chisty Prudy, and Elbey lived in Sosnovka almost year-round. But Giulara was never drawn to the dacha. She hated the sea. She preferred her city home with its third of an acre of garden plot to all the dachas in the world.

Both of Elbey's sons and their families lived abroad. Anar's office was in London, Elgiun's in Frankfurt. The sons usually came to their homeland once a year for a short time. They'd spend three to five days in Chisty Prudy and hurry back. Only the daughter, Giunel, and her three children, who'd been born at one-year intervals, bore the tyranny of Giulara. The daughter also gave birth to two sons and a girl. And as soon as the last was born, Giulara, without saying a word to Elbey, drove her son-in-law from the house. Now all Giulara's irrepressible energy was directed at raising her grandchildren. She intended to make her granddaughter a great composer, one grandson a great poet, and the other grandson no less great an artist, goals on which she spent all her burning, ill-tempered energy. "That drunk has disappeared again!" By the term "drunk," she meant the teacher of the middle grandchild, the well-known poet Giuliumjan Janday, who appeared twice a week to give the boy lessons of poetic mastery. Janday spouted rhymes, told his pupil interesting stories about well-known poets, and if he was in good shape—that is, only slightly drunk— he sometimes even played the *saz*, sometimes the *tar*, and with pleasure sang songs consisting of his own words, a lot of them set to music by the country's best composers.

In their passion for drunkenness, the other tutors—a composer and an artist—didn't differ much from Giuliumjan Janday, or as Giunel called him,

"Jynda" (Slutty) Giuliumjan. And from time to time they also disappeared, "off drinking and whoring," as Giulara put it. And then the voice of his wife, filled with malice and bile, persistently followed Elbey over the course of the day, driving him to trembling and poisoning his mood: "Find him, send him here! Do you hear? Fine, make it quick!"

Understanding that today's tragedy would be as annoyingly excruciating as Giulara's voice, Elbey left the door of his own office and decided to check whether his keys would open the other locked doors of Operations HQ. He tried the locks for seven of the seventy-two keys in succession, beginning with the door that sported the label "Human Rights Are the Principle of Humanism" and ending with the door labeled "Laboratory of the Soft-Hearted." Behind the latter door, under the banner "Glory to the Creator of the New Fatherland!" most of the weapons of a burst of patriotic joy were preserved; they gave off a sickly sweet scent that reminded Elbey of the scent at the bottom of his grandmother Gushver's trunk. All those doors opened. From that fact, he came to the conclusion that the operation had been carried out only on his office. After that, he grew a little calmer. His soul filled up with a strange pride mixed with burning sadness. "Ah, burn in the flames of hell, Eizengiul, mother mine! So, he hasn't decided to arrest me. Then what's he going to do with me?"

And hardly had he thought this than it was as if a thousand suns had lit up overhead, all at the same time. The whole eleven-hundred-yard corridor of Operations HQ was flooded with bright light and began to flash alarmingly with multicolored lightbulbs, and at that moment the national anthem began to sound. A door that until then hadn't opened for anyone emitted a whistle like a hedgehog and slowly dissolved. From the Department of Emotional Balance, an unknown person of between thirty and thirty-five entered and, with a confident, proprietary step, moved unhurriedly towards Elbey.

The violet-colored suit fit him as if it were brand new. The yellow-rose tie was reminiscent of an iris covered in dew. With a courteous nod of the head, he resembled an all-knowing, cultured, well-brought-up member of the Council of Europe who was well aware of his own worth, but with the lightly screwed-up eyes and official smile of the General Secretary of UNESCO. Glancing at that smile, it was impossible to doubt his love for the Glorious Allahabad Party, love that had cost at least fifteen thousand dollars. And it was impossible not to remember that star of the stage, the singer Balababash Jangiulium, who (if one believed evil tongues) received that very sum—fifteen thousand "greenbacks"—in a sealed envelope for every performance of a song glorifying the leader ("You're the same age as the sun, but you shine brighter").

And now that many-faceted person approached Elbey with enormous respect, glanced briefly at the bunch of keys Elbey held, extended his hand, and shyly said, "If you please."

Elbey placed the keys in the visitor's palm—the visitor who'd evidently only just come to him directly from Brussels or Strasbourg—then reached towards the holster for the pistol to which he'd become so accustomed over thirty or forty years that he didn't even feel its weight (more precisely, the weight seemed to him no heavier than a comb or handkerchief); he was preparing to hand that over, as well. However, the Euro-intellectual guest stopped him. "No! No! What are you doing? What are you doing?" he said smiling, this time in a colder manner, but with his former remarkable politeness painted with all the colors—no, no, not of the rainbow but of the national flag of the best country on the planet, headed by its immortal leader, who was the same age as the sun. And then, smiling, he added, "Please, there's a car at your personal disposal."

At that exact moment the lights went out. And to the sound of Balababash's song about the leader and the sun, the world plunged into darkness.

II

Elbey's official car stood in its former place. However, in place of his customary driver, another driver sat at the wheel. A Russian. A young man. Catching sight of Elbey, he jumped out of the car with the grace of a leopard throwing itself on its prey. And as if expecting that Elbey would speak to him in Russian, without giving him a chance to open his mouth, he said in pure Azeri, "I'm your new driver. My name is Kolya." He threw open the back door for Elbey and just as quickly returned to the wheel himself.

Elbey couldn't bring himself to ask about the fate of his former driver. Poor Mamed-aga, his former driver, escaping from Elbey's chest as a tortured sigh, began to withdraw from this world into some kind of otherworldly unknown—a place of uneasy fear, fear that filled all the living and unliving. As if from the depths of the underworld, the voice of Mamed-aga spoke when the new driver started the engine: "They arrested me, Master." And the days spent with Mamed-aga—days that would never come again—stood before the eyes of Elbey like some kind of heavenly vision. He woke from his reminiscences only after the car had already left the city limits. He looked around, but he couldn't figure out where he was.

"Where are you taking me?" Elbey asked in a shaking voice, and for some strange reason he heard the voice of Mamed-aga instead of his own.

"We're going to your dacha in Chisty Prudy," answered Kolya in a gentle voice, smiling broadly and speeding up a little.

"But I actually live in Sosnovka—" Elbey almost moaned, again in an alien voice, and thought with horror that he'd probably never again speak in his own former voice.

"Those are my orders. We're all soldiers here, you know. We have to follow orders."

"Who gave you those orders?" Elbey recognized the senselessness of that question; nonetheless, he asked another one, even more foolish. "Why didn't they take my pistol?"

"I didn't receive any instructions about the pistol. But they said the order about Chisty Prudy was given by some kind of DIV or DAV, I don't remember which, exactly, I'd never heard that word before. They gave your dacha in Sosnovka to the new chief. And they transported all your personal belongings to Chisty Prudy. Your two cars—the Mercedes and the Series 3 BMW—were left in Sosnovka. But they didn't take away this Mercedes S class. If they'd wanted to take it away, they wouldn't have changed the license plate."

Sitting in the car, Elbey didn't consider casting a glance at the license plate. But what he'd heard from Kolya had no effect on his mood. He very badly wanted to sleep through the current night, through tomorrow—until he got enough sleep, he wouldn't rouse himself from this nightmare. And then he'd think about the Master's reason for such a cruel deed. Freed from the most deeply settled internal deposits of black fear, he'd be able to sort out what, precisely, might have spurred the Leader to such a treacherous decision. Up until this extremely unlucky day, today, nothing of the kind could even have entered Elbey's head. Just three—yes, all of three—days ago the Master himself had telephoned and called Elbey to his office. "Come over, we'll shoot the breeze," he'd uttered in a tone of endless exhaustion.

"Have a seat. How are things?" The Master glanced at Elbey's red tie. "A wonderful tie. From London or Frankfurt? Only don't fib, tell the truth."

"It's from Turkey," answered Elbey honestly.

"You're lying, you wouldn't wear Turkish ties." He got up but didn't allow Elbey to rise. "Sit!" He walked to the window and stood with his back to Elbey. "What's with this weather?" he complained and returned to his place. "You know, of course, that tomorrow a large gang of foraging *farmazons* will arrive" (that's what they called foreign guests of all stripes in the Seat of Power: singers, writers, journalists, congressmen, athletes, and even the first personages of several states who had a base habit of receiving more than they gave). "We have reliable descriptions of all of them. Several have indicated the desire to promote our interests themselves. You see how it is: one has to bend over backwards each time to worthily meet and greet these insatiable idiots. Did we really live this way before? Then people had, at the very least... a conscience." He sat, grey, aloof, worn out with the ailments of an old person. Following his thoughts somewhere in the distance, he slid his gaze along the wall and over his own portrait and then with the deepest seriousness looked at Elbey. "They all profess the same faith, these *farmazons*: they take, and while they're doing it they never forget to put on the appearance of devotees."

Saying this, he devoured Elbey with his eyes as if, in place of the person he'd known from age nine or ten, there sat an unknown individual, and he was trying to figure him out. This behavior seemed extraordinarily strange to Elbey. He'd known about the *farmazons* for a long time. "Beggars" of a similar sort arrived in the capital just about every day, and he knew very well what it meant to "worthily meet and greet" them. The question could only be about which category of "worthy meetings." And only the Master himself defined it, from one hundred thousand up to one million, sometimes more. The principles had been established long ago. The mechanism was well-defined. If anything unpleasant ever happened, then it was only at the very start, mainly from mutual misunderstanding, sometimes from the stupidity and dimwittedness of some "congressman." Sometimes one flew into a rage, mistaking gifts for bribes. But later, thank God, they all came to their senses and became our people. They understood that every nation has its own customs and traditions that all who step on its soil must observe. In the end, "that pack of impotents, political scoundrels, and fakers"—as the Chief put it—from Europe and America understood things and figured out how they needed to conduct themselves with a hospitable people who possessed an ancient culture and with a country flowering inside its own heavenly borders far from planet Earth under its own bright Sun.

Thereafter, no further difficulties existed. Everywhere, now—from UNESCO up to the very bottom ranks of the UN—they knew (undoubtedly thanks to the Master's efforts, to his high intelligence and inexhaustible energy) that it was necessary to treat the ancient Allahabad culture with particular respect. No one understood that better than Elbey. One phone call from him had always been enough to properly greet any single, even a hundred *farmazons*. But what was happening now? Why did the Master call Elbey to his office for such ordinary matters?

"Come up with ten million—how long will that take?" he asked, glancing at Elbey with his supershrewd eyes.

"No time at all." Elbey jumped up.

The Head of the Main Building laughed loudly.

"Sit down, sit down!" His voice suddenly changed. "This time you're not going to give anyone a command. Bring it from your own money, what you're hiding at home. Of course I know you're loaded with money—where do you keep it?"

At home Elbey had secured approximately ten-and-a-half million. At first he wanted to deny it, to insist he didn't and couldn't have that kind of money. But, not for the first time, sensing the Master's invisible omnipresence, Elbey immediately understood that any excuse would bring nothing but trouble. It even seemed to him that the Master knew precisely that he kept exactly ten-and-a-half million at home.

"Yes, sir, *Ra*—" began Elbey, leaping again to his feet, but he stopped short, not saying the word *Rais*. He turned bright red, rooted to the spot with some kind of terrifying foreboding.

However, the Master liked the fact that Elbey had turned red, that he hadn't begun to spin some nonsensical story about his official honesty, and that he'd uncomplainingly acknowledged he had the money. Satisfied, he placed both hands on the desk. Even his withered, unsmiling lips trembled a little, and his eyes grew moist, freed of their former terrible impressiveness. He picked up the phone and said to the secretary, "Bring us some tea." Not taking his eyes from Elbey, he smiled. "These days I often remember my younger years. Believe me, in such moments the world becomes lighter." Having stunned Elbey with such unexpected candor, with his right hand he began to gently stroke his left, which was clenched in a fist.

Then he started to complain; he said what an unhappy person he was, that he'd had to traverse all the circles of hell until he'd achieved his current situation. He said that he'd had to fight his whole life with scoundrels and cheats for justice.

"I fought for a cultured, worthy, honest life for all my people, Elbey," he said with pride, continuing to scrutinize his listener intently. "But where, where is this honesty?" Staring at the glass of tea standing in front of Elbey, he fell into thought and then, lifting his head, carried on such a conversation that Elbey thought: Real, living jinns must work for this person.

"You're far too attracted to gold. I know. By the way, I've known for a long time. Your heart melts when you see gold coins. You come to life, you immediately light up. You dance the *Shalakho* from happiness. Don't worry, I don't hanker after your gold. Well, how much do you have? I'm guessing you've been able to collect five hundred pounds?"

Elbey didn't know exactly how much gold he had. But hearing these words from the Master, he there and then believed he had exactly five hundred pounds of gold. Maybe the Chief even knew where he kept the gold, he thought with fright, and had known for a long time. All of it was hidden at the Chisty Prudy dacha next to the sauna, behind the marble tiles of the swimming pool. Elbey had devised a completely unimaginable safe for it—even the most expert jinn wouldn't be able to find the door. If only the Chief didn't ask about the place where the gold was hidden! In that case Elbey would have to admit it without fail. For the present he was certain that no one other than himself knew about his treasure trove.

"I haven't weighed it," he answered, trying to hold himself together. "Fine, since you say it, let it be so—five hundred pounds. And all of it's yours, to the last ounce, I swear by the Creator."

"The Creator? Who are you talking about? Ha-ha-ha, he-he-he, ho-ho-ho!"

Elbey had never before seen that the Master laughed in such a terrifying way—putting his hand to his heart, asthmatically wheezing and groaning. His face reddened from laughing; tears appeared in his eyes.

"Tell me, Elbey, be a man, who created you?"

Poor Elbey, white as a corpse, wanted to say, "Allah," but he said, "You. You created me. Who would I be without you?"

"Fine, stop it! Enough! You've really made me laugh today. I don't even remember the last time I laughed so hard." Pulling out a handkerchief, the Chief began wiping his eyes in a leisurely way. "Let's say we've established how much gold you have. And who can weigh your diamonds?"

Elbey had more than once seen how the Master invited highly placed individuals to his office and amused himself with them in similar fashion. After such amusements those same individuals left either dead or alive. People close to the Master's office always turned away immediately from those who left *dead*. And they said about those who left the office *alive*: "He passed the exam," or "He crossed the bridge of hair."[1] On this day Elbey himself had to leave the office *alive*, no matter the cost. Because he understood quite well: leaving *alive* would be more precious than any diamonds or gold.

"On birthdays you always receive presents worth fifty to one hundred thousand. It's well and good. Don't be afraid. I'm simply asking out of interest: where do you keep those expensive things? They don't keep you from sleeping peacefully at night?"

"Sometimes, Ra—" Damn it, he'd almost said *Rais* again. "You're absolutely right, they are expensive gifts. But, in fact, I don't keep those things myself."

"Then who keeps them?" The Master asked, no longer hiding his anger.

"I just re-gift them—on holidays, birthdays. There are lots of occasions. Two sons, two daughters-in-law. Also Giunel and her three children. And Giulara herself loses her mind over diamonds, you know that well. She doesn't even let me glance at those expensive gifts. She snatches them up and keeps them herself." Elbey felt how his face was taking on a plaintive expression. As a matter of fact, that's exactly what happened; diamond rings, diamond earrings, diamond bracelets, diamond necklaces—in Elbey's opinion, all that had been created for women since the dawn of time. But now, in saying Giulara's name, he was pursuing a different goal. For Giulara was a close relative of the Master, his first cousin, the daughter of his father's sister. Elbey wanted to mollify him a little with that fact. "We're relatives," he wanted to say. "What belongs to me belongs in equal measure to your cousin."

"You, what, allow your wife to walk all over you?" Truly softened, the Master said these words very differently. In general he had a habit of changing roles as things went along. "Fine, go. Take the money *there*" (where *there* was, Elbey knew very well). "Come back and report to me." Elbey hadn't made it to the door when he was stopped by the Master's voice: "Listen. I need to know something from you. It's said that they've stuck me with a new nickname? You must know what it is."

"No, I swear to God! I haven't heard." In Elbey's head reality was getting confused with devilry.

"Well, how can that be, that you haven't heard?" the Master persisted, raising his voice. "Some pederasts, syphilitics, dirty dung beetles, parasites, idlers, impudent scoundrels, and destitute swindlers call me 'the DIV' and you don't know?!" He banged his fist on the desk as he always did when reaching a final decision, and a menacing expression of unpredictable intent froze on his face.

Elbey stood rooted to the spot, waiting for something even more terrible, something only comparable, perhaps, to the end of the world. The horror lay not only in the fact that he hadn't shown the necessary vigilance, hadn't informed the Master in time about his new nickname, but in the fact—and this was still worse—that in his terrible confusion he'd clean forgotten the intent of that simple word that meant fairy tale monster, strong man, sorcerer, and ogre, a meaning that was well-known to every milksop who'd just once in his life listened to any kind of old wives' tale.

And to think a person's mind could go blank like that! As if Elbey, who'd lived a whole sixty-six years on this accursed earth, had just then—around three days ago in the office of his Chief—heard that word for the first time. And right then, after it had provoked an attack of rage in the Chief, the true meaning of the word *div* came to him. And even after that, for a long time Elbey wasn't able to figure out who among the people known to him had thought up that moniker—at first glance an ordinary one, but one that reflected the character of the Master and his thoroughly satanic doings with devilish precision.

Later he thought of Faramaz Farasat, the drawing tutor of Giunel's youngest son—the one whom Giulara planned to make into a great master of the brush—who was, at a minimum, as good an artist as the current pride of the nation, Fatekh Faragat. Faramaz Farasat was a comparatively young artist but also well enough known in the country and no less famous in elite circles as an unsurpassed chatterbox and clown, good at all vulgar amusements. In his anger Elbey was even mentally able to send the court jester-artist to you-know-where—but then he suddenly remembered Nizam Shamistan, who'd once worked as an operations informant for the KGB and now, in his old age, from complete and unrelieved idleness had set out to become an academic. The Operations Chief had a good basis for suspecting Shamistan—it was certainly a proved fact that the ancient stool pigeon and newly minted academic had authored seven anecdotes in just the last half-month in which the *Rais* had been richly endowed with spit and mockery. That fellow had so flooded the country with his anecdotes that his fame had reached the minister of defense himself, the glorious commander of the strongest army on earth. And the minister had flown into a rage at the former Chekist, at first nearly sending his best tank division after him. Though the minister later reversed himself, he produced the following philippic in a rapid-fire burst (still not having dowsed the flames of his own anger) at one completely secret conference dedicated to the re-equipment of NATO's army with the newest Allahabad-produced rockets: "He's not an academic but a stinking swamp of gossip, and his gossip plays into the hands of our historical enemy, to the advantage of all Armenians and all non-existent and never-existing Armenia from sea to sea . . . fuck it!"

For the fact that that "stinking swamp of gossip" still hadn't been drained and thrice plowed over, Elbey himself was guilty. For some reason he pitied the veteran informer, that exceptionally hardy representative of the formerly powerful KGB. Elbey had lingered and lingered in informing his own Chief about Shamistan and consequently putting an old man behind bars to whom not long remained before he'd naturally and eternally lie down in a warm and cozy grave. It's hard to believe, but it was precisely then, when the grave with the body of the academic appeared before Elbey's mental gaze, that he—up until then blinded by fear—found his sight anew. In his memory petrified by horror, it was as if a magical explosion took place: something had been lit up like a match, and his brain was illuminated. Elbey finally remembered where, when, and from whom he'd first heard that nickname—"the DIV." He remembered to the minutest detail in what condition and even in which voice Faramaz Farasat had said it. And it had happened three weeks ago, at approximately nine in the evening, at a banquet in honor of his very own—Elbey's—birthday. At first Elbey had broken into a cold sweat at the insolent tricks of the artist, who'd become drowsy from vodka. He progressed to a fury and was ready to teach the impudent fellow a lesson, smash him in the mouth, and throw him out of the banquet. But then the sharp-tongued Giunel came to the aid of the artist. With hot women's candor she began to persuade her father that the conversation, she said, was in no way about some terrible *div* with a tail and horns who only thought about how to gobble up more living people. She said it wasn't even a word but a funny abbreviation of three words, moreover, three very good ones. They didn't in the least offend the acknowledged worthiness of our *Rais* but, on the contrary, would open yet another bright page in the life of that person who was talented in all things. "Papa, listen, just two or three days ago our Faramaz accidentally found himself near some kind of water main that supplies all the fountains of our megalopolis with water. And there, can you imagine, was He, himself—the Creator of the new Fatherland! And our maestro Faramaz saw with his own eyes how warmly our glorious plumbers, people who do heroic labor, toilers of a clean and proud profession, love the Master. They all looked so fine, so imposing—just like English lords. They conversed openly, sincerely, joking and laughing with the Father of the Nation. One of them even clapped the Master himself on the shoulder two times. And Faramaz, always clever in thinking things up, came up with a witty nickname for the Master—'the DIV,' which stands for 'Defender of Invaluable Vocations.' It's really quite amusing, right, Papa? Only, for heaven's sake, don't think there's any kind of insult hidden there. Invaluable— that means solid, important, worthy!" In a word, a lot of nonsense, complete rubbish. It was understood: the tipsy hooligan had decided to lightly tease the chief of Operations HQ Progress. But if it hadn't been for Giunel, Elbey wouldn't have forgiven the court artist that "brilliant invention" for anything. What can you do? Feminine cleverness turned out to be stronger than official duty, not for the first time. Elbey fell into the cunning, interlacing web of his beloved Giunel and, instead of teaching a dangerous joker a lesson, laughed from the bottom of his soul. He even nodded cheerfully to Faramaz Farasat, affectionately clapping him on the shoulder.

But Elbey wasn't certain the *Rais* had acted so cruelly with him for that particular treachery. He also wasn't certain that ill-omened nickname had originally been thought up by Faramaz Farasat. It was entirely possible that authorship lay with someone else and that Faramaz, through his own ingenuousness and inclination to brag, had simply presented it as the fruit of his own matchless wit.

Elbey wasn't surprised the word was able to make its way around town, but who in the Seat of Power might blurt it out, what's more, in front of a simple driver? Was it possible that some bold spirits had appeared there who'd stopped fearing the Master himself?

* * *

Elbey knew no fewer than a hundred measures by which his Master had abruptly changed the fortunes of people. That superman had long been convinced that the country belonged to him unconditionally. All the keys to power were in his hands, and no one doubted that he kept a list of names of all the residents of the state in his head. But, however paradoxically, he felt himself fully master of the situation only when he succeeded in discerning something low and mean in a person. In that country abounding in luxury and woe, submerged in a quagmire of secular prosperity, gasbags of various styles, toadies, and sponges of all stripes distrusted and feared one another but, most of all, each of them feared the Master. And he was able to appear differently in different situations and, in the confines of some two to three seconds, completely change his aspect. He possessed a remarkable ability to bide his time. And no one knew that better than Elbey. However, this time, three days ago, for some reason Elbey hadn't succeeded in using his brain in time to draw the necessary conclusion from the conversation with the Chief about *farmazons*. In fact, it was the first time the Chief had arranged the sending off of foreign guests by such a strange method—not at the expense of government agencies, like always, but at the expense of the person who was closest to himself in the Main Building. And Elbey—who until this time had never believed even a single word of the Chief—for some reason on that day believed his every word, accepted them as the highest truth, infallible in their rightness, like the chapters of the Quran. It might be because God had bestowed on the Master the special gift of persuading people. Or perhaps it wasn't a matter of any special gift; in fact, "to believe while not believing" was a daily requirement for every worker in the Seat of Power, their main responsibility. But, clearly, Elbey had lost his sense of reality and wasn't able to comprehend the Master's intentions in time.

"Always believe what you don't believe! Never believe what you believe!" That "philosophical maxim" was deeply imprinted on the brain, stomach, liver—on every organ of those who lived and ate at the expense of the Main Building. Otherwise, why on earth would Elbey, not having taken the trouble to think for a second, have sat exactly an hour and forty-five minutes in the Master's office just staring at him and blinking stupidly? And then he'd gone joyfully rushing around for money. And now just think about what happens to a person in that corner of the earth frozen with fear!

III

Elbey understood that ruin was breathing down his neck, but he didn't know exactly what the Chief was going to do next. His position was changing with such rapidity that from moment to moment he forgot what he'd just been thinking about. He wanted to question the driver, but he didn't have the heart for that. The road from the city to Chisty Prudy had never seemed so long to him.

He felt his eyes closing, but he wasn't aware of when he fell asleep. Elbey dreamed of a road, but it wasn't the road to Chisty Prudy. It was the highway that stretched through the fields in his hometown, the village of Giulliukend. The main road was located fairly far from their home, but he knew that road extremely well because his grandmother Gushver was constantly selling something or other there.

Gushver went out to that road early in the spring when herbs suitable for sale came up in the fields and mountains. She cut and collected bunches of longleaf, white swallow-wort, shepherd's purse, salsify, coltsfoot, mint, edible primrose, violets, and willows and carried them bright and early in the morning to the highway, close to the din of cars rushing by. Then the various berries and fruits ripened: sweet cherries, cherries, white mulberries, black mulberries, green cherry-plums. Then apricots and peaches and ripe cherry-plums came into season. Apples, pears, and quince ripened in the fall. And right up until winter itself, so long as it didn't snow, she left early in the morning and returned late in the evening.

Sometimes Elbey helped his grandmother; he clutched the heavy pail of apricots and cherry-plums or lugged a bag of green beans on his back. In the fall, when it got dark early, Elbey went to fetch his grandmother to help her return home. If sales were good, Grandmother hummed contentedly on the path home, rejoiced, laughed, and talked. She sang the only song she knew (and it appears she herself had made it up): "When she gave it up to him, night was dancing 'neath the window. . . ." One evening (was there ever really such an evening?), it had already begun to get dark; while waiting for Elbey, who was supposed to come for her, Grandmother saw a yellow spot on the asphalt in the middle of the road. When she went to see what was shining there, the yellow circle suddenly spoke in a human voice: "I'm a golden coin," said the circle. "Whoever finds me and takes me will possess exactly twenty-five pounds of gold." That night the joyous Gushver gave the coin to Eizengiul. "Protect it like the apple of your eye," she said. "If I die, sell it and give Elbey a luxurious wedding."

With regard to death, Gushver *arvad* had guessed right—she wasn't fated to live until Elbey's wedding. And not a year had passed since her discovery of the coin when—on the side of that same asphalt road, where she sat cross-legged on a mat under which was spread dry grass—Gushver *arvad* (according to her very own words) "was tenderly kissed on the buttock by some kind of shitty insect," either a sunspider or scorpion or black-bottomed flying ant. The spot of the "kiss" swelled overnight, turning into a wound. It grew red, blue, and black. And no kind of healing herb helped Gushver. Cursing both God and the devil, showering all her male and female kin with colorful language, the unfortunate Gushver was tormented over the course of four days and four nights before she died. Besides the found gold coin, she left behind a great number of one-ruble notes, three-ruble notes, and five-ruble notes that had been preserved in her always-locked trunk and her one and only line, the poetic expression of her eternal sexual thirst: "When she gave it up to him, night was dancing 'neath the window. . . ."

Now, dozing in the car, Elbey saw that same asphalt road. And he dreamed of the spot of yellow light right there in the middle of it that was in some ways reminiscent of a gold coin, in others of a ripe cherry-plum. He stretched his hand towards it, but the spot didn't stay in one place; it slipped away from him as if it were a stray sunbeam. It made Elbey devilishly angry—no matter how hard he tried, he couldn't pick up the gold coin resembling a ripe cherry-plum from the ground! He wanted to cry from frustration, and his heart was just on the point of jumping out of his chest.

Barely opening his eyes, he lifted his hand to his heart; it trembled like a wounded bird. And the first thing he thought about was that it was a good thing he'd hidden the gold not at the Sosnovka dacha but at Chisty Prudy—after everything, how could he possibly go back to Sosnovka for his hidden gold? However, his joy didn't last long. Black suspicion arose in his soul and immediately supplanted gold-yellow joy: who knew, maybe the staff jinns of the *Rais* had long ago sniffed out the place where the gold was hidden and it had been gone a long time already. . . . It felt unbearably stuffy to him; his woolen shirt was soaked. Elbey glanced at the road. The car had only just left the city.

"Listen," he yelled at the driver, "Go faster! What kind of driving is this?"

"Chief, I'm going over eighty," Kolya answered, smiling genially.

Elbey cast a glance at the speedometer and relaxed a little.

"You said, I think, that this DIV commanded that I live in Chisty Prudy. Who do you mean? Who is this DIV?"

Kolya reduced his speed slightly.

"I don't know, Chief. They just told me that the DIV ordered it. Maybe not DIV but DAV. Something like that. But the devil knows, maybe I just heard it that way."

"Who said that to you?"

"It was the first time in my life I'd ever seen that person."

"Was he wearing glasses?"

"No, no glasses."

"Was he tall?"

"No, short. I think with a moustache."

"In a general's uniform?"

"No, he was in civilian dress."

Elbey realized the interrogation wouldn't lead anywhere.

"Well, fine, drive," he said, lost in thought, his voice trembling slightly, looking through the car window at the darkened, ill-omened sun sinking behind the horizon.

When Kolya climbed out of the car and with difficulty opened the metal gates of the dacha, a strange smell—heavy and sickly—overtook Elbey, and immediately the deep sadness of infinite loneliness fell on him. Here everything looked like it was the eve of creation. It was as if time had frozen for good. The silence emanating from the depths of the garden evoked a new spasm of fear in him. With all his skin Elbey felt the enchanted depths into which he'd been cast by the wave of a single finger of the powerful DIV.

"Firdovsy, hey, where are you? Are you asleep? Drunk again?" Elbey looked all around in search of the caretaker. But there was no sound of him. From the other end of the yard, the plaintive howl of Hercules reached him, sounding like a child's wail. (It was Giunel who'd named the German shepherd Elgiun brought from Germany three years ago, still a puppy. And later she thought up two additional monikers, Hera and Hero. Elbey liked the name Hero, and that's what he called the dog.) "Here, Hero, come here, stop whining!" he said, flinging open the door of the room where the caretaker lived with a strong blow of his foot and, seeing that Firdovsy wasn't there, froze on the threshold.

"That means the gold—" thought Elbey, feeling the dull pain of fear penetrating every vein. Because that was the sole reason Firdovsy could have been kicked out of the dacha. Later Elbey would understand that a thorough search for the hidden gold had been conducted at the dacha. Then he understood that the DIV's staff jinns, his dacha goldseekers, would have been inconvenienced in finding the hiding place by the presence of the caretaker. But by what means, exactly, had they removed Firdovsy from the dacha? Did they arrest him, kill him, or simply say, "Get out of here, find yourself a new job!"?

Elbey felt sorry for Firdovsy. As a matter of fact, he had reason to feel sorry. If not for the caretaker's periodic drinking, Elbey would have valued him much higher than his former driver Mamed-aga; Firdovsy understood everything from the first word, was capable of gratitude, and looked after himself when he didn't drink or when he limited himself to his own "permitted" two shots. In "good times" (those times, according to Firdovsy, were up until 1990) he'd finished his studies at the institute and taught in his native village. And later (meaning when "nothing came even of teaching") he'd turned up at Chisty Prudy in search of his daily bread. At first he'd looked after the dacha of a solitary, aged professor for fifty dollars a month. But when Firdovsy's reputation as a good person and capable gardener came to Elbey's ears, he bargained for a whole month with the professor until he got his way and made the village teacher the caretaker at his dacha. Only rarely did he see Firdovsy, but he carefully ensured that the caretaker received his agreed-upon salary of five hundred dollars punctually because Elbey knew: with that money Firdovsy supported not only his own family but also helped his numerous kin.

"Don't look for him, Chief. He's not here," the imperturbable Kolya announced at last, attentively observing Elbey's actions.

"And where did he go?" Elbey shouted at the top of his voice, indignant at the omniscience of his new driver.

"He left, Chief. Went home to his family, his children."

"Fine, now it's time for you to take yourself home." Elbey pulled one hundred dollars from his pants pocket and held out the money to the driver.

The driver jumped back as if he'd been slipped not money but a live, poisonous snake.

"No, Chief, my orders are different. I've been told to stay here," said the offended Kolya, and his voice began to resemble the voice of Hercules, who hadn't stopped plaintively calling his master.

Elbey, who was dreaming of just one thing—to get rid of Kolya and check whether the gold was in its place—fell into a rage.

"A shit-eater told you that! Both he and his father!"

He patted down the driver to check whether he had a weapon on him.

But he didn't discover anything except a cell phone. Without returning the phone, he took Kolya by the collar and threw him out of the gates. Then he locked them and stood several minutes without moving, breathing heavily and pouring with sweat—and came to himself. But then it occurred to him that there might be other people in the dacha.

He turned on the car's headlights and, continuing to pour with sweat, checked the yard thoroughly, all the dark corners beneath the very high fences, behind every branch. Then he thoroughly examined both floors of the two-story house, noting to himself the cleanliness and order in the house. Only after that did he proceed to the covered swimming pool with a sauna located at the far end of the property and, with shaking hands, turn on the light. And here everything had been cleaned, washed, the swimming pool was full of fresh water—that picture sent chills down Elbey's spine.

The hiding place with the gold was located by the inside of a metal staircase attached to one wall. In order to reveal it, it was necessary to unscrew the risers connecting the steps with the floor, then lift the steps and, lightly touching one of the covering marble tiles, pull it out. And that's it—there's your very own gold!

Elbey nearly died as he hurried up to the staircase. And once he reached it, you'd have thought that he really had died. One of the screws was out of place. The second had been unscrewed but then more or less stuck back in place. Having already lost ten million, he didn't doubt anymore that he'd also lost the gold. Tears streamed from his eyes. He understood that there was no point in lifting up the stairs.

IV

Arriving home only at eight-thirty, the Master immediately sat down to eat. Breakfast and lunch for him were, in his words, "hasty affairs." He ate with pleasure only in the evening. And only in the evening did he drink a little cognac, which he preferred to other alcoholic beverages.

But today the Chief was hopelessly tired and didn't want to eat anything.

"What's hot?" he asked, looking without interest at the cold appetizers sitting before him and the tall, lean Ashpaz frozen in front of him with a foolish smile on his lips.

"There are dolmas. There's chicken *soyutma*, *basturma* cooked on the *saj*, there's *plov*—everything one could want."

Ashpaz reached out his hand to pour cognac for the Master. But the Master covered the shot glass with his palm.

"There's no need, wait. Apparently there's a kind of vodka called Beluga, you must know it. You've tried it, surely?" he asked in a mortally tired voice and, suffering from boredom, added, "Bring me a bottle, I'll try it."

Ashpaz quickly brought the vodka, but when he wanted to pour it into the shot glass, the Master once again covered it with his hand.

"Not here, pour it in a wine glass. We'll taste this 'beluzhka' that the people shower so much praise on." He drank the contents of the glass in one swallow, dipped lavash into the *qatıq* seasoned with garlic, and directed it towards his mouth. The bitter vodka spread sweetly through his body, warming every cell. In a twinkling exhaustion disappeared, and a blush rose in his cheeks. "That's excellent!" he said, straightening up sharply, like a snake preparing to strike. "Why didn't you say anything about it before?"

Ashpaz could do nothing except give his customary, foolish smile.

"Speak up, how long have you been drinking this?"

Ashpaz hadn't yet tried that vodka, which had appeared in the city only a few days previously, but he understood very well, as did everyone in the circle of the "Defender of Vocations," that if you want to keep your head, it's better to lie than tell the truth.

"I've tried it a couple of times. I ordered it just in case—you usually don't like vodka. You always just drink cognac."

"You're lying!" The crystal wine glass rattled from his roar. "You all lie to me! What the hell's going on with you people? Who's making you lie to me?"

"What hot food should I serve?" asked Ashpaz as if nothing had happened. For a long time now he'd borne all humiliations without complaint.

"Just bring what you want to. Did you say there's chicken? For now, bring it."

Ashpaz disappeared into the kitchen. The Master filled his wine glass a second time himself. But he didn't drink it. He again dipped lavash into the *qatıq* seasoned with garlic and began to chew slowly, recalling his last conversation with Elbey. Smiling, he thought, "I wonder what he's doing now. Most likely sitting and drinking, or already sleeping, or maybe calling who knows where and talking the devil knows what nonsense. It's impossible! Impossible to leave him unsupervised!" Suddenly his smile went out. "That scoundrel knows too much. It's a good thing he's a coward like a fox—greedy, naïve, and a blockhead. He's absolutely not dangerous so long as he doesn't do anything stupid."

By the time Ashpaz brought the food, the Chief was already calm. His face had cleared, a healthy light shone in his eyes, and the usual devils were dancing a polka.

"Perhaps also some *plov*?" asked Ashpaz. "I prepared a sauce from veal they delivered today from Kellekend. The meat's tender, like chocolate."

"What else did they bring today from Kellekend?" Kellekend was a little green settlement that, you understand, might be found either in the South, or the North, or the East, or the West, located somewhere in the boundless geographic expanse—wherever you please. It was the unforgettable place of the youth of our Father of the Nation—who now resided in the aureole of power—where the mountains smelled of thyme and wild mint, the foothills were fragrant with anise flowers, and the meadows by the banks of mountain streams shone with the colorfulness of nature from the beginning of spring until late autumn. There was a time when many people named their daughters after various flowers and now and then even contrived to gather the names of all flowers in a single girls' name—Eizengiul, for example, which means "all flowers" or "continuous flowering." Although many years had passed since he'd first found himself far from his hometown, he always remembered its clean air, blue sky, and the mountains smelling of thyme and mint. And he, who believed in neither God nor the devil, religiously believed in the taste and the benefit of everything that grew in the fertile soil of Kellekend. Meat, butter, cheese, honey, even pickles and onions were brought to him only from there.

However, the Chief's question "What else did they bring today from Kellekend?" put Ashpaz in a difficult position because the Master had never before asked him that.

"What would you like?" he asked, bending double so that with his own six feet of height he almost reached the Master's ears.

"Did they bring *chashyr*?"

"*Chashyr*? We do indeed have *chashyr*. I put some on the table." Ashpaz moved the plate containing the herb closer to the Master.

At the sight of the *chashyr* the Master chuckled, either because up until that moment he hadn't noticed it or because he remembered his late grandmother Bedimshakh—to this day he remembered the taste of the fresh *chashyr* she boiled in water and then fried in butter.

He ate quickly and with pleasure, trying to sit straight, head held high, and holding the fork in his left hand and the knife in his right, as was done among cultured people. The chicken was eaten swiftly.

"Fine, let's have *plov*," he said. "Somehow my appetite has been awakened. It's true what they say: for a good appetite, there's no bad food."

Ashpaz, nearly dancing from happiness, brought the *plov*. The Master again drank the wine glass of vodka in a single swallow and set to the *plov* with relish. Ashpaz, certain the Chief was satisfied with today's dinner, resolved to make use of the occasion, and he began in a roundabout way, in the sweetest of voices, "Today there was a huge sale of agricultural products in the city. Our oldest daughter also went to get some things for home. Coming back from the bazaar, she phoned and made me very happy. Two pounds of mutton cost three *manat*; beef was two-fifty, chicken two. And they were selling fruit for next to nothing. The girl spent all of seven *manat* and brought home a whole basket of food. 'Papa,' she said, 'the people are very pleased with our government. Everybody said prices had never been this low before.'" Seeing the Chief's glance fixed on him, Ashpaz faltered.

"Hold on, now, Tray, where's this, you say, that prices are so low?" asked the Master, laying the spoon on the plate and wiping his lips with a paper napkin.

Of course, the experienced Ashpaz knew very well: to gratify the Chief, it wasn't enough to hastily concoct any old kind of pitiful lie—the main thing was to lie with conviction, persuasively, ably, and professionally. In a word, so that the lie acquired a new composition of absolute truth, just as happens in a chemical reaction.

"It's that cheap everywhere!" he said confidently and with such a look that it was as if he were prepared to fight the Chief with his fists in the name of that unimpeachable truth. "Is anyone really going to deny that the people live much better today? To do that, you'd have to be without a conscience, or morals, or honor!" Ashpaz was even prepared to curse obscenely but contained himself. "Yes, there are some spiteful critics, I don't deny. That gang of mercenary parasites spreads dirty rumors as if in our country the law didn't command you but you, yourself, personally, commanded all the laws. That's despicable slander, the malicious invention of the opposition." With those words the extremely agitated Ashpaz concluded his speech and then and there hung his head, having stamped the petrified smile on his face.

The Master chuckled lightly, ran his index finger along his slender moustache, and again assumed a serious look. He kept people—even those who were near him every day—at a distance. To that old faker blinded by vanity, both truth and lies were equally distasteful. But all the same, he preferred lies to truth. Because it was easier for him to understand people deceiving him for their own advantage, and he could never grasp why people had to tell him the truth.

"Fine, Tray, have it your way," he said, having the ability when necessary to demonstrate leniency and even goodness, and having thought a bit, he uttered his favorite aphorism, which the cook had heard a minimum of three hundred times (although to this day he didn't understand the meaning that the all-powerful and all-knowing Chief put into the saying): "If you want to be first, don't stand in any line." And then with a satisfied sigh, he added, "I liked today's dinner. And the vodka turned out to be good. What do you think, perhaps I'll have tea? Yes, yes, tea with thyme and mountain mint."

The lanky and happy Ashpaz went to prepare the tea with that exact same smile frozen on his face. While he was there the telephone rang in the kitchen. Someone was calling from the city. It was Ashpaz's daughter, the one who supposedly had been at the market today witnessing the whole nation's joy. "Papa, Papa, the bazaar is in an uproar, Papa! Such high prices, it's an utter nightmare. Two pounds of mutton cost eight *manat*, beef seven-fifty, and chicken six. And the price of fruit rose so much, Papa! Apples are going for four *manat*. Potatoes and cabbage—"

"I'm extremely busy, daughter," Ashpaz answered, his voice shaking with fear. Replacing the receiver, he took the teapot and rinsed it with boiling water, continuing the conversation with his daughter to himself. "He knows about everything, daughter. He's aware of it all. That man never does anything without a reason, my own. And those high prices, believe me, he arranged that himself. He wants to test the degree of the people's stamina in order to find out how much more the people can take of him!"

Ashpaz was a good deal older than the Master, but he looked much younger than the Master did. He remained the same straight and trim person as in his long-ago youth when he'd worked as a waiter in the district capital, where there wasn't any place to eat besides the single public cafeteria. And he'd received his improbably funny nickname "Tray" then, in that very same small-town district capital, for his super-measured precision in serving clients and, more exactly, for the fact that he unfailingly served not only bread and hot food but even an ordinary salt cellar to clients only on a tray covered with a snow-white napkin.

Here, there, and everywhere he carried himself with dignity. But he did it with the face of a frightened child. While still a youth he'd delivered lunch every day with that same face (on that very same tray covered with a snow-white napkin) to the offices of various important individuals, beginning with the first secretary of the district headquarters and ending with the editor of the local newspaper, *Glorious Allahabad*, according to a strict schedule.

Later he worked simultaneously as head chef and director of the dining room. But he retained the face of a frightened child. Throughout his whole long life it didn't once come into his head to shake off the servile obedience that with time had turned into his second nature.

It's said the Lord God doesn't have laws on how a person should live in the world. When it comes to our Ashpaz, he hadn't even thought about how he lived in the world. He simply didn't have time for that. Since his youth he'd gotten up at dawn. He received deliveries for the cafeteria. He himself always boiled and fried all the food for the leadership and delivered it himself to the various impressive offices as before. Other than that, he loved to read books. He spent all his free time on reading and, afterwards, in thinking about what he'd read. There was one particular book, *Sword and Quill*, from which to this very day he prudently had never parted company, knowing his Chief valued it highly.[2] It was his own sort of self-defense; in every other respect he showed himself to be a creative nature and an extraordinarily clever person.

He was taciturn like a tray and imperturbable as a buffalo. Even though at one time he had been chief of the district trading organization, he still took lunch to the Master in his office with visible pleasure, prepared excellent Isfahan *plov* for him at home on holidays, and grilled *shashlyk* from pheasant and young wild boar for his guests on the bank of the river in the shade of a weeping willow. And even more important, he was a great master at holding his tongue, which was a character trait useful in the highest degree and made our Tray the eternal companion of the Master.

But Ashpaz wouldn't have been Ashpaz if he'd even once experienced the slightest degree of sincere feeling with regard to the Master. He remembered every minute that to co-exist with him was a hellish torment and to breathe the same air was a severe test. However, he bore everything without complaining, as if he'd become accustomed to living without air.

The Master didn't live himself and didn't allow anyone in his close circle to live. He was able to rape human will; those who surrounded him were able to somehow exist only by obeying the instinct of self-preservation. These people, it seemed, didn't differ from one another even on the outside. They worshipped only those who ranked directly above them and precisely because it was impossible to sort out who was for whom and who was against whom. And they never doubted that the Master knew them better than they knew themselves.

The Master's ears unfailingly detected whatever power needed at one or another critical moment. And power revolved around the axis of its Master as if it lived on its own—separate from the country and the people, like something invisible and unreal, however, in fact, more than real. Sometimes even the Master didn't manage to fully grasp the meaning of what he intended to do, as his wish was already being fulfilled with lightning speed.

Returning from the kitchen with tea, Ashpaz couldn't believe his eyes: the Master, who'd reclined in the soft armchair, slept sweetly. During his whole long service to that person, he'd never seen him sleeping. Now the Chief slept like a mere mortal, freed of any trace of impressiveness and grandeur.

Bending double, Ashpaz placed the tray on the table in front of the Master with the greatest caution and then, lifting his head, looked at him again and almost shrieked from surprise: Lord, how mightily the sweetly resting Master looked like his father! And to think it had happened to omniscient Tray— who'd seen hell and everything else—to live long enough to see before him the simple, provincial barber who'd died a thousand years ago now suddenly resurrected in the person of the Great Man!

Ashpaz almost jumped out of his own skin from unexpectedly cascading emotion, and he had only one remaining wish: to dash off out of the Chief's sight as soon as possible and withdraw to some secluded spot and begin to tell the endless prayer beads of his own, always heart-stirring, memories.

V

The Master's father had been known by the simple name of Piri, which was extremely common in his hometown. But the local people (were they one people?), having a special passion for salty language, had awarded him the heretofore unprecedented nickname of "Piri Preputsy."

The meaning of the word *preputsy* is unknown only to those of other faiths. No one, not even a person just learning to talk, can rightfully call himself a Muslim if he doesn't know that *preputsy* signifies the foreskin.

Piri's main work was to shave and cut people's hair but, besides that, it was precisely Piri's fruitful razor that turned many generations of boys into Muslims. The father of the current Defender of Invaluable Vocations not only clipped, shaved, and circumcised, he also had the ability to pull aching teeth firmly and with lightning speed. It goes without saying that Piri's multifaceted activity had to find a reflection in folklore, for example:

> *His pliers—from Tsar Nikolai's time long ago.*
> *His razor—a gift from old Noah.*
> *He never said morning prayers before vodka.*
> *Such was the Piri Preputsy we knew*
> *And his wife Baji* khanum *Gold Tooth.*

And this:

> *One p... cost fifteen pounds of wheat;*
> *From that wheat, his wife baked bread.*
> *He had the conscience of a sack of p... s,*
> *Piri cut the p..., hung it on a twig.*
> *He got what was owed and took off, Uncle Piri.*

Even those of other faiths likely know how slippery folklore can be. It follows, of course, that there were a few exaggerations in these "specimens of folklore." For example, in writing the line "He had the conscience of a sack of p...," the collective folk author exceeded the acceptable level of impertinence. Because the expression "a sack of p..." in our native provinces implies people who've strained themselves, that is, who are suffering from hernias. Our own Piri never suffered that kind of weakness. And also the line

"Baji *khanum* Gold Tooth" is, to put it mildly, composed of lies; Piri *kishi's* wife, Baji *khanum,* had all of one gold tooth in her mouth, and the other thirty-one were her own, white and healthy. But (what's true is true) those simple teeth constantly envied the gold one and, precisely for that reason, were in future to turn yellow and then black, so it ended badly for all thirty-two combined. But with regard to "hung it on a twig," the honest folklorist didn't deviate one bit from the truth. Because the people knew that after finishing the circumcision Piri would hang the clipped foreskin on a freshly cut willow twig and attach it to the wall above the bed of the newly made Muslim. And this was done not so it could be seen by those who came to congratulate the new Muslim in the literal and metaphorical sense as a member of the great family of Mohammed, but to serve as evidence of the certain medical knowledge of Piri. On the place where the cut was made, Piri poured a little pinch of ashes. With that he considered his work done. "When the twig dries out the boy can get up," he said and, according to the author of the amateur lines, having received what he was due, took off. The only thing, Piri advised the parents of the newly minted Muslim, was that they shouldn't throw away the twig with the skin flap in any old place but should bury it in the earth under a weeping willow or throw it in the clean water of the river when the new moon appeared in the sky. And it must be acknowledged that not one boy ever suffered from Piri's handiwork.

After four girls, Allah sent him a boy (in this manner, lightly tinged with socialist realism, our collective folk creator turns to the next page in the life story of Piri Preputsy, the happy father of a newborn son). His father's heart had given him early warning that this time Baji *khanum* would give him a son.

It was the height of winter—the last third of January. That year the winter had been without snow from the very beginning; snow fell all of once and thawed immediately. And all Kellekend waited impatiently for when it would snow again.

If you believe the oral folk tale, close to evening, at the first of his wife's contractions, our surgeon-barber-toothpuller—in whose ears the first shriek of the long-awaited child of the male sex was already ringing—ran, almost dancing from happiness, to the midwife Raziya, brought her home, and left her with his wife. He himself went into a small room and closed the door behind him so no one would disturb the day's happy solitude.

He'd prepared everything beforehand. In his cellar stood a three-quart container of mulberry vodka sent him in the fall by the accountant Gulu, nicknamed "Collective Farm" (his nickname doesn't appear further in our narrative), whose three sons Piri had circumcised at one time that spring. He filled a one-quart container of vodka and placed it on a shelf in the room. He arranged appetizers consisting of mutton *kaurma*, sheep's cheese, *chashyr*, and walnuts. And laying low in anticipation of the birth of his son, he prepared to surrender himself to drink all night long.

That night he really did drink a great deal, and he fell asleep close to dawn. Only Allah knows how long he slept. But he woke up to the shouts of the midwife Raziya. It turns out she'd been knocking on his door for a long time.

"Open up, you fornicator! Get up, you owe me!"

(The observant teller of folk tales, being able to share someone else's happiness and read someone else's thoughts from any distance, continues the story in the triumphant intonations of the midwife's lips.)

Having pulled on one trouser leg and holding the other in his hand, Piri Preputsy hastened to open the door.

"A boy?"

"Yes, a boy. And you've gotten sozzled again, you swine's swine. The whole house reeks like a latrine. Fine, put on your pants."

"A boy! A male!" muttered Piri, pulling on his trouser leg while hopping from happiness. "And he's a male in good order, Raziya? He has a thing?"

"He has, idiot! What else would be there?"

"His member stands up, right?"

"Yes it does, fuck you in the mouth. Compared to yours, it stands up like a nail."

"You, what, saw mine, you old whore?"

"Why would I need to do that?"

It must be said that at that minute Piri's member was standing up like a bayonet. If he hadn't known Raziya so well, he'd have squeezed her tight right then, laid her under himself like a pillow, and banged her a minimum of thrice, not once (but this is a lie, Storyteller!) removing his male spear from her feminine attractions the whole time. But Piri wasn't that stupid, that is, he hadn't lost his reason to such a degree as to accost Raziya—let's say, to grab either her breast or thigh—for he knew in that case he'd be beaten so badly that not a single tooth would remain in his mouth nor a single hair on his head. Raziya was known for her constancy to her husband. So what if she had a foul mouth? Everyone in Kellekend swore, with the exception of three or four people—the teachers, the mullahs, and the direct descendants of the Prophet. All of Raziya's whoring was concentrated in her tongue. If there existed a man in Kellekend for her, it was her husband Shorty Mohammed, chair of the inspection commission in the administration of the Kellekend collective farm, who stood just under five feet and weighed less than one hundred and twenty pounds. And who had to beg Raziya for three days for a single moment of pleasure.

With regard to "what was owed" (how passionately the wordsmith of folklore assures us of this!), Piri wasn't at all stingy. Not even having seen his son, he rushed to the henhouse and caught a strong rooster and laying hen for Raziya. Besides that he brought the midwife who'd told him the joyous news two pails of choice potatoes and an enormous, bright-red pumpkin from the cellar. Then he took a gold five-ruble coin saved up for the occasion from the safe and, in a mark of gratitude, laid it under Baji *khanum*'s pillow. And only after that did he take his son in his arms and cry sweetly. And then he looked in the yard and saw that a tremendous snowstorm was raging—you could cling to its tail and fly to the sky! It became an additional cause for joy. "You have a light foot, my son," said Piri. "With your arrival in the world, you brought sacred moisture to our land, and you saved our mountains and fields from mortal drought. Grow, my son, and live long, to the joy of all people."

He very much wanted to share his joy with someone (thus our indefatigable, pseudo-socialist realist continues his happy, cockamamie story, not at all ashamed at pretending to be a direct witness to some entirely unfunny and uncomical historical events). Piri stood a long time in the yard looking at the falling snow and racking his brains about whom to tell the happy news, but besides his friend Sadykhov, he couldn't think of anyone. Sadykhov had a first name too, of course, but in Kellekend and Giulliukend everyone called him simply Sadykhov. More exactly, Shroud Sadykhov. He'd received the nickname "Shroud" because, after becoming chair of the unified village councils of Kellekend and Giulliukend, he'd been waging a relentless battle against burying the dead in shrouds for more than ten years already. "In what law is it written that it's forbidden to bury the dead in their own clothes? Why do we have to listen to what the mullahs tell us when the proletariat of the whole world, united, is moving towards communism?" (when he said it, it sounded more like "gaminism"). "If the dead fall into heaven or hell, then it's *especially so*" (he always said those two words in Russian, with particular emphasis). "What's the unfortunate person going to do there in a shroud? Everyone who dies carries with himself two or three yards of white fabric. For what purpose? Our women can't find underwear to cover their private parts while going to a meeting. Our children run around the streets without trousers until age five or six. Wouldn't it be better to sew that fabric into underwear so our women and children can come to know all the sweetness of our new life?"

For ten years Piri Preputsy and Shroud Sadykhov together (continues the storyteller, clumsily flirting with historical events) fought shoulder-to-shoulder against kulaks and any kind of "alien elements" like *Sayyid* Miribrahim, who'd twice completed the *haj* before the 1920s. Together they also exposed Badger Mekhi, who hoarded seven sacks of wheat from the hungry poor at home; and Pockmarked Jabi, who slaughtered his own two heifers at night and made them into *kaurma* and stuffed two enormous clay pots with it rather than give it to the collective farm; and the miller Suleiman, who mixed wheat with pumpkin seeds and hazelnut shells in the time of famine in order to discredit Soviet authority and the glorious name of Comrade Stalin.

Had the village council been in their village, Piri wouldn't have given a second thought to the snow. But, alas, the council was located in Giulliukend, and it didn't appeal to Piri at all to drag himself to Giulliukend in such a storm. However, the class enemy of the miller Suleiman didn't think too long but drew back into the house and dressed more warmly in a thick wool sweater and new jacket (in those times people in Kellekend hadn't even heard about coats). He didn't doubt Sadykhov would have vodka; however, he seized a bottle himself, just in case, stuffed his pockets with shelled walnuts, and went on his way.

Hardly had he entered the yard of the collective farm's office in Giulliukend than, right there, he smelled the appetizing aroma of *shorpa* with *kaurma* seasoned with black peas. The warmth of scorching-hot coal blew over him even before he walked into the place (in villages at that time coal was only allotted for the heating of state enterprises and schools—ordinary people heated their homes with firewood, dung bricks, and other improvised fuel).

He shook off the snow in the corridor and entered. How wonderful is the warmth of coal—as if winter weren't even behind the door and last year's August heat had settled in here and stuck around! In the summer-like warmth and spacious, homelike room with high ceilings were the chair and secretary of the village council.

The chair, standing by the hot stove, was tasting the apparently ready *shorpa* with *kaurma* seasoned with the uncommonly aromatic black peas that had grown from time immemorial only on the blessed Giulliukend and Kellekend soil. The secretary (an actual official, not a girl who types), already drawing near to the border that distinguishes a girl from an old maid, the sharp-tongued and quick-witted Siddiga (we'll meet this woman a few more times in her capacity as the all-powerful head of the unified ZAGS registration and notary office, an institution named among the people with the appalling word ZAGSONOT), sat in her place in front of the wide, six-paneled window with a book in her hand.

Sadykhov rejoiced at the arrival of his old comrade in arms.

"Come on in, you came at the right time! Your mother-in-law, the old b…, obviously loved you, as the saying goes. It was probably difficult to get here in this storm—?"

Piri took the bottle of vodka from the inside pocket of his jacket and placed it in an inconspicuous spot.

"Don't start with my mother-in-law," he said, greedily breathing in the warm air. "Today her daughter bore me a son."

"Oh, that's wonderful! Fantastic!"

"Indeed, Sadykhov, today my son was born. And it seems everything's in good order with him. It's clear from his pecker," said Piri, nodding in the direction of Siddiga.

"May he grow big, Uncle Piri! And what did you bring us to sweeten the news?" asked the ambitious future female activist of the district Party organization, straightening her shoulders coquettishly.

Piri walked towards the girl, dumped a handful of shelled nuts on the desk, and seated himself there by the window.

"Try them, they're tasty nuts. The main refreshment comes later." In a fit of generosity Piri dumped out another handful of nuts.

Not taking her eyes off the nuts, Siddiga pulled the registration book from the drawer of the desk. "Shall we register the baby?"

"Go ahead, that's fine with me."

"And what's his name?"

"Skip that line."

"What, you still haven't thought up a name?"

"I have. I've considered thirty or forty names. But for now leave the place for the name empty."

"He was born last night?"

"No, this morning."

"That means we'll write him under today's date, the twentieth of January, 19—"

But here Sadykhov, standing at the stove, interrupted.

"You remember that time, Piri, the night of January nineteenth when that group of rebels poured out into the streets of the town? Those out-and-out rascals wanted to overthrow our authority! And your Mollavelli from Kellekend led them. You and I went through a lot early that morning, my friend Preputsy, when the adopted son of that swine Mollavelli—that diehard parasite and pervert Azhdar—rose suddenly from the grave, appeared right on the square in front of the Shah Abbas bathhouse, and declared himself the public leader of the whole unruly Allahabad mob! He said Allah had raised him from the dead for precisely that reason and sent him from that world to this for him to become a respected elder here. And everyone followed him with joy. 'Yes,' they said, 'he's the one who should be our leader! If Allah has raised someone from the dead and sent him to us,' they said, 'then we'll incur the anger of God if we don't obey him!'—that's what the adherents of that adopted child of Mollavelli wailed so heart-rendingly all over the square. Did you see what went on with the people? If the poets and writers hadn't intervened, believe me, we'd have lost power." Sadykhov sighed deeply. Then he ladled out a spoonful from the saucepan, blew on it to cool it, and stood still in that position, lost in deep thought.

"And it was all your fault, who else's? You didn't let them bury him properly in a shroud," recalled Piri. "'No,' you said, 'bury him in a suit!' Then he appeared and made all that fuss. In that January cold he wouldn't have made it to the square in front of the Shah Abbas bathhouse wearing a shroud. He'd have frozen to death on the road like a ground squirrel."

The secretary also became thoughtful.

"I simply don't believe that Azhdar rose from the dead." With exactly those words (if you believe the creator of this folk "epic") the bold village council personage entered the conversation, not agreeing with the opinion of the high-minded elders on the question of events related to funerals and graveyards. "It's simply that his death was a fake. He probably hid in some kind of cave near the cemetery and waited for a convenient chance. And when he saw the fuss was growing, he decided to go and fool the people—maybe something would work out to his advantage. Doesn't the success of those kinds of acts by rascals like Azhdar really lie in human ignorance?" Feeling that she'd spoken literately and almost in learned language, the girl couldn't hide her own pride. "Only books can save the people from ignorance." She bent down, lifted her knapsack of white fabric (the color of a shroud!) stuffed with books, and took out a slim, bright-red book, on the cover of which was depicted a smiling, mustachioed hulk of a person wearing an enormous, spherical *papakha* and a gold star on his chest. "Here, look: *Song of the Shepherd and Decorated Veteran*. I've already read this book two times, and now I'm reading it for the third time. You read and are astounded—what a great person this writer is! What a glorious country we have! It's not just the valiant labor by the glorious youth of the Soviet countries that's shown here. In this book the author angrily condemns ignorance and illiteracy and masterfully shows what an uncompromising struggle simple Soviet people wage against secret enemies of socialism such as the miller Suleiman, who mixed pumpkin seeds and hazelnut shells in the wheat to awaken hatred among the people for the great Stalin."

"They'll never succeed! No one can blacken the name of the great Stalin!" exclaimed Sadykhov, continuing to grip the spoon in one hand and the pot lid in the other, and again lost himself in thought.

But the girl's heart was overflowing.

"On the road to work today I met the teacher Durdana. She's been teaching literature for ten years already and is now director of the school. I asked her, 'Have you read *Song of the Shepherd and Decorated Veteran*?' 'No,' she says, 'I haven't read it.' I named around ten works, and she hadn't read a single one of them. If the director of the school doesn't read books—"

She suddenly fell silent, as if she'd used up all the reserve of her soul's anger on the unfortunate directress. Then, smiling, she added in a complete different voice, dreamily, sweetly:

"It's said that such a book, such a book is coming out, oy, mama! I myself heard about it yesterday morning on the radio. And the name is so romantic, mamochka—*Gored and Thrilled*!" Her hearing, possibly, had let her down (notes our scrupulous epic-neorealist here) because the title *Sword and Quill* had been spoken clearly on the radio.

Here the patience of Preputsy, who'd been dreaming of drinking, with God's help, his shot of vodka, was finally exhausted.

"We know, we know, daughter!" he said. "I swear on the grave of my father, we know all that! We weren't born yesterday—we know who's educated and who isn't. And who is that Durdana to compete with you in learning? If there are three to five cultured and well-read people to be found in the region, then you are first among them. All our people know that," he added, thinking to himself, "Eh, how I'd like to poke something in you now. Then you'd really be *Gored and Thrilled*."

It seems that the secret thought of our terribly happy father of a newborn son made its way to the old maid.

"Oy, I don't believe you. Are you telling the truth, Uncle Piri?" Happiness— at his words and at the secret thoughts she'd read—poured like balm into the heart of the young lady activist and passionate education advocate who'd long and not unsuccessfully been attempting to improve her social standing.

And while Piri was thinking about the fact that there are sweeter things in this world than hatred for the enemies of socialism—take, for example, nuzzling the luscious lips of Siddiga and whispering sweet nothings to them— Sadykhov the shroud-fighter returned to the sinful earth, and it became clear to everyone how high and far off his thoughts had been soaring when he (still with the spoon in one hand and the pot lid in the other hand) spoke.

"I just want one thing from nature, my friend Preputsy," said Sadykhov, looking from the room's intoxicating August heat out on cold January beyond the window, and with pure, Communist sincerity he proceeded to share his cherished dream with his friend. "'O, all-powerful nature,' I'd say, 'may the day come soon when I can feast my eyes on the five-pointed star above the Kremlin! If I can just once—be it from a distance—salute the great Stalin! And after that they can lay me in the ground, even in madapolam cloth—I swear by the memory of my father I'll go happily.'"

Having eased his heart and settled accounts with the world of reverie, Sadykhov checked the readiness of the *shorpa* once more, moved the pot slightly off the flame, ladled out two full spoonfuls of peas and two pieces of *kaurma* in soft lavash and, holding out all this to the lady lover of *Gored and Thrilled*, said, "You eat this, daughter, and take yourself on home. Take a bucket of water, carry it home. Make your old mother happy. No one else is coming today. Who's going to show up here in this weather? If it began as a hard snow, then it's going to fall all night."

(Here our collective creator of honest fables went for broke. Here's the end of that long-ago, moth-eaten history as he left it for future generations:)

But the snow stopped eventually.

Flitting with his thoughts among the far-off stars, the tireless shroud-fighter and authority on the dead had long ago fallen dead asleep in his own home. But as it turned out, the adventures of the happy father of a newborn son didn't conclude with that.

The famous virtuoso of circumcision, barber, and toothpuller also slept sweetly in complete solitude on a soft couch in the unified village council of Kellekend and Guilliukend, covered with the thick hide of a three-year-old pedigreed goat. But the base devil—who always finds ways to work his nasty deeds—taking the form of Siddiga this time, climbed into the dreams of our extremely well-fortified and sated Piri Preputsy and, systematically adding a little sweetness to his already-sweet dreams, concocted filth upon filth, following one single goal—to most cleverly and keenly corrupt the true son of the Glorious Party and father of a newborn child so as to disgrace his honest name in the eyes of all working people. That damned devil—singing lustily like a nightingale—in the name of the village council secretary overcome with reading, the virgin Siddiga, spoke such shamefully pleasant words that it's unlikely she herself could have uttered them: "I love you! . . . I'm giving it to you! . . . I'm coming! . . . I'm dying! . . . Screw me! . . . Kiss me! . . . Touch me!" etc., etc., all in that same indecent spirit.

"Never! For shame! Get away, girl! Go away, girl, stop! Keep away from me, keep away!"

But when Piri shouted "Keep away from me!"—and, really, this could only occur in a dream—another unexpected thing happened, something even the devil himself couldn't have thought up. The golden-red rooster Piri had given the midwife Raziya took off like an eagle into the heavens, spread his wings, and like a real eagle flew directly to the five-pointed Kremlin star! Knowing very well the outstanding ability of his former rooster to shit anywhere and everywhere he could (he'd given that particular rooster to Raziya for just that reason), the master was terribly worried. And when the rooster settled directly on the sharp points of the star, Preputsy's alarm changed to panic: "Shoo, shoo, be off, get off of that! Siddiga! Raziya! Ooh, ooh! Shoo, shoo, shoo!"

Thus, muttering "shoo, shoo" in his sleep, Piri Preputsy woke up the next morning at the office of the village council. And neither on that day nor ever after was the barber able to understand: was there indeed some sort of connection between the fact that Baji *khanum* bore him a son and that five-pointed star on which the red-winged rooster-conjurer in his strange dream almost shat?

PART TWO

prosaically realistic

In which we part company with the haplessly socialist-realist creator of a folk epic in order to continue our story in a realistic style more acceptable to the modern reader.

VI

Spring had arrived in Giulliukend. However, it wasn't the same spring that followed that January night when Piri struggled desperately with the impudent rooster in his sleep, but a completely different one many, many years later.

And this spring arrived so brightly and noisily that—speaking in the language of the residents of Kellekend and Giulliukend, who for lack of other activities usually joked around with words the whole winter long—"One should just look at the sun and howl from happiness!"

The mountain river bubbled up in its own particular way, flowing from the high mountains and running to Kellekend and from there rushing lower between the sharp cliffs and green meadows of Giulliukend with a roar. Its loud rumble rose up to the sun along with the whisper of green meadows. With identical fervor children, birds, foals, and lambs sang and neighed and bleated and danced to the drumbeat of the river's elemental force. The white flowers of the almond tree, the cherry-plum, and the cherry rejoiced at the river. It carried bitter notes of sadness to the souls of girls turning by degrees into old maids, and the hearts of blossoming young girls were filled with warm hopes and presentiments of happiness.

Throughout the region the mountain river spread the fragrance of snow melting on the mountain heights; of freshly lush, green meadows sprouting with mint, thyme, cow parsnip, and violets; and of the leaves of the silent weeping willows lining the banks from Kellekend to Giulliukend just barely, barely beginning to blossom. However, the wonderful expanse called Giulliukend and

Kellekend didn't consist of just rivers and streams, mountains and gorges, and the various birds and animals inhabiting them—in a word, not just of flora and fauna. Here lived people, too. And how could absolutely nothing happen in a place where people live? Among a number of events, we've already noted Piri's strange dream about the pernicious rooster impudently flying up to the Kremlin's five-pointed star. But it's still more remarkable that right after that escapade of the rooster, Shroud Sadykhov experienced a misfortune that may also be ascribed with certainty to a number of important events strongly tinged with mystery. The starry dream of the proclaimer of a new funeral tradition didn't come true, either actually or metaphorically, and the aroma of *shorpa* with *kaurma* and black peas had already long dispersed from the building of the village council; Sadykhov, accused of political sluggishness in the battle with "alien elements" (it was said that he'd been able to expose all of eleven such "elements" from the two villages and, contenting himself with that, had plunged headlong into culinary affairs), was sent to Siberia—evidently in order to meet up with the miller Suleiman and in the calm conditions of that place discuss funeral-related and other important issues with him.

In the form of additional information, one can say that, in the entire expanse of Allahabad, the most interesting events took place precisely in the cemetery. However—and this is known to us for certain—after the resurrection of Azhdar, no similar happening was noted, with one exception. According to rumor, that exceptional instance took place in Kellekend. Apparently, the night caretaker of the collective farm—"Mad Gazanfar" by nickname—was walking one night near the cemetery and saw the late Preputsy (completely drunk!) sitting on his own grave and crying bitterly. And apparently Piri, tears streaming, implored Gazanfar to inform the midwife Raziya that she should cut off the head of the rooster, boil it, add a pinch of black pepper, and feed it to her husband, Shorty Mohammed. Otherwise, that rooster would cause still more trouble. It goes without saying that this is old history. Because if it were recent news, the rooster Piri had given the midwife Raziya would have been, at the very least, twenty-five years old!

And if in some lands the more interesting events take place in the cemetery, is it possible that the appearance here of a certain book could also be a happening? In the marvelous land of Allahabad, it turns out, such a miracle could also happen.

And it happened! The book that was such an event was named *Sword and Quill*. And on this very day, a glorious spring day in Giulliukend, people awaited the arrival of the district policeman coming to look into the complaint of Firage, the head librarian. And the district policeman was tall, with a thin moustache and aquiline nose, a charming fellow—as you've already guessed, it was that same firstborn boy, son of that Piri Preputsy whom we last saw sitting on his own grave, drunk and crying.

The fact was that the former secretary of the village council and inveterate booklover, Siddiga—who'd long ago become the director of the highly profitable ZAGSONOT in the district capital and two months previously had married the editor of the newspaper *Glorious Allahabad*, the poet Khatam Vazek—on finding herself in Giulliukend for a short visit had borrowed that book to dip into for three days. But she hadn't yet returned it, and when Firage, fulfilling her official responsibility, demanded the return of valuable community property, Siddiga had cursed her with indecent words that until then hadn't been heard even in the Shah Abbas bathhouse.

Having found out that the newly named representative of authority planned to come to Giulliukend, Firage set to work at once. She swept and washed the floors in the library, wiped the dust from every book on the shelves, washed the windows twice, and also brought two pots of flowers from home—geranium and fuchsia—and with them beautified both of the library's windows. Now she sat with her former schoolmate and close neighbor Jinn Jamila in the library hall sparkling with cleanliness and carried on a pleasant conversation.

Having last year married the halva maker Abdul, a person many years older than herself, Jamila didn't last even ten days in her husband's home. On one of the darkest nights she left the district center on foot and, successfully completing many difficult climbs, reached Giulliukend towards morning. At night there are countless numbers of jinns on the road leading to Giulliukend, and there was no one in the village who wouldn't have known that. But Jamila didn't get her nickname for that reason. They nicknamed her "Jinn" because Jamila, whose most important activity was the resale of Iranian chewing gum, disappeared from time to time without a trace. As invisible as if she were a real jinn, she spent a little while somewhere and later reappeared just as unexpectedly. Some people maintained that this devilishly clever woman knew certain roads to Iran known only to jinns and used them periodically.

The other well-known activity of Firage's best friend was the composing of love letters from young fellows to young women and from young women to young fellows. When spring ran riot in Giulliukend, causing all the various animals and insects to climb on top of one another, the number of those who wanted to express their love also grew and multiplied. And it was no trouble at all for Jamila to concoct flaming love epistles for them. She opened up any page of *Sword and Quill*, which she had kept at home a whole month even before

Siddiga, and did this work easily. Because in no other book were there such profound and astonishing words as there were in that one. And there were no fewer connoisseurs of such words in Giulliukend than there were lovers of Iranian chewing gum.

And what words! "From the fathomless sea of my love for you, I take the thinnest threads of my heart! . . . The inspiration that love for you gives me can be compared with the richest library. . . . You're my first love, awakening in the spring of my life. . . . Love is like a seedling: it must grow and bear fruit."

And that's still not all! Jamila copied many other words from that book, words that were more precious than gold. For now she didn't allow them in circulation, so that the next generation of lovers would have something with which to caress the heart and inspire the soul. "Don't scatter before others the treasure taken from my soul. . . . Revealing her soul to you, the girl didn't show her face to the sun even then. . . . Isn't that first declaration of love dangerous for a girl desperately in love?" And still more, all in that vein. (Well, I hope you're now convinced that my inquisitive fellow villagers are passionately attracted to something besides the mysteries of cemeteries!)

"If I'd known this would happen, I wouldn't have taken the book from you. I'd have left it with you for another month. Too bad about that book. It outrages the heart to think that such a valuable book remains with such a witch." It appears that with these words Firage wanted to conclude the long-running conversation about *Sword and Quill* and "that trickster Siddiga."

But Jamila had still more to say about it.

"There's a character in the book—Saba *khanum*, that's what she's called— who's an exact copy of Siddiga! If you only knew what that Saba witch cooks up! She writes letters in the names of some people to others. She gets everyone fighting in the emir's court. They say that Siddiga also weaves such intrigues that even the sages of the district Party committee get flustered."

But Firage didn't read books; therefore, she decided to quickly change the subject.

"Did you see what her poet-husband got up to when he came to the village last summer? He throws his jacket over his shoulder, sticks his hands in his pockets, and strolls along the river bank as if he were Samed Vurgun himself.[3] What a husband that scoundrel found herself!"

Hardly had Firage said these words than a tall, well-built man with an aquiline nose appeared before the entrance of the library astride a white horse. He jumped to the ground with uncommon dexterity, threw the bridle on a dry branch of an old acacia, and in a moment appeared in the library.

Whether he greeted them or not doesn't concern us. But in an instant he was able to kindle the flame of joy in the hearts of the two readers of *Sword and Quill*.

At home Firage had brewed excellent tea in a thermos, and now she wished to serve her guest. But he didn't value her noble impulse.

"I didn't come here to drink tea," he announced, laying his hand on the thermos. "Which of you is Firage?"

"I am," said Firage, almost crying from the insult of a guest refusing to drink her tea.

"And who's this?" The representative of authority looked sternly down on Jamila.

"This is my friend, *Rais*. One of the active readers of our library."

It was evident that the use of "*Rais*" was very much to the liking of the inspector. He even softened a little.

"An active reader—that's good." The inspector began to roam among the shelves. "So, now, perhaps, you'll explain to us why you occupy yourself with such unworthy activities? What's this about letters you send hither and yon? There's not a single place you haven't written! It's still unknown whose sword and whose quill those are, and you've already alarmed the whole country with your letters."

"Don't say that, *Rais*! What have I done that's so bad? A library book is state property, and she's treating it like it's her personal property. And she doesn't even think that, besides her, hundreds of people want to read it." The aggrieved librarian swallowed tears.

"She's right, *Rais*," Jamila came to the defense of her friend. "Those who take a book from the library and don't think to return it are the ones taking part in unworthy activities. That's insolent and dishonest. There should be no place for those kinds of people in our cultured Soviet society."

"Ten people a day ask for that book," added Firage. "It's very valuable, everyone wants to read it. There have been seventy-five people waiting in line for it since January. And we have all of one book! We don't even have a second copy. What am I supposed to tell people? That Siddiga *khanum* wanted it that way?"

The representative of authority who'd arrived on the white horse was roaming among the shelves with a reproachfully cold look. He took one book after another from the shelf, unhurriedly leafed through it, checked its price, and put it back in place.

"There are so many books here, and you want to say readers can't find anything else to amuse themselves with?" he asked with sincere amazement.

"What can I say, *Rais*? I'm astounded myself. From the moment that book arrived, people haven't wanted to read anything else." Pouting like an aggrieved child, the librarian hung her head.

The reproachful expression that had been fixed on the face of the representative of authority suddenly disappeared. He laughed loudly, but the merriment changed almost immediately to anger.

"Because you don't have enough brains to promote the books! You waste time on writing letters all over the place. Instead of promoting books, you occupy yourself with unworthy activities. You disturb the schedules and the already-intensive work of the leadership!"

The inspector—who liked the word *Rais* when it was addressed to him— looked at the book he held in his hand with one eye and at the devotees of *Sword and Quill* with the other to see what effect his words had produced on them. There was such quiet in the room that if a fly had flown by then, it would have seemed much more like a helicopter. A lenient expression appeared on the face of the merciful representative of authority, who was satisfied with the effect he'd produced. He put the book back on the shelf, took another one, and continued, already amicably.

"I've read ninety percent of these books. But I still haven't read *Sword and Quill*, I confess. I haven't had time. On the other hand, I've read *Song of the Shepherd and Decorated Veteran* at least three times. It's an outstanding book. You know that, of course, but the people also must know what treasures are hidden in this small room. I just look at these books and my heart fills with pride!" For a short while he looked thoughtfully at the cover of the little book that he now held in his hand and then addressed Jinn Jamila: "Have you read this book?"

Seeing that the representative of authority held just that book about the shepherd and decorated war veteran, Jamila became as agitated as if she'd once again seen her husband the halva master.

"I've read it! I've read it!" she exclaimed, but because of the agitation enveloping her, she wasn't able to add another word.

"It's necessary to promote precisely these kinds of books among readers," said the inspector edifyingly, "because today's youth must understand which historical path the glorious Leninist Komsomol took!"

"Yes, remember that, and remember about the treacherous hypocrisy of our internal enemies such as the miller Suleiman, who was justly punished by our dear government!" Jamila supported the representative of authority from the position of an active reader.

But Firage's thoughts returned again to the thermos. The heart of the dismayed librarian, stunned by the brains and the knowledge of the young inspector who'd galloped up to her on a white horse, again trembled with the desire to serve him a glass of tea. Once again it didn't escape the perspicacious attention of the emissary of authority:

"One can sit in the library drinking tea and gossiping, chewing Iranian gum, writing letters on behalf of youths languishing from love, and infecting the healthy feeling of love in young people with harmful microbes. But even if that book hadn't been named *Sword and Quill* but *War and Peace*, not one sensible person would have written letters to the Mausoleum addressed to the Leader because of it!" The inspector angrily brandished *Song of the Shepherd and Decorated Veteran* and in a fit of temper flung it on the floor. "You wrote to the district Party committee—well, let's assume out of thoughtlessness! You wrote to *Glorious Allahabad*—fine. But tell me, where was your head when you wrote to Lenin's Mausoleum? Maybe you deliberately wanted to shame our leadership in front of the whole country?"

"*Ra—*" Firage began to babble and hung her head. Her tongue stuck to the roof of her mouth, evidently from fear.

And Jamila, having lost all her courage after the words about Iranian chewing gum and with it, seemingly, the last remnants of reason, began to rave.

"Yes, yes! You're right, so right! I share your opinion in full! What's the point of writing to the Mausoleum if the man is dead—" But here, mortally frightened, either at the word "dead" or at the responsibility for its inappropriate use, Jamila turned white and was only able to come to herself after a long pause. "You must have heard, *Rais*, may your parents be blessed: in our village there was a very fine shepherd. Young, with a beautiful moustache. One night it came into his head to write a letter to the Five-Pointed Star of the Kremlin. He said, 'I pledge that every sheep will give birth to seven lambs every year.' The poor fellow was dragged around everywhere and had to write so many explanations that in the end he became a writer."

The experienced gum trader might already be touched in the head, thought the young policeman, but he gave no sign of it.

"Fine," said the future *Rais*, "we'll wrap things up." He pulled an oblong paper from his pocket and laid it on the desk in front of the librarian. "Sign here."

"And what's this, *Rais*? What must I sign?"

"You're signing that you won't undertake any other unworthy activities of this kind."

"Please, with pleasure!" Firage began to babble, and she wrote her signature with such pleasure that it was as if she were registering her marriage at the ZAGS office for the first time in her life, what's more in the presence of Siddiga, who mortally envied her boundless happiness—Siddiga, with her poisonously furious physiognomy.

And at that same moment the projectionist Shirshirali (nicknamed "Get-in-Free"), who'd gone into town early that morning for the first film, walked into the library for the first time after the long winter months carrying a heavy package of books in each hand.

"*Sword and Quill!*" the projectionist proclaimed proudly. "Straight from the district Party committee. One book—I'm saying right now—rightfully belongs to me." He took a small pen knife from his pocket and deftly cut the strings around the bundles. There were ten thick books in each packet. He extracted his "rightful" book from one of the packages, happily thrust it under his arm, and not saying another word or looking at anyone, left.

The inspector took one of those twenty books himself.

"I'll read and return it without fail in nine days, at the very latest," he said politely, smiling like the spring sun. "And now, beginning this very minute, we need to prepare for a big event. In two days or so we'll conduct a vigorous *subbotnik* here. We'll begin a great work to upgrade our roads. It's a much-needed and serious undertaking. We'll dig up the weeping willows that grow in great numbers along the river by their roots and transplant them along the highway. Let our willows delight the eye of everyone who goes by! Let journalists and other important people following our asphalt roads contemplate the beauty of our land! And let our good neighbors—the Armenians and Georgians—abundantly admire our weeping willows, which clearly testify to our ancient culture. We must work together so that the life of our people turns every day into a holiday!"

After that the well-built man with the gaze of an eagle leaped on his white horse, and galloping by the library, he affably waved his hand at the two devotees of *Sword and Quill* frozen by the window.

After the representative of authority disappeared, raising a cloud of dust that flew from the horse's heels, for some time the friends lapsed into thought, only rarely exchanging meaningful glances. In our opinion, two circumstances might serve as the reason for such deep thought. First of all, both were delighted by the beauty and intelligence of the representative of authority of the new type who flashed like spring lightning in the sky of Giulliukend, which had slept lazily all winter long in the shadow of the old mountains. Secondly, the news about the *subbotnik* being prepared stirred the hearts of the lovers of *Sword and Quill* and fired new hopes and wishes in them.

All the same, the friends—the true meaning of whose philosophical silence was known only to themselves—couldn't remain inactive for long. From the library they rushed straight to the school. And there it became clear that not even school director Durdana understood the meaning of the word *subbotnik*. They were somehow able to explain to her what a "Leninist *subbotnik*" is; however, they were completely unable to make the director of studies understand. "It's a long way from rural inspector to Lenin," he said, a bit mockingly. "Go find yourselves something useful to do."

That day the friends ran around the whole village, door to door. They knocked on every door. They poked their noses into houses. They called people from behind fences. But no one answered the call. It was as if the village had gone extinct. In fact, however, everyone was alive and healthy. People hid in various places—one in the cellar, one in the cowshed, another in the outhouse. And all because no one expected anything good from those meddlesome friends; when they threw themselves into action, sooner or later some kind of misfortune would happen in Giulliukend.

Moreover, the peasants of that time already knew quite well that any decree from on high was the devil's work and that it exceeded human understanding to make sense of it. People interpreted such directives as fateful inevitability and understood quite well that trying to evade the inevitable was an entirely useless and hopeless undertaking. Those who willingly undertook to fulfill that sort of appeal automatically became relatives and comrades-in-arms of the devil in the eyes of the rest. Also eternally on the invisible list of the devil's relatives were all the members of their households and the friends of those who, in concert with Satan, diligently fulfilled the idiotic orders from above. And everyone in the village knew it was necessary to be especially careful with such people. By general acknowledgement of the villagers, the incautious were unconditionally considered to be dimwitted, at the very least. In such situations a smart person is smart in being able to find a way out of the situation and save his or her own skin. And the people had neither the time nor the desire to think about how that kind of "skin-saving" philosophy turns out in the end to be still more unfortunate. The devil is the devil precisely in that he's always full of time and desire to carry his affairs to a successful conclusion.

* * *

Apparently only Samandar, the chair of the Giulliukend collective farm, was little interested in his own skin. The chair understood the meaning of *subbotnik* quite well, but he simply couldn't understand the undertaking to transplant willows from the river bank to the side of the highway. More precisely, he wasn't able explain to anyone that there existed a time-tested method of transplanting willows and that there was absolutely no need to dig up trees. It was enough to cut a single branch, plant it where you liked, and it would take root, so long as you watered it continually.

For three days before the *subbotnik*, the chair tried three times a day to telephone the second secretary of the district Party committee in the center, but he heard exactly the same response each time: "Don't oppose the event!" But in fact, that same second secretary had drunk vodka in the shade of those willows no less than fifty times, eating wild boar *shashlyk*. And now it was as if the scoundrel had gorged himself on apples and left the Garden: he didn't understand a single word, it was as if he didn't care about either the willows or Allah. Only the word "event" stuck to his tongue: "Don't oppose the event!"

On Friday (that is, the day before the "highway phantasmagoria") the chair appeared in the office at dawn. It was as if he'd had a dream that today someone would surely telephone from the center and announce the cancellation of the "event." And the chair of the inspection commission (formerly known to us as the beloved husband of the midwife Raziya), Shorty Mohammed, now considerably older, also appeared early in the morning and, still sleepy, sat down next to the chair.

"Maybe I should drive to town, try to find at least one reasonable person there, explain the heart of the matter to him? This is real sabotage, what they're planning to do with our willows," the chair started to consult with the sleepy and therefore nodding Shorty Mohammed.

"There's no need," answered Mohammed, opening one eye with difficulty.

"I'm afraid they won't phone themselves," began Samandar, not taking his eyes off the telephone.

"They already called. They won't bother to call again."

"Aren't you sorry about the willows?" said the chair loudly, hoping that the chair of the inspection commission would finally wake up.

"I'm sorry about you, not the willows," responded Shorty Mohammed, half-asleep.

"Why in the world are you sorry about me?"

This time Shorty opened both eyes.

"Lots of heads are going to roll because of that young fellow."

"Are you serious? That's something new!" It seemed to Shorty that the chair's voice trembled slightly.

"They say he was strolling around the cemetery the other day." Shorty Mohammed's eyes closed again.

At the word "cemetery" the chair himself trembled.

"Enough with the sleeping! Open your eyes and say something like a real human being. What was he doing in the cemetery?"

"How should I know what he was doing there? Probably he was thinking up something, since he was walking." Shorty opened his eyes and yawned. Then he straightened up and shook himself, demonstrating to the chair that he wasn't sleeping any more. "To tell the truth, that type is capable of raising the dead from the grave. That inspector isn't of human birth. That type swarmed around here during dekulakization."

"Oh, leave it, for the love of God!" Samandar waved his hand, losing hope of hearing anything sensible from the lips of the chair of the inspection commission.

"They say he wrote down the names of all those who organized the *shakhsey-vakhsey* ritual in the village and sent that list to the KGB."

"Listen, what are you talking about? Which *shakhsey-vakhsey*?" The chair was losing patience. "You just think how long it's been since *Muharram*. He wasn't even inspector then! You've lost your mind from senility."

"That's why they chose him to do this job, stupid! After he presented that list. Why else would they suddenly have decided to make the son of that rogue Preputsy an inspector?"

The chair plunged deep into thought, not taking his eyes from the telephone.

"What, you don't believe me?" Shorty Mohammed laughed his old, wheezy laugh. "However, don't worry, they won't let him linger here long. They'll promote him and take him somewhere higher up."

And about that the chair believed Shorty Mohammed one hundred percent.

"From your mouth to the ears of Allah," he said and again grew absorbed in waiting.

The silence of the graveyard reigned over the office.

VII

In the same kind of sepulchral silence, Elbey stood motionless in the fairytale luxury of the enormous Finnish bath, having now finally understood that he was irretrievably ruined. Unimaginable exhaustion suddenly bore down on him. Sitting by the pool on the sofa covered with beige cashmere, he saw and felt nothing for some time. The mournful howl of the dog reached him from the yard as if from another world. He wanted, very much wanted, to shout something to Hercules, to calm the dog, but he didn't have enough strength even for that. Elbey wasn't even able to open his mouth before sleep overwhelmed him. And it was an astonishing thing: in that strange condition of semi-consciousness in which he was carried from the present to the past, calm was granted to him, and there appeared hope that life would go on. . . .

Giulliukend. A cloudless, dazzlingly bright sky. It was a long time ago, but he remembered everything to the most minute detail.

Near evening that day in Giulliukend it was as if the air itself had been pierced by some kind of imagined, caressing gleam of light. The sun just about hidden behind the mountains to the west threw a yellow-rose light on the opposite mountain, and the mountain, illuminated by that light, seemed to smile on everything living and non-living, lighting up the soul with a soft and quiet heavenly caress.

The leaves of the willows planted along the highway were still green. Because August hadn't yet arrived. The river water didn't roar but coursed calmly along its thousand-year-old channel. In August when the river dried up completely, the willows drinking the water flowing from the weir along the narrow channel would begin to dry out, and not one would live until autumn.

But it was still a long time until August. It was the middle of June. The cherry-plums and cherries had only just ripened. There were two weeks left until the ripening of the mulberries and apricots.

Two people stood on the asphalt road, a boy and a woman. One of the pails beside the woman was empty. The second was completely filled with ripe, amber-yellow cherry-plums. Because the cherries that Gushver had brought to sell that day had all been sold, but no one had bought the cherry-plums.

Elbey, certain that sooner or later the cherry-plums would find a buyer, stood beside his grandmother and suddenly saw a white horse galloping along the road, a horse on which he himself had flown along countless times in his dreams. And the horse was galloping right towards them. Coming close, the horseman stopped the horse.

"What's this commotion you've stirred up here, old woman? Collect your wares and get out of here!" The horseman squeezed the horse with his legs, demonstrating that he was angry.

Gushver sat calmly on the overturned empty pail. At the croaking of the *Rais* she straightened up and walked directly towards the horse.

"'Old woman'—that's your mother, Baji *khanum* Gold Tooth!" she shouted. "And your father, Piri Preputsy, who's now stuffed in his grave, was always stirring up a commotion! Why are you shouting at me? My name is Gushver. And I gave my only son for your fucking authority."

The *Rais* sprang evilly from the horse. His face turned white. His eyes were about to fly out of their sockets.

"What's this nonsense you're talking, woman! Do you know who I am?"

"Oy, you scared me, oy, I'm frightened!" Gushver answered in a mocking tone. "Just look at him posing there! To me you're shit, just shit. Go find yourself someone more timid and yell at her as much as you want!"

The *Rais* was squeezing the bridle of the horse in one hand. What to do with the other, he didn't know.

"You, come along with me!" he commanded. "I'll put you behind bars, then you'll find out who you're talking to."

Gushver stood bravely in front of the horse.

"Well, let's go, take me to jail! Go ahead and rape a soldier's sixty-five-year-old mother. I see you're capable of that!"

Now the *Rais* lost his head. He turned towards the mountain that not long ago had been yellow-rose and had now become the color of dark coffee. Then he turned again towards Gushver and asked in a calm, even embarrassed, voice:

"Who was your son?"

Although Gushver was seeing him for the first time, it seemed she knew the nature of such people very well. She knew one should never give in before a power-loving gang. If you give in, all is lost: they'll sweet-talk you and then run you over. Therefore she decided not to change her "offensive strategy."

"My son was a man and the son of a man. He cultivated the collective farm's land honestly, harvested wheat for himself and others. He earned his honest bread sparing neither sweat nor blood, and he didn't transplant willows to the road so that soft-butt fat-bellies driving by in cars could look at them and glorify him! It's early now, but just you wait, when August comes, then we'll see what you do!"

Gushver's strategy proved to be one-hundred-percent correct. After that additional attack by the militant mother of a soldier, the *Rais* retreated still further. He was so frightened that he couldn't even hide it from Gushver.

"And what's going to happen in August?" he asked in a whine.

"Your death's coming!" Gushver raised her voice still more, seeing that her opponent was retreating. "You're from Kellekend: do you really not know that in August the water in the river dries up? If you didn't know, you should've asked someone who did. Or are you just like your good-for-nothing papa, Piri—the only thing you know how to do is guzzle vodka?"

The *Rais* put his foot into the stirrup.

"Don't talk about my father," he said, trying to make his voice authoritative.

"I will talk about your father! Every year I gave him a pail of cucumbers and tomatoes from our garden. And that buffoon didn't once pay me a kopek."

"It seems you're looking for a fight," muttered the *Rais*, leaping onto the horse. "It's better to keep away from you in future!" And he galloped off, tormented by fear.

"Let's go, little son. Clearly, no one's coming to buy our cherry-plums today. You take one side of the handle, and I'll take the other, and we'll trudge along home slowly. These beautiful cherry-plums, just like amber. I'll put them on the roof and let them dry out. God willing, we'll sell them this winter."

They had left the highway and were slowly heading in the direction of the village when suddenly the *Rais* on the horse once again blocked their way.

"Give me the pail," he said, leaning down from the horse.

"Why should I do that?"

"I can help carry it. Let's go, I'll take you home. What direction is your house?" he asked in a shaking voice, obeying an overwhelming feeling of guilt.

"This village only has two sides, not eight. We live on this side of the river." Gushver, noting the embarrassment of the *Rais*, softened. "If you want, carry it, that's fine with me. Only, hold the pail tight."

The *Rais* took the heavy pail and put it in front of him.

"Well, let's go."

"Take the child, too. Don't you see the way he looks at the horse? I'd like to sit on your lap myself. But I won't do that, not for anything. I'm afraid you'd feel me up! It's scary how much you look like your lecher father."

The *Rais* lifted the boy and sat with him in the saddle.

"You have a tongue in your head!" he said, trying to make his voice sound lighthearted. "This is the first time I've ever seen such a sharp-tongued person!" He loosened the reins slightly so that horse walked more slowly.

"You should've seen your own father! Forty years he walked around our village and not one person ever heard a single decent word from him."

"You're obsessed with my father. What did he do to you?"

"What could he do to me? I'm obviously not a boy he could catch and circumcise!"

The *Rais* didn't say anything. They moved silently for a long time, and then he cautiously asked the boy, "Did your father die at the front?"

"No, he didn't die," the boy exclaimed happily, with the faith in immortality characteristic of childhood. "He's a commander there, and he has a horse just like yours, white and beautiful."

The *Rais* led the horse slowly so that Gushver could keep up. And the boy, finding himself on a horse for the first time, looked around in delight. And from the back of the horse, the world presented itself to him as miraculously limitless and wonderful because the child was above and the world remained below. Between the ground and Elbey was an immeasurably enormous distance.

The boy wanted the road to go on for a long time so that he could see more and more of the world from that enchanted height. But at the same time, Elbey wanted to arrive in the village more quickly because the village boys had never seen him high up on a horse. And he also wished the pail were full of gold instead of cherry-plums—just like the gold coin his grandmother had found on the road—and that he could scatter those gold coins along the path so his grandmother could pick them up and carry them home; then she'd never again have to walk to the road to sell various edible and inedible things from the first day of spring to late autumn.

"Do many people in the village talk all kinds of nonsense about my father, or are you the only smartypants?" the *Rais* asked extremely cautiously before they came to the entrance of the village, trying to put a brave face on a sorry business.

Gushver *arvad* was a sharp enough and wise enough woman. But even she couldn't have guessed what long-range plans the *Rais* might have in asking such a question.

"And why just me? Everyone talks that way. Or are you planning to renounce your own father?"

"They can't all talk that way! Tell me the names of each of them."

"You want me to list the whole village for you?"

The *Rais* was silent again for a long time and then, right at the entrance to the village, once more started the conversation.

"They say there were people in the village who created rhymes about my father. Do you know who they are?"

"Look for them in your own village! There were no poets in ours."

"But they say there were."

"Well, if there were, that's good. The only thing to do with a person like that is to create obscene verses—everyone who was circumcised knew him. I swear to you, he was an excellent fornicator! Very happy, sharp-witted. It seems you didn't inherit that part of his character. It seems you're very stern. I'm afraid you'll turn into a dragon in the end. Ugh, what a shame that would be!"

Elbey remembered very well that when they arrived at the gates, they were flung wide open, and his mother Eizengiul was putting the samovar in the yard.

Everything from the gates to the veranda was swept clean. In the recently watered yard it smelled of fresh earth; and of the pleasant, slightly intoxicating smoke from the samovar; and of the hardy mint that had finished flowering, which grew in abundance along the sides of all the irrigation canals. (For the rest of his life, his memory of childhood would retain the image of his mother in a reddish, rose-violet dress; her matchless beauty, which until that night he'd never noticed; the happy mooing of the cows returning from the pasture; and the voices of women urging them into the houses to be petted and milked.)

In front of the gates the *Rais* handed Elbey down first. Then, bending low, he gave Gushver the pail. And when he'd already turned the horse, intending to gallop away, he saw the young woman of extraordinary beauty hurriedly coming towards him.

"Come to us, brother—it's not customary to turn back at the threshold at this hour of the evening! We have tea and dinner already prepared. Come in, you'll be our guest," she said, smiling a sad and at the same time slightly coquettish smile and, as if mastering herself, added in a stern voice, "You'll find a place to tie your horse in the yard."

The *Rais* turned and looked at Eizengiul. She also glanced up from below and looked at him. What did the innocent little boy notice in the glances of those two people who'd never before seen one another? Why was he suddenly so frightened, so frightened that he cried?

It was as if those glances also frightened the horse. The *Rais* wanted to turn him and gallop away, but the horse didn't want to move from the spot for anything.

A little later the *Rais* did gallop away, and his mother took Elbey by the hand and led him into the house. There she washed his hands and feet, fed him, and put him to bed. In the middle of the night he woke up in tears and wept bitterly, breathing hoarsely and convulsively, as if demons were tormenting him in his sleep. His sobs were torn from such depths of his soul that it was beyond the power of even his mother to find the source.

VIII

Elbey was awakened by his own scream, his face wet with tears. And the horror of his current situation seized him so swiftly that not a trace remained of the cheerful atmosphere of his childhood dream. He resolved to go to sleep again so as to forget everything. He took off his coat, leaned against the back of the sofa, closed his eyes, and letting his head fall on his chest, dozed off. Not a half-second had passed when, from a long-ago, intolerably hot summer day, Elbey heard the voice of the *Rais*, naked to the waist, sweaty, standing next to his young and beautiful mother. "I also dropped by to drink some *ayran*," he said, toweling sweat from his forehead with a large bath towel.

Elbey woke up from that fleeting dream covered in cold sweat himself and tried to shake off the horror he'd dreamed. But the meek, frightened face of his mother with her smooth, silky skin remained before his eyes. Her mouth slightly open and a guilty expression on her face, she was looking at him with a kind of despair, and her eyes sparkled to an unusual degree. She bit her lips, trying not to cry, and trembled. Elbey distinctly remembered the expression of her face; it had tortured his memory for many years already, causing hellish torments. He was firmly convinced that it was the fault of his beautiful, grey-eyed mother that he'd become who he'd become. "Ah, you loathsome bitch!" Elbey said aloud, catching his breath with difficulty and, rising abruptly from the sofa, ran feverishly into the yard.

In the yard he felt the exact same stuffiness that had followed him two hours ago in the long corridor of Operations HQ for the Restoration of Progress and Pluralism. Not a swallow of air to breathe, not a single sound— exactly like the grave. And the strangest thing of all: he no longer heard Hercules barking.

Elbey climbed up to the room with windows looking out on the sea where he usually slept when he came to this dacha, turned on the light, and went out on the balcony.

The cloudy, grey sky sprawled along the horizon like a giant, dying seal. And it was as if not a single sound remained in the world besides his heavy breathing, whistling like the sound of the death rattle. For Elbey, in whom life had welled up day and night for many years, it was terrible to spend that autumn night all alone at his own dacha. That night had already nestled inside him like a snake in hiding, waiting for the right chance to inflict a fatal bite. He still couldn't understand clearly whether all this was really happening or whether he was imagining it.

He wanted to calmly consider his situation but was overcome by yet more anxiety. The more he remembered his mother, the more repulsed he felt in his soul. He no longer controlled himself, imagination drew pictures for him with extraordinary clarity of that intensely hot summer day after which, it now seemed to him, he'd also become a different person. As if his carefree childhood had irrevocably left him at just that moment. . . .

That night after her son and mother-in-law had fallen asleep, Eizengiul went carefully out into the yard. The moon shone. Light alternated with shadow, shadow with light. Her eyes sought the *Rais* in all the places hidden in shadow—under the trees, the bushes. She quivered with every rustle in the bushes, with the light trembling of leaves. Eizengiul already knew she was in love, and she realized that love was marked with the stamp of shame by the right hand of Allah himself. And in that alarmingly worrying night she sentenced her love to death, firmly resolving never again to allow the *Rais* to approach her, and if she gave birth to a child, to kill herself. And from the next day forward to never let Elbey out of the yard so that the *Rais* would never be able find her alone.

Fortunately, she was not pregnant. For several days Elbey's sheep grazed right in the yard. And Gushver, weary from the everyday trek to the highway in the August heat, decided to stay home for a while. The love that had unexpectedly blazed up in Eizengiul's heart died down by degrees, turning to ashes. And then the *Rais* was transferred to a new position in the district center; he stopped appearing in Giulliukend. And only much later, after seven or eight years (the summer Elbey finished school), for some unknown reason he suddenly remembered the in-no-way remarkable Giulliukend boy who on one intensely hot summer day had caught him with his mother.

And it was precisely about that intensely hot summer day that the *Rais* began to talk at that first meeting with Elbey in his spacious and cool office.

"Well, let's get acquainted," he said, his face inscrutable, extending his hand to Elbey, who gaped at him, open-mouthed. "What, you're afraid of me? Don't be afraid. Do you remember that you and I drank *ayran* together in Giulliukend? I remember it well! And I know you behaved yourself like a man then and not like a gossipy woman. I know you never told anyone about that, how you and I drank *ayran*." He glanced approvingly at Elbey and, having turned his face to the light pouring through the window, became sadly thoughtful. "Oh, it's burning, everything's burning! Kill me, kill me!" he heard the voice of Eizengiul from the far off, unforgettable past, and that voice, perhaps for the thousandth time, resounded in his soul with the tender song of love.

Elbey was seized by utterly unimaginable fear when he remembered and again relived that terrible night when he'd dreamed of his mother in a pool of blood that poured from her womb and the then-*Rais* standing beside her with a bloody red towel around his shoulders, dripping with sweat. And possibly the *Rais* in his dreams drenched with blood and pain had been exactly the same then as he was now: powerful, authoritative, and dangerous. Elbey felt himself caught like a bird and almost wept.

"I know you've finished school," said the *Rais* almost tenderly. "You aren't going to study at an institute because you were a poor student—I know you never got more than passing grades. What are you planning to do now? Do you have some kind of goal?"

"I'm going into the army," Elbey answered. More than anything, he wanted at that very moment to run away from the office of the *Rais*; he was afraid of him.

"You're not going into the army!" the *Rais* said decisively, stood up, and quickly went to the window.

The window of his office opened onto a little yard. Two elms with yellowing leaves, three or four stunted pomegranate bushes, and a hazelnut bush grew there. He looked at them a long time, then returned and sat down at his desk.

"I'll hire you to work for me. You'll get a good salary. You'll work some, find out about life. You'll earn some money and help your mother. I'll arrange housing for you, you'll be comfortable. I'll take care of the question of your draft notice myself. Now you're going home, but tomorrow morning you'll take the first bus and come here."

To this very day Elbey remembered how happy he'd been when he tore himself from the office of the *Rais*, although the little town was swimming in an intense haze of heat under a sun that melted anything and everything. He walked under its fiery rays understanding very little, but with some sort of consciousness that something fateful had happened in his life—that something had gone out of it to which there was no return. (Elbey would live fifty years in the world after that day and still not understand whether the *Rais* had remembered him and hired him because he'd told no one, not even his grandmother, that he'd seen the *Rais* alone with his mother—although over time he'd realize that, more than anything, the *Rais* valued the ability to be silent in people. On the other hand, he would understand—it was impossible not to understand—that human submissiveness was the very air his protector breathed.)

And precisely because the strength and authoritativeness of the *Rais* were insurmountable, Elbey appeared before him the next day exactly at the appointed time and drove himself into the earthly hell that he was destined to bear within himself for many years. Precisely because of his fear before the *Rais*, he shut his mouth with a lock and uncomplainingly endured thousands of humiliations and insults. Elbey lost the feeling of time and stopped being master of himself. He didn't find and didn't even look for a path to be saved, the only road along which he might have escaped. And years later he was perplexed about why his life from its very beginning had not been in his own hands but the in hands of some other person.

It seems (O Noble Reader!) that complicated philosophy wants to climb into our simple-hearted narrative, although it's possible to avoid strained philosophical maxims in speaking about the insurmountable power of fear.

Probably everyone knows what fear is, but hardly any of us contemplate the impenetrable abyss where it builds its nest. Keeping in mind how Elbey, having observed the secret glances exchanged by his mother and the *Rais*, was frightened one evening on the threshold of his own house, we (with the help of Freud) can suppose it was precisely then that the hidden fear that would ruthlessly devastate his soul took root in Elbey, nesting there once and for all.

Let's say it all happened exactly that way. But how can we find an explanation for the incontrovertible fact that it was by no means Elbey alone who trembled that way before the *Rais*? All my beloved land with its mountains and plains, houses and roads, mosques and minarets, with its mystically plaintive cemetery music and people full of love, sated with reading *Sword and Quill*, shook before him.

"Fear of him makes even curly-haired men bald" is what my most courageous fellow villagers said about him to one another in secret, after which they lived day and night in an anxiously melancholy condition, fearing that someone someday would inform the *Rais* about what they'd said. And if there was no evil power mixed up in that, then from what unknown depths did that fear—by which my beloved fellow villagers were deprived of will and now all good Allahabad folk (who once weren't so submissive or cowardly) tremble—take its beginnings? (O Reader, don't leave me alone with my fear!)

Perhaps it only seemed to my courageous fellow villagers that they were going bald just then, but in fact they'd been that way since their very birth, and it was necessary—if not for Allah, then in any case for his Prophet-Messenger—to see them that way. Especially because not one of my fellow villagers was granted the ability to even conceive that the *Rais* was also afraid of them, and that he was so fiercely cruel and free of all morals because their *Rais* had also been "bald" from birth, and that he derived his power from the weakness of people.

And in that lay not his strength but his weakness. And that's why he constructed his path with threats and coercion; a master of disguise, he loved to blackmail people and twist anyone around his finger in any way he needed.

But that's still not all, if we're speaking about the philosophy of fear. Fear is earthly hell for the human soul. In that hell everyone suffers the same but each in his own apartment. Of course, the *Rais* didn't willingly choose his own hellish apartment. People forcibly drove him there, and he hated them intensely for that, hated them because all of them together had turned his father into a general laughing stock, thinking up humiliating, cockamamie stories about him, rhymes and all kinds of other filth; hated them because in school the hooligan boys had mocked him, and the girls' contingent out of stupidity had whispered hurtfully every time he appeared, whether in the street, at a wedding, by the river, by the spring. . . . Wasn't it really because of human meanness that he'd had to tear himself from his first sweet love, whose place in his soul was taken by incessantly throbbing and bleeding pain? And in that fateful hour for Elbey when the *Rais* had suddenly remembered the in-no-way remarkable boy from Giulliukend, his soul, without any doubt, was seeking not Elbey but Eizengiul; however, he didn't allow himself to risk his career another time, not even in thought. On the contrary, he was constantly punishing himself for that long-ago risk and had already for many years rejoiced every morning when he woke up that no one, thank God, had found out about that *special*, fleeting portion of his life. God forbid anyone should find out in future. That fact alone would be more than enough for enemies to crush him and for all the people to curse him for all time.

And enemies were ubiquitous. The *Rais* constantly felt their spittle mentally aimed at him from every dark corner. And that strengthened his thirst for power. For him, the obstinacy of Hercules was indeed necessary in order to defend himself from enemies and enter the very height of authority where, it seemed to him, there wouldn't be any fear, any humiliation. (But we know well, Reader, what hellish torments of fear he endured even at the height of authority, trying to keep himself there for us even after his time had passed!)

IX

Lost in the chaos of thoughts and feelings, Elbey now thought about Firdovsy. It would probably have given him even more joy to discover his caretaker here now than all the gold that the staff jinns of the *Rais* had found (probably after examining every square inch of earth with special instruments and finally reaching the swimming pool).

It was surprising, but he received more pleasure from a couple of hours' interaction with Firdovsy than with a gaggle of highly placed personages practically lining up to land him as their guest. With Firdovsy he really rested, relaxed. If he got free time he left work and came straight here. And sometimes he even sent a car for Firdovsy to convey him to Sosnovka. Not often, but perhaps once a month they got together. They ate, drank, laughed together, and parted lightheartedly. And strangely enough, no matter how much Firdovsy drank in Elbey's company, not once was he unbecomingly drunk.

Elbey consumed the excellent vodka with mushroom *shashlyk* and chicken *chykhyrtma* that Firdovsy masterfully prepared with pleasure. And he heard the poems created by Firdovsy with the exact same degree of pleasure. Here it's necessary to note that besides *Sword and Quill*, Elbey had never in his life finished a single book. And Firdovsy didn't think of himself as a poet; however, Elbey ranked the very silliest of the caretaker's poems higher than the doggerel of Giulara's beloved Giuliumjan Janday, considering them much more beautiful, smarter, and richer in content. He particularly liked Firdovsy's poem about Gorbachev. He sometimes remembered individual lines even at work, and now and then they distracted him, delivering him from a bad mood. Here's an example:

> *The brother of Satan himself, despicable Gorbachev,*
> *Arranged himself on top so as to shit on us all.*
> *He took the pants off the country, stripped folks down to threads.*
> *Gave freedom to the shriekers, streamed shit on our heads.*
> *You, O Honest Person, believe, believe you me,*
> *Better than the USSR I will never see.*

It's hard to understand why Elbey liked this poem so much, for in reality it was thanks to the disintegration of the USSR that he'd become the possessor of such wealth and thanks to the political short-sightedness of Gorbachev that he was able to make use of the current inconceivable privileges. If we grant that fact, then Elbey certainly shouldn't have liked the poem "The Dragon"; on the contrary, he should have thrown Firdovsy out of the dacha once and for all for such a creation. Just think:

> *Everyone everywhere roared that people power would win,*
> *People would get their freedom, live to their hearts' content.*
> *But then a black wind blew; the Dragon showed his face*
> *And squeezed the people tight, tight, tight in his embrace.*
> *Do dragons love their people? No one thinks that way.*
> *Save us, Heavenly Lord, from this Dragon's embrace.*

Is it possible Elbey that didn't guess which dragon was meant in those venomous lines improvised on the fly by the former teacher of literature? Perhaps for the chief of the Operations HQ for the Restoration of Waterfalls it was that same terrible person who'd squeezed the people so cruelly deceived by him in a fatal embrace. Or was it a different kind of monster, one who had driven the country into the very heart of a historic spiderweb, who had changed History Itself into a sinister dragon's dungeon so as to himself shine as its brightest star, to become a symbol of all-encompassing happiness and an idol of all-encompassing worship? That's too complex a question for us. But in any case, every time he heard that poem Elbey remembered to protect himself: "How well you depict that Armenian Kocharyan as the dragon," he kept repeating. "Or maybe you're mocking Bush here? Or did you have Putin in mind for the dragon? Ha, ha, ha!" Elbey laughed with gusto.

He thought he'd never see Firdovsy again, and his mood was utterly ruined. Even the sea bored him; he went back into the room, thought he'd turn on the television but didn't. He suddenly remembered that for a long time he'd wanted a drink—he'd drunk hardly anything since early morning. Elbey went to the kitchen to relieve his thirst, but when he walked in, his eyes opened on the most fantastic scene of the spectacle prepared for him today by the great Defender of Vocations. A snow-white cloth was spread on the table, and laid out on it were a freshly roasted piglet, various types of *shashlyk*, Erzincan meatballs, Kellekend dolmas from grape leaves, caviar (black and red), French cognac, Italian wine, Russian Beluga vodka. . . . Most of all, Elbey was struck by the fact that while searching around the whole house earlier, he apparently hadn't noticed anything of the sort. "Mamochka, what's this?" moaned Elbey and began to hammer his sweaty chest with his fists. Was it possible that the

Master had found one more scorpion-like way to bewitch people, to lull a person to sleep with sweet dreams in order to chop off his head?

He drank some water, and having relieved his thirst, he suddenly thought that perhaps the Master intended to appear here to personally sniff out what smelled, to find out what was now sustaining Elbey—whether he was prepared to silently bear the punishment intended for him—and also to conduct an edifying conversation with Elbey to warn him against taking a "false step." No one could really predict what additional devilish bedlam he was prepared to arrange for Elbey. And that bedlam might begin at any time: tonight, tomorrow morning, and possibly right now—in one, two, three minutes. Yes, the Master was always able and loved to manipulate the emotions of people in order to bring everyone to full obedience. Even in those situations where he sentenced people simply to an inglorious death without resorting to crude violence. But was he really going to do that with Elbey? To take him and throw him in the trash can like a half-eaten apple? They were like relatives, after all! For a hundred years before the Main Building, Elbey had already known him as his chief-for-life: *Rais, Rais, Rais. . . .* And for more than ten years now they'd inhabited the very heart of Power together. And there was no person who could have been better informed than Elbey about everything that had happened and was happening in the Seat of Power.

As if from the thick darkness of the underworld, the voice of the *Rais* suddenly reached Elbey: "If you wound a snake, you must finish it off!" And Elbey shook from that sudden splash of memory. As if the wounded snakes of the whole world had lifted their heads, pointing at him! Yes, those were *his* words. He always said them with special cruelty, even fury, leaping up, his face changing sharply.

Elbey collapsed weakly on the sofa. And at that same moment the sound of a cell phone reached his ears, ears that were worn out with hallucinations.

An ordinary local number beginning with 012 lit up the screen. But the frighteningly menacing voice Elbey heard belonged to the person who'd just promised him a terrible, snake-like death.

"Listen, what did you just dare to do?"

"What do you mean?" His own voice sounded strange to Elbey.

"Why did you insult that Russian fellow?"

It was necessary to know the DIV well to understand why he started the conversation that way.

"Who . . . I didn't insult . . . anyone," said Elbey haltingly.

"You threw the driver out on the street. Do you really not know how dearly that's going to cost you?"

"I know."

"What do you know?" Now he was shouting at the top of his voice.

"Exactly what you say, *Ra*—" That damned habit! Elbey had almost said "*Rais.*"

"*Ra, Ra*—Listen, what's this with *Ra*—?" The voice changed a little. "You say 'Mus—' and don't finish 'Mustafa'? Thirty years ago I was your *Rais*, and you still can't break yourself of the habit of calling me that. You say '*Ra*—' and look blank, like a ram. Because you are a stupid, dim-witted animal! And you don't want to grow, become a person."

"Well, I . . ." Elbey wasn't able to utter another word.

"That's what I mean!" The Defender of Vocations was seized with laughter. "Well, so, you won't make any more mischief?" he asked, his laughter finished.

Elbey was silent, clenching his teeth. A careless word might lead to new unpleasantness, he knew that exceedingly well.

"Why are you silent? Maybe you're offended by me?"

"No, why would that be? I don't have any reason to be offended by you."

Now the Master was silent for a while. Possibly it seemed to him that he hadn't given his voice the required authoritativeness.

"Well, that's right. Good for you, that you're not offended. It means you understood everything and drew the correct conclusions. You really don't have any reason to be offended by me. I gave you what I've never given anyone in my whole life. You sat in your chair only because I sat you there. But now I can't let you remain in your former job, even if I really wanted to. I don't have the moral right. Because you started to be naughty, Elbey. You created a state within the state. Who named the head of the district? Elbey, of course. Who authorized the building of the wine factory? Elbey, again. There isn't an outhouse in this country into which you haven't poked your long nose. To what didn't you put your mangy hands? You forced judges and prosecutors to crawl on all fours in front of you. You turned the police into menageries. All the heads of the executive branch, like true dogs, were only concerned with collecting gold for you. You started to bite the hand that feeds you. How could I leave you in a responsible job after that shame?"

"I didn't do anything without your orders," said Elbey, barely audible, and understood immediately that he ought not to have said it.

"No, you didn't understand anything. You still don't understand anything! And it seems you're not able to understand!" Not anger but rather insult, even sincere regret, began to sound in the shaking voice of the Master. Perhaps he hadn't expected to hear anything like that from Elbey. Or, in starting the conversation, had he intentionally wanted to see whether Elbey would say something like that? The chief of Operations HQ should have remembered how his own Chief was able to mask his true thoughts.

"Forgive me, I made a mistake. I won't say that again. All that was unlawful, what you said—it's on my conscience alone." Elbey said this in a barely audible voice, trying to suppress the flood of anger that had arisen inside.

The Master was again silent for a long while. Elbey understood that he'd told the truth for nothing. He should have immediately taken all the sin on himself, ninety-nine percent of which he'd committed under the personal orders of His Satanic Majesty, the Father of the Fatherland.

"Look here," the Master sighed, deeply and sadly. "Listen to what I say. What's done is done. So let everything you collected and hid remain with you. But on one condition: keep your mouth shut!" He was again silent for a while. "Understand?"

"I understand, how could I not?" Elbey sat, burying his head in his hands, and it was as if he were swimming in the dark.

The phone was silent again. This time the quiet lasted much longer.

"How are things at the dacha?"

"Everything's fine."

"I ordered them to leave it in good shape."

"They did, I'm grateful to you."

"I ordered them to leave you something to eat."

"They did, thanks."

"I'll find the time—I'll come over myself. I just need a little while to come to myself."

"I'll wait with impatience." Elbey himself didn't understand where those foolish words had come from.

"You've started to talk a bit too politely. It's evident that you've watched some television. Fine, don't even think of bursting into tears," he added generously, not hiding his malicious pleasure at that.

"No, I haven't turned on the television yet." Elbey thought that now the official part of the conversation was finished, the artistic part, the "amusement," as they called it in the Main Building, was beginning. But he still had to endure more than a few tormenting minutes, listening without complaint and swallowing lie after lie.

"You don't miss your poet?"

"Which poet are you talking about?"

"Well, you had a caretaker—a poet-faggot. I know you cared about him a great deal."

Elbey felt the urge to ask what had happened to the caretaker. Was he alive or . . .? But he didn't ask. He understood that this was not yet the final thrust; the final thrust was still to come.

And the Chief continued with his characteristic harshness:

"You remember how much trouble I took to make you read *Sword and Quill*? I was always fussing over seeing you develop, become a cultured person. It didn't happen, you didn't want that. You showed rare speed only when you smelled gold and dollar bills and connected yourself with people as primitive as you are yourself. How am I guilty in that?"

"I remember," said Elbey, "I remember very well. . . ." For some reason the mournful, grey eyes of his mother suddenly appeared before his mental gaze, looking at him from a far-off, intensely hot summer emptiness.

"I recruited that Russian fellow so he'd protect you. So he'd be your servant, so he'd help. If you don't want him, no need, I won't interfere in your affairs. But I wouldn't want all that rabble to get established in your dacha. Chatterboxes like that Giuliumjan Janday. I asked around, and now I know precisely: he's the one who thought up that stinking DIV catchword, and that what's-his-name—that one who's straight like a stick, the ignorant and good-for-nothing idler and hack artist whose instinct for self-preservation obviously failed—spread it around." He said these words all in one breath, trying not to show the infirmities of his age, but Elbey couldn't fail to notice his heavy breathing and, having known his Chief since day one, suddenly caught on. Could the Chief himself have thought up that nickname and spread it around the country in order to once and for all settle accounts with any remaining enemies he suspected of being discontented with the regime? To arrange a last, colossal roundup and eradicate the manifestation of any form of dissent?

"No one will come to the dacha," Elbey assured him and thought to himself that it would have been a good thing if Giuliumjan had been at the dacha today; he would have gotten it out of the poet and found out what other gossip was going around the city. He would have gotten him drunk, forced him to recite poems and, look, the night would have been over.

"And you want to say you don't know who called me that? You knew! You've known a long time! Your poet-faggot, whom you paid five hundred dollars a month, who lived at your dacha and composed epigrams against me! And you listened with pleasure. What a scoundrel you are, Elbey!"

For the umpteenth time this day it went dark before Elbey's eyes. There was no possible doubt that the family of Firdovsy had been left without a breadwinner. And they'd probably done something with poor Mamed-aga. And of course they'd fired Kolya; a person couldn't hang around the Seat of Power who hadn't been able to fulfill the will of the Greatest of the Great.

"What a blockhead you are, Elbey! I dreamed up the best job in the administration for you; I racked my brains for a whole month creating the name for your good-for-nothing institute! And after eleven years you haven't even learned to pronounce it correctly. Go ahead, Elbey, say the word 'pluralism.'"

"You thought that name up for yourself!" Elbey snapped angrily in his thoughts and was silent, experiencing the taste of bile in his mouth.

"Well, Elbey, say it: 'plu-ra-lism.'"

"Pullarism," muttered Elbey and heard the black whistle of fear clearly in his ears.

"Pullarism![4] Oh, you! Look what your rotten mind cooked up! And do you remember how you disgraced yourself in front of the whole country on television by addressing your opponent as 'Mister Impotent'?"

"Yes, I remember," affirmed Elbey in a sepulchral voice, although he knew very well that nothing of the sort had ever happened.

"Eh, what happened? Where did you go? Are you really embarrassed about your disgusting behavior? Listen, if the idiotic thought suddenly pops into your head to take off abroad—don't do it!"

"Yes, sir!" Elbey was barely able to utter. "What would I do abroad?"

"Exactly, so sit where you are in your dacha and enjoy life! You always enjoyed life. You lived it up, and I suffered. You'll be all right if you behave yourself—you'll have enough for bread and butter." Through the phone a wheeze could be heard, torn from his chest. "Today I'm very tired. I'll go rest a while, and you remember my words: breathing in is easier than breathing out." With that, the telephone call ended.

X

Hardly knowing where he was, Elbey lay on the sofa for some time gazing at the ceiling. Then he felt thirsty again. Opening a bottle of water, he drank it all down, straight from the bottle. Suddenly his glance fell on the boxes standing near the refrigerator: two boxes of Beluga vodka. It was as if Elbey had been struck by a current of electricity. It occurred to the former chief of the Department on Questions of Pluralism that one of the simplest methods the Master used to eliminate people was to gradually instill a passion for drinking in the undesirable person and get rid of him that way. In fact, those cunning and deeply confidential tasks had even been handled by Elbey. This was done mainly with worthless "tender-assed" and "shit-headed" people and always led to the desired result. Moreover, Elbey himself very much liked that method, first of all because in saying "get rid of that enemy" the Master didn't consider it necessary to eliminate the enemy physically (he was, undoubtedly, a great humanist). The point was just to gradually remove the undesirable person from the public sphere. The Chief himself composed the list of those he suspected of dissatisfaction with the regime. And following that list, Elbey made drunkards out of some with the best French champagne or cognac and others with ordinary "factory" vodka. For example, in just three months Elbey had made a drunkard of a fifty-year-old People's Artist, the poet Gyrchyn Darchynly (who'd once incautiously expressed doubt about the genius of the Master at someone's funeral feast), with cheap "factory" vodka—after which they solemnly, with great honor, accompanied that unfortunate person on his last journey. Seventy-seven-year-old composer Shabustar Subkhany had been able to savor French champagne for all of forty-seven days. And world-renowned master of the brush Fatekh Faragat (who'd gotten his first real taste of French cognac only at age eighty) was now destined to "heave a parting sigh" in just two months, according to the preliminary prognosis.

Elbey kicked one of the boxes with such force that the pain in his foot was answered with an echoing ache in his brain. "No, Master, that's not going to work with me," he said in a confident voice in his head, and he looked with hatred at the bottle of Beluga standing on the table. After that he opened the refrigerator that was stuffed completely full, pulled out a roll of sausage, cut it in half, and went into the yard to visit Hercules, whom he called Hero.

When he was ten to fifteen steps from the dog's cage he smelled such a stench that he stopped and pinched his nose shut with his fingers—so that was what "dog stink" was! Clenching his teeth, he took another few steps. It was not necessary to go further: *the dog had kicked the bucket*! Moreover, it looked like the unfortunate Hercules had experienced an excruciating dog's martyrdom. It seemed the hatred of all brutally killed dogs was realized in his clenched jaws and the teeth bared before death. His black fur had acquired an earthy hue.

Elbey ran with all his might, tearing off a sprig of cilantro from a bed along the way. Bruising the herb, he lifted it to his nose to mask the stench, if only just a little. The most terrifying, bared dog fangs still stood before his eyes.

He climbed to the balcony on shaking legs. This time the sea presented itself before Elbey's gaze not as a dead seal but as an all-powerful dragon that, jaws gaping, was prepared to swallow all living things. Elbey wasn't the slightest bit surprised when that sinister dragon in a human voice spewed forth, "If you wound a snake, you must finish it off!"

There was hardly a man in his native Giulliukend who hadn't killed a snake or two in his time. And he himself had killed a great number of them. And now it was as if all of them had suddenly come back to life and appeared before him: the saw-scaled viper, the black adder, the smooth snake, the Levant viper, the cobra, the steppe ribbon racer. He remembered how long it takes and how excruciating it is for snakes to die. "A snake hasn't breathed its last until it sees the stars"—all of Giulliukend, from three-year-old children to grey-haired old people, knew those words. Elbey knew very well: in order to kill a snake, it was necessary to crush the head. While the head was intact the snake would live, even if you cut the body into a hundred pieces.

"If you wound a snake . . ."—that fragment of a phrase had whirled obsessively around Elbey's head even before the phone call from the *Rais*. But now he believed, it seems, that it wasn't in the plans of the Chief to finish him off. Otherwise, why would he have sent him here? He could have sent him to an entirely different place. And perhaps while he considered it necessary for now to send just Firdovsy and Mamed-aga to that "other place," he was going to dig up more dirt on Elbey. With Mamed-aga all was clear; he'd only just been sent to the "other place." But poor Firdovsy had probably been there a while. And they'd put the unfortunate dog in his metal cage most likely when they'd come for Firdovsy. Perhaps Firdovsy himself had locked up Hercules when they arrived, those who later caught him and shoved him into a car. How many days had Hercules sat in that cage? And having stuffed the refrigerator with food, why hadn't someone thrown a piece of bread to the dog? Perhaps because nothing had been ordered with respect to the dog, just "Put the dacha in order. Arrange food and drink of the best sort. Gold. . . ." No, those who cleaned up the dacha wouldn't have known anything about the gold. The gold was the business of one, at most two people. Everyone did his own task at the personal order of the Chief. And with regard to the dog, evidently, there had been no instructions. Even a dog couldn't live in that world without *his* imperial command. . . . But had Hercules really starved to death? Elbey was worried by a sudden suspicion: if that were the case, where did the stench come from? Was it possible that a dog who'd died from hunger just a few hours previously could stink so badly? Because Hercules had been whining, calling Elbey to help the moment he'd stepped into the yard. That meant they'd *poisoned* him—? That thought stunned Elbey because it was fully plausible. Only the *Rais* could resort to such Jesuitical methods to frighten, humiliate, and morally annihilate a person who'd uncomplainingly served him over the course of many years branded with the stamp of damnation. It was undoubtedly his last warning. The Master was saying, "Look at the dog and think of yourself. If you don't hold your tongue, the same dog's death awaits you."

Elbey once again sensed the stink emanating from the depths of the garden. Had the scent ever left his nose? It seemed to be everywhere: in the dacha, around the dacha, even in the sky and the sea.

Elbey returned to the kitchen—it stank there, too. He decided to go to the bathroom to take a shower, hoping to get rid of the stinking smell. He took off his jacket and threw it on the sofa. When he unbuckled his belt, he discovered that all this time he'd been wearing his pistol, and at that he lost the desire to take a shower. With horror he suddenly realized the diabolical thought that had probably led the Master to leave him the pistol: "If you want to shoot yourself, that's easy—go ahead, shoot yourself, and that's that."

Already frightened of his own pistol, Elbey sat on the corner of the sofa and fixed his gaze on the food. Perhaps it was necessary to be afraid of even the food? Or perhaps of the large bottle of Beluga standing on the table?

With shaking hands he poured himself a glass of vodka. He drank, but the vodka didn't act on him in any way. He had to pour another glass. He drank it in one mouthful and finally felt an easing, experienced how his soul was freed from fear, from all the horrors of the day he'd just lived through. A pleasant warmth spread over his whole body. The stench receded. And at that moment the phone came to life.

Giunel was calling.

"Yes, daughter, I'm here," answered Elbey in the most cheerful voice possible.

"Papa! Papa! How are you?" Alarm sounded in his daughter's voice.

"Excellent. Absolutely outstanding. How are things at home?" Elbey really did feel superb.

"Everything's fine at home. Tell the truth, Papa, how do you feel?"

"Fine, honestly. And when I heard your voice, everything became entirely perfect."

"Papa, do you want me to come and stay at the dacha with you for a while?"

"No," Elbey's euphoria began to fade a little. "It's not worth it, daughter. I want to rest alone for a couple of days. Come to myself a little."

"Well, then, rest, Papa. You really haven't had a break for a long time. Do you want Mama to come?"

"No, no need. There's no need for anyone to come here!" Elbey began to get angry. "I want to be alone a little."

"Fine, Papa, whatever you want. I like your voice, it's cheerful, thank God! Will you promise me to always be so cheerful? Don't think about anything bad, okay, Papa?"

"It's already late to worry about anything, daughter."

"That's true, Papa. A person can't stay in a good job forever. Sooner or later you'd have left yourself."

"That's true, daughter."

"Mama says to tell you hello. We all love you very much."

"Thank you, I love you very much, too."

"Okay, rest well. If you need anything, say so."

"I'll let you know, my daughter, I'll absolutely let you know."

"Kisses, Papa, good night."

"Good night, my little girl."

God's world plunged anew into quiet, as if the angel of silence had flown over it. And in that immense quiet he saw himself, defenseless and boundlessly alone, having nothing to show for himself now besides his sixty-six years. He swam in the cloud of a hangover, and in that half-light the dog was again before his eyes. The fact that the dog still lay in the yard aroused a sharp anxiety in him. He regretted that he'd driven Kolya away and was already thinking about whether to throw the dog's carcass away somewhere himself or dig a hole at the dacha and bury it. Drinking still another full glass of vodka, he firmly resolved that the time had come to call Giuliumjan Janday; then even the problem of burying the dog could be resolved quite simply. But it was a strange thing: although the entire universe practically rang with the voice of Giuliumjan Janday, the heavy shovel somehow turned out to be in the hands of Elbey himself. He himself would have to dig the grave, but he just couldn't, no matter how hard he tried; the earth wasn't the local sort, soft and sandy, but the kind of earth in his native Giulliukend, hard and stony. And when he tried again to dig, suddenly his grandmother Gushver began persistently calling Elbey in her cheerful, battle-ready voice: "Time to get up, now, get a move on, we're already late getting started." The visions changed from one to another with the swiftness that's possible only in dreams; the next minute Giuliumjan in the flesh (tipsy, as always) already stood in the kitchen. Waving his hands, he bawled verses:

> *Powerful and glorious, great and mighty,*
> *Bright like a star, like a ray of sun.*
> *O brother of all, father, and true friend,*
> *Eternal benefactor, to you I bow down.*

Even asleep, Elbey understood where the poet had gotten his mad inspiration, undoubtedly from the abundance of victuals on the kitchen table. But the former chief of Operations HQ for the Restoration of Fountains was able to remember the lines from the long poem dedicated to himself, Elbey (on the occasion of one of his birthdays), thanks only to the magic of dreams. Until then, for the life of him he'd been unable to recall a single line of the multifaceted creation of Giulara's favorite poet. And if it weren't for the magic of dreams, then how could the eyes of the piglet roasted over wood chips from an oak stump turn out to look so terrifyingly like the eyes of the well-known court poet Giuliumjan Janday? Mutual respect and love could be read in the glances of these two strange beings fixed on one another. "Hey, wait a minute!" shouted Elbey evilly, with even a little bit of hatred for Giuliumjan, seeing that the poet was preparing to dig into the piglet. "First go bury the dog. Burn everything there so the dacha doesn't smell like carrion. Then come back, then we'll enjoy life until dawn!" However, Giuliumjan, who over the last five to ten years had visited the shrine in Mashhad four times, Karbala three times, and completed the *haj* twice (on the orders of Giulara and the money of Elbey), mutely salivating, continued to look fixedly at the piglet. "Hey, I'm talking to you!" Elbey shouted loudly but didn't hear his own voice. He wanted to get up, grab the shovel, forcibly shove it in the poet's hand, and direct him to work, but no matter how hard he tried, he couldn't move from his place. And then his grandmother Gushver began pestering him anew: "Sleep, my son, sleep deeply," she said first in a voice from beyond the grave, and then she sang a song unknown to Elbey: "What's lost is gone for good, la-la-la, le-le-le, lo-lo-lo, loi-lo. . . ."

Elbey wanted to go to the swimming pool, collect a whole pail of gold, and give it to his grandmother, but the dream continued to work its wonders: the radiance of the gold coin found long ago by Gushver struck Elbey in the eyes, but just as before, he couldn't move from his place. He wasn't even able to lift his eyelids to look at the gold. The telephone exploded with rings either from London or from Frankfurt (or perhaps Giuliumjan was calling). But the dream immediately translated those rings into its own language. For example, Gushver's empty pails softly jingling along the road as she returned from trading, or an enormous dog bursting from its rusty shackles somewhere and preparing to attack Elbey. . . .

And he himself, having drunk a bottle of Beluga, lay on the sofa as he was, in his clothes, and dreamed his unhappy dreams.

It was still early, very early—all of eleven minutes before eleven.

* * *

That night, having slept a little, the Master woke up anxious and animated. He wanted to fall asleep again but couldn't. However strange it was, desire suddenly came to life in him. He wasn't able to control his imagination, and with unusual vividness it drew for him one picture sweeter than the last. Something warm and light crept into his soul, something that resembled what he'd experienced long ago before his meeting with Eizengiul; once again, he desperately wanted to embrace, kiss, and love her. . . .

A a month went by after those glances he and Eizengiul had exchanged, but the woman continually stood before the inspector's eyes. And on that day, not having closed his eyes until morning, he understood he wasn't able oppose the call of body and soul any longer. First he rode to the highway where Gushver usually traded to satisfy himself that the old woman was in her regular place. The *Rais* didn't worry especially about the boy; he'd often seen how the boy grazed the sheep the whole day. But so that no one among the villagers noticed him, he approached Eizengiul at the height of the intense noontime heat when everyone hid from the heat in their homes and not a soul remained on the street.

Setting out when the sun stood at its very zenith, he left the horse on a slope between Kellekend and Giulliukend and arrived at her home by a path he'd selected earlier. The meeting about which he'd long dreamed finally took place (and everything happened as it should have).

Returning by the same path on which he'd arrived, he climbed down towards the river. The intense heat haze shimmered in the air, but the heat didn't seem tormenting to him; on the contrary, it spread as healing medicine through his body, as if absorbing in itself the tenderness and sweetness of that half-hour he'd spent with Eizengiul. The burning desire to embrace her once more tormented him. From that intense heat, from the river's coolness, from the earth on which he walked, all around he heard Eizengiul's voice: "Oh, it's burning, everything's burning! Kill me, kill me!" Having "killed" her several times and having himself died a similar number of times during that half-hour in her tender embrace, he was still not sated with her. And he didn't believe he could ever be sated. Saitsfying himself that the horse was grazing in the same place where he'd left him, the *Rais* lay down under a spreading oak in a green glade a little way from the river and slept deeply until evening.

And waking up, he undressed and threw himself in the very deepest part of the river. There he embraced the water, gentle like the satin skin of Eizengiul, and assured himself that the feeling of happiness they'd both experienced in that half-hour hadn't left his breast, perhaps would never leave. The *Rais* had previously had secret meetings with women, but not once had he experienced such delight. (Yes, Reader, the then-*Rais* guessed correctly that he'd never again be granted such happy embraces.)

PART THREE

fully plausible

In this penultimate chapter of our not-uncompromising narrative, we're carried once more into the past life of today's leader-for-life, the Father of our Fatherland, this time attempting to single out several indisputably documented moments of it that are characteristic not only of our main character but of the whole motley international brotherhood of lovers of power.

XI

In my native land with its plaintively mystical music, where even the curly-haired grew bald from fear before the *Rais*, there was now a new representative of authority. His main task was to walk the crowded places of the town, glance into the bazaar, the two tearooms—one next to the bazaar, the other not far from the Shah Abbas bathhouse—and the cafeteria located in the center of the little town, listen to the conversations, and report daily about everything to the *Rais*.

In the first days after he'd become the representative of authority, Elbey walked around the cafeteria and tearooms with pleasure because he could eat to his heart's content and drink tea there. (The *Rais* never stinted on money for his underling.) But over time he began to notice that people eyed him suspiciously and quite often with open disdain. And once it came to his ears that they were laughing at him, changing one letter of his name and calling him not Elbey but Albey, meaning "tame bey." From that moment, his appetite disappeared.

There was no one in that land who wasn't afraid of the *Rais*. But when it seemed to the Master that individual people stopped trembling before him, he instantly found the means to unite them in a monolithic, easily directed crowd. For example, on Saturdays and Sundays he closed the cafeteria and both tearooms; all the cooks and tearoom workers had to take part in *subbotniks*. In the center of town where the shops of the tailors, barbers, and blacksmiths were crowded together, he ordered the opening of an Alley of

Honored Repose and the transfer there of the graves of people who'd displayed courage on the home front during wartime. (Compiling the list of such people was entrusted to the head of ZAGSONOT, Siddiga, and her husband, the editor of the newspaper *Glorious Allahabad*, the famous poet and publicist Khatam Vazek.) He gave orders for the House of Culture to conduct mass events on Sundays, for example, on a theme found with the help of the afore-mentioned poet: "With our mighty sword and quill, we'll slash the scoundrels till they're killed."

Not a single social event was managed without the participation of the *Rais* and of personages from a list personally composed by him, on which were inscribed the exact same, more-or-less publicly recognized names of important figures in writing, singing, the visual arts, etc. who were prepared to greet any of his initiatives with stormy, prolonged applause. Like an alchemist, he mixed lessons extracted from his prior shortcomings with today's successes, always achieving the desired tomorrow.

In a word, in my native land there was no power capable of opposing the *Rais*. He understood that, and understanding made him stronger still. However, the *Rais* wanted my poor fellow villagers to bow down to him out of something beyond fear. The people must truly respect and value him, must know that the *Rais* toiled only in the name of the people and that his single goal was for people all around to find out about our land, for poets to create poems about it, for singers to sing songs, and for the mountains and springs of his Kellekend to be captured in all their beauty and glory on the canvases of artists. He was a cruel person but also partly a dreamer. He wanted to be the all-powerful *Rais* and at the same time the Master of the People's Soul. But on that precise point he had no success; it seemed to him that until such time when there were no people left who remembered his father Piri Preputsy, no one would respect him. And he couldn't do anything about the base, obstinate memory of the people.

And then there was his aunt, the actual sister of his father!

Aunt Dilber had married long ago and for more than thirty years had lived in the town and worked in the Shah Abbas bathhouse as a cashier-purser, a fact that, naturally, did not increase respect for the *Rais*. He implored her hundreds of times to leave that job and stay at home. But all for nothing: every time her nephew started to go on about that, she raised a shout. "Let your fellow town-dwellers choke on their respect for you! I don't need that kind of respect. My daughter studies in another city, and I have to send her money every month."

"I'll give you that money."

"If you have that much, buy diamonds, let your wife hang them on her you-know-what. I don't need your money."

Several times he dispatched the glib Siddiga to his aunt. But even the eloquent Siddiga, whose tongue could charm a snake, couldn't convince Dilber.

Strictly speaking, the only person who warmed the heart of the *Rais* was that same Siddiga, the head of the powerful ZAGSONOT and the wife of the poet-publicist Khatam Vazek. The *Rais* valued highly the advice of that experienced woman about whom he'd heard since childhood. For many years she was his most dependable source of information. He talked with her by phone every day. If necessary, he went to visit her at home. Siddiga valued his trust, knew her business very well, and understood the *Rais* from a single word. She was even able to read in his eyes what he didn't want to express in words. Let's say that if one day the *Rais* spoke about his father in front of Siddiga, the next day a large article would appear in *Glorious Allahabad* about the heroism displayed on the home front during the war years by the unforgettable Piri. Clear evidence that Siddiga was able to read the Master's wishes in his eyes appeared in the fact that three poems signed by Khatam Vazek and dedicated to "Piri, Hero of Labor" had been published in the newspaper during the previous month, one in the classical style and two in fashionable blank verse. Moreover, the whole town was talking about the still-unfinished long poem dedicated to the most high and wise father of the *Rais* by our poet-publicist.

In developing written literature this way, the *Rais* undoubtedly wanted once and for all to be done with oral folk works. However, it wasn't so simple to shut everyone's mouth. Rumors traveled around the town that several newly appeared makers of a stinking oral epic apparently were already creating a malicious "Legend of the Rais and Siddiga" and had named their indecent nonsense "Sword and Quill." The role of carrying the sword was allotted to the *Rais*, and the symbol of the quill was meant for Siddiga, although in fairness that role should have been destined for Khatam Vazek because in our land he was actually the principal literary flatulist. But there was also a reason for the choice of Siddiga, and it lay in the fact that no matter how the imagination of Khatam Vazek gushed forth, it was the power of Siddiga's pen that had been known long and well by the people.

Thanks to that pen, any fifty-year-old person could become sixty years old tomorrow and peacefully start receiving a pension. Even young girls for whom there were still one to five years until the age of matrimony could grow up in an instant and receive corresponding legal papers from ZAGSONOT. On the other hand, overripe girls became younger thanks to Siddiga's office—some a year younger, some even ten years. That pen had begun to show its strength back in the war years, raising the age of some and arresting that of others. As subsequently became known, Siddiga had freed at least one hundred people from the army.

* * *

"Who, exactly, if not she, lived a sweet life here in the most difficult years of the war?" Ibadulla (a representative of the oldest dynasty of Allahabad tearoom owners) was saying to the well-known halva maker Abdul while warming the large, four-bucket samovar and polishing its side with a towel the color of coffee. "She lived even better than those who occupied positions higher than hers. And she told ridiculous stories, she said, 'I don't take bribes of any sort.' But she took everything—including even pickles and rotten pumpkin jam. Every day they brought her butter with honey from all over the whole countryside." But Abdul, the famous master of preparing halva (that same person who for all of ten days had been the husband of the Giulliukend chewing gum trader Jinn Jamila, the lover of *Sword and Quill*), listened unwillingly to the tearoom owner, lazily reflecting on his own concerns.

It was still early in the morning; the sun's light had just barely touched the heights of the farthest mountains. More than an hour remained before customers would appear. And Abdul had dropped by not just to drink tea. He and Ibadulla had a long-standing business agreement. Every day Abdul brought seven pounds of halva he'd prepared to the tearoom, which the tearoom owner always sold in full. In exchange, the halva maker brought Ibadulla twelve pails of water from the town's best source by hand cart, and while waiting for the samovar to boil he conversed with the owner of the tearoom.

Cars drove from time to time along the road that ran about ten to fifteen yards from the tearoom because it was the very center of town. The mosque, the only department store in the whole town, and all the governing institutions were located on that street. The four-story building of the district Party committee on the other side of the street was the only multistory building in town, specially built to that height in order to in itself camouflage the pitiful throngs of single-story hovels. Fifty to sixty yards from it stood the building of the district executive committee. The department of public education, the police department, ZAGSONOT, the editorial offices of the newspaper *Glorious Allahabad*, the post office, and the House of Culture were also situated on that same street, standing at a considerable distance from one another. And the smithy, the tailor's shop, and the barbershop were located in old, one-story buildings on the site of the former bazaar between the district Party committee and the district executive committee. And Abdul, talking with Ibadulla, constantly glanced towards those hovels.

"Where did I leave off, Abdul?" said the tearoom owner a little louder to attract the attention of his friend, who was listening with half an ear.

"You were saying that that Siddiga really put out when she was young."

"No, I didn't say 'put out,' I said 'took.'" The tearoom owner lifted a full scoop of coal from the sack, threw it into the mouth of the samovar, and then again began polishing its side with the towel the color of coffee. "On the subject of what she put out—I haven't heard about that, Abdul, I'm not going to lie. But on the subject of bribes, they say even now she takes them hand over fist. It would be interesting to know if she shares them with the *Rais.*"

"You don't share them, you won't get them," answered the halva master shortly and unequivocally. And from the way he smartly crossed one long, thin leg over the other, it was clear that he was very satisfied with his own answer. (Abdul had the reputation of being an educated person because in former times he'd worked a whole nine years as a proofreader at *Glorious Allahabad.*)

"Here's what I think the reason is, Abdul, that such insatiable people live in these two villages, I mean Kellekend and Giulliukend: maybe our seed is defective." The tearoom owner finished fiddling with the samovar and sat down next to the halva maker. "If we'd been normal people, would you really have chased that Giulliukend beauty out of the house in the middle of the night?" Ibadulla tenderly smoothed his black moustache, unusual for his age, and laughed slyly. "Listen, did you at least manage to enjoy her? She was really much younger than you."

"I'll tell you the truth about that, Ibadulla, she was a sweet thing! Only, the bitch wouldn't put out. She made conditions: once every two days, and just once each time. That night I begged her for four hours, went down on my knees in front of her. And she—no way! So I drove her out. 'Beat it,' I said, 'go sell your chewing gum. I didn't take you to wife so you could set up your own motherfucking way of fucking. I took you so you'd put out when I had the desire!'"

They sat silently for a little while. The hands of both were thrust into their pants and placed on their private parts as if on their hearts—both of them daydreaming passionately about feminine caresses.

They were still lost in sweet reverie when they suddenly saw Elbey, right in the middle of the road, coming towards them with a pile of newspapers.

"He's bringing the papers again," sighed the tearoom owner. "Seems like they're up to something new. Otherwise he wouldn't bother to deliver newspapers at this early hour."

"Most likely Khatam Vazek finished his new poem about the *Rais'* father, Marshal Preputsy," responded the halva master mockingly. "The samovar's boiling. Make the tea."

"Wait, let him come in," said the tearoom owner without stirring, following Elbey's approach. As he came up to them, Elbey pulled several newspapers from the pack and threw them on the table.

"Let people read them here, and don't let them filch them to take home," he said and was getting ready to leave, but here Ibadulla, hiding a sarcastic grin in his moustache, asked in a serious tone:

"And what, son, is there any news?"

"Read it, you'll see. I haven't read it yet myself."

"They say our *Rais* is getting ready to go back to the big capital. Did something happen, Comrade Chief?"

"Yes, getting ready. What's it to you?" Although Elbey answered in that offhanded way, he rejoiced in his soul: if even the tearoom owner knew the *Rais* was going somewhere, then he really was going! And Elbey wanted that more than anything because when the *Rais* went anywhere, he, too, considered himself a person.

"It's just interesting to a person, Comrade Chief." Abdul managed to keep his face solemn. "He's our helmsman, and we want to know ahead of time when he's getting ready to go somewhere. So we can beg Allah to send down a good journey and safe return for him."

Elbey understood the halva maker's sarcasm immediately. But he didn't consider it necessary to answer.

"I've got to get to ten places," he announced. "And let the newspapers lie there, people will come and read them. Only don't let them take them home," he reminded them.

Still smiling knowingly in his moustache, the tearoom owner said, "Yes, sir, Comrade Chief. Tell the *Rais* not to worry—those who don't read the paper today won't get any tea from me," and turned away so Elbey wouldn't see he was laughing.

Then the tearoom owner began to brew tea, and he remained standing beside the samovar; only from the movement of his moustache was it evident that he was cursing someone for all he was worth. And the halva master laid a newspaper in front of him and began calmly reading it, but then he leapt up and exclaimed so loudly that the tearoom owner shuddered.

"'The Center of Our Town Changes Its Look!'" announced the former proof-reader of *Glorious Allahabad*—these words were picked out in large type at the top of the first page. In the article that followed, what everyone already knew was discussed: the park, the Alley of Honored Repose, the old buildings that would be demolished, the new trees that would be planted, the power of labor, the singing of birds, the joy of young children, and the wonderful future of the ancient town. Khatam Vazek concluded his article with verses of his own composition:

> *O, my town, my cradle,*
> *My honor, my courage, my pride, my name.*
> *For you a new dawn is arriving.*
> *Return to your youth, my ancient land.*
> *Become young again,*
> *Open your arms to weeping willows filled with catkins!*

Having read Ibadulla the newspaper article in full and declaimed the poem with feeling, the former husband of that Jamila who was so stingy with her passion said "Bah!" and spit on the paper, then swore colorfully. "Where's that tea?"

"What do you want to eat?"

"What do you always give me?"

"Today I've also got honey."

"Bring me bread and cheese, but eat the honey yourself."

The tearoom owner brought Abdul his customary breakfast—a hunk of *brynza* cheese, lavash baked in the tandoor, and a glass of sweet tea—and put it on the table. He also poured himself some tea and sat down opposite Abdul, who was uncommonly stingy in his household but more than generous as a man—the same Abdul who hadn't received satisfaction over the course of ten days from a woman forty years younger than himself and for some reason was living a miserable bachelor existence to this day.

"And did they write in there when they'd demolish the small shops?" he asked, indicating the newspaper.

"When they want to, they'll demolish them. Who can stop them?"

"Did you hear what the tailor said to him that day? 'Well, *Rais*, if we aren't allowed to work here, we'll work at home. At least for now, thank God, the house is ours.'" The tearoom owner abruptly guffawed. "Just think how much deep meaning there is in those words!"

Taking his time, Abdul swallowed a piece of cheese and drank a mouthful of sweet tea.

"You say those words to smart people. But our *Rais* is a person with a double bottom. What's in his head is what's in his stinky intestines. He'll spit on the tailor and his wise words," he responded irritably, and haughtily turning up his nose, he added decisively: "And look, the smith Husein said what needed to be said to him. 'Bring your father's grave here,' he said, 'and shove it in our eyes every day, block our eyes, take God's light away from us. You really need for us to all be blind together so we can't distinguish light from dark, can't see anything except your glory. You alone see everything ahead for everyone.' They say that after those words he dropped everything in the smithy and went home. Meanwhile, the barber's holding firm to his shop. 'I feed five children with this trade,' he says. 'If you take away my business, I'll cut all five of their throats.'"

But here the conversation of the renowned tearoom owner and excellent halva maker was interrupted because a movie reminiscent of Italian neorealism was starting to play in front of the barbershop.

At the beginning, twenty policemen appeared instantaneously, as if from underground, and surrounded the doomed barbershop with a living wall. Then up drove the car of the *Rais*, horn blaring, and the Master himself got out of it.

At the same moment, the obstinate barber unexpectedly climbed into the frame, taking up a spot next to the *Rais*, and hundreds of people began assembling from all sides like a flock of birds, promising a still more interesting continuation of the film.

The barber stood surrounded by the crowd. His five children from ages one to ten were also there. It wasn't clear whether the very littlest one held in the mother's arms was a boy or girl. Of the remaining four, three were boys. Pressed one against the other, they stood calmly near their hovel. And the barber himself held the hand of the only daughter, who was three or four years old.

When the noise began, the daughter was the first to cry. She was seconded by the infant in the mother's arms. And after them all the other children wailed in chorus.

"Well, come on, *Rais*, what are you waiting for? Come on, cut off their heads!" roared the barber.

The *Rais* stood, not moving, with his hands thrust in his pockets.

For the first time in his life, that experienced conductor of the secret music of the lower spheres and leader of dark forces saw the absence of fear in front of a mighty authority. He stood, tormented by a presentiment of shame at being made a laughing stock in the eyes of the crowd.

The policemen tried in every way possible to drive the people away from the barbershop, but no one wanted to leave. The efforts of the police elicited only laughter from the people, and the children, frightened at what was happening, wailed still louder. The chaos grew enormous.

However, for all its apparent similarity, one particular of this "film" didn't correspond to the style of Italian neorealism: the *Rais* lost face—it disappeared! In any case, it now bore absolutely no resemblance to the face the people were accustomed to seeing. A distorted mask appeared in place of that face, and (believe me, Reader!) from the look of that mask, a stream of vital energy began to pour into the blood vessels of the people. (Partially risking falling into the mysteries of the unknowable, we can suppose that the face of the *Rais* in that moment was reminiscent of the turkey-like mug of that depraved rooster—who was hardly likely to be alive now—that at one time Piri Preputsy had happily given to the midwife Raziya).

If *Sayyid* Mirmovsum-aga hadn't arrived in time at the barbershop, it's unknown how this "film" might have ended—as a *shakhsey-vakhsey*, or with a tear jerker finale in the spirit of Indian movies. First the *sayyid* took the barber aside and whispered something in his ear. At that moment the barber disappeared with his family from the frame. Then, with a single gesture of the *sayyid*, the "extras" began to break up. As soon as the ability to move returned to him, the *Rais*, shaken by what he'd seen, sat in the car and disappeared, quick as lightning. The movie was finished.

With that, early morning concluded in one of the wonderful corners of the country that we call Allahabad. At last the sun came out (having lingered behind the mountains, it goes without saying, from modesty) and smiled so tenderly on the people that it was as if it were right now preparing to sing—in the tender voice of Balababash Jangiulium—"You're the Same Age as the Sun," the song we already know.

XII

Still deeply shocked by what had happened, the *Rais* returned to his office white as a corpse and sat down heavily in his chair. The tall, grey-bearded, placidly calm *Sayyid* Mirmovsum remained standing before his eyes.

For the first time in his life, the *Rais* doubted the omnipotence of authority, and that doubt made everything, even the desire to wield power, useless and meaningless in his eyes. "In order get respect from these scoundrels, it's necessary to be either a descendant of the Prophet like that *sayyid* or to become strong, more terrible than the Prophet," he thought, seized by a terrible presentiment and overwhelmed by a kind of deep melancholy that until then he'd never known. He sat at his desk for some time without moving, in a state of complete apathy. Then, as if remembering something, he opened the desk drawer, pulled out *Sword and Quill*, and having barely opened the book, was struck by words he'd underlined thickly at some point with a red pencil: "Admitting defeat in any of its manifestations is baseness." Those words from his beloved book calmed him a little. At that moment Siddiga phoned, and the conversation with her brought relief.

"Hello, *Rais*! How are you, how are you feeling? That son-of-a-bitch barber probably spoiled your mood?"

"No, not him. It's—"

But Siddiga didn't let him finish.

"I know, I know. Mirmovsum's appearance distressed you."

"Do you know that *sayyid* well? It is true he smokes opium?"

It appears the words of the *Rais* astonished even Siddiga, who had seemingly known all his devilish contrivances very well.

"No, *Rais*, that scenario won't work," Siddiga said with chagrin, dragging out the words.

"What, not even his sons smoke?" he asked, grey with fury.

"No."

"How can that be? What, there's no opium in town?" he exclaimed, turning crimson.

"Opium can be found in town, *Rais*, but the *sayyid* doesn't have sons. He has only two daughters, and both married elsewhere."

The *Rais* thought for a moment, clenching the phone in his hand. Siddiga was also silent.

"Fine, come over here," said the *Rais*, swallowing the bone of his malice and hearing how the air was torn from his lungs with wheezing.

Siddiga came into the office pressing a thick book wrapped in newspaper to her breast and giving off the scent of perfume.

"You're still roaming around with *Sword and Quill*, Siddiga *khanum*? You haven't had your fill of it yet?" The *Rais* said these words simply to have something to say and, turning his face to the light streaming through the window, fell into thought.

Instead of answering, Siddiga placed the book in front of him, sat down opposite, and said, "The times of *Sword and Quill* are long gone, *Rais*. Now they're publishing the kind of books that you read and are simply struck with wonder! Of course, one feels the influence of *Sword and Quill* in them. And that's entirely natural. Because the new writers must continue the traditions of the old masters." For a second she was buried in dreamy thoughtfulness, an enigmatically mild expression on her face, and then she continued with the glittering eyes and voice of a bird of prey. "You won't believe it, *Rais*, our Khatam has written a big novel: eight hundred and eighty-one pages, imagine that! I finished reading it late last night. Sheer lyricism, just like reading poetry. And the title corresponds with the general tonality of a modern lyric-epic novel, *Weeping Willows along the Highway*—that's what our Khatam named his novel!"

Siddiga spoke with unexpected emotion for the chief of a respectable office, choking on the words, panting and puffing from heat and excitement. Looking at her, it was possible to think that she really was delighted by the newly created great novel and that as an experienced connoisseur and genuine expert on literature she sincerely rejoiced at its appearance. In fact, it was part of her astutely planned—to the tiniest detail—scheme: first it was necessary to bring the *Rais* back into good spirits after what had happened and then decisively set forth a projected plan of attack.

But the *Rais* didn't have the patience to hear out her prepared monologue.

"Hold off with the literature," he said, trying to contain his anger. "So, you say that *sayyid* doesn't even drink vodka?"

"No, *Rais*, what are you saying? There were no drinkers at all in their clan." A smile flashed across Siddiga's serious, worried face. "I know what you want. When you asked me on the phone about the *sayyid*'s children, I understood everything. But it won't work with Mirmovsum-aga. Don't compare him with our country people. And then, they're terrible fanatics—they'll raise the whole town against us. Better not get involved in that." A poisonous smirk wandered across Siddiga's face. "But while I was walking here, an idea came to me. Hold on, I'll explain everything now." She unwrapped the newspaper in which the book she'd brought was covered and opened the book up to a previously bookmarked page. "Here's everything you wanted to know about the *sayyid*. He's part of a clan from the Iranian town of Zanjan. His father Miribrahim Shapur moved here along with his whole family in 1882. Because he was a *sayyid* and had completed the *haj*, they exiled him to Siberia in 1939."

But the *Rais* didn't want to hear Mirmovsum's biography.

"It's all clear, close the book. You're right, there's no point in getting involved with this scion of the Prophet. But you say you've thought of something. What, exactly?" He fixed his eyes on Siddiga, impatiently awaiting her answer.

During the ensuing monologue the color of Siddiga's face changed several times; at first it colored a little, then went grey, then again was covered with a flush.

"What if your late father Piri becomes respected, holy *Miri*, essentially the same as a *sayyid*? We'll say that, fearing repression during the years that ate men alive, he needed to renounce his legacy of being a *sayyid*." Siddiga laid her palm on the book as if she were swearing on the Quran and, being a person who wasn't stupid, noted to herself—not for the first time—that a person mad for power couldn't be made to listen to reason. "They always say, 'truth will out.' And this book even suggests where to look for that truth! Everything that happens in the world today is forgotten the very next day. But what's written down on paper today will tomorrow become an incontestable fact of the biography of any of our citizens, dead or alive. For you, I'll do that on this very day." Having pierced the *Rais* with her fox-like slits-for-eyes, she smiled girlishly and tenderly and, after being silent a few seconds, added enthusiastically: "And Khatam will have something to work on. We need to print a weighty article immediately in the newspaper: repression, arrests, exile in Siberia. . . ." At that she gave a triumphant smile, as if she were the heroine of her made-up tale finding an enchanted lamp. "And also about Stalin's crusade against our religion. About the torments endured by your father, needing to renounce his own true name, Miri. Then, if needed, Khatam will find a couple of people who'll give the newspaper the requisite interviews. Do that many people really remain who remember those times? So, let a dozen gossips whisper for a few days, and then even they will shut up. And no one will dare commit an outrage against the grave of your father on the Alley of Honored Repose, the construction of which will speedily take place with your diligence and the help of Allah. Be assured, they'll fear you! I know the local people very well. Although they're clever like foxes, they're also more cowardly than jackals."

Here Siddiga, burning like a coal in the oven of the Giulliukend village council, threw a fleeting glance at the *Rais*, and her ardor suddenly went out. He sat clasping his head in his hands, infinite sadness in his eyes. Behind his back the dull, grey shadow of the heat-scorched elm with stunted, trembling leaves fell on the wall.

"How did this happen, how did I turn out to have so many enemies?" said he, in the barely audible voice of an endlessly lonely person.

When the *Rais* lifted his head, Siddiga saw his eyes were wet from tears; it staggered her that such a person also could cry. And she remembered the day the *Rais* was born, the insane joy of Piri, crazed with happiness. The snow in the yard. The oven heated with coal. Shroud Sadykhov's beloved *shorpa* from black peas with *kaurma*. . . . She also wanted to cry. But instead of that she pursed her lips and shook her head.

"Why are you upset, *Rais*?" she asked. "Perhaps I've somehow distressed you?" Taking on the sorrowful look of a weeping willow, she meekly and tenderly looked at the *Rais*, although her heart seethed with hatred, and the bile of malice flickered in the depths of her fox-like eyes.

"Sister, you've given me strength! You've poured balm in my wounds!"

Siddiga's face lit up. First of all because it was the first time she'd heard herself addressed as "sister" from the lips of the *Rais*. And still more because her plan had succeeded, and that meant that the effort hadn't been in vain.

"But first of all, it's necessary to do one more thing, *Rais*. It's very important," she raised her gaze to the ceiling.

"What is this thing?"

Siddiga transferred her gaze to a pink ray in which the shadows of the elm leaves now trembled like butterflies.

"It's not very complicated. During the first few days after the article appears, it's necessary to commission all the mullahs to start a conversation about this at all funeral feasts. They have to convince the people that everything really happened that way. That is, to convey the truth to the people."

"And do we have a lot of mullahs?" A shadow flashed again on the face of the *Rais*, which had been clearing up.

"Enough. And among them are even some literate ones capable of reading the Quran. One of these is the Giulliukend mullah, Nizam Jafar. I'll take it on myself to persuade him. And another is Mullah Husein Rafi, who was born in Kiurdamir. During the war he got married here, and here he stayed. There are also Mullah Mahmud, Mullah Yagub, Mullah Murtuz, Mullah Novruz Jahrili. . . ." Siddiga noticed the anxiety in the glance of the *Rais* and broke off her count. "Fine, I'll take it on myself to persuade forty mullahs." She had good reason not to doubt her success, insofar as she'd helped fifteen of those mullahs evade call-up to the army during the war. "And if you're able to persuade only one mullah, Yasin Mollazadze, that would be a big thing in itself. I know he'll be stubborn: he'll say, 'I don't know anything, it's against my principles, my education doesn't permit. . . .' By the way, he really is highly educated. They say he knows the Quran by heart. And he's read the New Testament and the Torah. Therefore he eternally shows off, just like our *Farmazon* Firage." At these words, Siddiga was seized with laughter. She laughed so infectiously that it was as if she'd decided to expend her entire annual reserve of gaiety here and now.

"Fine, sister, I'll take on that Mollazadze myself. After the article comes out I'll invite him here and have a talk with him," said the *Rais* with a cold smile and thoughtfully added, "Perhaps even Tray could be attracted to this work. Let him assist people in carrying out funeral customs—give them tea, prepare food."

"It's not worth it," objected Siddiga. "That Tray only looks like a quiet person. In fact, he has a very high opinion of himself. Imagine, the other day he brought Khatam a whole notebook of strange poems, in one of which he exhibits open sympathy for the miller Suleiman—as if the slander of envious people had had him sent to Siberia illegally! And that's evidence that Tray still isn't firm enough ideologically; you know, even your late father took part in unmasking that enemy element Suleiman."

The *Rais* at first smiled and then burst out in a loud laugh.

"What are you saying, who are you talking about? That Tray's a coward, like a hare. Well, fine, we won't include him. Let him write poems."

Siddiga pulled a handkerchief from the neckline of her dress and wiped the sweat from her face.

"Well, whatever, time will tell us what kind of person he is, your Tray," she said, smiling a very meaningful smile. She got up pressing the fat volume to her breast and, warmly exchanging parting words with the *Rais*, left the office.

Returning to her own ZAGSONOT along the empty, scorching hot streets, she thought furiously, "My own Lord God, how little of a person is left in him!"

That day only the lack of wings kept the *Rais* from taking to the air. But as evening approached, Aunt Dilber thoroughly spoiled his mood for him. The *Rais* remembered her doing the same thing even in Kellekend. She loved to lay out everything that was in her head and, not shy in her expressions, cut immediately to the heart of the matter.

"I've heard you want to transfer the dust of my brother and bury him here," she said in a threatening voice on the telephone. "Look, don't do such a stupid thing."

"Don't you get mixed up in these things," answered the *Rais* as gently as he could.

"How do you mean 'mixed up'? What, you want to say you know people better than I do? Or do you want all our clan to be forever accompanied by a curse?"

"No one will do anything," answered the *Rais* in a barely audible voice.

"They will so!" Dilber had never been able to speak softly, and now her voice roared like a tractor's engine. "You drop your fucking inventions! I won't allow people to shit on my brother's grave because of your crackpot plans. The devil only knows what you're doing with the living—at least leave corpses in peace!"

"Don't shout. I know what I'm doing!" The infuriated *Rais* didn't hold back.

"Oh, up yours!"

With that, the conversation ended. The cashier-purser of the Shah Abbas bathhouse spit angrily and hung up the phone.

XIII

On the day the article appeared, all Allahabad was thrown into alarm. And exactly two days later all the mullahs started up the tear-jerking, sad story with shameless importunity after every *fatiha*—the story about how that true representative of the holy class, Miri, the father of the *Rais*, had to become "Piri" because of the cruelly troubled times when a dirty lie ruled the whole country in the form of sacred truth. Mixing up Piri with Miri and Miri with Piri, they wished first Piri, then Miri peace and prosperity in the heavenly kingdom, and with that they so confused the people that in the end even the relatives of the deceased didn't understand whom, exactly, they were mourning.

The well-defined plan thought up by the impertinent admirer of *Sword and Quill* fully justified itself. The attention of the whole town was riveted on what the mullahs said at the funerals and memorial feasts. Few doubted in their souls that it was all a tall tale, but in the event no one even dared to open their mouth, afraid to attract the anger of the devil to themselves. In doing so, good people all unwillingly fed the demon, despite the fact that each one in his own way was suffocating from fury; but an until-now unprecedented, thick indifference rose in their souls from their own powerlessness, an indifference that spread, becoming a mass epidemic.

People fell into mysticism, which had happened often with them even before, but never before had life seemed to them so mortally paralyzed. Several even imagined that they didn't live in time itself but in the space between two times where a dead father is suddenly made the living representative of a sacred clan by the will of a son, and the living son steps forward in front of him like the terrible commander of a certain non-corporeal army, accompanied by a many-thousand-strong detachment of trumpeters but without a single foot soldier, and it was impossible to understand which of them was more alive— and which less dead.

And the cemetery theme again played a role when once, in the middle of the night, the late Gushver knocked on Jinn Jamila's window. It goes without saying that Jamila didn't open the window, but in the morning she discovered a letter in a crack under the window frame. In it, Gushver swore on oath in support of the *Rais*' father's legacy of being a *sayyid* and, as an emissary of the other world, authoritatively stated (she said) that the torments of hell awaited whomever didn't believe in the holy pedigree of Piri Preputsy (more correctly, Miri Prygutsy) on the terrible day of judgment.

It might also seem strange that when Piri turned into Miri without impediment, people began talking about things that up until that time they'd have preferred to keep quiet.

They said that in Kellekend some old woman had boiled milk for an entire hour, but the foam never rose to the top. That in Giulliukend someone's *kaurma* was covered in white mold, and someone's black peas all suddenly turned bright red.

That kind of talk, of course, couldn't spoil the wonderful mood of the *Rais*. On the contrary, he experienced a secret pleasure from it because that kind of talk awoke touching memories of his childhood and youth. He knew *kaurma* can be covered with mold in only two cases: when it's not fully cooked, or when less fat is added than required.

And the talk about black peas carried him back to the memory of that blissful day when the velvety, coffee-colored flowers of black peas in Eizengiul's yard had seemed implausibly beautiful to him. The grumbling of the Kellekend women on the subject of milk awoke warm memories of his late mother Baji *khanum*.

And precisely during those days when the *Rais* was successfully establishing his family connections with the Prophet himself, he'd begun to grow decidedly *younger* in the eyes of all the people. Still more surprising was the fact that, having earlier felt repugnance towards all types of singing, the *Rais* himself suddenly began to sing. Every day at dawn he sang one and the same song, not suspecting that in a few years the whole country would sing it in chorus: "I wound around mountains, glanced through meadows with the crane-like eyes of native springs. From far off, I heard the noise of reeds. You're my breath, my flowering garden, Allahabad, Allahabad."[5]

Yes, the affairs of our *Rais* went, as they say, full steam ahead. Siddiga's prognosis with regard to Mullah Yasin proved correct, too. He sat a full hour in the office of the *Rais* declaring on his oath that he didn't have anything against the much-respected Piri turning into the venerable Miri. But to personally take part in that necessary development "under the current ethical-moral-pedagogical situation" he considered undesirable for the successful achievement of the intended goals. "For which goals, exactly?" asked the *Rais*, sneering sarcastically, and after long consideration Mullah Yasin gave a still more evasive answer: "The ultimate goal of any goal is to attempt the main goal." Understanding nothing from that unintelligible answer, the *Rais* drew a pistol and shot three times in the air, at which point thirty to forty policemen encircled the mullah, who was farting from fear, and they dragged him out of the office by the feet and tossed him in the street. The tragicomedy achieved its climax when the fantastical memorial of the universally recognized successor to a holy pedigree and the "Father of all Fathers"—as was written in Khatam Vazek's poem that was printed in *Glorious Allahad* on the day the Alley was opened—was erected among a small number of others in the cool shadow of weeping willows in a prominent spot in town; not one single person remained anywhere who even in his dreams would have allowed himself to commit an outrage against that memorial.

The Alley of Honored Repose became the most crowded place in town, despite the fact that every time they visited it, people inexorably aged. Several cases were recorded of people who'd entered the Alley as curly-headed youths and exited entirely bald—not to mention that, on visiting that strange object, a few very young schoolchildren had even become covered in grey hair. With the appearance of the Alley, *Sayyid* Mirmovsum vanished without a trace. Then Mullah Yasin Mollazadze left this life—he died of diabetes and burning envy at the unprecedented luck of Mullah Novruz Jahrili, who after the impious campaign known to us had become practically the best friend of the sheikh-ul-Islam himself. He wasn't even able to leave behind a will. On the other hand, the anonymous—until that time—author of the still-unfinished folklore version of "Sword and Quill" left behind a sizable legacy; he hung himself in the intense noontime heat on the branch of an apricot tree to the unbearable droning of dragonflies. The famous tearoom owner Ibadulla closed the tearoom, having signed up for the choir circle organized not long before at the House of Culture named in honor of the poet-publicist Khatam Vazek. And the famous halva master Abdul stopped cooking halva and got together again with Jinn Jamila, and the two of them set up a profitable and now-legal trade in Iranian chewing gum.

For Elbey that campaign turned into a wonderful pastime. A personal car was at his disposal around the clock. He drove from village to village. He'd sit an hour at one funeral feast, a half-hour at another, eating his fill of *plov*, halva, and persimmons. He heard the tall tales of the mullahs about the legend of Miri and Piri—which they told with much more heartfelt emotion than the sad stories of the misfortunes of the sainted Imam Ali and the Imam Husein—and communicated all the operations-related information to the *Rais*. He made reports every evening.

Some things just can't be avoided, as they say. It was precisely during that period that the first significant page in the now-sixty-six-year-old biography of Elbey also opened up. And it coincided with the time that the daughter of

Dilber—the beloved aunt of the *Rais*—having finished her studies, returned to her mother. Wearing a tight skirt, with short hair, overdressed and made up, she strolled along the main street twice a day thirstily catching the attention of the men. Naturally, the *Rais* didn't like that.

On one of those intensely hot August days, he called Elbey to his office and said to him, "I'm going to marry you off," to which Elbey obediently replied, "Yes, sir," and colored deeply.

When the *Rais* walked through the gate of Aunt Dilber's old, one-story little house that had stood from time immemorial opposite the Shah Abbas bath-house, Aunt Dilber was sitting on a stool under a quince tree and loudly cursing at her daughter—who was listening to a tape recorder on the veranda—in the kind of words that not even the most thoroughly foul-mouthed people of Kellekend had ever heard. One might have imagined she was ready to strangle her daughter.

"I didn't deprive myself of things here and send them to you for three years so you could take up whoring there! You left here with your cherry intact and came back with it popped. Not even—"

Seeing that her nephew had arrived, Dilber fell silent. But Giulara, turning off the tape recorder, threw herself at the *Rais* with shouts of "My brother! My brother!" Then she brought a chair from inside and placed it next to the stool on which her mother sat. Although Dilber was also pleased at the arrival of her nephew, her wrath still hadn't cooled.

"You've disgraced your brother, too, you whore! You've dishonored him in people's eyes. What should he do with you now? You went off to study, and you lost your honor!"

"And it was the right thing to do," answered Giulara insolently, not in the slightest embarrassed by the presence of her cousin. "I think I got lucky. Would it have been better to come back here and sit in front of you as an old maid?"

"Do you hear what that fat-ass tart allows herself to say?!" exploded Dilber. "She not only admits it, she even boasts about it! I spit on you, Miss Insolence!" Dilber reached for the sugar bowl to fling it at her daughter, and Giulara ran into the house.

"And you could speak a little more politely, Aunt. You don't respect me as the son of your brother—you don't have to. But you should at least respect my office," advised the *Rais* cautiously.

"Has that whore left me even an ounce of politeness? Not only does the cursed heat not let a person live, but I also suffer because of that slut," Dilber sobbed, and two tears even appeared in her eyes.

At that moment a light breeze carried over the town. The leaves of the trees began to rustle softly. Aunt and nephew thirstily gulped the fresh air, and because of that their mood noticeably improved.

"Ah, at long last, the air stirred a little! I've been suffocating for ten days already." Dilber got up and started to fan herself with the hem of her wide skirt.

"Well, fine, sit down. Tell me what happened. Let's talk like human beings, if only for five minutes," the *Rais* forced himself to smile.

"So what else could happen? Your cousin left, shared the honey from her honey pot, and returned."

Her nephew understood, of course, what his aunt had in mind when she said "honey pot."

"Then why are you screaming about it to the whole world? Let's marry her to someone; she'll hide her sin, and we won't be disgraced."

Dilber was instantly transformed.

"You've found that slut a husband? Who in the world is it?"

"There's someone here. And I know him very well. It's that Giulliukend fellow who works for me. I've already talked with him. If it all works out, I'll promote him."

"Ah, I understand, you mean Gushver's grandson, that *malbey*." No matter how happy Dilber was that she'd be successful in getting rid of her daughter, she couldn't refuse herself the pleasure of wounding that fellow, thus showing the scorpion's poison of her own character.

"Why is he a *malbey*? An excellent fellow!" Giulara's voice was heard from the veranda, Giulara who not long before had been pretending the conversation of her mother and cousin was of absolutely no interest to her. "Brother, do you mean that fellow who brought us watermelon the other day? I agree to marry him." And fearing the next attack of her mother, she hid herself from view.

"You see what she gets up to? She hasn't just shamed us, she's not embarrassed to snap at us, either!"

The *Rais* got up.

"It happens that you even get shamed in life," he said, turning his aquiline gaze to the far horizon. "But any shame must be concealed before it's too late. Moreover, it has to be done so that people who've laughed maliciously at you today will envy you tomorrow." The *Rais* pronounced this aphorism standing on the porch of his aunt's house as if on his own future pedestal. Finding himself on the street, he sighed with relief and pronounced still another aphorism: "It's great to think about tomorrow when you own today."

PART FOUR

sublimely anxious

In which we'll tell you a secret: everything that happens further in our narrative could also happen in any country where the authorities are more powerful than the people and the people are stupider than their rulers.

XIV

Firdovsy turned up unexpectedly. The man himself: the short, dark, thin poet-member of the opposition and dependable dacha caretaker.

God knows when that was, during the day or at night. Elbey had already lost all sense of time. Either the fourth day or the fourth night had arrived since he'd found himself stuck hopelessly at the dacha. He didn't go up to the gates, didn't telephone anyone himself, and didn't answer anyone's calls. And he was tormented by the question of how Firdovsy could turn up in the dacha if the gates were locked.

Of the two boxes of Beluga that had stood in front of the refrigerator, one was empty. Part of the food on the table had already gone bad, and the rest had begun to stink. To that stink was added the stench of the dead dog in the yard.

"I hid the gold, Master. When those thieves arrived with their metal detector, I retrieved all the gold. Here it is, see? It's all here."

Firdovsy stood in the doorway, hesitant to enter, as if afraid to wake the master, and Elbey wanted to invite him into the room, but in the stupor of sleep he wasn't able to speak or move to go to the door to see about the pail the poet had brought; could it really contain the gold he'd saved from the Master's jinns?

Drowsiness continually overcame Elbey, and he was greatly bothered by the irregularity of his breathing. When he lifted his head to breathe a little more deeply, the pail appeared before him, but Firdovsy was again nowhere to be found. Elbey was alarmed. It seemed to him that he was stuck in some kind of swamp, and from somewhere in the remote distance the tearfully sad voice of Firdovsy reached him: "Here's your gold, Master. It's all here. I didn't take a thing myself. I won't come back, Master, goodbye. You need to get out of the dacha quickly, too. But be careful. A Dragon is lurking in the yard."

Heeding the words of the faithful caretaker, Elbey tried to get up, leaning his hand on the wall, but couldn't. However, he saw the pail filled to the top with gold coins. And when he looked at the pail again a moment later, there wasn't any gold in it at all. Ordinary cherry-plums lay in the pail, ripe, amber-yellow. The same cherry-plums that Gushver, lingering all day at the highway, just couldn't sell.

And there are so many wonders in this world: in the last moment of life, Elbey wanted cherry-plums. He put out his hand, but collapsed into a place where there were no cherry-plums or gold, not even a Dragon who'd supposedly been roaming around somewhere on the grounds of a large dacha.

He lay face down on the floor, two steps from the pail of cherry-plums that so shamelessly resembled gold coins. And reflected in his eyes—even a very long time after death—was a yellow gleam. The gleam of either gold or cherry-plums. Is it possible for a person to go off to the other world while the lively gleam in his eyes remains behind?

Unfortunately, that's not given to us to know.

* * *

The Defender of Invaluable Vocations found out about Elbey's death at five-thirty in the evening. At six he was supposed to receive a delegation of five women who'd arrived the other day from Europe to familiarize themselves with the state of freedom and democracy in Allahabad. They'd spent one day in Kellekend and two in Giulliukend and were now returning to the capital. Having thought a little, he changed the reception to tomorrow, and calling his assistant, he instructed him to develop a cultural program for the guests and present it to him. Knowing that the Master might at any moment change plans, they'd planned such a program in advance in the Main Building and, seeing on the list the names of five men who were to brighten up the leisure time of those five women "to the highest degree," the Chief laughed loudly.

"Those deputies do enjoy themselves. What, are all the visitors young? Or are our young men not squeamish about old women now?"

"The majority of them are young—from forty to fifty years old. There's even a girl among them, it appears."

"A what?" At that the Master had an uncontrollable fit of laughter. "You say there's a girl? A girl!" He calmed himself with difficulty. "But you should warn them, otherwise they'll get too excited and up and fuck this fucking European democracy. I wonder, do they themselves know what they're so persistently asking of us? What do they have themselves, other than belonging to some kind of stinking civilization that sows the seeds of debauchery and phrasemongering all around?" He breathed heavily through his nose like a hedgehog, dreaming of that happy time when he wouldn't need to curry favor with any foreign power.

The assistant also attempted to laugh, but failed. It had occurred to him that the five fellows who would defend the glory of the motherland in all kinds of ways today would certainly draw the fury of the Master tomorrow, and he was afraid, not knowing why himself.

"What other assignments are there?" The assistant looked servilely at the Master.

The Defender of Vocations was in deep thought, or perhaps simply tired. That condition often came over him, especially closer to the end of the work day. And then he gave the impression of being a weak, insignificant person.

"Pay serious attention to the funerals," ordered the Defender of Pluralists in a tired, hoarse voice. "Everything should be done as is customary."

"It will all be done," answered the assistant and turned to leave.

"Wait, I've still got something to say to you." He laid his palms to his temples and massaged them. "Do you have information about the Old Dacha? Call them, let them know. And have Ashpaz go there immediately." He looked at his wrist watch and, already much more animatedly, added, "I'll leave for there in an hour."

It was amazing: when his mood changed, he was always drawn to the Old Dacha.

On the ride the Master wept soundlessly. Sometimes he was overcome that way. It happened when he felt himself the loneliest man in the world. Because he considered the people surrounding him only conditionally to be people, and periodically he longed for an ordinary person of flesh and blood. He arrived at the Old Dacha in exactly that darkly sentimental mood. Whether it was somehow connected with the death of Elbey—he didn't think about that. But there wasn't the slightest doubt that the news of Elbey's death could have taken the Master unawares; he'd waited for it from day to day.

However, getting out of the car he felt things had grown brighter before his eyes. He wanted to stroll a little along the shore, but hunger and weakness compelled him to give up that intention. He decided to drink a couple of glasses of cognac, eat something, and then stroll along the shore as much as he wanted.

Ashpaz, who'd learned of Elbey's death not long before noon, guessed with some kind of uncanny intuition that the Master wouldn't drink Beluga with dinner tonight. Therefore, reckoning the *Rais* would drink cognac, he'd prepared *plov* from chicken and raisins with special effort. It was precisely the food the Master preferred with cognac.

The Master's condition wasn't concealed from Ashpaz, but he didn't risk speaking of it and asked his habitual question:

"Should I serve tea before the meal?"

"No, no need for any tea," answered the Chief in a weak voice. "I think I'll drink a little cognac. Hurry up, bring the food."

"The *plov* is ready," announced Ashpaz joyfully. "It's infusing." He brought a bottle of cognac from the bar in the kitchen, opened it in front of the Master (as was the custom), and poured a glass. Then he served the *plov* and stood a little while admiring how appetizingly it steamed and went back to the kitchen.

Ashpaz knew with what speed the Chief ate if he had an appetite, of course. But when he returned to the table to add cognac to the glass, he didn't believe his own eyes: in five to ten minutes the Master had eaten all the *plov* to the very last grain of rice, and the large bottle of cognac was half-empty. Now he sat on the sofa in front of the window and, deep in thought, admired the sea. So as not to disturb him, Ashpaz wanted to leave quietly. However, the Master, not moving and not looking at him, said softly:

"Don't go; come over here and sit a minute."

Ashpaz went up to the sofa but hesitated to sit.

"I'll go and brew the tea."

"Not yet. I'm going to take a little walk. Make it when I get back." And seeing that Ashpaz wasn't sitting, a little louder and a bit angrily he ordered, "Sit down, already!"

Ashpaz had been waiting a long time for the Chief to talk about Elbey. Therefore, receiving the order to sit down, he thought the time had come for that conversation. However, the Father of the Fatherland led such a conversation that Ashpaz, who'd seen how that person could bully people, completely lost his nerve.

"Today I found out that you at some point wrote poems and included in them some very interesting ideas. You showed real bravery defending the unfairly condemned miller Suleiman in your poems. Be a man, Tray, tell the truth: did that really happen?"

"Yes, that might have happened, truth be told," said Ashpaz cautiously and glanced fearfully at the face of the Chief, but he understood there was nothing to be afraid of; in the eyes flickering with yellow light there was neither fury nor malice, nor even laughter. His look was sad and sincere, and it wasn't even directed at the sea but towards some unseen expanse.

"I know that to this very day you're never parted from *Sword and Quill*, isn't that right, Tray? Why don't they write such solid books now?" His voice, sad and lonely, sounded as if it came from some unknown distance. "I was twenty-six when I first read that book. How short human life is," he whispered, agitated by his memories.

"What are you saying, what are you saying?!" energetically protested Ashpaz, contrary to his custom, who dragged that book around with him only to disguise his true thoughts. The naiveté of the Chief, so uncharacteristic for such a base nature, surprised him. "You're strong, like steel. And your health—" he spit quickly three times so as to ward off the Evil Eye, "is like iron!" He thought for a moment. "A steel character in an iron body, that's precisely how the author of *Sword and Quill* would have described you, had he lived to our time." The goblets jingled with the bravura of Ashpaz's voice. "Just now you drank a half a quart of cognac all at once. If I'd drunk even half of that, I wouldn't still be standing on my feet."

The Master laughed from the bottom of his soul, without any nastiness, just like an ordinary person.

"You've started to speak very literately," he said, wiping eyes moist from laughter with the back of his strong hand, and he suddenly felt that his "masculine spear" had also gained strength. "Oh, it's burning, everything's burning! Kill me, kill me!" the sweet woman's voice reached him from that long-ago hot day, piercing his whole body, heating him with the pleasant warmth of the first spring breeze. Thrusting his hand into the pocket of his pants, he tenderly stroked his own enlivened "spear," and the hot wave from that spread to all his nerve endings. In his imagination the cold sea beyond the window turned into the weir of the Kellekend mountain river, into the tenderly satin water into which that far-off, dreamlike, sweet time had frozen forever.

"Mr. Lanky, will you be offended if I ask you something?" Finally tearing his gaze from the sea, he looked at Ashpaz. "How many women have you tasted in your life?"

"Even now I have that pleasure from time to time," Ashpaz wanted to answer, but thinking the Chief hadn't known that kind of happiness for a long time already, he guiltily and modestly said:

"I don't even know, can one really count them all?"

"You're lying," retorted the Master firmly. "It's possible to count, it's possible. Every woman gives pleasure, but in his soul a man forever treasures the happiness given by just one. You, Tray, evidently haven't had that happiness; you don't understand the difference between male need and love."

"But I haven't really experienced other women besides my poor wife," Ashpaz attempted to correct his mistake. "It's necessary to think about her now and then. When we forget our wives, they become worse than witches."

The searching glance of the Master again returned to the sea. Under a sky covered by clouds, without moon or stars, the sea was sunk in gloom. The bright light of the floodlights turned on for the occasion of his arrival lit up only a small strip of the coast.

"In your opinion, what governs this world, Lanky? Only don't talk about God, I know that myself."

"Strong people like you govern the world. And God always helps them," answered Ashpaz without hesitation.

"No, you're lying again. Fear governs the world, only fear! The more a person fears, the less he understands. That means it's unprofitable even for God when a person understands a lot, Lanky, because even God knows that if a person doesn't fear anything, the world will collapse. And you're doing the right thing to satisfy your wife from time to time out of fear. Tell me, honestly, how often it happens—once a week?"

"It's always possible, if my wife wants it." Ashpaz was so enthusiastic about the disposition of the Master today that in just a minute he would have broken the etiquette of the Seat of Power—he would have started a conversation about Elbey himself. But here the telephone rang.

"Answer it, find out who it is," said the Master tiredly, and seeing that Tray was hesitating—no one except the Master himself dared touch that telephone—he repeated louder, "Go, answer it!"

Ashpaz timidly approached the telephone, and his voice, reminiscent of the clang of knives and forks, carried quickly around the whole room.

"People from the Administration are asking where to bury Elbey *muallim*."

The Master heard the question extremely clearly but for some reason didn't answer immediately.

"Tell them to bury him in the same cemetery where the great poet Khatam Vazek snoozes," ordered the Defender of Vocations, cynically mocking both of the dead men at one time. Then he added, "Let them bury him in the Alley of Honored Repose." But having understood that Ashpaz wasn't able to manage that, he came himself and angrily took the phone.

"Well, what's the problem? Why can't you let a person sit in peace?"

"There's no longer an Alley of Honored Repose there," they answered on the phone.

"How can that be? I myself founded it in my time."

"Last year they built the new headquarters building of the GAP in that spot."

"What's a GAP? What's that about?"

"GAP—the Glorious Allahabad Party!" One could only guess what the clerk at the other end of the line was thinking to himself.

"Fuck your mother! Not a day passes without a new party being created! Are you listening?" he shouted loudly, as if he'd called for help.

"Yes, sir, I'm listening," they answered on the phone.

"Let them bury him where the widow says," he ordered in a voice turned to stone and, laying down the receiver, added, "How wonderful it is when a person dies a natural death." And then he sat down again on the sofa and, turning a nostalgically thoughtful look towards the sea immersed in gloom, said, "Come here, writer. I have something serious to talk about with you."

At the single word "writer" it became hard for Ashpaz to breathe, and going closer and glancing at the face of the Master, he understood with his animal senses: this was the end.

The Master was so white that it was as if he'd just arisen from the dead. His everyday, colorless appearance didn't have anything in common with his usually commanding core. He pressed his right hand to his breast, and to Ashpaz's horror his left held a familiar, thick notebook. He looked at the notebook as if it were his own heart.

"Are you going to sit or stand?" the Master asked, indicating the armchair across from the sofa with a nod.

"Better to stand," answered Ashpaz in a sepulchral voice. He could never have foreseen this kind of horror, not even in his worst nightmares.

"It turns out that you, Tray, didn't just write poems but got up to mischief with a diary, evidently in order to secretly write your name in history behind our backs."

Ashpaz's legs stiffened, and his heart almost stopped. He'd begun keeping a diary relatively recently and, of course, hadn't imagined it would fall into other hands. How had that happened? Had his son-in-law, who'd not long age begun working in the Ministry of Economic Development, turned out to be such a loathsome swine? And how did he find out where his father-in-law kept his diary? Because Ashpaz had hidden it in his bedroom in an extremely secure place, or so it had seemed to him.

"Take it, read it," said the Chief, becoming animated.

Glancing at the notebook as if at his own tombstone, Ashpaz took the diary submissively.

"Well, go ahead, read. Don't be afraid!" the Master ordered in a thunderous voice. It seemed to Ashpaz that that voice came from the heavens.

He began to read, not understanding anything.

"*October 20. Sunday. Tonight I dreamed of enigmatic silver willows. And yesterday I dreamed of a forest glade overgrown with field violets—*"

"Wait! What are you reading? Enough of your nonsensical dreams! Read what I underlined in red pencil."

"*He was partly—*" began Ashpaz, but suddenly he was attacked by the hiccups; his legs buckled and, weakened, he sank mechanically into the armchair.

"*He was partly—*" mimicked his Master, and snatching the notebook from Ashpaz's hands, he himself began to slowly read: "*He was partly a person touched in the head, and while sowing discord among people, scheming, he temporarily forgot what sorrow and boredom were. Scheming was something of a sport for him.*" The Master coughed, then continued. "*He surrounded himself closely with people who'd never had anything before and now had everything. These people wove a web of lies all around, creating every kind of obstacle in the path leading to truth. And they had their own, secret state inside the official, universally recognized one.*" The Master paused, experiencing the prick of wounded pride in the depths of his soul. "Are you listening?" he asked in a voice shaking with fury. "Listen to this: *He substituted the love of power for corporeal love.*" He gasped from anger, and the flame of madness danced in his eyes. "So, that's how it is, Tray? That's how it is?! But listen further: *Last night he charged me to lay out a luxurious table in Elbey's dacha. The food on that table would have been enough for fifty people. And two whole boxes of Beluga! Elbey will probably drink himself to death. He's not the first, he won't be the last. Misfortune inevitably lies in wait for anyone marked out for his favor.*"

He was already reading frenziedly. The feeling of bitterness in his voice increased at the speed of light. "Ah, you pig shit! You act as though I'm already dead!" He began to wipe his brow as if escaping from a brain hemorrhage and, having somewhat restored his mental equilibrium, continued to read. "*The blindness in this country has in fact taken on the character of psychosis. The imaginary liquidation of unemployment, the trivial additions to salaries and pensions, the construction of infamous highways and factories for war materiel, the erection of numerous fountains, skyscrapers, sports complexes, and entertainment venues—that's the miracle-working economic takeoff.*" Suddenly, completely unexpectedly, he had an attack of laughter, from which a sparkling, silver-blueish shine appeared in his eyes. *"For the people there's no greater misfortune than this kind of psychosis.* Psychosis, psychosis, psychosis!" he repeated three times with unbelievably expressive artistry in his voice. *"This is the epoch of fictitious development, for which the time will come to settle accounts not only in blood and the loss of material assets but in long years of decline, disbelief in everything, universal devastation, general fear of any kind of ideology, indifference to politics, an attraction to philistine prosperity, and nihilism."*[6] He was now reading enthusiastically and excitedly and even, it seemed to Ashpaz, with great pleasure, as though it conferred on him the gift of being a great artist. *"Having completed the first betraying step, a person rushes to plunge into his betrayal as quickly and deeply as possible and hurries to chop off all restraints so that nothing connects him with his former life. A real leader assigns meaning to lives, his role is precisely that. But* he *does nothing but make the lives of people meaningless. Good God, what's going to happen to our children in this country?!"*

He stood up from his armchair and immediately sat down again. And he began to speak, his voice sharply changed.

"And I thought nothing could surprise me anymore. You've surprised me, Tray, surprised me a great deal! But these aren't really all your words. You copied many of them from somewhere, that's for sure. Tell me, confess, for once in your life don't lie to me: where did you dig up such learned words?"

"I…" said Ashpaz. "I, I, I, I…," he continued stammering and crying. After that, he was able bring forth two more sounds: "*RA*. . . ." And he wasn't able to make another sound.

The Master sat, hands folded across his chest, not taking his eyes from the notebook. He looked gloomy and pitiful, as if a sudden black wave of fear had rolled over him.

"How nice it would have been, Tray, to meet again in the other world," he continued in a cracked voice and for a second was immersed in silence. He added, almost calmly, "But I don't understand one thing—what could have propelled you to such baseness. Now, stand up, if you can."

Instantly looking drawn and seemingly aged by fear, Ashpaz could get up only on the third attempt.

The Master also stood up.

"Well, go. Go, don't be afraid, no one will touch you."

When Ashpaz was already at the door, he yelled loudly after him:

"Go out to the road—get on the blue bus. It'll take you where you need to go."

Instead of an Epilogue

On the unholy day that followed, the Master, having planned to be at work at twelve-thirty, suddenly changed his mind a half-hour before leaving the dacha, delaying his departure for a whole hour. Panic began in the one-hundred-thousand-strong squad of highway police. Because automobile traffic from the Old Dacha to the Seat of Power had been completely stopped forty minutes ago, and now the army of traffic cops didn't know how to deal with the thoroughly girdlocked city transport system.

The chaos became monstrous, creating a traffic state of emergency in the city. The ceaseless honking of horns mixed with the barking of police megaphones, the glass shook in building windows, the men's and women's underwear spread out to dry on the balconies fluttered bashfully in the wind. The street dogs all hid in the bushes, and the cats in the houses crawled under the bed. Even the *plov* being prepared in the homes of well-heeled citizens lost its taste.

The city was filled with curses. The taxi drivers, remembering Soviet authority with kind words, urgently spread gossip. For example, they talked nonsense that Shirinbala Shekerli, the person in charge in the city highway police, had shat himself in a car and that the car stank so terribly that the driver lost consciousness and to this moment still hadn't come to his senses.

During the course of a half-hour, thirteen drivers and the same number of bus passengers experienced heart attacks. More than one hundred people suffering from psychiatric disorders were transported, some to the police, some to the asylum. In a word, the unexpected order of the Master entirely changed the city dwellers' customary way of life. Because of the *Rais'* change of plans, the situation became so inflamed that social stability thoroughly threatened— like a millstone pinned to an axle and very firmly fixed inside the geography of the country—to develop a serious crack. Things went so far that the Armenian propaganda organs were already preparing to paint the cultural face of the ancient capital with black paint, and new (moreover, extremely well-founded) measures for that situation were being developed in a number of secret organs.

Having gotten rid of the chief of Operations HQ yesterday, and having fifteen minutes ago today ordered the release of his "two blockheads"—the "poet-faggot and lunatic driver"—the Defender of Invaluable Vocations suddenly remembered the dream (a mystery!) he'd had the previous night, closer to morning. He'd dreamed of a Kellekend springtime and his old father.

His father was sitting in the yard under a luxuriantly flowering apricot tree. And on the tree, their golden-red rooster-conjuror had found himself a new amusement: sitting hour after hour among the white-pink apricot flowers and periodically defecating from above. "Come here, catch that swine!" his father commanded him to help. "Today we'll cook a superb soup from him with excellent black peas for lunch. I see how that bastard is planning to rain down as much liquid shit on my head as possible!"

What the devil could that dream signify? What meaning does a golden-red rooster have in dream language? Was it a good thing to see a flowering tree in a dream? Wasn't it a bad thing that for the last three or four days he'd dreamed twice of his father, about whose existence he'd forgotten long ago? And those strange words of his: "You sat Tray on that blue bus for nothing, my son. His poems about me were far better than Giuliumjan Janday's poems extolling and lauding you."

These musings fatigued the Master extraordinarily and were the reason a great number of people—included among them, undoubtedly, even well-known people—were stuck in endless traffic jams. A few of them, settling comfortably into soft seats, waited patiently for the opening of the road. Others, impatient, scratched their seats and bit their nails. There were also those who saw a spark of future popular good fortune in that bedlam, and they surreptitiously gave themselves up to dreams about the inevitable end of the regime, clean forgetting the simple rule of contemporary history: what appears outrageously extreme today will be accepted as the ordinary way of things tomorrow. One of the people who turned out to be in that unprecedented traffic jam was Nizam Shamistan, already known to us as an uncommonly remarkable personality born for a by-no-means quiet life.

Headed to the opening of a ceremonial event by the name of "Year's Best Novelist," which was conducted every year by the independent television company PAMPERZS-PREZERVATIVOS, and having taken a taxi so as not to be late to the important event, the academic got stuck at the intersection of two streets named in honor of glorious bridge builders and courageous plumbers. For around an hour already he'd amused himself in conversation with the driver. In Arabic he poured forth the chapters of the Quran. In Russian he cursed the

former leaders of the Popular Front. He declaimed long poems, recounted friv-
olous anecdotes. In the end it got to the point that the taxi driver was certain:
this person was from the state security organs, from *There*.

"For the love of God, Nizam *muallim*, please, speak a little more softly.
Really, I'm not deaf," said the driver, risking attracting the anger of the learned
passenger.

The academic from *There* probably didn't even hear the taxi driver's
request because his thoughts were occupied with a prognosis of political development in the country, and he'd already marked this traffic confusion for himself as proof of the paralysis of authority.

"A traffic jam! A fantastical traffic jam!" exclaimed the inspired academic.
And he added, equally fervently, "You could name a novel that. *A Fan-tas-
ti-cal Traffic Jam*. It sounds great, doesn't it?" Turning his face towards
the driver who was suffering from his talkative presence, he announced
ardently, "That novel might have astounding success! They could even
give the author a Nobel Prize. But we don't truly have real novelists. And
those we have give their pitiful writing stupid names: *Blue Sea*, or *Hot Sun*.
Or *Sword and Quill*, *Zaur and Ziba*. . . . You have to give a good work a sonorous name. Our writers don't understand that. Because all of them are complete idiots. And their bravery doesn't go further than the red underwear of
their Armenian wives—"

Intending to buttress his argument with another chapter of the Quran
so that the taxi driver wouldn't have any further doubt about the fact that
he himself was a leading theorist in the genre of the novel, Nizam Shamistan
discovered that the driver wasn't in his place; he was extraordinarily surprised
(evidently this superannuated KGB man, this clamorous politician and noted
demagogue, didn't have information at his disposal about the fact that the
driver was a refugee from Agdam and had a great deal of experience in making
hasty getaways).

Meanwhile, the driver was already far away from the dangerous passenger.
More than anything in the world the poor taxi driver now wanted to take cover
in the nearest café and drink a shot of vodka. Gnashing his teeth from hatred
towards all television shits with their stool pigeon academic chatter, he swore
colorfully—like everyone from Agdam—as he walked. "Sit, sit, wait for me,
dirty-ass, hope that we'll see each other soon. You are a . . . and your mother
was a . . . and I'll be a . . . if I ever once sit at the wheel of that fucking car again
after this. Up yours! You'll find out who I am. They didn't name me 'Kasum
from Agdam' for nothing. I don't give a damn about you or that car as ancient as

Tutankhamun, that Zhiguli. Let the son of that cross-eyed Mesrop, that Gagik, fuck my grandmother Melek if I ever, even once, remember that clunker!"

The strangeness of the situation lay in the fact that poor Kasum Agdamsky, not yet having lost his taste for life, rejoiced with all his soul that he'd escaped from both his antediluvian Zhiguli and his super-talkative passenger.

Along with large-scale events such as the academically weighty prognoses of Nizam Shamistan (that we, from our perspective, can certainly assign to the genre of political masturbation), other different, less meaningful happenings that didn't have universal significance were also taking place in the city.

For example, coming out into the city, the well-known opposition poet-publicist Matakh Murovdagly—having just turned in his great book under the name *A Cucumber the Size of a Pumpkin* at the publisher Giant— accidentally met the former owner of the Zhiguli. Now, being treated with "factory" vodka as the driver's guest in a café named Moonlight, he was very emotionally reading Kasum Agdamsky an excerpt from his new poem, "His Star Shines On, Shines On," which was dedicated to the newly chosen president of the Union of Glorious Creators, Tokhiazar Tezbazarov. The happy Kasum Agdamsky listened to him in wild joy, although to be fair, he didn't understand a single thing in the poems of the excited poet—in the first place because even in his long-ago school days the owner of the now-abandoned Zhiguli hadn't understood anything in poems, and in the second place because even the most complete connoisseur of poetry would hardly have been able to understand the lines pronounced by the poet in an excitedly anxious voice. Lines of this sort: "To destroy Agatha's Mousetrap to him alone is given. And he'll drink to brotherhood with Bradbury over 'dandelion wine.'"

The famous poet Giuliumjan Janday burned to death in his luxurious, new foreign car a hundred yards from the enormous building of the FSMICM—the Fund of Spiritualist Mythmaking of Imposing Carpet Makers—on Gyrchyn Darchynly Street. Either he'd been consumed by a homemade bomb thrown from the side of the Iranian embassy, or else he'd been punished by the Lord of Sainted Mecca himself, where the poet had drunk holy water from the Zamzam well a minimum of three times—punished because even after that, he hadn't refrained from the loathsome habits of guzzling vodka and eating pork. And of the renowned poet, supposedly, only one pitiful ash remained, the color of baby shit. On the other hand, that good-for-nothing idler and hack artist Faramaz Farasat had been very lucky. The estimable traffic cops who carried his body to its final rest—almost intact and fully fit for honorable burial—were practically wearing general's epaulettes. It was known for certain, too, that the world-renowned

master of the brush, the eighty-year-old Fatekh Faragat, had parted from life forever in the back of an ambulance in that fantastical traffic jam.

And if to some extent we take into account the opinion of the many-
thousand-strong crowd of pedestrians finding consolation and joy in the
day's automobile bacchanalia, then it's possible to believe that in that
extraordinary situation, one alone of all the star celebrities was able to preserve (in the literal and figurative sense) his own authentic self: Balababash
Jangiulium. Having fallen into the traffic jam thirty yards from the Seat of
Power, he sang to the whole country for exactly half an hour without stopping the most profitable song of his whole, rich repertoire, the one about
that very person "the same age as the sun" who, regardless of any meteoro-
logical anomalies, shone brightly in the cloudless sky over the glorious land
of Allahabad.

* * *

Coming out of a building in which he'd never before been but which—from
the long, half-lit corridors and small, metal-clad doors stretching out as he
walked along—he'd named the "maternity hospital" to himself, Mamed-aga
was joyously heading home when he suddenly stumbled across the "fantastical
traffic jam." "Well, well, well!" he exclaimed. "This is really something, what's
this fuckery?! Yes, that shitty oil will give us a fever, I swear on Etaga's grave!"
Following that, Mamed-aga cursed both the Popular Front and Gorbachev
at the same time in choice words. But don't think that Mamed-aga's mood
was spoiled by that traffic jam or that he became irritable and cursed like a
sailor because of it. On the contrary, his mood wasn't just good, it was simply
superb. They hadn't tormented him in the "maternity hospital," they didn't
even try to scare him. They spoke politely and in a civilized manner with
the former driver for an hour at most, at the very most an hour and a half.
More precisely, until that moment when the black telephone in the office
rang. The person conversing civilly with Mamed-aga said only two words on
the phone: "Yes, sir!" after which he hung up, politely conducted Mamed-aga
to the door, and said, "Go, brother, look after your children,"—and, moreover, shook his hand powerfully, wishing him and his children a happy life in
the inevitably bright future. And Mamed-aga didn't leave that polite remark
unanswered. "Yes, may Allah protect your children, too," he said, "And I have
three hero-sons, all three prepared to turn their hands to winning back our
dear Karabakh tomorrow!"

Leaving the "maternity hospital," he headed in the direction of the Alley of Heroes, and there he saw an old man sitting right by the road. Taking him for a beggar, Mamed-aga stuck his hand in his pocket for change. However, coming closer, he understood that this wasn't a beggar but an ordinary seller of sunflower seeds. He handed the man a *manat* and, alternately spreading open both pockets of his jacket, filled both of them with sizeable scoops of seeds. Walking further and nibbling the seeds, Mamed-aga looked around and saw a person who resembled Firdovsy walking down that same road along which he himself had just walked. Clearly, Firdovsy had come out of a different door of the very same "maternity hospital" and was headed into the city.

"Firdovsy, is that really you?" The joy of the unexpected meeting compelled Mamed-aga to shed a few tears. "Where are you coming from, brother, and where are you going?"

"I'm not coming from anywhere and not going anywhere." The official tone of Firdovsy made Mamed-aga laugh.

"Listen, how solemn you look! Don't you sound imposing?! I almost died of laughter!" Mamed-aga looked in the eyes of the dacha caretaker and became unexpectedly serious. "Were you there long?"

"I? No. Really? It wasn't. It won't be." Firdovsy was in a slightly abnormal state; his speech was inconsistent and somehow not of this world.

"Okay, fine, don't tell lies!" Mamed-aga was losing patience. "I'm asking if they kept you long in the 'maternity hospital.'"

"Of course not, I confess!" Firdovsy was saying, as if in a dream. But suddenly it was as if he'd awakened. "Maternity hospital? What maternity hospital? I don't know any maternity hospital."

Mamed-aga pulled a handful of sunflower seeds from his pocket and forced them into Firdovsy's palm.

"Chew on these, the seeds are good. What did they ask you about there?"

"Well, not really about anything! No one asked me about anything. We conversed very politely. In a very civilized manner. . . . With great respect. . . . Then he got an order over the phone, said, 'Yes, sir!' and released me. He said, 'Go, brother, look after your children.'"

"Did he shake your hand?"

"He did, I swear by Allah! Really, really powerfully, in a very civilized way. And I said to him, 'May Allah protect your children, too.' I said, 'I have a one-year-old son. He'll grow up soon and, God willing, go off to liberate Karabakh from our historical enemies.'"

"You did an excellent thing in saying that, very original!" Mamed-aga thought deeply, his face becoming unaccustomedly serious. "And they didn't ask you about Gorbachev?"

"No, they didn't ask. They only ordered me not to write any more poems. They said that very politely. And I answered just as politely, 'A curse on the father of anyone who ever starts to write poems.'"

"You never said a truer word," praised Mamed-aga, giving his voice a certain lyricism. "Yes, and all the current poets are shits, the ones who have the impudence to write poems after the late Vahid."[7] He sighed deeply and continued, "And, look, they asked me about Gorbachev. I answered that he's a very base person. On the other hand, I praised Chernomyrdin highly."

From where, and why, did words about Gorbachev and Chernomyrdin come to the former driver? Not even Putin himself could answer that question now. However, it's certain that such a conversation hadn't happened and couldn't ever have happened. To whom and for what purpose would Mamed-aga's opinion about Gorbachev have been interesting when the city was choking in a traffic jam? Uttering that nonsensical lie, Mamed-aga peeped into the eyes of the former poet-gardener, and he saw so much suffering and hopelessness in them that he was prepared to burst into sobs like a child.

"Let's go unwind in a kebab house. We'll eat, drink, and relax like human beings," Mamed-aga proposed cheerfully, seizing the former prisoner by his buttons.

But Firdovsy answered in a sad voice, "I'm busy."

"Busy doing what?"

"I'm going to devote myself to bringing up my son so he—" Firdovsy stumbled, and he sobbed so loudly that Mamed-aga almost began to cry with him. "They've entirely 're-educated' the poor man" thought the devotee of Aliagha Vahid's poetry.

"Why are you in such a hurry to get to your son? He won't go anywhere. Wait, the traffic jam will clear up—we'll go to my place. God sent you to me. Otherwise you'll loaf about all night in the streets and towards morning become a bum." He took Firdovsy amicably by the arm. The friendliness of the former driver cheered up the former dissident and maker of poems.

"Are you able to go to Chisty Prudy?" asked the father of the future courageous warrior.

"I can go, if you're asking. To do what, exactly?"

"I have a request. Will you do it for me?"

"Of course I will!" answered Mamed-aga with quiet confidence.

From an inner pocket of his jacket, Firdovsy pulled out a packet covered in newspaper showing a photograph of Balababash Jangiulium—who, as the caption under the photo noted, had been awarded the title of People's Artist for the third time the other day—and held it out to Mamed-aga.

"This needs to be given to him."

"To whom?" asked Mamed-aga, taking the packet.

"To Hercules, who else? Throw it to him, let him eat. The poor thing has been sitting there starving for five days."

"What is this, pieces of meat?" Mamed-aga sniffed the newspaper packet. "No, it seems to be ground cutlets. What, they fed you cutlets in the 'maternity hospital'? And you say you don't know any 'maternity hospital'!" The former driver was purposely prolonging the conversation. Because to drive out to the dacha of his former master with that ridiculous packet seemed to him to be an entirely unthinkable errand.

"What have you thought up—a 'maternity hospital'?!" Firdovsy wiped his tears with the back of his hand. "If you won't take it, just say you won't take it. What does this have to do with the 'maternity hospital'?"

Mamed-aga had fallen into a difficult situation and was, it seems, deeply entangled. First he looked all around. Then he fixed his astonished gaze on Firdovsy. Then he put his lips to the ear of the former gardener and whispered, "Are you completely out of your mind—to feed a dog cutlets?!" He shoved the packet in Firdovsy's pocket. "Is it possible you liked the 'maternity hospital' that much?" Mamed-aga was sincerely perplexed; did Firdovsy really want to send him to Chisty Prudy only for the sake of the dog?

"So, you won't do it?" Firdovsy's face fell. "Then go ahead, chew on your seeds. Maternity hospital! Maternity hospital! What are you, an academic?"

And Firdovsy disappeared—as if blown away by the wind.

Mamed-aga looked all around for a long time, but Firdovsy wasn't any-where, and a deep sadness came over him. Upset, he took out the sunflower seeds and, in a fit of anger, dumped them onto the ground. "Everyone's lost their minds from that cursed oil," he muttered and looked around. Cars were everywhere, huddled one next to the other, an ocean of cars that, it seemed, had neither beginning nor end. And it seemed to Mamed-aga that this traffic jam would never disperse.

Bestowing on "black gold" still one more indecent epithet—"slut for sale, from the family of train station whores"—he spit with gusto in the direction of the "maternity hospital" and with quick steps headed towards a café with the strange name of Solar Eclipse.

February–December 2010

Farewell, Aylis

An Afterword

No, I'm just speaking about scum. In any time of transition this scum, which exists in every society, rises to the top, not only without any purpose but not having even a glimmer of thought, just expressing its anxiety and impatience with all its might in itself. Meanwhile, without even knowing it, this scum almost always falls under the command of that small handful of "advance guard" that operates with a definite goal and directs all that trash where it pleases so long as it doesn't consist of complete idiots itself, which, by the way, also happens. . . . What our troubled time consisted of and from what to what our transition was—I don't know, and no one, I think, knows.

—Fyodor Dostoevsky, *Demons*

i

President Ilham Aliev and I sat along the bank of the river in Aylis.[1] Rolling up his pants, the president lowered one foot into the water and stretched out the other on the young grass. He was merry and infinitely happy. His squinting eyes sparkled with a strange, almost child-like delight.

It was early in the morning. Everything seemed better than it could possibly be in real life. The sun was brighter than sun, the grass greener than grass, and the water cleaner and clearer than water. And you yourself, Mr. President, were more friendly and sincere than in everyday, grey ordinariness.

You rapturously took in the small river stones and lively, playful fish darting about in the water that now and then lightly touched your foot. And besides those fish, there was not a single other living creature around.

The river ran in a low-lying area, so Aylis remained much higher than we were. More precisely, not all of Aylis but one of its picturesque riverside quarters.

In that quarter cool springs spurted from beneath the earth, windows opened to meet the innocent morning sun, and ravishing gardens spread out in front of the houses.

I saw all of this—and you didn't. Because you'd never been to Aylis before. You hadn't yet seen anything here except the river bank on which we were sitting. Had never washed up with the water from the spring in that same quarter. Had never once admired the dawn from the balcony of one of the neighboring houses.

And you didn't know a single one of the inhabitants of those houses. But I knew them all. And I was acquainted not only with their houses but with every tree growing near those houses. There were fruit trees that the local inhabitants had cultivated from time immemorial, tending and fussing over them, receiving a generous harvest in return: apricots, mulberries, pears, plums, almonds, hazelnuts, walnuts. ...

A church once stood in that quarter, Mr. President; it was called the White Church. It was destroyed back in the 1930s, and the stones were carried away in trucks and used to construct a canning factory in Ordubad. Only two walls were left from the church. Enduring much rain and many snowfalls, those walls remained the exact same blinding white from year to year, and no one in Aylis knew what remarkable kind of lime covered them. On the other hand, everyone knew to whom the two houses located closest to the former church belonged.

One of them was the house of Tamara, daughter of the cross-eyed saddle maker Bega, who was the only Armenian remaining in Aylis after the death of Anykh (Aniko), the wife of Mirza Vahab Gasanzade whom, incidentally, even your late father knew well. Tamara didn't speak Armenian and, in fact, didn't know it, and she was so assimilated with the Muslim population of Aylis that no one cared about her Armenian heritage.

Well, and the second house belonged to the old woman Nisa, the mother of Tamara's beloved Habib, who left this life before his time.

Living so closely together, Tamara and Habib fell in love with one another while they were still children. They studied in the same class and finished school at the same time. And they always went to the fields of the collective farm together. Seeing how they went everywhere together, everyone around them understood that it wasn't just friendship, no; herein, probably, lay something more serious. Something akin to the story of Majnun and Layla.[2]

Many in Aylis wished Tamara and Habib happiness. But there were also those who didn't. And to the joy of the ill-wishers, that happiness simply didn't come to pass. Habib's obstinate mother Nisa didn't permit her son to marry an Armenian. What's more, she bustled around and very quickly married him off to another girl so that he'd forget Tamara once and for all. At that wedding a real tragedy played out: the groom was accidentally poisoned by drinking homebrew, and at the very height of the celebration he gave his soul to God.

After that, the devout Nisa, who'd always fasted and completed her prayers, lost her faith in Allah forever. She never again completed any devotions and didn't even attend funeral feasts. And on the night of January 13, 1990, that same Nisa, accidentally meeting Tamara by the ruins of the White Church, said these terrible words to her: "Leave this place, daughter of Bega. Leave before your unclean blood is spilled. Don't force us Muslims to take sin on our souls."

That very night five fellows, hearing about what was going on in Baku, conceived the idea of displaying their patriotism and demonstrating that Aylis fully supported the capital. They broke into Tamara's home, killed her with an ax, and carried away the corpse and threw it in one of the Armenian cemeteries.

I know it's extremely unpatriotic to write these things. But, excuse me, Mr. President, why the hell do you need so many patriots? In the Writers Union alone you have no fewer than two thousand of them. And I want to serve my motherland not as a patriot but as a writer. And a writer without mercy—that's almost like *plov* without rice.

A writer is always in the service of God, even when God seems unfair to him in the highest degree. A writer is free in all his actions and activities, which are controlled only by his conscience. He's capable of standing the world on its head even with his eyes closed, as I was able to do in this enchanted dream.

There we sat on the bank of the river. Above us were the houses, balconies, gardens, and two snow-white church walls, still pleasing to the eye. Near the church grows a mighty mulberry tree, and the sunlight streamed through its spreading branches, through the bright-green leaves. From time to time one of the rays fell on your face, and you rejoiced like a child.

From the very first moment when, by the will of Allah, we met there on the bank of the river in Aylis, I wanted to ask you a few questions. But I somehow couldn't bring myself to do it. Because those questions weren't simple, and I initially doubted the majority of them even had answers. For example, I couldn't wrap my head around the idea that a person who'd been born in a country that advocated internationalism, a person who'd received an excellent upbringing and education, could so deeply hate the entire Armenian people. That he could consider someone who'd used an ax to hack his sleeping fellow student to death to be a *chevalier sans peur et sans reproche*.[3] Perhaps upbringing and education don't have any importance in politics. And it's only an illusion to seek conscience and mercy in politics.

What marvels there are in dreams! While asleep, I imagined the president and I had been sitting there on the river bank for a very long time, almost since the moment the world was created.

But I needed to take you somewhere, Mr. President. I needed to show you what makes Aylis—Aylis.

You absolutely had to see the monastery in the Vang quarter of Aylis. You had to thoroughly survey that place's majestic church inside and out. And then we would have drunk some water in the holy monastery spring and gone down below towards the center of the village. You would have looked at Aylis from above and understood what it is about this place (I always take all my acquaintances who come here along that route).

But unfortunately, I was not fated to show you my Aylis, even the ruins of which have silently testified to the magical creativity of human hands and to the grandeur of the human spirit for a long time now. And what a shame I wasn't able to convince you of that, even in a dream. Honestly, it's as if the devil himself intervened! We weren't able to move even a step from the river before that same omnipresent devil whispered to me that the monastery no longer exists. In its place now stands a mosque, and although the mosque was built five years ago, not one inhabitant of Aylis has dared cross its threshold even now. You see, everyone in Aylis knows that prayers offered in a mosque built in the place of a church don't reach the ears of Allah. For that's wrong in human terms—to tear down one of God's houses ostensibly to build a different one.

What a good thing, then, that we didn't go anywhere. How splendid that we didn't see that mosque erected in place of the monastery church. What's the point of a person looking at what the Lord doesn't want to look at?

Allah saw me that day on the river bank, do you hear, Mr. President? He sent down his divine light to me. And I generously shared it with you. Because it's a sin not to share the light sent from on high. And only the Almighty has the right to extinguish it.

When I was only fifteen or sixteen I carried that light from Aylis to Baku. And I've been able to keep it safe to this day, to protect it from an abundance of evils. And thanks to that light, the Aylis I saw in the dream really did shine so brightly and was so wonderful.

So who commanded you to extinguish that light sent down to me personally by the Lord? That's also what I wanted to ask you in that dream. But I didn't ask. I decided not to spoil your wonderful mood. Nevertheless, I'm certain that the hour will arrive when, without fail, someone will ask you that question.

I want to assure readers that this dream, quite astounding even to me, isn't an artistic gimmick and isn't used to create any kind of superficial effect. It's possible to perceive certain symbols and a hidden meaning in it, of course. But oddly enough, I did in fact dream all of it. I even wrote down the dream in my diary, in which I write very rarely, and made this feverish note: "August 7, 2016. Saturday night into Sunday. Hellishly hot in Baku. And I'm forbidden to leave Baku. The dream I dreamed tonight was a real miracle. Aylis. Early in the morning. The two of us sat on the river bank: Ilham Aliev and I!"

ii

I've said many times that *Stone Dreams*, my little novel-requiem, doesn't have a direct connection with the Nagorno-Karabakh conflict and wasn't intended to study the difficult machinery of relations between nations or to analyze the reasons for the historical Armenian-Azerbaijani hostility.[4] In neither its ethical nor moral dimensions does it support one or the other given national idea.

It contains none of the appeals to peace and friendship traditionally met with in classical works by Azeri authors of various times.

But for some reason, none of those who politicize this novel want to consider this simple truth.

The principal theme of *Stone Dreams* is the tragedy of the main character, who can't find a place for himself in a society that has turned political amorality into a national idea and who, therefore, stands alone against the times. Without a shadow of a doubt, any unbiased reader could confirm this.

The last days of 1989: the real war was still ahead. But the seeds of enmity and hatred had already been sown between two neighboring peoples who'd lived through the entire Soviet period without quarrel or conflict. Who sowed them? Where did that bitterness come from? Here, like it or not, it's necessary to mention the book *Hearth* by the Armenian writer Zory Balayan, who was little known until that time.[5]

I'll say it frankly: that wasn't a book but a foul death sentence for everything good that more or less united Azerbaijanis with Armenians. In fact, that book demonstrated what terrible consequences a writer's malicious recklessness might have for the fragile organism of relations between nations.

The atmosphere of universal psychosis provoked by Balayan's book nurtured new writers, poets, historians, and journalists. It wasn't difficult to understand that. What was impossible to understand was something else—the distinguished veterans of science and art who just yesterday had been champing at the bit to extol friendship and the brotherhood of peoples and who today readily joined that new wave.

Jingoism can't exist without poisoning ethics and morality. The blind, uncontrollable hatred in both Armenia and Azerbaijan drew embittered failures—and at times out-and-out scoundrels and rogues—into public life. And even the truth sounded like a lie on the lips of such people. Doesn't the reason for their historical worthlessness—first of all to their own nation—lie in this?

I don't know why people love Zory Balyan in Armenia, I only know very well why I don't love him.

Did all those people, I wonder, really always love their Motherland so passionately? Was I for some reason unable to recognize it earlier? Is such mass and sudden patriotism even generally possible? Perhaps they were simply tired from the long Brezhnev period—boring and sluggish—and now, activated in the Gorbachev era of *perestroika,* they burned with the desire to write themselves a more interesting and content-rich biography.

Everyone was happy and glad. But glad about what? Where did that energy and excitement come from? In what did the evil recklessness of these people lie? What guided them? I could never make sense of it in my head. But my heart felt there was something otherworldly in that sudden fervor, something diabolical, and that it would sooner or later lead to monstrous consequences.

With unbelievable enthusiasm the Azerbaijani service of Radio Liberty— broadcasting from Munich and supported by the United States—advocated aggressive nationalism in all its programs.[6] Zory Balyan's book obviously made the work of the leading announcer of the station, Mirza Khazar, much easier. Could an ordinary citizen of Azerbaijan who'd appeared from who knows where—only superficially speaking the Azeri language and seeing its beauty only in hasty, cheap, nationalist opuses of poetry—really influence the national politics of the United States? Perhaps the American government didn't know about the programs of that ill-intentioned journalist inciting his fellow countrymen towards a bloody clash with Armenians. Or perhaps the US had its own interests in that bellicose propaganda. I confess, I'd never have thought that the propaganda coming from the US could sink so low. A gigantic intrusion of ignorance in all spheres of life prevailed in the programs of the Azerbaijani service of Radio Liberty.

The facts were devastating. It suddenly turned out that over the long centuries of its development, the world hadn't changed one iota—the cruel, merciless world that crucified Jesus, burned Giordano Bruno at the stake, confined Galileo under house arrest for life, and in the course of a single century caused the massacre of two peoples, Armenians in Ottoman Turkey and Jews in Auschwitz—it remained exactly the same, that world!

Everyone was in it together, everyone was in concert. And I alone turned out to be the stranger among my own people, solitary and outcast. And this new loneliness didn't resemble that other loneliness I'd already come to know in childhood and later accepted willingly as destiny. This was a tedious, everyday loneliness, far from any kind of romantic ideal.

Earlier, in moments of disappointment I'd found books from my home library coming to my assistance. Time after time, in difficult moments of life I reread the works of Chekhov, Bunin, and Saint-Exupéry, or plunged into the humor of Zoshchenko and Ilf and Petrov. So what happened to me this time, then, if even these beloved authors suddenly lost their former attraction for me? Even such geniuses as Shakespeare, Cervantes, Dickens, Balzac, Tolstoy, and Dostoevsky standing on the shelves of my library now seemed to me as powerless and defenseless as I was myself. There had been so many geniuses in the world, all of them coming and going, and yet evil remained. What, then, was the point of writing?

We all lived in conditions of earth-shattering evil. It seemed to me that evil, as a matter of course, lived in every person. All around were the boundless hypocrisy, militant cynicism, and unheard-of insolence of self-proclaimed patriots toadying up to the shrieking crowd. The most holy feeling of national worth was subjected to complete destruction, and the idea of constructive patriotism lost any meaning.

Violence took away faith, carrying a lie in itself. Everyone was supposed to serve the heroic optimism that arose from God knows where in a fit of civic watchfulness. I'd never known such a mockery of the elemental norms of conscience.

Perhaps I'd lost my mental equilibrium. Did I lack the brains or intellect, perhaps, to understand the changes taking place in the world? Freedom, independence, democracy—it seemed to me that ordinary people living their natural lives had never needed any of that, and that behind all those ideas stood the devil attempting to prevent a person from living in a normal, human way. People need water, bread, love, joy, and other blessings created for them by God. People can live their lives without war and revolution if outsiders don't interfere in their lives and if those who've never created anything themselves don't encroach on what others have created.

iii

Freedom, independence, democracy—so far, each of those words has brought Azerbaijan only misery and suffering. Those who hadn't found their own path in life easily adapted themselves to pointing out a path to others. And that path led two neighboring peoples straight towards war. First on Theater Square in Yerevan (Armenia), and then on Lenin Square in Baku (Azerbaijan), rallies of many thousands of people took place, rallies that were called, it seems, to inform the whole world about the inevitability of that war. Well, and the world didn't give a damn! Even the all-knowing CIA apparently never guessed that such a bloody conflict would flare up in the Caucasus. Is that possible? And if it's possible, then in whose voice was Mirza Khazar so furiously calling two peoples to a bloody fight on the air of Radio Liberty?

After long and wearisome doubt, I finally came to the conclusion that the events in Theater Square in Yerevan and Lenin Square in Baku were directed from a single center. Who played first violin is not given to me to know. It's undoubtedly possible to suspect the KGB, which had a strong grudge against the Kremlin and, having undertaken to organize disturbances in the country, might have done it to take revenge on Gorbachev, who'd deprived it of its former might. As for Azerbaijan, it, like all the other former republics of the USSR, was swiftly losing hope in the Kremlin.

iv

Mirza Khazar can insist all he likes that Azerbaijan "languished two hundred years under the Russian yoke"—I don't believe a single word of it. Because the Azerbaijan about which he spoke in a false, sickly sweet voice never really existed. But a little Muslim country did exist where thousands of schools, kindergartens, medical institutions, and libraries appeared precisely with the help of the Russians. Every year Azerbaijan's publishers produced hundreds of thousands of books in my native language, and the print run of popular journals was not less than fifty to sixty thousand. In Azerbaijan we had our own Academy of Sciences, Conservatory, and Philharmonic. This country was proud of its renowned scholars, artists, singers, and composers. And thanks to the efforts of Russia, we lived peacefully side by side with the Armenians for seventy years. In order to deny this, I'd have to renounce my conscience and memory.

However, every time Russia loses its strength, nationalism lifts its head in the adjoining countries, and ethnic and religious conflicts arise.

The Nagorno-Karabakh conflict—which had already begun to develop in 1987 and became more serious with each passing day—coincided, not at all by accident, with a period of Russian weakening. What happened in Karabakh on the threshold of the breakup of the Soviet Union had much in common with the events of 1917 that took place after the fall of Tsarist Russia. And this similarity was displayed especially vividly in the degradation of the Russian army. As the Soviet Union was falling apart, Russian soldiers, understanding earlier and better than everyone else that the Russians were losing their leading position in the region, clean forgot whom they served and lavishly sold arms both to the Armenians and the Muslim populations of Karabakh—precisely as they had done back in 1917 in Nakhchivan. With the help of those arms, the 1917 Nakhchivan Armenians for a little while withstood the Muslims who inflicted cruel slaughter and pogroms.

After the fall of Tsarist Russia, the fate of the Nakhchivan Armenians was finally sealed with the introduction of Turkish soldiers to the region.

I don't know when the Turks entered Aylis, or where or how long they took up positions there. But from my grandmother, mother, and many other inhabitants of Aylis, I heard over and over about the horrors committed by the Turks in my hometown on December 24, 1919. And if I hadn't heard about them all my conscious life, it's possible that it would be as difficult for me as it is for many to believe in the reality of the historic crime that goes by the name of the "Armenian genocide." But I believed, in fact, that that catastrophe had really taken place. And perhaps that's precisely why I was experiencing the new, oncoming tragedy in advance—I was experiencing it both for my own people and for others.

And I didn't have a shadow of a doubt that the tragedy was unavoidable.

V

The first act of that new tragedy played out in Sumgait in February of 1988.[7]

I found out that something bad was taking place in Sumgait that very evening in the foyer of the Moskva Hotel from the Armenian writer Vardges Petrosyan.[8] But I didn't pay attention. It didn't even occur to me to ask why he was so agitated.

The reason for my indifference to the news was that, first of all, at that time there were just too many rumors and too many people spreading them. And, second of all—and the most important reason, the memory of which is disagreeable to me to this day—was that although I had often met Petrosyan at various events sponsored by the USSR Writers Union, I was only superficially acquainted with him and didn't know what kind of person and writer he was. With some kind of bitter prejudice, I considered him one of the literary high muckety-mucks of Armenia who held all of Azerbaijan and all Azerbaijanis in contempt. Precisely for that reason, I met his anxiety with mute indifference.

I remember quite well how my reaction disturbed and upset Vardges. He stood as if thunderstruck and then swiftly walked away. Apparently, my indifference was enough for Vardges Petrosyan to clearly imagine me as one of the hangmen of the Sumgait slaughter. Only much later did I find out about his sharp speeches against war and nationalism. And where now can I track down Vardges, and with what words can I beg his pardon?

vi

Armenians and Azerbaijanis have so much in common. For example, the word *dolma*, which we use for stuffed grape leaves, doesn't belong to either Turkic people or Armenians. It's an age-old Greek word. And in the original it sounds like this: *dolmades*. The whole territory of Greek vineyards is hardly less than the territory of Armenia and Azerbaijan put together. And meat is meat everywhere. Why in the world did the rolling of meat in grape leaves suddenly become such an important national question?

You know, being Turkic and Muslim, we people of Azerbaijan are at the same time also people of the Caucasus. It's precisely this fact that to a significant degree distinguishes us from all the other Turkic peoples. From time immemorial we and the Armenians have danced to the exact same melodies at weddings and feasts. Have you ever heard those melodies at the celebrations of other Turkic peoples such as the Turkmens, Uzbeks, Kazakhs, Kirghiz, and even the Anatolian Turks, who are very closely related to us? So why in the world have we now decided to divide the indivisible? Why has it now suddenly become so important for us to decide to whom *dolma* or lavash belongs, and why doesn't anyone have enough courage to stop the mouths of "patriotic" provocateurs who are prepared to do anything to turn friendship into enmity?

Why are there more supporters than opponents of criminal acts? Why did they turn out to be so much stronger than us, the simple people? And why, after all this time, have we still not revealed the terrible crimes committed in Sumgait and in Khojaly?[9]

vii

Or what happened in Baku?

Just imagine this scene: everyone who turned Baku into an Armenian meat grinder on January 13, 1990, was dressed in a black trench coat. Their job was to kill defenseless people. All with one face, indistinguishable from one another either by height or build. Who put that uniform on them? From where did they find so many hangmen and set whole flocks of them on the city?

Those people in black trench coats strolled around Baku like its masters. Without a shadow of fear they attacked the homes of Armenians and tortured and killed those who lived there, sparing neither old people nor babies. Moreover, they lit bonfires in several parts of town to burn the corpses of those killed.

It was as if the collapse of the world had been ignited. Terror crawled along the streets of Baku. Even teenagers took part in the anti-Armenian psychosis. They were informants going door to door, seeking Armenians everywhere.

It was a nightmarish day. First and foremost because on that day, for the first time, we became witnesses to how hundreds and thousands of innocent people were facing death.

On that day conditions were also alarming for my family. For many in Baku I was already considered a suspicious type, sympathetic to Armenians. It hadn't been a year since the Moscow journal *Druzhba narodov* had published my March 1989 article, an article in which I spoke out against the wave of nationalism. In connection with that, an emergency meeting of the Azerbaijani Writers Union had been convened, and a group of writer-patriots declared me an "enemy of the people" and "a traitor to the motherland." After that, the usual persecutions began throughout Azerbaijan. There were denunciations and all that's customary in these situations: insults, slander, terror by telephone. . . . I received dozens of threatening letters. And even back then, several threatened to burn my books. Of course, all of that was of recent memory. And it meant that on that terrible day of January 13, 1990, danger might also threaten me and my family.

There's no greater misfortune for a country than that kind of psychosis. Fear held sway all around. The city rolled towards the precipice, having lost every shred of spirituality and humanity. It was impossible for the mind to comprehend the horrors that were taking place. According to unofficial data, more than sixty people perished that day.

My situation at the time was reminiscent of the situation of the main character of *Stone Dreams*, Sadai Sadygly, before he was beaten up by monsters and fell into a coma. If I'd left the house that day to save some innocent Armenian, the very same kind of misfortune might have happened to me.

My artist-protagonist absolutely had to die precisely when he did, on the night of January 12, 1990. For he had to die on my behalf as well, so as not to see what happened in Baku on the unholy day that followed. Surely it's better to die than to live as someone who has recognized his own helplessness in conditions of universal ill will?

viii

They killed Tamara in the middle of the night of January 13, 1990, Mr. President!

The sincere, good, pure-as-the-driven-snow Tamara Atabekyan—the last Armenian in Aylis, who didn't even know Armenian.

A piercing wind blew that night in Aylis; it snowed. Tamara's killers didn't go to much trouble. Wrapping the corpse in a sheet, they carried it to the nearby Armenian cemetery, threw it in there, and coolly left. And the snow came down and came down for many days on end.

And until it thawed no one knew whether Tamara was alive or dead.

When the snow cleared, the shepherd Mamish, tending his sheep near the cemetery, discovered the corpse. Digging a grave, he buried Tamara. And while he did that God knows what words fell from his lips. But when he'd buried Tamara's body and returned the flock to the barn, he appeared in the busy tearoom; they say he was beside himself. Afire with anger. He shouted in a voice that wasn't his own. He even wept.

"Can we be people?!" said Mamish to the tearoom regulars. "No, no, and again no! What wrong did that unfortunate woman do to us? Did she even once insult any one of us? Whose life did she disturb? The poor thing didn't even know her own language, so she loved our language. But no—someone had to kill her. Kill her and throw her in the cemetery. Who are we, after this? We aren't people but wild animals!"

The eyewitness didn't tell me what other things Mamish called the people of Aylis, but the words he addressed to my fellow villagers at the end of his speech deserve to be written in the annals of recent history.

"Do we consider ourselves to be people?" he said softly. "Who are we? On what path do we walk and what awaits us if we don't change our ways?"

With those wise words Mamish left the tearoom. It's a good thing he was the one who found Tamara's corpse. Otherwise, believe me, no one would have known about the murder. And those who did know would have sealed their mouths shut. Because the inhabitants of Aylis absolutely did not want to be even indirect witnesses of such a crime committed in their village. The death of one Armenian woman mustn't spoil the reputation of Aylis! In general, it would have been better for the inhabitants of the village if Tamara hadn't died but had lived.

If the shepherd Mamish hadn't discovered Tamara's body and informed all Aylis about it, then, most probably, she would never officially have died. One night she would have "run off to the Armenian side" in Meghri or Kapan. Or else (also at night) some "base Armenian" from the other side would have arrived, killed Tamara, burned the corpse in order to cover his tracks, and cleared out. You see, that was supposedly the ancient custom of Armenians—to kill their own and blame everything on Azerbaijanis! As some accuse them of having done, for example, in Sumgait.

The most difficult thing is to learn to lie. But as soon as you learn, everything goes forward smoothly.

ix

A torrent of lies suddenly overwhelmed my homeland, and what a torrent, Vardgesdjan![10] I know your homeland couldn't withstand that torrent, either. But did they really shoot you on the threshold of your own home because you didn't want to hear and speak lies? If not for that reason, why, then, did they kill you?

On the one hand I'm sorry for you, and on the other hand I envy you, do you hear, Vardges? They say you also looked a lie in the face. You knew that to live, enduring a lie, is worse than death. Now do you understand, Vardges, why I envy you?

A damned lie is the kind of thing that, if you let it catch hold of you even once, will never release you. And the most vile and ugly lie is one that comes from above. Because those who sit on high aren't so naïve, they know the difference between the truth and a lie. And your task is to piously believe that those who sit on high are smarter than you. "If I tell a lie, then what right do you have not to lie?"—that's how they think, the power-loving petty tyrants who have the impudence to control the whole country by themselves. And if you want to survive in such a country, you need to always remember that axiom.

I always knew this. But strangely enough, I managed to live my far-from-simple life without lies and hypocrisy. I saw cowardly editors, evil censors. Not one of my creations was ever printed without obstacles and impediments. But I bore my writerly cross with stoicism.

When the Soviet Union collapsed, I rejoiced. I thought the hard times for writers were behind us. Bureaucratic control over artistic thought would be finished once and for all. And no one would be able to tell us what we could and couldn't write. Perhaps it was precisely that idyllic illusion that subsequently cost me so much.

They didn't shoot me, Vardges: they took away my Aylis. They said that even it belonged only to them. That absolutely nothing in this country was mine. They said that what I had was given to me by the people and that now they, the people themselves, were taking it away from me. And that they themselves were the people—and I was no one. And that I didn't even write my own books. How could I have written them if the people hadn't given me the talent? And that the people had also given the order to burn them. And that I should even have said "thank you" that they decided to burn just books and not me personally.

Did you know anything about Aylis, Vardges? You probably knew at least something. And it seems that Hrant Matevosyan knew everything.[11] Once when I was in Yerevan in Soviet times I asked him about it. Hrant suddenly stopped short. He even turned pale. He looked at me with suspicion and hurried to change the subject. And at that moment I understood that Hrant knew all about the Aylis massacre and was avoiding that conversation because he wasn't entirely certain whether my ancestors had either directly or indirectly taken part in them.

I also asked Anait Bayandur, my acquaintance from Moscow's Literary Institute who had translated Hrant's work into Russian, about Aylis. Anait said openly that among her ancestors were writers and clergymen, that they were connected with Aylis from ancient times, and that some of her relatives were even buried there. Needless to say, all these conversations took place in Soviet times. Now neither Hrant nor Anait is alive. And neither are you, Vardgesdjan. And I don't have much time left.

And even Aylis is dying, little by little.

X

February 9, 2013, turned out to be the most terrible day of my life, as well as an unexpected turning point in my fate: on that day, in my native village, they burned my books!!!

In Aylis February is reckoned to be the coldest month, with a great deal of snow. However, in the video I watched on the internet, there was no snow visible. But I saw a great number of people, the majority of whom came from Ordubad itself, the district capital. Many people from neighboring villages were gathered there. Also in that crowd were several of my fellow villagers—fifteen to twenty people. And from the way they were dressed, I understood that February temperatures there were below freezing.

The action occurred in the place called the bazaar, which formerly really was a bazaar. Located on high ground, the main market square of Aylis had once had the good fortune to be one of the lively points on the Great Silk Road. Camel caravans arrived from many countries, and carriages stopped from Tabriz, Ardabil, Isfahan, Izmir, Tiflis, Yerevan. . . . There they sold excellent Iranian rice, Iraqi dates, Indian and Moroccan spices, and, it goes without saying, the fruits of Aylis itself: walnuts, almonds, dried mulberries and apricots, and the renowned Aylis silk valued more highly than gold. And it was right there one summer that one-eyed Farhad, the brother of the butcher Mamedaga, shot the son (who had studied in Paris) of the landowner Arakel—Arakel who himself had completed the pilgrimage to the Church of the Holy Sepulchre in Jerusalem and received the religious title of *mugdisi*.

Now the administrative center of Aylis was located there: the executive committee; post office; first aid station; and the pompous, two-story House of Culture whose doors opened only occasionally when meetings were conducted and regularly scheduled elections took place.

The House of Culture didn't appear in the video. But I easily imagined the people collected right in front of it, people who'd come from all corners of the district for this "historic event." Under the feet of those people I saw not just grey asphalt but the sandstone and stones—now hidden under asphalt—that my bare feet had once touched. A little way off stood the mighty, aged plane tree—the beauty and pride of the former Aylis bazaar. No one knew how old it was, just as they didn't know the age of the bridge nearby. And a little below that bridge once stood the luxurious, three-story mansion of *Mugdisi* Arakel that had now turned into a melancholy ruin.

That day, looking at the people who'd crowded into the square, I saw all those places where the Aylis churches once rose and all the flower and vegetable gardens established there now to hide that fact and deceive history. I saw my own home, built with my own hands all of twenty-five years ago, and every tree and bush I'd planted.

Among those people on the square, was there even one person who knew why he'd come there? If all that brouhaha were indeed connected to *Stone Dreams*, wouldn't it have been possible to organize it just a little more plausibly? You know, my work still hadn't even been published in Azeri. And the journal *Druzhba narodov* in which *Stone Dreams* had been published in Russian was arriving in Azerbaijan in just two copies at that point. So that meant no one cared what *Stone Dreams* was about or why it had been written; one part of the crowd appeared there for the free spectacle, the other part hoped to find something to their own benefit from that spectacle.

It is real torture for a writer when a people turns into a mob literally before his eyes. And having blended into the mob, a person immediately becomes not just faceless and soulless but horribly corrupt. You see, just ten days before this "rally" practically all of them had been proud of me as their famous writer and distinguished deputy; their children knew me from their schoolbooks. And now, having turned into a mob, they'd already forgotten all that. For them, I no longer existed as a creative person. And, believe me, *Stone Dreams* interested them no more than any of my other books collected from all the city and village libraries of Nakhchivan so they could burn them right there in Aylis itself. Not one of them had read a single phrase of *Stone Dreams*. If they had read it, it would have made absolutely no difference. You see, the most active participants in that mob were people of approximately my own age. They certainly knew everything I'd written in *Stone Dreams*.

All of them knew that there had once been a number of churches in Aylis, thanks to which the town was known not only in Nakhchivan and Yerevan but in many countries of both the Christian and Muslim world; there was a time when Aylis was called Little Istanbul.

How could those people so quickly forget the massive destruction of churches and cemeteries that had begun in Nakhchivan all of ten to fifteen years previously? And is it really possible that people born into and living in the Ordubad district hadn't heard at least once about the Armenian pogrom that took place at one time in Aylis? Consequently, they'd come there to "execute" me for the fact that in my novel I proclaimed a certain truth that was well known to them all. "Akram is an Armenian! Akram is a traitor to his motherland! Death to Akram!"—on that day they were courageous in their curses addressed to me, as if the demon of aggression had awakened in them.

I knew the faces of practically all of those who'd gathered on the market square in Aylis. I'd seen them many times at meetings I held in 2005 at the time of my election campaign when I ran for deputy.

One pot-bellied hulk, a person I'd often met on the main street of Ordubad, conducted himself particularly aggressively. He was shouting in full voice, shaking his fists, demonstrating his unprecedented bureaucratic zeal to the higher ups. Earlier that person had been a police inspector, and now he'd become the director of the local history museum. And every time I'd met him, I heard the exact same phrase from him, pronounced in a typical Ordubad accent: "And when are we going to get together and drink a shot of vodka?" Apparently, the thirst for that shot he'd once promised me now compelled him to howl so savagely.

The rotten, nauseating smell of everyday Armenophobia hung in the Aylis air. A strange expression was frozen on the faces of several participants in the meeting—a semblance of bewilderment mixed with fear. Mainly it was the Aylis women who'd been driven there by force, threatened and belittled. And the male half of Aylis was represented by out-and-out loafers who loitered there the same way every day not knowing what to do with themselves. Their sly smirks were striking.

Well, and among those who came to the rally from the district center were many men and women who clearly enjoyed participating in such an important event: petty officials fed with crumbs from the state budget. It was simplest of all for me to understand them because I knew very well what the main responsibility of a state official consisted of in the prevailing moral-psychological atmosphere of Nakhchivan, where the authorities did anything they wanted and compelled everyone to dance to their tune. If you dance, you're with them. If not, good luck finding yourself a place under the sky. And under what sky can a person find a place if even the sky belongs to them, the powers-that-be? And if behind them stands all the might of the govern-mental machine ably constructed in its time by that leading builder of an authoritarian regime, Heydar Aliev?[12]

State officials, and not only they, now had to behave themselves much more obediently than in even the worst times of the all-encompassing Soviet ideological yoke. It was as if history were moving backwards to the time of moral-ethical genocide. No other path was left to a person than to constantly demonstrate his own devotion to the leadership. And many rally participants were proud and happy precisely because on that "important" day for the whole country, the authorities hadn't forgotten about them, hadn't overlooked them. Instructions came from the very top, from Ilham Aliev himself.

I wanted to shriek, to tell them, "I'm not any sort of Armenian, and every one of you knows it! I don't extol Armenians but simply write the truth. And writing the truth is my responsibility because I'm a writer. And I love you and don't want you to be deceived and cheated by the authorities above, for whom a lie is the only correct truth. Wake up, understand who I am: I'm not any kind of traitor but simply a victim of the same shameless regime that's made you so pitiful and weak-willed."

xi

I was never closely acquainted with Ilham Aliev. But I knew his father Heydar Aliev very well and repeatedly met and spoke with him in private.

With regard to Vasif Talibov: both during the lifetime of Heydar Aliev and for some time after his death, Talibov was favorably enough disposed towards me.[13] He even visited me several times when I was in Aylis. And I always openly expressed to him that I thought the mass destruction of Armenian monuments in Nakhchivan was a great shame of our nation. In the spring of 1997 when that monstrous vandalism had just begun, I considered it my duty to send Heydar Aliev a telegram in which I expressed my opposition to what was happening.

Heydar Aliev and Vasif Talibov are undoubtedly not comparable as great figures. But it turns out that miracles sometimes happen in politics. Having worked only a couple of years with Aliev in the Supreme Assembly of Nakhchivan, Talibov to such a great degree made Aliev's administrative-ruling style and methods his own that after his new, upward takeoff into big-time politics, taking the Nakhchivan seat of his own chief, he was able to become the all-powerful master of Nakhchivan and its permanent ruler.

Talibov was born in a typical Norashen village to the family of a collective farm worker in an atmosphere of patriarchal obedience. I don't know if his environment was religious or what impressions of religion he himself had. But in spite of all the prohibitions and persecutions of the atheistic Soviet regime, the people of Norashen, like everyone in Nakhchivan, always remained Muslim and to one degree or another believed in Islam. For Muslims, the destruction of churches is beyond the pale. And the defiling of any cemetery, no matter whose, where the spirits of the deceased live eternally—the disturbing of whom might attract shattering calamity to humanity—is strongly condemned.

How is it that yesterday's worker in a third-rate knitted-goods factory suddenly became a bold, intrepid spirit, the new khan of Nakhchivan, ordering hundreds of cemeteries and churches to be wiped off the face of the earth?!

I'm prepared to forget Vasif Talibov, his visits to me in Aylis, even the numerous poisonous letters and telegrams sent from Nakhchivan to my Baku address at his personal command, and even those sinister bonfires of my books blazing on that cold February day in my native Aylis.

But I haven't forgotten—I will never forget—how an ordinary mortal can change into a moral monster when he loses his immunity to lying.

xii

I can't remember how I slept that night or what I dreamed. But waking up the next morning, I felt such calmness and ease in myself that those feelings will always stay in my soul and memory. That was a condition of spirit greater than happiness itself. And I understood that something had taken place in my life that was more important than anything in all the preceding time of my existence under God's heaven.

For the first time in my life I understood clearly that my fate stands behind me. It's mine, only mine, and no power of any kind over it has been given to anyone besides me.

For the first time in my life I was convinced that if a person retains the ability to be greater than his own suffering, it's impossible to deny him all joy. And thanks to that same Aylis that long ago gave me my first bitter lessons in life, I've turned out to be quite patient and hardy.

How old was Aylis that morning? I was seventy-five. And all my life, wherever I was, Aylis was always with me: in my student years in Baku and Moscow and in numerous creative business trips to the various corners of the Big Country.

In Germany, England, Norway, Turkey, Mongolia, Poland, Hungary, the US, Yemen, everywhere, in all the countries where I've had the good fortune to be, I looked for a little piece of Aylis, and I always found it. I've lived a long creative life, and in all my stories and novels Aylis is unfailingly present: its rocky mountains laughing under the sun, the stony earth groaning from the intense summer heat and thirsting for moisture, and the people worn out from the heat. The inexhaustible spiritual energy of Aylis coursed without stopping through my veins, helping me defend myself in the face of violence and injustice.

And now, look: Aylis was no longer mine. And would never be mine again. Lord, why was I rejoicing, then?!

Suddenly, the blessed weight of the Aylis mountains that I'd always felt in my chest disappeared, evaporated. It seemed to me as if Aylis had never existed at all. As if no one else besides me had ever seen the Aylis that I carried in my soul all my life like an ache, like hope, like warmth and light.

Perhaps I experienced such relief because the Aylis taken away from me that day by the potent hand of the authorities hadn't been my Aylis for a long time already. It was their Aylis: without God and without Memory, without History, and without a Biography.

That morning I was inspired with the hope that even if their Aylis lasts a hundred years, *my* Aylis, which God created especially for me, entrusting its joy and sorrow only to me, will also exist in the world. For the Almighty decided, evidently, to also entrust to me alone the sacred mission to tell people about that Aylis. I've spent almost all the years of my life telling people about my Aylis, and it seems that I've been able to do that colorfully and attractively enough in my writing in the bright searchlight of my dreamy, supersensitive childhood. How wonderful that my labors haven't fallen by the wayside! My books have found a place on bookshelves in hundreds of thousands of libraries in many countries far and near.

Let some in my motherland think I'm not a writer: so be it. I don't need honor or glory in a country where they burn books and a killer with an ax is elevated to the rank of hero.

xiii

Stone Dreams belongs to my second trilogy (the first, *People and Trees*, was written in the 1960s). *Stone Dreams* is the second story of this new trilogy; the Moscow journal *Druzhba narodov*, evidently in view of the timeliness of the subject matter, decided to publish it first (*Yemen*, of course, was published before the breakup of the USSR). I thought it necessary to call this story a "novel-requiem" because the work doesn't meet the requirements of a tradi-tional novel, and the disclaimer "novel-requiem" seems to me to give the reader advance warning of that fact. The third part of the trilogy, *A Fantastical Traffic Jam*, was supposed to be published in one of the next numbers of *Druzhba narodov*, and its publication was officially announced in that same number of the journal where *Stone Dreams* appeared. But the echoes of the commotion caused by *Stone Dreams* in Baku quickly reached Moscow, and the frightened editorial staff obediently halted publication of *A Fantastical Traffic Jam*.

Was the publication announcement for *A Fantastical Traffic Jam* known in Baku's official circles? Undoubtedly, it was. Six or seven months before publica-tion of *Stone Dreams* in the Moscow journal, the entire trilogy had been published in Baku in a small printing. Probably the ruling elite knew about that, too. And if, as many people think, the reason for my persecution really lies in *A Fantastical Traffic Jam*, then the question naturally arises: why did that part of the trilogy in particular cause such bitterness and malice at the highest echelons of power?

A Fantastical Traffic Jam is written in the style of magical realism in the satirical, ironic manner of García Márquez. This third novella of the trilogy por-trays the symbolically named Allahabad, an imaginary, oil-rich Muslim country corrupt to the bone.

In Allahabad, a country rapidly losing its moral character, toadying and bootlicking are held in great respect. All-powerful ideological officials are cou-rageous patriots in word and petty, mercenary little people with a brute hatred towards human individuality and any kind of non-conformity in deed. And the frightened and obedient educated elite of this country can barely be called an intelligentsia.

Was Azerbaijan really the prototype for Allahabad, and were those people who created that atmosphere of hopelessness and despair really seated at the height of power in Azerbaijan? Not a single state official is mentioned by name in *A Fantastical Traffic Jam*. And if someone in authority in Azerbaijan suddenly saw himself in those personages, in what way is this author guilty? How could I convince those same authorities that my story was by no means written with the goal of shaking their "throne"? No artist's word can end evil if the machin-ery of the state supports it. In *A Fantastical Traffic Jam* I described only the vis-ible side of hidden processes that take place behind tightly closed doors, and I tried to give my writer's forecast about what terrible consequences they might have in the future.

A writer's forecast can be correct or mistaken; every normal society inter-prets it that way. But to my great regret and tremendous surprise, in this case my forecast was one-hundred-percent correct. In the last few years numerous facts have surfaced about corruption and theft at the highest echelons of power in Azerbaijan—mysteriously enigmatic arrests in the ranks of the Ministry of National Defense, the whole press filled with articles and notices about thieving ministers, judges who are scoundrels, generals who are butchers, and deputies who are crooks—it is precisely about this societal vileness that my *Fantastical Traffic Jam*, a novel written almost ten years ago, tells the story. Wasn't this the reason that the powers-that-be punished me so harshly? Why didn't they want to understand that with their recklessness they were digging not only my grave but undoubtedly their own?

To mistake an artist's representation for reality is inexcusable ignorance. This is direct interference by the state in the creative affairs of a writer and bureaucratic control over artistic thought, the sort of control that was widely applied back in the time of Stalinist aesthetic utilitarianism.

With regard to *Stone Dreams*, I had a premonition that publishing it might present me with such "surprises," and I clearly realized that with its publication I couldn't expect anything good. But I was unable to even imagine the bitter bias with which it would be read not only by politicians and patriots but also by writers of my close circle—yesterday's like-minded people who'd often lifted a glass with me to the health of the Armenian people and the prosperity of Armenia at the celebratory meals that were fashionable in their time, a time when exchanging declarations of love and respect between an Armenian and an Azerbaijani was not considered a grave crime.

My comrades in the writer's guild immediately denounced me as their long-time enemy, as if they hadn't known me before, or knew only bad things about me. They gave the impression that they'd never heard anything about the repression of 1937 and didn't have the slightest idea that it was precisely under the flag of such patriotism that all the campaigns of denunciations against the creative intelligentsia had unfolded in the years of the all-shattering Stalinist moral terror.

Members of the political opposition who'd earlier sympathized with me didn't spare me now, either, unanimously accusing me of unforgivable, pro-Armenian views and failure to observe balance in describing the conflict between the two opposing sides.

"Twenty percent of our land occupied," "more than a million refugees and internally displaced persons," "Zory Balayan," "Armenian fascism," "Khojaly, Khojaly, Khojaly"—with these words everyone found it convenient to shut me up.

Not having read my work, even international diplomats and political commentators seriously questioned it: might this book in fact distort reality, and might the authorities simply be fulfilling the will of a whole people by punishing its author?

And no one cared that my miniature novel has nothing to do with the Karabakh conflict. It is from top to bottom about a person and a human tragedy—about the spiritual suffering and psychological shock of the main character. And about what kind of "balance" could one possibly speak here if there isn't even one weak hint in the novel that its author has the slightest intention of playing the role of arbiter, daring to take it on himself to give a comprehensive appreciation of the centuries-old and highly complex conflict between Turks and Armenians?

A writer is free to choose whether or not to defend the transient national interests of his own country. But he's always responsible for the moral appearance of his own people, for the spiritual state of his own fellow citizens. A writer is a writer because he may have interests beyond the narrowly nationalistic. And how is it possible to live a creative life while consciously yielding to the general psychosis always sowed by state ideology?

Friendship between Armenians and Azerbaijanis is not high-flown rhetoric for me but an extremely important question of principle. I sincerely value this friendship and consider it a historically important cultural heritage of my people. For me, this friendship is worth much more than all the material blessings achieved by my country during all its years of independence. For a long time I've perceived the current enmity and estrangement sowed between us by shortsighted politicians as my own personal tragedy.

"He wanted Armenians to like him!" "He wanted to get the Nobel Prize!" "He was jealous of Orhan Pamuk's laurels!"—such are the gifts prepared for me by long-suffering fate because I just couldn't strike a bargain with my own conscience.

xiv

On that morning of February 10, 2013, the day after my books were burned in Aylis, for the first time I came to believe in the uniqueness of my own fate. The realization gave me a strange, almost mystical joy. Never before had the world seemed so transparent and vast to me as it did that morning. My mind grew clearer; my spirit underwent revitalization. It was as if everything around me had been illumined with some kind of new light; everything began to breathe anew. Moreover, imagine: this happened after ten days of unrelieved stress.

On one of those ten days, like real jinns from a fairy tale, some spawn of the New Azerbaijan Party (YAP) suddenly bust into the yard of my building, lit a bonfire of my books, and in voices that weren't their own shouted: "Death to Akram the Armenian!"[14]

On the next day more rootless urchins from that same party of authority with rapturous enthusiasm carried my symbolic coffin around the city.

On the third day the Milli Mejlis met with its full complement of chosen patriots.[15] Demonstrating yet again their boundless tolerance, the patriot-deputies celebrated important news for the whole country with great enthusiasm and continuous, wild applause—that is, my birthday as a new-minted Armenian, enlarging the ranks of the "thirty thousand" fortunate Baku Armenians.

On yet another of those memorable days the authoritative literary men—the experienced wheeler-dealers in literature and high muckety-mucks who'd permanently headed the two-thousand-strong army of writers for thirty years already—released a declaration written in flawlessly clear YAPist-Stalinist-Zhdanovist-style language.[16] And in that declaration my closest friends of yesterday informed the people with true writerly zeal that I was, it turns out, no novice in base, pro-Armenian transactions but a very experienced traitor to the motherland and had been so practically since birth.

The declaration by famous writers could not, of course, escape the notice of the Head Mullah of "Allahabad." It was received by him as a message direct from God on high, and our venerable sheikh-ul-Islam immediately called together his brotherhood in the religious guild and slandered me in such an ugly way that all the Talysh people—his tribesmen—were ashamed of him for a full forty days.

I'd anticipated all kinds of hard knocks from the authorities, experienced first-hand almost all possible models that authority uses to deal with dissent, but I wasn't going to give up. And still the press continued to attack me, demanding immediate surrender.

A writer can be killed by deference to rank and by ceremonial honors, but it's impossible to kill his faith in mercy. I considered it to be a sacred debt to pay for all those killed, tortured, and ruined.

XV

The bonfires of my books in Aylis were probably calculated to break me once and for all. To some extent, they succeeded. My Aylis—sunny and bright—suddenly disappeared from my dreams. Now, even finding myself there in my dreams, I was always searching for my own bright Aylis.

Now it had turned into a dead, uninhabited place—grey, without sun or moon, shrouded in eternal silence.

And in that grey silence, I saw my own father for the first time in a dream, my father who died at the front when I was still a very small child. Holding a rifle in place of a shepherd's crook, my father stood among the naked Aylis cliffs behind a fantastical flock of sheep reminiscent of stone statues and looked in bewilderment at the endless cemetery that stretched out beneath.

Another night I heard the trembling voice of my mother, full of tears, from beneath the tombstones of that same cemetery at which my father had looked. And in that voice she told me again, word for word, that terrible tale about the events she'd witnessed while just a little girl and had been unable to forget for the rest of her life. "Airanik, Aleksan's daughter, had two twin daughters who looked like two halves of the moon. She took one of them by the hand and held the other in her arms. The bearded sergeant Mehmet, may he be cursed a million times, seemed to turn into a wild animal in a single second. Lord, with what fury he took Airanik's children from her and dashed them on the ground! And the unashamed Mirza Vahab, who read the Quran every day and was reputed to be a scholar, stood on the side and cheered the killers on: 'Use your bayonet, bayonet them, save your ammunition!' Those dishonorable people didn't pity even decrepit old people. They drowned Armenians in their own blood and then went to rob their homes."

Now I often have nightmares. In place of the unfortunate and angry local women whom I earlier met frequently in the streets of Aylis, I dream now of a disheveled Leila Yunus, now of Khadija Ismailova in torn clothing.[17]

In one of those nightmares the long-dead Hrant Matevosyan appeared. He stood in the middle of the carriage road that wound like a belt around the mountain named Khyshkeshen and looked with strange interest at the roof of our old house, which had belonged to us since time immemorial. And by the look of his eternally sad eyes, I concluded that to this day he still wasn't entirely certain that my ancestors were innocent of the crimes committed in the former "Little Istanbul" on that day of judgment for Aylis when it was crucified by Turkish butchers.

And Anait Bayadur was also there, searching in one of the old Armenian cemeteries of Aylis for the graves of her kin.

And Tamara, embracing Habib's grave in the Muslim cemetery with both arms.

Lord, isn't all this a mystery! And with what words will I be able to convince the reader that the Aylis sun returned once more at the moment in one of those dreams when Azrail, the angel of death, rose over my head.

"What do you want to take from this world?" he asked in an imperiously calm voice, looking through the window on the expanse of the entire universe covered in bright light—the entire universe, which seemed to be contained now within the boundaries of just little Aylis.

"Aylis!" I said without hesitation. And suddenly awakening, I remembered my earlier enchanted dream on that hot August night in 2016. Aylis. Early in the morning. The ravishing world, where the sun shone brighter than sun, and the grass was greener than grass. And there on the bank of the small mountain river, two people were sitting quietly: THE HAPPY PRESIDENT AND THE FREE WRITER!

And then, with tears in my eyes I said, "Farewell, Aylis. Don't call me. I won't come."

Winter 2017

Instead of an Epilogue

(The text of a speech for the Venetian literary festival Incroci di civiltà, March 2016, not delivered because I was denied permission to leave Azerbaijan.)

Back in Baku when I began thinking about how I should start this speech, if there was a need for me to speak here, these next, anxious words immediately came to mind: "Before you stands a completely defenseless person." And then I heard my indignant inner voice: "Don't whine," it said, "don't grumble like an old man. You aren't the only one in the world in this kind of situation—there are people who are more defenseless!"

Unfortunately, that's the truth, my dear colleagues! Now we are all defenseless before these inconceivably cruel times.

There are periods in history when nothing can fill the emptiness of the human heart: not religion, not science, not literature.

Spiritual and artistic authorities, it seems, have become a thing of the past. The state institutions of the most developed countries have been unable to propose any reasonable means of releasing us from this moral and spiritual dead end.

At one time my fellow countrymen and brothers in faith cursed Soviet authorities for the fact that they shut the doors of our places of worship in our faces. Now the number of mosques in my country will soon be comparable to the number of schools, but none of my fellow countrymen have become closer to God because of it.

It's cramped in churches and mosques, and in heads, too. People no longer have the spiritual strength to look to the future with hope, and they don't have the time to look into their own souls. The bar of culture has fallen throughout the world. People have understood that culture won't save us.

Lord, I'm freezing in this world,
I'm sorry for wearing a coat indoors,
What's yours here is already destroyed,
And nothing of ours can keep us warm.[18]

It's hardly possible to express the pain of our hearts better than the young Russian poet did in these four lines.

We've all turned out to be powerless now. Not only have individuals turned out to be defenseless, but whole peoples and nations.

No one is going to take responsibility for the criminal political adventures in Chechnya, Yugoslavia, Iraq, Libya, Syria, Yemen, and the Donbass that have taken hundreds of thousands of lives and maimed the fate of millions.

If this continues, then in the very near future a real torrent of the most terrible crimes will pour forth in the world, crimes that will be and forever remain unpunished.

As Solzhenitsyn said, violence and lies—these two things have always gone hand in hand. Violence doesn't exist and is unable to exist alone; it is unfailingly accompanied by lies. Violence has nothing to hide behind except lies.

Violence isn't just confined to the terrorist acts being carried out now in the world in unprecedented numbers, acts that evoke anxiety for our lives and the fate of our families and friends in each of us. Violence is not any less terrible when it surreptitiously penetrates our consciousness, corrupting our hearts, killing faith in goodness and justice in them, and making us helpless before ignorance and obscurantism. It ruthlessly mixes up good with evil.

Taking refuge in the so-called "national idea," a vast number of people—people who don't have anything to support their spirit or who carry an ominous emptiness in their souls—sow the seeds of hatred with impunity between peoples and nations that just yesterday were living peacefully side by side with one another.

The nationalist is terrible because his character is that of a heartless optimist who, in rejecting a tragic perception of life, fundamentally contradicts truth. This is a revolt against reason and humanity. Nationalism is a naked lie uttered by devilishly embittered people who with great impudence proclaim themselves as the bearers of the only correct idea and as the true fighters for the people's happiness. Patriotism imposed from above gives such fascist bastards great opportunities to turn the people into a brainless mob. But we know that those who stand nearest to the mob are also the most corrupt. And that to appeal to the masses as a people is to condemn them to a long and evil obscurantism.

When you live among sinners, sin sticks to you, too. But a writer's a writer in that, even in the most extreme conditions, he's able to protect within himself the quiet awareness of a deeper truth.

"The truth is greater than Nekrasov, greater than Pushkin, greater than the people, greater than Russia," wrote Dostoevsky in his time.

"Beware the writer who sets himself or herself up as the voice of the nation," warned another writer, our contemporary Salman Rushdie.[19]

To be beloved by the masses, it's possible to write however you want and whatever you want. But the ability to develop a kinship with your reader is given to only a few writers.

A writer isn't a writer because he's adored by a mass reading public. He's a genuine spokesperson for eternal moral values to whom the people entrust their own pain. And when the people start losing their identity, writers suffer from that more than anyone else.

A writer is a teacher from the heart of the people, and he's not in the least to blame when politicians fail to understand his magical ability.

The psychology of power can't stand writers who have their own view of fateful events taking place in the life of society. The authorities punish those writers cruelly and terribly. And in my case they acted with similar cruelty and pitilessness.

But I won't say more about that. I don't want to shame my little country in front of a foreign audience, my little country that I love no less even after all its current rulers have done to me.

There's much sadness in my story, but there's also been much that's useful and instructive.

It seems to me that with my little work, published now in Italian, I've been able to accomplish my main goal: I've saved many Armenians from hatred towards my people.

And I've come to understand that in this bloody conflict, neither we nor the Armenians are to blame—the two peoples would never have gone to war if politics hadn't interfered in their lives.

And I'm further convinced that our two peoples are each good in themselves, but together they're simply great.

I've always known that only through personal suffering are we able to see what's invisible in our ordinary lives. Now I've walked that path with my own two feet, trying not to stumble or fall. Apparently, my soul had to be completely exhausted in order for me to realize and get to know myself anew among the great number of people who are susceptible to the current corruption and seasonal treachery.

There are episodes in life that are worth more than many lifetimes. In this episode of my life I was a hero for some and a traitor for others. I myself didn't doubt for a minute that I was neither a hero nor a traitor but simply a normal writer and humanist with the ability to feel pity for another's pain.

I've found myself in Galileo's situation—Galileo, who didn't doubt for a second that he was correct but, even while indisputably correct in his own opinion, was unable to knock on the rusty hearts of the guardians of universal dogma and make himself heard.

I've been deprived of peace and prosperity for the sake of a small step towards bringing together two peoples connected not only by geographic proximity but also by centuries-old historical fate. And my most cherished dream is to see them together again once more.

And I very much want to live until that joyous day.

Akram Aylisli—
A Writer for His Time

What can an eighty-something writer from an obscure country in the Caucasus tell us about the world we live in? Quite a lot, actually, despite the fact that his work is rooted in the reality of late Soviet and post-Soviet Azerbaijan, a country little known to the larger world and one whose writers have generally not made a big impression on the international literary scene. As the reader of the three novellas presented here will see, however, Akram Aylisli manages to tap the history and reality of Azerbaijan to provide exceptionally enlightening commentary on major political, psychological, and social trends that far transcend the specifics of his own country. And while there is no doubt that his fiction is tendentious and idea driven, his approach is sufficiently literary to ensure that the work almost never reads like a thinly veiled tract.

At the center of Aylisli's stories is a consideration of the ways in which individuals are tossed about by political and social forces significantly more powerful than themselves. He focuses the novellas in this collection around the demise (figuratively or literally) of a relatively weak central character who gets caught up in the maelstrom of events. To be sure, the theme of the "little man" has been a staple of Russian literature (and it is from Russian/Soviet literature that Aylisli's work undoubtedly grows, although there are other influences at work as well), starting at least from Pushkin's narrative poem *The Bronze Horseman* (written in 1833). In that poem, the hero Evgeny's hopes for a happy domestic life are destroyed by the death of his fiancée in a flood that engulfs the city that Peter the Great erected on an inhospitable swamp. In the poem's climactic moments Evgeny, driven mad by his loss, curses Peter and is then pursued across the city by the vengeful Tsar's statue, eventually dying a solitary and pitiful death by the Neva River. In Aylisli's work, the "little men" are not quite as little as Pushkin's hero, nor are they always sympathetic. Regardless, each of them is crushed by political currents greater than themselves.

In *Yemen* (1992), the little man is Safaly *muallim*, former rector of a Soviet literary institute, whose life is ruined by a series of accidents that commences during his time as a member of a delegation to Yemen in the mid-1960s. In the Soviet context, Safaly *muallim* is not a true little man. The opportunity to travel abroad (even to an allied country like Yemen) was afforded to only a very few people, including those like Safaly who were in positions of some authority. Nevertheless, Safaly's rank does not protect him when he falls under suspicion. Unable to sleep in his hotel after his arrival in Sana'a, he takes a walk in the garden, and his disappearance from his hotel room prompts the paranoid and venal leader of the delegation, Ali Ziya, to conclude that he has decided to escape and ask for political asylum in the US Embassy. This supposed defection is enough to ruin Safaly's career. The basis for the story is thus a tragicomic accident, and the "fall of Safaly" is a kind of anecdote that provides an excuse for a story that broadens to consider many other themes in a style reminiscent of the oeuvre of the great Soviet Abkhaz writer Fazil Iskander (1929–2016). While readers feel a certain sympathy for Safaly after his fall from grace, a number of clues in the story tell us that although he was never one of the worst Soviet careerists, he was far from a paragon, as illustrated by his previous willingness to write sycophantic reviews of the work of various official writers, including Ali Ziya himself.

In *Stone Dreams* (2011), Sadai Sadygly, the main character who spends almost the entire story in a coma, is by far the most sympathetic of Aylisli's little men. Sadygly is a leading dramatic actor in Baku, and as such and like Safaly *muallim* he is part of the Soviet cultural elite. Unlike Safaly, however, he is portrayed as an almost completely positive figure, although he is consistently linked to Don Quixote, a traditional symbol of dreamy impotence. Like his avatar, Sadygly is simply incapable of accepting the boorish reality of the surrounding system. His acting talent allows him to avoid following the crowd in its slavish admiration of various generations of autocratic leaders and even, from time to time, to get away with speaking truth to power. When Soviet authority breaks down in the late 1980s, Sadai Sadygly is disgusted and horrified by the pogroms against Armenians that became the defining feature of life in Azerbaijan. Badly beaten by a mob as he tries to help an Armenian, he is brought to a hospital; most of the story takes place in his comatose dreams as he slowly succumbs to his injuries.

While *Yemen* is told in a rambling style that recalls the work of Iskander, Aylisli's approach in *Stone Dreams* is much more closely connected to the narrative style of the great Yugoslav writer Ivo Andrić (1892–1975). Weaving contemporary historical tensions between Armenians and Azerbaijanis with historical materials from as far back as the seventeenth century, Aylisli tries to recapture the aura of the little town of Aylis in the distant province of Nakhchivan, recalling Andrić's recreation of Višegrad in *The Bridge Over the Drina* (1945) and Travnik in *Days of the Consuls* (1945). As in Andrić's novels, Aylisli shows that tension and conflict have always been at the center of the relationship between ethnic groups, although in moments of serenity both groups have been able to flourish.

The "little man" of the novella *A Fantastical Traffic Jam* (2011) is simultaneously both the highest placed and most abject of Aylisli's heroes. Elbey is a nonentity who has spent his entire career as a toady to the leader of the fictional land of Allahabad, which bears an uncanny similarity to Aylisli's Azerbaijan. He has spent his career sucking up to the great leader, amassing enormous wealth in the process. The story revolves around the loss of his position and eventually his life at the whim of the leader whose will he had served. Unlike Safaly and Sadygly, Elbey is not at all an attractive little man. And even as we see him gain a glimmer of insight into his position during his abrupt fall from grace, we find it hard to develop any sympathy for him.

It is important to reiterate that the specifics of the immediate political situation do not change the fates of individual characters in Aylisli's fictional worlds—whether they live in Soviet, transition, or post-Soviet times, they have little or no ability to change the course of history that is dominated by autocratic and arbitrary leaders and mob violence. Nor does it seem to matter whether they are actively opposed to their reality (as is the case with Sadai Sadygly), passively opposed (Safaly *muallim*), or active in aiding and abetting it (Elbey). There is simply no escape for the individual, at least not in the world of reality.

While the trope of the individual crushed by larger forces is pervasive in Russian and Soviet literature, Aylisli's other main theme, the exploration of the tyrant's mindset, is less common in the tradition. Indeed, it is somewhat remarkable that, given the Russian state's autocratic traditions, Russian literature has focused so much more frequently on the oppressed than the oppressor. Although there are exceptions, such as Tolstoy's treatment of Nicholas I in his great novella *Hadji Murad* (posthumously published 1912), outside of the literatures of the Caucasus it is hard to find as sustained a treatment of this topic as we see in the two later novellas of Aylisli.

In *Stone Dreams* our understanding of the machinations of power within the Soviet state apparatus is filtered through the words of Sadygly. Describing the largesse of the country's leader, he recognizes that the system functions on the basis of a mutual pact between the ruler and the ruled. "He makes friends by dishing out delicacies from the common pot—our common pot—as if it were his own. He gives everyone something, taking away the most important thing in a man—his dignity. He castrates the soul of the people so as to make everyone quiet and obedient" (p. 84). Sadygly understands that a state built around the cult of a leader's personality is condemned to a kind of eternal return. Thus, when told by the theater director Maupassant Miralamov that under the newest leader things will change for the better, he retorts, "[N]othing will change.... And you won't do anything to hurt the former Master, as they call him to this day among the people, even if you revile him still more loudly. Now you plan to pile all the guilt for your own servile obedience on him so as to get out of that shit with clean hands" (p. 138). Given that the Azerbaijani state today remains of the type Sadygly reviles, it is easy to see why Aylisli's work has gotten him into considerable political trouble, even if no names are officially named.

If the currency of power is gift giving that enforces subordination, the lubrication of the system is fear, a topic explored explicitly in *A Fantastical Traffic Jam*. In this novella we do not simply see the system at work through an analysis by a character who understands its basic underpinnings. Rather, we observe it from the inside through the interactions of some key players, one of whom is the leader himself. And what we see is decidedly unnerving. The Master (or *Rais*), as he is called, wields power based on his ability to exploit his subjects' worst instincts. As his flunky Elbey recognizes: "In that country abounding in luxury and woe, submerged in a quagmire of secular prosperity, gasbags of various styles, toadies, and sponges of all stripes distrusted and feared one another but, most of all, each of them feared the Master" (p. 176).

The most salient characteristic of Allahabad is the inversion of truth and lying, with strong preference going to the latter. As the narrator tells us, channeling the thoughts of the nation's leader using *style indirect libre*:

> The Master chuckled lightly, ran his index finger along his slender moustache, and again assumed a serious look. He kept people—even those who were near him every day—at a distance. To that old faker blinded by vanity, both truth and lies were equally distasteful. But all the same, he preferred lies to truth. Because it was easier for him to understand people deceiving him for their own advantage, and he could never grasp why people had to tell him the truth. (p. 185)

For Aylisli, power is based on the ability to control narratives and to instill fear.

> Probably everyone knows what fear is, but hardly any of us contemplate the impenetrable abyss where it builds its nest. Keeping in mind how Elbey, having observed the secret glances exchanged by his mother and the *Rais*, was frightened one evening on the threshold of his own house, we (with the help of Freud) can suppose it was precisely then that the hidden fear that would ruthlessly devastate his soul took root in Elbey, nesting there once and for all.
>
> Let's say it all happened exactly that way. But how can we find an explanation for the incontrovertible fact that it was by no means Elbey alone who trembled that way before the *Rais*? (p. 217)

Even more interesting, however, is the insight that this fear travels in more than one direction. It rules the ruler himself, who is as terrified as any of his subjects:

> Especially because not one of my fellow villagers was granted the ability to even conceive that the *Rais* was also afraid of them, and that he was so fiercely cruel and free of all morals because their *Rais* had also been "bald" from birth, and that he derived his power from the weakness of people. And in that lay not his strength but his weakness. And that's why he constructed his path with threats and coercion; a master of disguise, he loved to blackmail people and twist anyone around his finger in any way he needed. (pp. 217–218)

The only escape from fear, we discover, is a retreat into childhood, the period of life before humans recognize how irredeemably horrible the adult world is. Again, this trope is a commonplace of Russian and Soviet culture, dating back to Leo Tolstoy's iconic novella *Childhood* (1852). According to Tolstoy's vision, which was eventually codified as a central myth of Russian culture, childhood is the happiest time of life, a period in which the innocence of the young person has not been corrupted by hypocrisy and lies. In each of the stories in this collection, the desire to regain a kind of childhood purity animates the characters, providing at least a partial refuge from the culture of lies and fear that characterizes the adult world.

In *Yemen* we first understand this when Safaly enters the garden next door to his hotel on the infamous day of his supposed attempt at defection.

The garden is both an avatar of humankind's original paradise, the Garden of Eden, and simultaneously the actual garden that surrounded Safaly in his childhood home town of Buzbulag.

> When he'd fearfully opened the door, Safaly *muallim* went into that garden; then not only did he forget his fear, but I would even say, if you believe me, that he even completely forgot that he was a Soviet citizen.
>
> What was that, O Lord: a revelation, an inspiration, an awakening, or just that Safaly *muallim* hadn't noticed that at some point he'd died, and had now arisen and found himself in that scrap of "Yemeni Buzbulag"? In spite of his sleepless night, Safaly *muallim* felt unprecedented vigor and ease in that garden; it seemed to him that if he wanted to, right now he could fly above the garden like a bird and, in the twinkling of an eye, find himself in Buzbulag and there, in the yard of Khyzyr *kishi*, sit on any tree, on any branch. In that garden, it was as if Safaly *muallim*'s memory and consciousness had awakened from many years' death-like hibernation: he saw his entire half-century's life as if it lay in the palm of his hand—and the very best moments of that life, similar to the strange spring breeze, were affectionately, tenderly seeping into and wandering about his body and blood. (pp. 18–19)

Although Safaly's visit to that garden would have fateful consequences for his career as a literary critic and university administrator, its liberating potential is even more consequential. Given that, as Czech writer, statesman, and dissident Vaclav Havel put it, life under communism meant living a lie, Safaly has had his eyes opened. He can now, at least from time to time, escape everyday reality by returning to his childhood paradise.

For Sadygly in *Stone Dreams*, childhood paradise is the small village of Aylis in Nakhchivan. Specifically, in his comatose state Sadygly returns to one transcendent moment of his childhood when a beam of sunlight fell on the cupola of the partially destroyed Armenian Vang church.

> Once Sadai Sadygly, being in a fine disposition of spirits, had compared that light—first appearing, then slowly fading and disappearing from the church cupola and the crest of the mountain—to the smile of God and the radiance of the Almighty's eyes. God himself had sent that light. Without His blessing, how could Sadai Sadygly, currently unconscious in a Baku hospital, so closely, so distinctly see the Vang Church in Aylis, the

yellow-rose light on its cupola, its yard, garden, and that same tall cherry
tree disappearing as if it were a poplar into the height of the sky? (p. 101)

This vision allows Sadygly respite from the terrible world of *perestroika*
Azerbaijan, in which Azerbaijanis and Armenians are at each other's throats and
pogroms against the Armenian population of Baku seem to repeat the history of
the Armenian genocide of the late 1910s. Ultimately, it is the attraction of that
childhood vision that leads to Sadygly's refusal to struggle with death, whose
embrace he accepts at the end of the story.

Childhood's salvific powers are less apparent in *A Fantastical Traffic Jam*,
perhaps because the main characters are more irredeemably hopeless than
Safaly and Sadygly. Nevertheless, even for the thoroughly evil *Rais* childhood has some pull, as instanced by his recollections of his home region of
Kellekend:

> Although many years had passed since he'd first found himself far from
> his hometown, he always remembered its clean air, blue sky, and the
> mountains smelling of thyme and mint. And he, who believed in nei-
> ther God nor the devil, religiously believed in the taste and the bene-
> fit of everything that grew in the fertile soil of Kellekend. Meat, butter,
> cheese, honey, even pickles and onions were brought to him only from
> there. (p. 183)

Akram Aylisli is both a chronicler of the difficult reality of late and
post-Soviet Azerbaijan and a trenchant critic of the modern post-truth
state. In a literary idiom influenced first and foremost by the Russian literary tradition and the broader literatures of the Soviet Caucasus but infused
with elements of European and American modernism and Latin American
magic realism, he weaves compelling narratives. He is particularly adept
at teasing out the toxic interactions between the autocratic ruler and his
willing subjects. As one figure characterizes it in *A Fantastical Traffic Jam*,
such interactions produce an "epoch of fictitious development, for which
the time will come to settle accounts not only in blood and the loss of material assets but in long years of decline, disbelief in everything, universal
devastation, general fear of any kind of ideology, indifference to politics,
an attraction to philistine prosperity, and nihilism" (p. 261). It would be
difficult to find a better characterization of our world in the era of Trump,
Putin, and Erdoğan than this.

As is frequently the case in the Russian/Soviet literary tradition, Aylisli is better at elucidating the "accursed questions" than he is at answering them. But to quote the final line of Mikhail Lermontov in his author's introduction to *A Hero of Our Time*, "It's sufficient to diagnose the disease. How to cure it, God alone knows."

Andrew Wachtel
Narxoz University,
Almaty, Kazakhstan

Glossary of Terms

ayran: A sour drink prepared from fermented milk.

Albey: A name meaning "tame bey."

arvad: A wife. Used as a polite way of addressing a married woman.

ashpaz: A head chef, usually invited to cook *plov* for weddings, housewarmings, and religious and other holidays.

babki: A game of ancient origin played by throwing animal bones or other small objects.

baji: A sister. Used as a polite way of addressing an unmarried woman.

basturma: Dried cured beef.

bey: A courtesy title for men.

borsch: A sour soup made from beets. Borsch is a part of Russian, Ukrainian, and many other Eastern European cuisines. During the Soviet era it was an extremely popular dish.

brynza: A salty, creamy cheese made mostly from sheep's milk.

chashyr: (Lat. *ferulago*) A mountain plant (herb) from the umbellate family.

chykhyrtma: A traditional Georgian soup made with rich meat broth thickened with beaten eggs and flour.

chyrakh: A sanctuary.

dacha: A country cottage used by urban dwellers, especially in the summer. During the Soviet period, the government distributed dachas only among prominent Communist Party members and the newly created academic and cultural elite. Towards the end of the Soviet era, dachas became more accessible to the middle class.

daijany: Used as a polite way of addressing an uncle's wife.

div:	A fairy tale monster, strong man, sorcerer, and ogre.
Eizengiul:	A name meaning "all flowers" or "continuous flowering."
Elbey:	A name meaning "chosen one and defender of the people."
elektrichka:	A suburban train in the Soviet Union.
farmazon:	Derived from the French *franc-maçon* ("freemason"). In local jargon it signifies "dandy, slave of fashion, windbag."
fatiha:	The opening chapter (sura) of the Quran. Recited at the beginning of every prayer cycle, including during funerals.
garabasma:	"Black misfortune" in Azeri.
gardash:	A brother. Used as a polite way of addressing a person of the same age.
jinn:	A supernatural creature, spirit, or demon (English variant: "genie").
jynda:	Rotten, slutty.
hai:	The Armenian term for one's Armenian nationality.
hajji:	A person who has completed the *haj* to Mecca.
kafir:	A non-Muslim; an infidel.
kaurma:	Mutton thoroughly roasted in its own fat that's intended to be stored for a long time.
kerbalai:	A person who has completed a religious pilgrimage to Karbala.
khanum:	A respectful way of addressing a woman of high social status derived from the feminine equivalent of the male title *khan*.
khash:	A dish of boiled cow or sheep parts.
kishi:	A man. Used as a polite way of addressing an older man.
Komsomol:	The All-Union Leninist Young Communist League, or Young Communist League, was a Soviet political organization that helped instill Communist values in young people. Its members received social, political, and (during *perestroika*) even commercial advantages throughout the Soviet period; many members went on to hold positions of power in the Soviet government.
lavash:	A soft, thin, oven-baked, unleavened flatbread eaten all over the Caucasus and Western Asia.

malbey: A cattle baron.

manat: The basic monetary unit of Azerbaijan.

matyshki: A contemptuous way of addressing adherents of a different religion derived from the Russian *matushka* (a diminutive form of "mother").

miri: A term of respect for a religious figure. Can be used in conjunction with *sayyid*, a direct descendant of the Prophet Mohammed.

muallim: A teacher. Used as a polite way of addressing a professor.

Mugdisi-Makhtesi: Derived from the Arabic for "someone who has visited Jerusalem," this term indicates Armenians who have completed a pilgrimage to the Church of the Holy Sepulchre in Jerusalem.

Muharram: A holy month for Shiʿa Muslims, during which they perform *shakhsey-vakhsey*.

nomenkla-tura: The privileged class of government managers and bureaucrats under the Soviet system of government. Almost all were members of the Communist Party.

papakha: A wool hat worn by men in the Caucasus.

perestroika: The official government policy of reforming and restructuring political and economic realities during the last decade of the Soviet era. The policy was most closely associated with the leadership of Mikhail Gorbachev.

pir: A Sufi shrine, often linked to pagan traditions. Considered to be a place of magical influence. Also refers to a Sufi spiritual guide.

plov: A dish in which rice is cooked in a seasoned broth. Plov is a staple food and a very popular dish in many countries of the former Soviet region.

preputsy: The foreskin of the male sexual organ.

qanat: A type of underground irrigation canal.

qatıq: A fermented milk product. Qatıq can be described as a more solid form of yogurt.

rais: A leader. Used here in a general sense to mean the highest official in the country.

saj: A special kind of frying pan.

sary: An Azeri word meaning "light-haired."

saz: A string instrument; usually a saz is a long-necked lute.

sayyid: A direct descendant of the Prophet Mohammed.

shakhsey-vakhsey: The Shiʿa religious ritual of self-flagellation connected with the death of the grandson of Mohammed, the Imam Husein.

Shalakho: A popular dance indigineous to the Caucasus. The Shalakho is usually danced by two men and one woman. However, sometimes men perform this dance alone. Men dance quite rapidly, while women move slowly and lyrically.

shashlyk: Meat grilled on a skewer kebab-style. Shashlyk is one of the most popular dishes in the Caucasus.

shorpa: A rich meat and vegetable soup or stew.

soyutma: A dish made from lamb, onions, and tomatoes and garnished with sour cream.

subbotnik: Derived from the Russian word for "Saturday," a subbotnik is a day of unpaid work on weekends. Working a subbotnik was initially voluntary after the Russian Revolution, but gradually it became de facto obligatory to such an extent that people quipped they were working "in a voluntary-compulsive way."

tar: A long-necked string instrument.

toman: A Persian monetary unit, used also in Azerbaijan briefly after the Second World War.

Yallı: One of the most popular folk dances in Azerbaijan.

yerazy: An abbreviation meaning "Yerevan Azerbaijanis," ethnic Azeri refugees from Armenia.

ZAGS: An abbreviation derived from the Russian [*organy*] *zapisi aktov grazhdanskogo sostoiania* meaning "civil registration office," the government office where all births, marriages, divorces, and deaths must be officially registered.

zurna: A woodwind instrument used to play folk music.

Notes

Yemen

1   The reference here is to Heydar Aliev, formerly a major general in the Azerbaijani KGB and during this period First Secretary of the Communist Party of Azerbaijan. In 1982 he became a member of the Soviet Politburo and First Deputy Premier of the Soviet Union. He later became the third president of Azerbaijan. [Translator's note]

2   The Sumgait pogrom began on February 27, 1988, when gangs of ethnic Azerbaijanis broke into Armenian apartments, attacked and killed Armenians on the streets, raped and killed Armenian women, and engaged in the destruction of Armenian property. The police did not intervene to stop the murders or the looting, and chaos reigned for three days. The death toll is widely disputed and ranges from 32 (official Azerbaijani sources) to 450 (Armenian sources). For more on the Sumgait events, see Joshua Kucera's introduction on pp. x, xv. [Series editor's note]

3   The reference here is to former Soviet leader Mikhail Gorbachev. [Translator's note]

Stone Dreams

1   *Majnun and Layla* is a love story, originally in Arabic, set in pre-Islamic Hejaz, concerning the love of the seventh-century Bedouin poet Qays ibn Al-Mulawwah (known in the story as *majnun*, meaning "madman" in Arabic, Persian, and Azeri) for Layla. The most influential version of the story was the Persian version of the poet Nizami of Ganja (present-day Azerbaijan) in 1188. As a result of this story, the word *majnun* became synonymous with an extreme form of romantic love in Islamic culture. [Series editor's note]

2   This is a humorous verse that actually exists in Aylis folklore; it's not intended to be spiteful. [Author's note]

3   These lines are lightly paraphrased from the play *Vagif* by [Soviet Azeri poet] Samed Vurgun (1906–1956). In their original language, the lines rhyme sonorously. [Russian editor's note]

4   Caucasian Albania refers to an ancient territory (4th BCE–8th century CE) that overlapped with present day Azerbaijan and southern Daghestan. It was a multiethnic region that had its own language (related to Udi, a modern language indigenous to the northeast Caucasus) as well as Middle Persian. [Series editor's note]

5   *The Diary of Zakary Akulissky* was published by the Academy of Sciences of the Armenian SSR in Yerevan in 1939. All citations are from this edition of the diary. [Russian editor's note]

A Fantastical Traffic Jam

1   According to Muslim belief, this is the bridge by which the soul of a dying person will either cross to heaven or slip down into hell. [Russian editor's note]

2   *Sword and Quill* is a graphomane's pseudo-novel on a historical-patriotic theme by the hugely popular Azeri writer Mamed Said Ordubadi [Məmməd Səid Ordubadi]. It's a literary forgery stuffed with cheap aphorisms and banal love intrigues. [Author's note]

3   Samed Vurgun was the standard-bearer of Soviet-era Azeri poetry. [Russian editor's note]

4   *Pul* (Azeri) is money, *pullar* is a lot of money. [Russian editor's note]

5   This is a lightly paraphrased version of the very popular poem by Samed Vurgun. [Russian editor's note]

6   The passage that references "psychosis" is taken from the book *The Abyss* by L.V. Ginzburg, 1967 (text slightly changed). [Russian editor's note]

7   Aliagha Vahid [1895–1965] was a popular Azeri poet who wrote mainly on themes related to love in the style of medieval poetry. He was famous among the people as a person who ignored the ruling Soviet ideology. [Russian editor's note]

Farewell, Aylis

1   Ilham Aliev (b. 1961), the son of Heydar Aliev, is the fourth president of Azerbaijan, in office since 2003. [Series editor's note]

2   The story of Majnun and Layla is partially retold in *Stone Dreams*, see pp. 100–101. [Series editor's note]

3   The reference here is to the 2004 Budapest murder of Armenian army lieutenant Gurgen Margarian by Azerbaijani officer Ramil Safarov. See p. xiv of Joshua Kucera's introduction for further discussion of this event. [Series editor's note]

4   For more information on the Nagorno-Karabakh conflict and hostility between Armenia and Azerbaijan in general, see Joshua Kucera's introduction. [Series editor's note]

5   Zory Balayan is an Armenian novelist (b. 1935). [Series editor's note]

6   Radio Liberty is a broadcasting organization founded in 1949 that is based in the United States and broadcasts to 23 countries in Eastern European, the Caucasus, and Central Asia. [Series editor's note]

7   The Sumgait pogrom began on February 27, 1988, when gangs of ethnic Azerbaijanis broke into Armenian apartments, attacked and killed Armenians on the streets, raped and killed Armenian women, and engaged in the destruction of Armenian property. The police did not intervene to stop the murders or the looting, and chaos reigned for three days. The death toll is widely disputed and ranges from 32 (official Azerbaijani sources) to 450 (Armenian sources). For more on the Sumgait events, see Joshua Kucera's introduction on pp. x, xv. [Series editor's note]

8   Vardges Petrosyan (1932–1994) was a prominent Armenian novelist and poet and editor-in-chief of the Armenian magazine *Garun* (Spring). He was assassinated in front of his house in Yerevan. [Series editor's note]

9   For discussion of the massacre of Khojaly that resulted in the death of many Azeris, see Joshua Kucera's introduction (pp. xv–xvi). [Series editor's note]

10 Vardgesdjan: the addition of the *-jan* suffix is a form of endearment to underscore the author's affection for Vardges Petrosyan. [Series editor's note]

11 Hrant Matevosyan (1935–2002) was a prominent Armenian writer of fiction and drama for stage and screen and head of the Armenian Writers Union from 1995 to 2000. He opposed the Soviet cultural doctrine of socialist realism. [Series editor's note]

12 Heydar Aliev (1923–2003) was the First Secretary of the Communist Party of Azerbaijan, a member of the Soviet Politburo, First Deputy Premier of the Soviet Union, Speaker of the Milli Mejlis (National Assembly) of Azerbaijan, and third president of Azerbaijan. [Translator's note]

13 Vasif Talibov (b. 1960) has been chairman of the Supreme Assembly of Nakhchivan and de facto ruler of the Nakhchivan Autonomous Republic within the Republic of Azerbaijan since 1994. [Series editor's note]

14 The Yeni Azərbaycan Partiyası, YAP (New Azerbaijan Party), is the ruling political party of the Republic of Azerbaijan formed in 1992 by Heydar Aliev and currently led by his son, Ilham Aliev. [Series editor's note]

15 The Milli Mejlis (literally "national assembly") is the legislative branch of the Republic of Azerbaijan, with 125 deputies. [Series editor's note]

16 The term "YAPist-Stalinist-Zhdanovist" refers to similarities between policies advocated by the YAP (New Azerbaijan Party) and the repressive measures of the Stalinist period, during which Andrei Zhdanov's infamous 1946 "Zhdanov Doctrine" required Soviet artists, writers, and members of the creative intelligentsia to exhibit ideological conformity with official Community Party policy. [Translator's note]

17 Leila Yunus (b. 1955) is an Azerbaijani human rights activist and director of the Institute of Peace and Democracy; she was given a prison sentence of eight years in 2015 on widely-contested charges related to her human rights work and released in 2017 for health-related reasons.
    Khadija Ismailova (b. 1976) is an investigative journalist and radio host for the Azerbaijani service of Radio Free Europe; she was arrested in 2015 on widely-contested charges and released on probation in 2016. She is a recipient of the Right Livelihood Award (2017). [Series editor's note]

18 "Gospodi, ia zamerz v etom mire" [Lord, I'm freezing in this world] by Vladimir Shchadrin (1937–2004), *Novyi mir* 5 (1997). [Translators note]

19 Salman Rushdie, "Notes on Writing and the Nation," *Harper's Magazine*, September 1997. [Series editor's note]

Recommended Further Reading

Aldstadt, Audrey L. *Frustrated Democracy in Post-Soviet Azerbaijan*. New York: Columbia University Press, 2017.

de Waal, Thomas. *Black Garden: Armenia and Azerbaijan through Peace and War, 10th Year Anniversary Edition, Revised and Updated*. New York: NYU Press, 2013.

Goltz, Thomas. *Azerbaijan Diary. A Rogue Reporter's Adventures in an Oil-Rich, War-Torn, Post-Soviet Republic*. Armonk, N.Y., and London: M. E. Sharpe, 1998.

Grant, Bruce. "The Edifice Complex: Architecture and the Political Life of Surplus in the New Baku," *Public Culture* 26, no. 3 (2014): 501–528.

Grant, Bruce. "Cosmopolitan Baku," *Ethnos* 75, no. 2 (2010): 123–147.

Herzig, Edmund. *The New Caucasus. Armenia, Azerbaijan and Georgia*. London: Royal Institute of International Affairs, 1999.

Karny, Yoav. *Highlanders: A Journey to the Caucasus in Quest of Memory*. New York: Farrar, Straus and Giroux, 2000.

Niekerk, Carl, and Cori Crane, eds. *Approaches to Kurban Said's Ali and Nino Love, Identity, and Intercultural Conflict*. Rochester: Camden House, 2017.

Said, Kurban. *Ali and Nino*. Trans. Jenia Graman. New York: The Overlook Press, [1937] 1999.

Swietochowski, Tadeusz. *Russia and Azerbaijan. A Borderland in Transition*. New York: Columbia University Press, 1995.

CPSIA information can be obtained
at www.ICGtesting.com
Printed in the USA
BVHW040019060319
541858BV00008B/106/P

9 781618 117946